P9-APO-081

HAWAII'S OWN LOVE STORY is the poignant romance of Parker Kealii, a Hawaiian man of the sea, and a pretty mainland wahine, Anne Blair.

LEGENDARY WAIKIKI IN 1949 is the setting. Only the pink towers of the Royal Hawaiian Hotel are taller than the coconut palms and the locals are especially nice to visitors since they haven't the luck to live in Hawaii.

THE BEACHBOYS, Parker's friends, are famous for their rascal charm and for seducing tourist ladies with scandalous ease. But Parker, the ex–nickel diver with the Huck Finn grin is different. At the age of 36, for the first time, he falls deeply in love.

ANNE, THE PALE, SLENDER BRUNETTE with an air of privilege could hardly be less suitable for Parker. Still, their love fulfills the desires of both. But Waikiki is changing. The construction of the first high–rise hotel marks a turning point in Hawaii's destiny.

A TEST AWAITS PARKER in which he may destroy what he cares for most.

WITH A LOVING EYE AND AUTHENTIC PEN, Jean MacKellar celebrates the Hawaiian people, their aloha and hospitality, their love of their land, and the sea.

SECTIONS OF THIS NOVEL won awards in fiction contests.

READ IT with your heart.

Way Out Here!

HAWAII'S OWN LOVE STORY

JEAN MACKELLAR

GLEN PRESS ◦ BERKELEY

Copyright © 1988 Jean MacKellar
All rights reserved

Published by
Glen Press
P.O. Box 7708
Berkeley, California 94708-0708

Cover illustration by Radu Popescu

Printed in the United States of America

Typesetting and book design by Cragmont Publications

Printed and manufactured by Edwards Brothers, Inc.

This is a work of fiction. All characters, events, and details of the plot are imaginary. Any resemblance to persons living or dead is purely coincidental.

Library of Congress Cataloging–in–Publication Data

MacKellar, Jean Scott.
    Way out here!

    I. Title.
PS3563.A31343W38   1988   813'.54   88–11306
ISBN 0-9603518-6-8

For Katha Wehelani
keiki o ka aina

Chapter One

THE COCONUT VINE AT WAIKIKI HAD IT THAT PARKER KEALII WAS in trouble at home. For more than a month he had been sleeping in beds that were not his own. Mostly he stayed in rooms of beach boys who had other arrangements for the night. For awhile he used Pekuela's cubby hole in the rooming house on Koa Street, Pek's wahine having taken him on a trip to Hilo. Before that, Parker doubled up with Horse at Kunia's place. Kunia, a fireman, was in the hospital recovering from burns he got when Pee Y Chong's went up in flames. Earlier Parker had stayed at Spam's when Spam went to the mainland with his music group to appear on the Arthur Godfrey show.

From time to time Parker also spent the night between the canoes on the sand in front of the Outrigger Club. All the beach-boys did that at one time or another. Usually it was because they were drunk and it was too much trouble to walk the block or two home, although sometimes it was to get away from an over—enterprising wahine, or to be with one who wouldn't go with them to their room.

But Parker Kealii differed from most of the beachboys. In the first place, he was married. This already was pretty original. The beachboys generally managed their lives better than that. Pekuela was in his forties and still had a procession of grateful tourist ladies buying him meals and clothes. Parker was not known to have such advantages. He was not only married but stuck with children. Six, in fact, although various sources on the coconut vine pointed out that some of them didn't look much like him. That wouldn't have been important if he had been satisfied.

Now, clearly, Parker was dissatisfied. Although he didn't complain about whatever kept him from returning to his home nights in Palolo, it had changed his habits radically after all these years. Gossip about Parker was quite out of the ordinary. More than anyone else he represented order and stability on the beach. At age thirty–six he had become a sort of anchor figure. He was the guy you counted on because he was kind, and always there.

Parker headed the city and county lifeguards. He'd been in the work since long before the blitz. During the war the beaches had been sealed off with tangles of barbed wire but since 1945 he'd been back on duty, usually under the big banyan at Waikiki. Before becoming a lifeguard, putting his relationship with the sea into service, so to speak, he'd had a glorious past as a Kakaako Wharf Rat. Now he was considered an old timer, a senior. Only Duke Kahanamoku commanded more respect among the locals than Parker Kealii.

Parker's appearance did not recommend him as a lifeguard. He was not tall, with square shoulders and a profile meant for surveying the sea. He was only five feet nine and looked even less, the thickness of his arms and legs tending to foreshorten his height. He had not the good looks, for instance, of the beachboy, Sunshine. Sunshine, tall, proud necked, his cheeks and eyes so charmingly molded in lush Polynesian curves. Parker was not like that. No. But he was Hawaiian, at a glance, his skin burned to a deep mahogany, and he had a white smile with even teeth that transformed his face into friendly territory. On duty he paced the beach in a rolling, bowlegged walk, carrying his head erect, chin tucked down, with what seemed a kind of personal reserve. His features were undistinguished, plain, until he smiled. In his smile the man was revealed. Even if it was the first time, when he smiled at you, you felt you knew him—the good nature, the shyness, the steadiness.

For the past month Parker had been taking two meals a day at The Blue Lagoon. It was here he was headed for breakfast about eight–thirty one fine morning in June of 1949.

❂   ❂

Scuffing stiffly down Kaiulani Avenue toward the beach, Parker felt the effects of the night before. His body ached, his left hip was sore. But he had more important things to think about than how he felt. In one hand he carried the unfortunate folder. He was dressed for work in his faded blue trunks with the Red Cross badge and a fresh white cotton tee shirt. Its short sleeves stretched a little tightly over the husky brown arms. His hair was

2

neatly parted, the waves flattened for the moment with water. His legs gleamed with the light polish of coconut oil he rubbed into them each morning. Slung over one shoulder was the towel with which he would rub down after his swim at the end of a day of watching everyone else swim.

Already the sun peered over the Koolau range, backlighting the coconut grove of Waikiki. In the light breeze palm fronds rustled. Japanese doves purled. On bushes where anyone who wanted to could take one, a fresh supply of pink and red hibiscus unfolded for the day.

As he trudged the familiar sidewalk Parker enjoyed the morning scene. From the open doors and windows of the little bungalows, half a dozen to a block, he picked up clues on the life within. In one a phone rang and a woman's voice said "Hello." In another a washing machine placidly thumped. Several houses had radios turned to J. Akuhead Pupule who was saying that his sponsor, H.C. and D. actually stood for hot coffee and doughnuts. Local humor. People didn't care much for Honolulu Construction and Draying until Akuhead made the joke. Early morning bathers passed, still dripping, with cheerful nods. It was the kind of morning Parker was used to. Still, he found pleasure in it.

At Kuhio Avenue he glanced toward his favorite sight, dark, rugged Diamond Head, rising above the palms. On the beach he'd have a better view. His body's aches came from sleeping on the floor of Melvin's room. Melvin had quarreled with his wahine so he needed his bed. Parker had to make do with a towel on the floor. The soreness would go away after he walked up and down the beach a bit. He chose not to think about the circumstances that made it necessary for him to sleep on someone's floor. It was the report he had to write this morning that occupied his thoughts.

Once a month he was required to hand in a record of events on the beach—the rescues, accidents, and calls to the police. With him, in the folder, lay copies of the preceding months' reports. He had only to change a few words here and there to bring the new one up to date. Still the task seemed like a mountain looming between him and rest of the day. The trouble was, his handwriting and spelling weren't too good and he esteemed his boss so much

3

that he wanted the report to be absolutely perfect. It should not have a single blot or scratch–out on it. Often he had to copy it over half a dozen times. This seemed the only way to do things for a boss he respected as much as Kanekini.

Parker didn't blame Kanekini, but this report which he found so oppressive was part of changes taking place that were making his duties more and more disagreeable. In the old days, if a swimmer got in trouble you rescued him and that was all there was to it. You just had to keep your eyes sharp and be brave and strong. Now there was a procession of papers to deal with. Nearly every week the office sent around a mimeographed sheet advising the boys on new procedures, new rules.

Even more responsibilities lay ahead for Parker soon. His seven man team was to be increased by two more lifeguards. Since the tourists had been arriving in larger and larger numbers it was decided that the Halekulani and Ala Moana Park now needed guards.

Parker enjoyed keeping the beaches safe for tourists. Each day was fresh and interesting for him. He thought he had one of the best jobs in the world. Although he'd known some hard times he still had a sense of life as good fortune. He'd been born a Hawaiian and that already seemed to be a seal of love. Hawaiians had a lot of rotten things happen to them, but at bottom they had what they were, and what went with that—the sense of ease, and of gifts to be shared. The music, the land, the sea, the aloha. Around The Blue Lagoon it was said that more than forty people were alive today because Parker Kealii had been there when they needed help.

Parker snapped his towel at a cheeky mynah bird, sassing him, not moving, on the sidewalk ahead. At Kuhio Beach, where he stood guard, a huge banyan sheltered many tribes of mynahs and even more chittering sparrows, kamikaze divers for the crumbs of the lunch wagon nearby. Kuhio was considered the local end of Waikiki. The classy side lay between the hotels—the Royal Hawaiian and the Moana. That was where the starlets and oil barons' families amused themselves, with the help of beach-boys like Sunshine and Pekuela.

4

At the corner of Koa and Ulu Niu, although he knew what would happen, Parker cut a diagonal across the half acre of well kept lawn belonging to the Niu Cottages. A family of water buffalo couldn't have dented the tough hilo grass but at once an angry female voice shouted "Kapu! Kapu! Don't you see the sign? Keep off the grass!"

The beachboys always tried their luck as they passed, to see if just once they could walk on the Niu landlady's grass without being hollered at. Her dog, a black and white terrier, yapped from the lanai. No one knew if the terrier told the landlady or just backed her up.

"Okay! Okay! Sorry!" Parker yelled back as he continued across the grass.

Already the sun was hot, stinging his skin when he emerged from the shade. On Kalakaua Avenue three people waiting for the bus stood in a line behind the telephone pole, taking advantage of its shadow. An electric bus slid to a stop and Beef, sleepy eyed, stumbled off. He must be coming from a night with his haole wahine, Doris, Parker thought. She was crazy about him but her family, prominent kamaainas who lived in Manoa were against Hawaiians, or at least for their daughter. Beside, haoles weren't supposed to sleep with someone until they'd had a massive wedding at St. Andrews. The wahine had to sneak Beef into the gardener's cottage to have a night with him. Beef gave a gruff "Howzzit!" as he passed. Parker chuckled. Beef didn't look like he'd surf much today.

The Blue Lagoon was one block away, on the corner of Liliuokalani, facing the great banyan and the sea. A simple place, it was owned by a skinny, worried looking Japanese named Hiro who was also the cook. A dozen small wooden tables were ranged within its wide door, five more stood under the umbrellas on the setback from the sidewalk. Here the honest smell of steaming laulau and of onions frying in chop steak mingled with the scent of the sea. Whether they ate or not most of the locals dropped by several times a day. This was the heart of the coconut vine.

Recently there had been a new addition to those who sat under the yellow umbrellas regularly, a fair–skinned malihini, with a book of all things. Democratically the locals nodded to her, and while she gravely watched them, they also, in their own way, "sparked" her.

The word "local" is very precise in its meaning for those to whom it applies, although they have a wide range of backgrounds. They include those whose ancestors fought for and against Kamehameha the First, Chinese, Japanese, Portuguese, Filipino, Korean, Puerto Rican and mixtures of these bloods in many wonderful combinations. The gift of life in Hawaii meant they were all naturally born to aloha. There were also haole mixes and a few pure haoles, although the whites who were born in the islands or lived there a long time were usually called kamaainas. But they were another story.

John Parker Kealii, born of Hawaiian parents on the Parker Ranch, Kamuela, the Big Island, was about as local as you could get. Since there was no doubt at all about the blessings of his birthright, why, as he headed for the Lagoon, did he begin to think about someone who distinctly was not local on this lustrous Island morning?

Chapter Two

S HE DIDN'T FIT. THAT WAS WHY PARKER WAS THINKING ABOUT the new haole wahine at the Lagoon. Why was someone like her eating regularly at a place for locals?

Most tourists hated local food. They sampled the poi, pronounced it no better than library paste and went back to their steaks and club sandwiches. This girl ate lomi salmon and laulaus all the time. He'd watched her.

Another thing—the girl had a special air about her. Looked as though all her life she'd had special privileges. Not that she said or did anything remarkable. It was the way she carried herself. As if she'd been trained to hold her head and use her hands in a certain way, but so long ago that now it was natural. She didn't talk to people. Even after a couple of weeks she said only a few words to the waitresses. There was something shy about her. How could she look vulnerable and stuck up at the same time? She was said to be from San Francisco. A debutante. Whatever that was. Really, she was a puzzle. If she was so privileged and all, why wasn't she up at the high class end of the beach instead of down here among the locals? And then there was this habit of carrying a book. Even for a tourist she was strange. Her name was Anne. Why was he thinking about her?

There were too many tourists around these days. That was part of the problem. Before the war things had been different. Waikiki was like a village. You knew everyone by sight except the tourists. Since they hadn't the luck to be born local you'd be extra nice to them. Aloha was a natural feeling. He'd been happy to see these people who came to look at his island, happy to share it with them.

Now, every ten days the *Lurline* brought in three or four hundred new people and you could hardly catch your breath between the strange faces. Just as you were getting used to one batch, they'd vanish and new ones would appear. The locals didn't smile and speak as warmly as they had before. Parker felt bad about that although he felt less like greeting the newcomers on his beach himself.

Maybe that was why he hadn't yet spoken to the haole wahine. What for? She probably wouldn't be around long, anyhow. But then he spoke to a lot of other people he knew would soon be gone. Maybe he was changing.

Waikiki was changing. That was sure. An example of that hurt his eyes right now. The Moana Cottages, about twenty of them scattered among the tall, sweet palms, were being demolished. As he stopped to watch, a roaring bulldozer backed for a headlong crash into one of the stripped frame and screen structures. In a few strokes it went down. The driver turned his attention to a plumeria tree nearby. The yellow and white flowers of the plumeria made Hawaii's favorite lei. Crisp and fragrant, they were easy to string, remained fresh for hours. With one heave the great blade sheared the rubbery trunk through. The crown of green with its galaxies of pale blossoms went over softly, without recourse.

Parker turned away, his stomach qualmish at the sight. The white cottages had always looked cozy to him, each one private but easy with the others. In winter they rented for months at a time to rich folk, and movie stars too. "Flappers' Lane" the place was called because so many single ladies stayed there. A famous writer had scandalized a lot of people with a story about the parties that went on, and the ladies' romances with the beachboys. But what he wrote wasn't a tenth of it.

Now the little houses were being razed to put in something the haoles probably considered grander. That was their way. They'd probably build something two stories high and park the tourists up in the air, instead of on the ground among the growing things, where they belonged.

Parker crossed Kalakaua Avenue for a look at the sea. He had a better sense of the day after he'd renewed his connection with the sea. And with Diamond Head. Dominating the far end of the beach, alone, the massive extinct volcano lifted its lordly profile to the Pacific. Light from the east skimmed its dark, furrowed flanks, still brushed with green from the spring rains. Parker studied the rocky slopes and arches for a moment with gratitude.

He wouldn't have traded the sight of Diamond Head for any other in the world. The haoles said it looked like a sphinx without a head, its paws reaching toward the sea. But that was a poor way to describe it, to compare it with something else. They didn't know how full of its own singular mana Diamond Head was, a power not to be confused with any other.

Under the still meek sun the sea paraded its familiar succession of combers. Rising in the dark blue when they struck the reef, they mounted, tipped over and dropped thunderously. Today the combers were high, their foaming crests brilliant and furious. Good sport for the surfers. Parker checked the well known surfing breaks, Public Baths, Popular and Queens. Already a dozen boards were joyfully sliding shoreward. It was the resplendent beginning of a perfectly ordinary Waikiki day.

No one was swimming yet in the pale green shallows that would be his particular charge after 10 a.m. In the lacy wavelets that expired on the beach a pop bottle tumbled. Parker waded to it, picked it up before it broke and slashed someone's foot. A movement within the clear glass caught his eye. A baby squid had sought refuge there. Parker studied the little fellow. Then he hurled the bottle as far as he could, into the sea.

Tramping back across the sand toward the Lagoon, Parker glanced at the damp greens of the Koolau range in the east. Somewhere in the stretch of homes climbing Palolo's hillside his kids had already left for school. No use thinking about that.

There seemed to be half a dozen figures under the yellow umbrellas that sheltered the restaurant's sidewalk tables. Parker made a decision. This time he would speak to the new wahine, Anne. He had this report to write so of course he'd be busy with that. But he would at least speak to her. He'd been putting it off so long that now he was just about afraid to. Of course, she might not be there.

As he approached, his eyes quickly sorted through the tables. Payoff was there with his wahine, Lois. Miriam and Kawehi were sharing a plate of scrambled eggs. Anne sat beside the panax hedge. And next to her, his hand hung on the back of her chair, was Sunshine. Parker could hardly believe it. This wahine had never spoken to anyone. Now she sat with Sunshine, of all

9

people. Sunshine, whom he liked less than practically anybody. And his arm draped as if he owned her.

What was Sunshine doing at the Lagoon, anyhow? His territory was the Royal, mostly, and the Moana. He was usually too busy hustling his rich people to come slumming down at this end of the beach with the locals. And what was he doing up so early in the morning? Sunshine rarely got to the beach before noon. He must have an angle. Sunshine always had an angle.

He wore his trunks but was dry, his wavy hair combed back from his face in that new style, like he was in a convertible, headed into the wind. Sunshine kept up with that kind of thing. Leaning toward Anne he shaped something in a precise gesture with his right hand. He looked at her, then his hand, then again at her. He smiled. Sunshine's sickening smile. All those teeth. That way he had of making what he said seem so personal.

Because of the explanation with the hand neither of them noticed Parker as he took a table near them. Not that he cared for the view, but it seemed like a good place to write his report. If this strange wahine, Anne, wanted to be taken in by Sunshine it was nothing to Parker. Still, all that greasy chuminess was pretty hard to ignore.

And then the girl, herself was so odd looking. So terribly haole. In profile you couldn't help but notice her nose, like a sparrow's. Hawaiian noses were more human. Worse than the nose, she was pale as a dinner plate. She'd been around long enough to look better than that. Maybe she liked being white. A strange idea. She looked too frail to surf. Probably didn't weigh much over a hundred pounds and none of it muscle. She was the sort who belonged on a lanai in Manoa Valley, stretched out on a piece of white wicker furniture, with a book.

Well, the book she had with her today, as usual. She held it against her, spread across her chest, almost as if to defend herself. There was something else. Her lips were smiling, a polite smile, Parker thought, amused, a bit flattered too, perhaps. But she was leaning to the side of her chair, not touching the back, away from Sunshine's hand.

Sunshine laughed, pushing his voice into a falsetto. Then he interrupted to talk some more. Parker couldn't hear his words be-

10

cause Lois was nagging Payoff in her loud, scratchy way. "You not goin' to eat them *together* are you?" Payoff was spooning opihis out of a mayonnaise jar onto his plate with jelly doughnuts. Lois was crazy about Payoff.

Rose came for Parker's order. "Later," he dismissed her easily, opening his repellent folder. There was no reproach in the set of Rose's sturdy shoulders as she softly scuffed back inside the restaurant. The Lagoon waitresses were plain as water to look at but they were so good-natured everyone was fond of them.

Sunshine glanced over. "'Ey, howzzit!" Then, to Parker's astonishment, he said something to Anne and left her. Moved to Parker's table. It was almost like something planned.

"How's things on the beach?" he asked. Cheery. Pressing interest on him. As if they were the best of buddies.

"Jus' fine," Parker kept his voice even. Trying to figure it out. He stared gloomily around. At Kawehi's waist-length wavy hair. At Miriam's strong legs and luau feet. Lois was making gagging sounds as she watched Payoff eat the opihis with his doughnuts.

Sunshine studied the sea. As if he remembered something he chuckled, turned his elegant neck to full face Parker. "D'you hear about Horse?"

"What about Horse?" Parker didn't keep up with the Outrigger beachboys although occasionally their stories drifted his way through Melvin.

"Las' night he was swimmin' in front of the Moana with this new wahine. Things were goin' fine. He'd got her top off and then she panicked. He was holding her top and his own trunks. She grabbed her top out of his hands, his trunks got loose too. She ran off, he couldn' fin' his trunks. Was lookin' all over for them...."

"Maybe a eel got 'em!" Parker hooted.

"Horse didn' know what he was gonna do, all those haoles up there on the courtyard lanai. He sneaked around the rocks over to Hale Auau, got a surfboard. Carried it in front of him to cross Kalakaua Avenue, get home."

Parker thumped the table, grinning.

"Dede foun' one of his boards missin' this mornin'. Couldn' imagine who would swipe a koa board. Horse jus' grabbed the first thing he could travel with."

"Horse," Parker said, shaking his head, seeing it.

He looked across at Anne, wondering if the story was actually for her. But she had her nose in her book and Sunshine sat with his back to her.

Wipeout, wearing his orange Primo Beer shirt lumbered up. Parker liked Wipeout as much as he disliked Sunshine. The dishevelled, sad–faced giant had lost his job at Hickam a few weeks earlier and looked more mournful than ever. He greeted them but didn't seem about to stay. Rose waffled her hand to him in the motion that meant "No" and shook her head. Morosely Wipeout ambled on.

Parker had his own story. "Had to call the Shore Patrol yesterday."

"A fight?" Sunshine looked ready to smile.

"No. Jus' a drunk. Fell asleep on his back in the sun. Out. Really out. His eyes was a li'l bit open an' his eyeballs got sunburned."

"Yeah?"

"He woke up an' started screamin'. Runnin' aroun' like a crazy man. 'I'm blind! I'm blind!'"

Parker ran his thick hand over his face at the memory. "We had to catch him, hold him down. Shore Patrol took him to the Navy Hospital."

"Always sumpthin'!" Sunshine pronounced cheerfully.

From across the street came a yell. "Parker! 'Ey!" Zarko and Jojo of The Useless Bunch galloped over. They were in their trunks, trailing sea water. They looked furious.

"Parker!" Zarko began again, panting. His chest heaved, his face was a storm. "You know that dolphin comes in sometimes, plays around the canoes?..."

The girl would certainly look over now. "M'yeah?" Parker said carefully, since his authority was being drawn on. She might not have noticed how often lifeguards were needed. "That's Frisky."

"A haole out there's tryin' to spear 'em."

12

Parker forgot Anne. "Where?"

"By the reef." Jojo pointed left, toward Chris Holmes's.

"Usually Frisky's over by the Outrigger," Parker muttered, trying to see it. Dolphins moved in small groups and rarely came close to shore. It was a rare and wonderful thing to have a dolphin around but this one appeared every year about the same time for a few days.

"Me an' Zarko was out at Popular jus' now an' we saw this dark shape go by. Fas'. For a minute I thought it was a shark. Then I saw the shape of his back an' I knew who it was. He went by so fas'." Jojo smacked one palm off the other. "Then I see this haole a few yards away, bringin' in the line of his spear gun. He'd shot at Frisky."

Parker's stomach gave a turn.

"I yell, 'It's a dolphin.' I thought maybe he took it for a shark. Crazy haoles will shoot at anything. An' he yells back, 'I saw 'im first.' Like it was his right to shoot at it."

Jojo's Portuguese features were twisted with fury, his thick eyebrows almost a straight line above his dark eyes.

"Li'l moah I'd a drown' him," Zarko fumed. "But he had this gun. He went off...."

"No law 'gainst shootin' fish," Sunshine observed.

"Dolphin's not a fish," Jojo snorted.

"Same thing," Sunshine cut him off.

"What kin we do?" Zarko demanded of Parker.

Parker was thinking. In the old days it had been so much simpler. When someone got out of line you just shaped them up. The locals fixed things among themselves. You couldn't do that now. The police came in and wrote citations for every little disturbance. Since he represented the city and county on the beach he wasn't supposed to encourage taking a case into your own hands.

"You know this guy?" Parker stalled. "'S he a local?"

"Haole. Brown hair. I nevah saw him b'fore." Zarko spat contemptuously. "Lousy haole."

"M'yeah. Pointin' his gun like he'd use it on us if we came closer. Some day I'll catch him on land. He won't always have his gun."

13

"You beat 'em up, you'll be in the wrong," Sunshine pointed out. "He can bring charges." He looked cagey as he said it, as if he was measuring it out. Deciding if it was worth it. Parker knew Sunshine liked a fight as much as anyone, but he was also shrewd.

"Thass' the trouble nowadays," Parker growled. "Police come 'round for ev'ry li'l thing." Burned at Sunshine for sticking his nose in.

"If you see the haole guy on the beach, come to me," Parker told Zarko and Jojo. "I'll talk to him."

"You could check with the Board of Forestry and Fisheries," Sunshine pointed out. "There's a law, I think, about dolphins. They could tell you what to do."

Parker looked sidewise at Sunshine, his fury tinged with respect. He himself loathed calling government offices, never did it if he could think of something else. Office people's voices sounded so educated. They used big words to ask questions. Leave it to Sunshine to know about government boards, like that. He was smart as a haole. There were rules for every thing these days, and someone at a desk in charge of those rules. Parker found the thought depressing.

Zarko and Jojo, only half satisfied, loped off. Parker signaled Rose. He was hungry and in forty minutes he had to start work. He wondered why Sunshine was hanging around. Whatever he'd come for had yet to take place.

"The usual, Rose. Large poi." She nodded, shuffled off to give his order to Hiro.

Sunshine stretched magnificently. Then, as if it had just come to mind he exclaimed, "'Ey! I hear they gonna hire two more lifeguards."

"You heard right!" Parker's tone didn't give away a thing. "When's that?"

"Coupla weeks." Parker found Sunshine's interest unlikely.

"I wanna take the test."

"You?" Parker almost laughed out loud. Sunshine tied to a city–county job? He couldn't mean it. Sunshine did so well on his own he didn't even have an arrangement for chits with the hotels or the Outrigger. He wasn't popular with the other beachboys but every time the *Lurline* sailed, the heart of some lady tourist aboard was breaking for Sunshine.

The expression on Sunshine's face was surprisingly earnest. "I wanna be a lifeguard," he said. "I thought about it, an' I decided."

Parker looked across at Sunshine, the broad shoulders, the handsome head set on a straight pillar of a neck. He was wearing a new gold cross and chain. It gleamed against his bare, golden brown chest. Sunshine wasn't as dark as most of the beachboys. He had Chinese blood. It showed in the sleek look around his eyes, too. Apparently the haoles considered him handsome.

"I thought you was goin' up to the mainlan' to be in the movies. I heard you had an offer."

"M'yeah, I had an offer. But I don't wanna go. Other boys went to Hollywood, like that. Mostly it doesn't work out. They're back in a few months. An' *glad*."

"Buster did okay."

"M'yeah, but how many Tarzans do they need? Naw. They can keep the mainland. I'm gonna start with sumpthin' I *know*. Not wait for the haoles to fix me up with a contract." Sunshine made a grimace, gestured. His hand dropped to the table near Parker's, a golden brown next to Parker's lava rock darkness. "An' the tourist wahines...I'm gettin' tired."

"You, tired?" Parker gave a short, unconvinced laugh. Rose settled a plate of two eggs, Portuguese sausage and two scoops of rice with a cup of coffee in front of him. "Don' forget the poi," he reminded her.

"I know," she said patiently. "Large."

"Lotta guys take the test?" Sunshine's eyebrows were drawn, his look keen.

"Usually fifteen, twenty."

"I really want this job, Parker." His voice almost humble.

"How come?"

"I wanna settle down. I might even get married. This running around is o.k. but I want my own...you know, some of these wahines make you sick. If I had a reg'lar paycheck.... Look, Parker. Do what you can for me, uh?"

15

"I'll put you on the list for the test. The rest is up to you. Read up on your Red Cross procedures."

"Can you put in a word for me to Kanekini?"

"I'm not here for that." Busy with his eggs and sausage.

"M'yeah. Well. Okay, Parker." Sunshine slapped the table with punctuating good humor as he stood up. "Anyhow…thanks, uh? I'll be there for the test."

Before leaving he spoke again to Anne. His face took on another expression as he bent, said something into her ear. She looked up, made a flustered movement. But he didn't linger. With a bantering laugh, which he prolonged to hold her look, he went off down Kalakaua.

Parker watched Anne watching Sunshine. She was smiling a queer little smile, almost as if she didn't want to. Parker had never begrudged the other beachboys their easy patter and quick pickups. On the contrary, he admired them for an art he'd never acquired. It was a funny thing. He wasn't shy with the people on his beach. He wanted them to feel at home, to enjoy themselves. So every day he initiated small exchanges with whoever was there—tourists, service men, crippled up old folks, school kids. He found them all pleasant and interesting. But he could not start talk the way Sunshine and the other beachboys did, to make time with a wahine.

His being stuck in his marriage with nothing on the side for as long as anyone could remember was doubtless due to just this failing. Not that he worried about it or tried to do better. No. He had plenty to enjoy without dodging some girl from a month earlier, after a parade of new ones in between.

In some ways, of course, the beachboys' life had a lot of appeal. What they did with their wahines, according to Spam and Kunia, didn't match anything in Parker's experience. But then he was married. Marriage was for children. They'd taught him that at the Salvation Army Boy's Home.

Really, it was incredible the way Anne was reading her book, not paying any attention to the morning around her, to the sunshine, the air, the happiness in the breeze. Anyone who thought that what was in a book beat what was going on in real life— well, that was almost pitiful. But she always had her book, as if it

16

were her friend. Her only friend, maybe, and she wouldn't be caught without it. The coconut vine had it that she was running away from something. That was why she was here instead of in one of the valleys.

She wore her usual clothes today, white saila–moku pants and a tee shirt that revealed small breasts and pale, useless looking arms. Her dark, straight hair was shoulder length, parted on the side and held back from her face with a bobby pin. She wore flat sandals made with gold straps. They seemed oddly classy to Parker.

He raised his hand to Rose, made a mime of scribbling. Then he stood to go to the counter and pay. Anne's table was on his way. She glanced up.

"Howzzit!" he said affably. He'd have said it to anyone sitting there.

For the first time she was looking at him while he was looking at her. This gave him an unusual sensation. Her eyes had something in them. Curiosity? A flash of mischief? It wasn't what he'd expected from her dainty, aloof way of acting.

"Howzzit!" she returned politely.

At the cash register Mieko made change from a five into his palm. He was putting the bills into his wallet as he passed Anne's table again. "That book mus' have some good pictures," he joked. "You' always lookin' in it."

She hadn't really appreciated Sunshine's attentions, he'd thought, but now she seemed glad he'd spoken. She touched the book with an acknowledging gesture. "No pictures," she said. "It's about old Hawaii. No pictures then." She added, "But strong people."

He liked her saying that. "M'yeah. They was real strong in the old days."

As if this were a pretty good thing to agree on they both smiled. Her eyes, he noticed, went over his tee shirt and arms. Not that there was anything special to see, but she didn't seem to disapprove. He stood there, feeling chunky and awkward but flushed with pleasure.

"You're Hawaiian, aren't you?" It was a statement the way she put it.

He chuckled. "You could say that." Not wanting to seem to brag. He turned the subject back to her. "New Hawaii more bettah," he suggested with a grin. Making a gesture, palms up, around them. "Technicolor!"

She burst into a delighted laugh, her eyebrows lifted.

His feet seemed to want to leave. Parker put down a quarter tip, picked up his folder. He hadn't done a thing on his report but the sky was a splendid blue. Sunshine wasn't the only one who could make this tourist, Anne, smile.

Chapter Three

PARKER HAD LEFT POLLY AND THE KIDS WITHOUT A MAJOR FIGHT, nothing worse than usual. One night he simply hadn't gone home. He'd phoned and left a message with Paul that he wouldn't be there. The freedom of the first night had led to a second, then a third and fourth. Polly, furious, came looking for him at his station under the banyan tree. She'd thrown a fit right there during his work hours, yelling and trying to tear up his face with the car keys while the people on the beach gaped. It was only when, ducking and cursing, he'd shouted to Dede at Hale Auau to call the cops that she'd finally lumbered to the car and left. Then, for sure, he didn't want to go home. The humiliation of that scene, undermining his authority where he worked, bothered him more than anything in a long time.

Soon afterwards he'd returned to the house for a few clothes and his ukulele. He could get along on very little. For years, as a wharf rat he'd done fine with only one change. He knew how to wash his clothes every night. His chief problem was lack of money to get a place of his own. Polly had picked up his last paycheck at the office before he could get it. Had signed his name to cash it. That wouldn't happen again. For the moment, until he got another check, he had to stay here and there.

Beyond keeping away from Polly and the house, Parker had no clear plans. Eventually, he supposed, he'd go home. Because of the kids. In the back of his mind was a vague hope that if he stayed away long enough, something would change. Polly would start to act differently, or he wouldn't mind the way she was. After a rest of a few months perhaps he'd be able to bear her better.

He did not discuss his problems with the boys on the beach, not even those with whom he stayed. This was partly because he wasn't used to putting such things into words, and partly shame. He knew that most of them, if they heard about Polly's shouting and trying to leave all the work around the house to him would have a very simple prescription: "Belt her one!"

19

Parker hated to admit that he couldn't hit his wife. After all the fighting he'd done in his life, all those gang battles when he was a Kakaako Wharf Rat, he didn't have the stomach for hitting a woman. He knew what his fist could do. But it wasn't just that. He couldn't even slap Polly. Which was ridiculous, because Polly was built solid as a refrigerator. She could pick up a six year old and give him a whack that sent him flying like a tennis ball. Once she'd knocked a neighbor's kid back over the fence that way.

Parker's failure to deal with Polly lay in some kind of revulsion against hitting a woman, or at least her. When she got into one of her moods, yelling, he didn't feel like much of anything, except turning away. His blood would rise for a moment, then he'd get a sickish feeling. He'd just walk off making a face like he was sick. It made her furious when he did this. She'd start hitting him, which didn't do much good; her fists would bounce harmlessly. Sometimes he bore it, keeping her out of his face, just waiting for her to run down. Sometimes he grabbed her wrists and held her while her face turned all colors. When she got loose she'd stand off and throw things. Shoes, if they were in the bedroom, fruit and pots if they were in the kitchen. There was no longer anything in the living room that could serve as ammunition, except occasionally a stray toy. The statuettes, plants and ashtrays had all been used up.

When he could, Parker left the house during Polly's moods. But mostly he couldn't, because she played music three or four nights a week. So it was she who left and he who was stuck with the mess and the kids. Daisy was sixteen, Ruth fifteen and Leilani fourteen. They were old enough to take care of the younger ones. He hoped they were doing it now.

Being on the loose evenings as he was put him in the way of connecting with a new wahine if he cared to. Several times Punch tried to take him to one of the parties at the Moana. Parker always refused, but one night he thought: Why not?—and went.

The party was given by four stateside wahines in the room two of them shared. The bottles were open, Pek and Morgan were already drinking when Parker walked in with Punch. One of the haole wahines at once snagged Parker. How she looked didn't make much of an impression on him except that he noticed she had terribly long red fingernails. She patted his chest a lot. They were sitting on the bed, the others were in the wicker furniture of the spacious old, high–ceilinged room. The beachboys made jokes about Hawaii and the haoles as they drank. Parker kept looking at the wahine's long fingernails, trying to imagine what they'd be good for. He didn't think they'd be useful for making leis. Maybe there was something else that he couldn't think of right off, like cleaning fish hooks.

The way she patted him on the chest made him more nervous than happy, although he tried not to show it and always said "Sure," when she asked if he was ready for another drink. This, Parker told himself, was what those famous Moana parties he'd been hearing about were like. Finally he thought of a use for her fingernails: stripping the center rib out of ti leaves. They might be good for that.

Morgan suggested a muumuu float and that seemed like a good idea. Muumuus were found for both the women and the men. They undressed inside the wide, floor length gowns, laughing a lot over the outlandishness of the men's appearance. Pekuela complained he wanted a zipper or at least buttons in the front of his, in case he had a need. Parker couldn't get his thick shoulders and arms into anything with sleeves so they found him a blue and purple scoop–necked muumuu that tied with straps. He clowned and teased with the rest. Then they ran barefoot, whooping, down the stairs, across the broad lanai and courtyard into the sea.

The point of a muumuu float was to trap a lot of air in the yards of fabric so you'd bob around like a big, fat jelly fish. It was necessary to show the malihinis how to catch air inside the wet cloth and this required a lot of groping about. No one had anything on under the muumuus. It had been agreed earlier, only a chicken wore something under a muumuu.

Giggling and splashing they practiced inflating their garments, learning to capture air and hold it in place with knees and toes. When this had been more or less mastered they moved on to tickling and kicking, trying to ruin one another's balloons. The wahines began lifting their muumuus and casting them outward from their bodies like throw nets in increasingly daring displays.

At first they were standing in water up to their breasts, but then they moved into the shallows until the water barely covered their thighs. Laughing and shrieking, they lifted their gowns and threw them, then knelt and bobbed. The men, not to be outdone, lifted their muumuus to their shoulders, bellowing, Parker as game as the rest. When everything that each had to offer had been seen, the group began to break into pairs, melting away from the Moana's spotlight on the green night water into the darker areas on each side.

Parker found himself alone with his wahine who seized him around the neck, playfully mashing the balloon of his muumuu. Pressing against him, she ran her hand the length of his body. He could feel her searching for the hem of the gown, pulling it up. With her clasping him like that and laughing in his ear he was in fact ready to go for broke until he felt her nails digging into his neck. That reminded him of just how long they were. Those claws could not only clean fish hooks, they could make ribbons of an ule. He didn't want that to happen to his. With a chill, he felt his whole body retreat, like an eel diving back in its hole. Tonight wasn't the night. This wahine wasn't for him.

❁   ❁

Parker tramped the beach from Hale Auau to the stone wall and back, his head erect, chin tucked down. With a quick grin he greeted those who looked his way, but his thoughts were elsewhere. His eyes checked the kids close to shore and the surfers in the distant breakers but what he was thinking was: I guess I'll have to learn to get along without a wahine. I don't know how to go after one and if one comes after me, even if I don't want to, I just scuttle off sidewise like a crab. I guess I'm stuck with Polly. But I don't want Polly, so I guess I'll just have to do without.

But then for years he'd been without a wahine. When he was young he'd loved sports so much he hadn't thought about girls until Polly started looking for him at the nickel diver's shack.

The way the songs talked about having a sweetheart—he'd never had that. Ei nei. Kuu ipo. Before he'd known it could happen in just three times, he'd become a father. He'd never thought of Polly as his wahine. At first she was just a girl who came around, and then he was stuck with her as his wife. Polly certainly wasn't the one. Polly, yelling, slamming things around, cuffing the kids, always in a hurry, always on her way out.

To get a wahine for whom you had the feelings in songs perhaps first you had to do something special. Like in the movies, when there was a daring rescue or a fierce chase. Perhaps he had never done anything special enough to earn a wahine. He wished he could work on an underwater demolition squad. He knew how to handle explosives. During the war that had been his job. He'd been on a gang unloading dynamite and ammunition at Pearl Harbor. If only he could swim explosives out to an enemy ship, wire it up in the dead of night. Something like that.

Would Anne be impressed? He had no idea what to do next with a girl like her. Besides, he didn't know why he thought about her at all. She might seem pretty to white people but she was too puny for his taste. Too mysterious.

It wasn't really Anne he thought about as he pondered his problem with wahines. It was someone he could talk to, share a laugh with. Like this morning, he'd burst out in a whoop over an item in the Advertiser. There was a story that a whorehouse had been busted on Hana Malie Street, which was where the Chief of Police lived.

It always tickled Parker when the police got caught out. Polly's father was Assistant Chief of Police. That was one reason she was so sassy, accountable to no one. No matter what she did, her father could always fix it up for her. She was her father's pet. When she was a kid she'd tried, with another girl, to burn down Lunalilo School. Started a fire in the girl's bathroom with toilet paper. The father had managed to have the affair smoothed over even though there'd been several hundred dollars worth of damage.

Parker's own kids were getting into bad stages now too. Daisy was a fighter. Unfortunately, she took after him when he was young. She'd beat up anybody she thought needed it. Leilani was moody—sometimes wouldn't speak to anyone for days. Ruth was sweet natured but she'd been caught shoplifting at Benson Smith's Drugstore. Well, all kids did that at one time or another. When they didn't have money for something they just took it. He wished he had more money to give his kids.

Lying on Melvin's bed, listening to the Hawaiian music that was on KGMB every night from nine to ten, Parker noticed how often the word aloha appeared in the songs. There wasn't a Hawaiian song that didn't have the word aloha in it. One song titled "Three Important Things," talked about "faith, hope and aloha, but the best of these was aloha."

There were, of course, different kinds of aloha. He had a special kind of aloha for the people who swam at his beach and entrusted their lives to him. He'd stand there beside the banyan some days, watching them, the sunbathers sitting or stretched out on their towels, always with their feet toward the sea, soaking up the gorgeous day, the bright, peaceful sky sheltering them, and he'd feel good all over at what was in his heart for them. The little keikis shouting and jumping in the shallows gave him especially tender feelings. Whenever one came by, he'd touch the keiki's head. What he felt for keikis was a very special kind of aloha.

He had another kind of aloha for his boss, the chief of the Parks and Recreation Department, Kanekini. Kanekini was a Portuguese Hawaiian, heavy set, gentle, near retirement age. He had one eyelid that drooped so he seemed to be considering something when he looked at you. But he remembered everyone's name, and when you talked, he smiled as if he were glad you'd come to see him. Parker would do anything for Kanekini. To have a boss for whom you could feel such aloha was really great luck.

And then there was the aloha he felt for the musicians making this nice music, right now, on station KGMB. He listened, grateful, attentive, hoping that one of their numbers would be "Beyond the Reef." The song seemed wonderfully sad to him. It just fit the feelings of lonesomeness he had these days. He could almost imagine he had lost such a great love, who sailed away over a sea that was dark and cold.

A great love, Parker supposed, would include great sex. Something like what Pekuela, them, talked about. With Polly his sex life was miserable. For the last ten years it had been reduced to a brief, faceless combat in the early morning. Before they were sufficiently awake for their latest antagonisms to be remembered was the only time they could share one another's flesh. Every few days, their eyes still glued shut, they fumbled and struggled familiarly in the sagging, wrinkled heap of the bed. The blind tumble seemed almost a part of the night's dreams and shadows. Polly's bulk—although she was not much over five feet she now weighed as much as he—was no more than a familiar hive to which, by instinct, he mechanically droned. Boring as these encounters were, they remained as evidence that something called marriage existed.

Four times he'd been chagrined to find Polly pregnant. When Paul was born he'd resolved never to let it happen again. He'd always taken care. Even with sleep weighing his eyelids down, heavy as poi, he'd never missed. That was why, with his perfect record, he felt so betrayed and mad when Polly got pregnant again. It wasn't easy in those stuporous morning struggles to make himself withdraw, but he always had.

Polly got pregnant, not once but twice more after Paul. Of course she tried to make it out like it was Parker's fault. That he had missed, that the kids were his. But he knew better. And when they were a year old you had only to look at them to know they were not his kids.

If he had cared more for Polly he could not have accepted the betrayals as easily as he did. But after the first fury each time when Polly denied all his charges, he'd just given up and accepted her dishonesty as one more of life's strange burdens.

Polly made good money, for a woman. She had two jobs. Her father had made her a matron in the women's side of the city jail, where she could be late and goof off and no one could do a thing about it. Evenings, three or four nights a week she played guitar with Annie Lo's group. But in spite of the fact that she contributed a lot to the family finances she did not seem like a partner to Parker. Rather, she was like a dreadful piece of baggage with which he was inexplicably stuck. The chaos that surrounded her, the noise, confusion and blame that were a part of her presence seemed worse to him than the bills she paid.

At ten, when KGMB's program ended, they had not played "Beyond the Reef." But there were other songs he enjoyed, especially "Blessed are those who have kissed in the rain...." Switching off the radio as a mystery came on, he sighed with wasted pleasure. He stood, threw the paper towel in the trash basket, went to the bathroom where he washed his crotch. Better men than he had been reduced to the same. At least he wasn't worrying about long red fingernails and the problems he suspected would go with the fingernails. He was a free man, he could tell himself. Nothing on his conscience. Not even about Polly.

He threw himself on the bed again, despondent. What would it be like to have sex with someone you really loved? He tried to imagine it. Would it be like a conversation, each of you saying something nice to the other? Could the feelings be as sweet as those in "Beyond the Reef?"

With a groan Parker turned and buried his face in Melvin's pillow. It looked as though he'd never know the real thing.

Chapter Four

PARKER STAMPED THE LENGTH OF HIS STATION AND BACK AGAIN, tense, aggravated, his eyes on the sea. This was one of the worst days of the year for a lifeguard.

The weather was beautiful, idyllic even, but it was deceptive. Far out in the Pacific, summer storms had churned up savage currents of energy that raced toward the islands in the most violent surf of the year. Newcomers generally didn't know this. They saw only the serene white clouds piled up in fairy tale castles over Ewa, felt only the kiss of the trades, carrying off the heat of the sun. Waikiki's waves, blues and greens to saturate the greediest eye, looked innocent and tempting. They mounted, crested and tumbled in joyous abandon, the menace of the plumey cliffs hard to imagine as the surfers used them to slide shoreward. One of the smaller surfs, Popular, churned four feet high and Canoe Surf was giving the outriggers more of a ride than some of the tourists were ready for. Out at mighty Castle Surf, which rarely appeared and once had been reserved for Kamehameha and a few favored alii, monster waves now lifted dragon heads of foam.

It was on just such days that tourists often decided to learn to surf. Without any thought of danger, they rented boards and threw themselves into the sea. Parker shook his head constantly at what he saw. But there was little he could do except be there if needed. His stomach was tight from keeping such a sharp lookout, left and right, near and far. No time for exchanging pleasantries with people on the beach as he usually did. In surf like this even decent swimmers could founder and accidents were common.

At three in the afternoon Parker had already treated two swimmers gashed by loose boards and a man who was knocked on the head. He'd been sent to Emergency for an x–ray in case he had a concussion. Parker watched two young servicemen going out on boards. He'd seen them clowning earlier, noticed their swimming didn't amount to much. How much trouble would they get into before they gave up? What would it take to convince them that surfing was more than just standing on a board, one foot forward, as if you were having a beer at a bar?

Parker had a poor opinion of malihinis in general. Although he enjoyed them as individuals when he got to know them, he found the species just about hopeless in the things that mattered. For some reason his thoughts went to Anne. He wondered if she would do anything so dumb. Why did he so often think of her? From the looks of that white skin she didn't surf, apparently she never even swam. He'd never seen her on the beach. With those weak looking arms she wouldn't last ten minutes in the waves today.

Something new caught his eye, a swimmer cutting through the water on a diagonal, toward the lifeguard tower. Usually swimmers came in perpendicular to the shore. There was an air of urgency to the fast, choppy stroke, even though the head and thin arms looked small. Parker strode to the water's edge to meet him.

It turned out to be a kid, not more than twelve, probably Hawaiian–Filipino. A skinny little wretch. He reminded Parker of himself when he was that age.

"A small boat turned over," the kid panted, standing in the shallows. His bony ribs heaved as he swallowed, wiped at his face.

"A boat? Where?"

"Out there." He pointed a brown arm like a stick, far out.

"You mean by Cunha Surf?" Dismay swept through Parker as he imagined the kid out there in those bone crushers. And he didn't even have a board. Surfing on his ribs.

The kid nodded, gulped. "I guess. Two people," he added. "They're holding on to the boat."

That sounded wrong to Parker. Why didn't they turn the boat right side up? Or, if they couldn't turn it over, why didn't they leave it and swim to shore? Parker scowled, trudged with the kid through the warm rumpled sand to the tower and mounted it. Of all the idiotic problems to give a lifeguard! And now, of all times! He looked hard at the seascape's shifting horizon line but the rising files of waves obscured the water beyond.

28

He shouldn't leave his post. Anything could happen in the forty minutes or so he'd be gone. Agitated, Parker glanced at the cavorting forms in the spangled water before him. But he couldn't let a call for help go unanswered either. He came down from the tower. The kid's face was so earnest there was no reason to doubt him. Torn, Parker made his decision.

"Thanks, kid," he said. He turned and hurried to Hale Auau for a board. "I'm going out on a rescue," he told Dede. "If Kunia shows up, tell him to watch the beach for me."

Sloughing his board into the shallows, expertly Parker mounted it. The first thirty yards were mechanically smooth. He pulled with both arms in the butterfly stroke, his chin low on the dark, varnished board for maximum purchase. He'd chosen one that was extra long and heavy, in case he had to bring both exhausted people in on it. One or both might be injured. That might explain why they hadn't tried to come in on their own. Why did he feel that this was some kind of folly he should not be involved in?

Buffeted by increasingly stiff waves Parker plowed his board forward. His heart pounded strongly as he thought of what might lie ahead. It was always a test. The sea was terribly unforgiving of foolishness. And people, when panicked, did strange things.

In his twelve years of rescues he'd just about seen it all—drunks, would–be suicides, would–be heroes trying to save someone and going under themselves. One afternoon in a sudden storm he'd had to pull out five swimmers, one after another, some fighting like cats. Occasionally he was called when it was too late. Once it had been for a kid with his head split almost in half. He'd hit a rock as he dived. Why would two people be hanging onto an overturned boat?

Larger waves, already broken into foam, rolled toward him, one after another in quick succession. Heading his board directly into them, Parker was hit in the face by several feet of white water, carrying him back toward shore. He let his arms and legs hang over the board to create a drag against this movement. As best he could he stayed on course toward the point which, according to the kid, was his goal.

He'd forgotten to ask the kid his name, he realized. A plucky little fellow. Ragged trunks, not an ounce of meat on him, shivering with the prolonged cold. Probably hadn't eaten all day. Still, the kid had watched him leave with an air of regret, as if he'd like to go with him. Parker remembered when he'd been that age, when he'd had nothing but the sea. He'd been beaten almost daily for running away to it, but neither the belt nor the broomstick had stopped him. The next day he'd go back. Quite simply, the sea was worth the beatings.

Rolling in from Cunha's, the waves were eight footers and more. Some of the best surfers were riding the smoothly churning cliffs of water. He had to guard against a collision as the riders veered their boards sharply left and right to prolong their rides. His wrists felt the strain of holding the board steady to go through the great wheels of water.

Now he was in intermediate water, a deeper blue, between Cunha and Papa Nui, the surf named by Duke Kahanamoku in honor of the big boards used by old timers, much like the one he was using now. The surfers were behind him. They had sport enough in Cunha's and to the left, over toward the monsters of Publics and Castle. He was alone.

The water was so choppy it could make you seasick, but for the moment Papa Nui was not up. He stroked hard to get past where he figured the waves would soon be rising. It was up and down in gullies and peaks, his board rocking and dropping, slamming stiffly into brute hills of white-capped blue. As he tossed in the troughs he couldn't see he was making any headway at all. He began to fear he was actually losing ground. A glance back at the shore would not show that, although he did line up the tip of the Royal Hawaiian's tower with a cleft in the vegetation of Manoa Valley behind it for a point of reference later.

The sun was still bright in a sky of scattered, harmless looking clouds, but it had lost some of its warmth. Sharpening behind him, the wind whipped the edges of the tossing water into lacy foam. His arms and shoulders began to tire in this struggle which as yet had no clear goal. Then, in the distance, he caught a glimpse of an irregular, white bobbing object. The boat was there. The sight of it gave him new strength. When he was close enough to make out two heads in the water beside the boat he let out an encouraging shout, "Hui!"

It was a haole and a girl, he saw. The man held awkwardly to the boat's centerboard which protruded only a few inches above the water. The girl hung on to him from behind, both arms desperately encircling his neck. Her terrified face was unfamiliar.

As Parker stroked toward them the man waved his free arm, shouted. He was deeply tanned, with a peeling pink nose. Mainland men didn't have wrists that brown, hair bleached to straw. A local should know better than to be in this mess.

When the boat and board were only a few yards apart the heaving seascape presented new dangers. The closer Parker drew, the greater the risk that the sudden lift of a watery hill could slam them into one another. Parker had very little control against the shifting water and they had none at all. He decided not to close the distance. Feathering to keep his place he yelled, "Swim to me! I don' wanna bring the board nearer."

"She can't," the young man yelled back. "She can't swim."

Jesus, thought Parker. Oh, Jesus.

"Can you swim? Can you bring her to me?"

The young man looked unenthusiastic. Parker couldn't blame him, the way the girl was clamped on, her arms around his throat as if she'd rather die than let go. The guy was letting the girl jeopardize them both. They must be bone cold, Parker thought. With all his exertion, even he was cold. And they'd been out here in this dark water with the big fish for a long time.

It was dangerous for them to let go of the roughly bobbing boat even for a moment. As if he knew this the man made several tentative movements before he braced his feet against the side and shoved clear. But he let the girl keep her stranglehold on his neck, an idiotic thing to do. As he breaststroked toward the board his head was underwater half the time, the girl's pale, stricken face just skimming the lacy surface. Parker maneuvered the board toward them carefully, keeping an eye on the boat as it sloshed up and down the watery hills and gullies.

When they were within a few strokes Parker slid off the board and held it sidewise so he could reach the man and help him ease the girl off. She couldn't seem to let go. It was necessary to pry her loose, and she was no help at all about climbing on the board.

"Come on, Pat!" her friend shouted at her. "Throw your leg over. Try, Pat! It's going to be all right now. Come on. Do it!"

They pushed and pulled her onto the center of the board, all the time bobbing and jerking this way and that in the water themselves. Finally they had her chunky body lying chest down in place. She wore a loose yellow shirt and blue shorts. Her legs were surprisingly long and tan.

She clutched the plank the way she'd hung on the man's neck. Really, she was a case. It dawned on Parker that the little boat must not have had life preservers. This man had taken a girl who did not know how to swim out in the heaviest seas of the year, without life preservers! He talked like a local. His face even seemed slightly familiar although there were a lot of straw blonds with peeling pink noses around.

Parker glowered across the lurching board at this local idiot and wondered if he was going to want a ride in. The stinging salt water that slapped his face every few moments blurred his vision.

"Can you make it to shore?" he shouted. In the tumult of the waves, his ears full of water, a shout seemed the only way to be heard.

"Of course," the man yelled back, his tone peevish.

"Good." Parker was so glad to be rid of him he couldn't resist adding, "Cunha's huge."

As if dismissing the obvious the man nodded but then he lifted his chin in a comradely salute. "Thanks, uh?" He headed off with a strong overhand.

The girl may need medical attention when we get in, Parker thought. I should have reminded him. Maybe he'll think of it himself. It's his friend.

He lifted himself onto the board, submerging it slightly for a moment. The girl gave a cry that ended in a coughing fit as some loose water smacked her in the mouth. Her legs slid sidewise. He had to pull them back on, maneuver her into position. She seemed to have lost her ability to react properly to anything. Authoritatively Parker separated her stiff knees and pulled himself up between them so his shoulders were above the small of her back. The board's tail dragged low in the water but she was out of it from the breast up. Settling himself on her body, his chest pressing her buttocks, he began to stroke with alternate arms as a change from the butterfly.

Almost a mile away stretched the beach with its sprinkling of low structures. Behind rose the cool ridges of the Koolaus. The cleft in the vegetation he'd lined up earlier with the Royal's pink tower was now to the right. That was good. They'd be to the left of Cunha going in.

He rode high on the girl because their weight was further back on the board than normal. That was for extra safety when they got into the surf and the waves began to pass over them. He wanted the board to be almost vertical when a wave struck. This wahine was too unpredictable. He couldn't count on her to help stroke, he couldn't count on her for anything. He didn't dare try to catch a wave with her. With one of these big rollers propelling them twenty–five miles an hour they'd be in like a shot. He'd have to do it the hard way. The main thing was to keep her safe until he got her on land. Eventually they'd get there. Eventually it would be okay. This poor panicked creature taking water every minute didn't know how to swim. That really struck him. He couldn't imagine what she'd done with her life until then.

As his arms reached and pulled, attempting to set a smooth pace against the perverse action of the water, he was aware of the cold lumpiness of her body under his. She had not addressed a single word to him, poor girl. His exertions were generating a warmth between them. Perhaps that would reassure her, help her to relax. "You' doing' fine," he encouraged her.

The heaving waters piled up, closer than he'd expected. They were nearing the reef. He could feel the rumbling roll of an un-formed wave pass under them. He should tell her what to expect.

"We're goin' into the surf," he shouted forward to her. "You stay steady...." He caught a faceful, had to shake his head to clear his hair, streaming into his eyes. "You stay like you are on the board...." He was going to say, "And when a wave comes, hold your breath." There wasn't time. Suddenly there was an ex-hilarating lift, as of a great beast moving under them. The water dropped from in front of the board, fifteen feet down, in a roaring, vertiginous cliff.

The girl screamed.

All was confusion. They didn't sink back from the edge of the cliff, letting it move out from under the board, as he'd planned. The top broke on the right and raced toward them. Several feet of suffocating white foam hurled into their faces. The girl's body wrenched and the board's weight tipped forward. Its rear end was caught with a savage energy by the main thrust of the wave, behind the white water, and they shot toward the bottom.

With the water sucked up into the cliff the reef might be only a few feet under the surface. But whether they piled headlong into a wall of coral with the force of a charging bull was out of his hands. He had two things to do. One was to hang on to the girl, the other was to get away from the lost board so it wouldn't kill them. If they did not resist, the rotary power that pounded them downward would also bring them back up. Provided, of course, their brains weren't dashed out on the bottom. Grabbing the girl around the waist with both arms he hugged her as a child hugs its pillow, his face pressed hard into her back. At the same time he kicked the board away. It would go down, then shoot straight back up and out of the water like a trout snapping at a fly.

The concussion of the wave dazed him but as they churned in the great wheel of water he automatically gave into it, holding his breath, knowing they were safe. They had not hit the reef. All they had to do was wait for the rise to the surface. As they somersaulted and rolled, she writhed against his chest. At one moment her hip jammed hard against his balls in a clear single sensation among all the others. Keep her from swallowing too much water, he prayed. If she'll just hang on, we'll soon be on the surface again. He wished she would trust the water and save her strength. Of course it was natural to fight for your life. He'd get her out of this, even though they'd lost the board.

His lungs were tight as they rose through the last few feet of water then broke into the marvelous, lifegiving air. In an immediate reflex he lifted the girl clear so that her head was high above the water to get all the air she needed. She gasped deeply in an intake that convulsed her whole body, almost like vomiting. But there was little time for recovering. Another wave would be along in seconds. Usually they rose in sets of seven, sometimes nine, before there would be a rest of some minutes. He had no idea how many were to follow, when he could hope for a rest.

The girl's first reaction when she got back some of her wind was to twist in his arms and try to grab him. That would not do at all. He was not going to let her hang on him the way the haole guy had. Parker cupped her chin with his experienced hand, held her at arm's length in his strong grip. She thrashed as if to break off the stem of her neck but he held firm. Men bigger and more powerful than she had not been able to break his hold. It was the safest carry, and they had a long way to go, he stroking on his side. He wished she would stop yelling.

Another wave was on its way toward them. This time he was ready. He stopped and righted their bodies so their feet were pointed straight toward the bottom. At the last moment he turned around so they caught the charge on their backs. The battering wall of water swept by with a minimum of shock. Anchored by their vertical positions they were soon left behind in calmer water.

When she got some of her breath back again she struggled desperately. Parker yelled into her ear, "Don' be scared. We're doin' okay." In spite of the punishment they were taking Parker had a fierce sense of being alive.

Half a dozen more waves swept by, each pushing them closer to shore. Between waves he gained a few yards in swimming. His head low in the sidestroke, he dimly heard her yelling. Each time she opened her mouth she caught more water and went into a coughing fit. He held her head as high as he could but there was no way he could spare her entirely what they had to go through. He pitied her from the bottom of his heart. She was depending on him to save her life. The thought gave him a sober joy. Out of all the people in the world he was the one to whom this had been entrusted.

On the right side of Queen's Surf the waves were high but less punishing than what they'd been through. The girl's struggles were more feeble and he was thankful for this. His own strength was giving out. The surfers at Queen's dashed shoreward on their boards not far away but none of them seemed to see him. He hadn't the extra resources to try to hail one of them sliding by on his far left. Doggedly he pulled on.

The water was steadier now, between the waves, combed out by the procession of breakers. His arms ached, his kick felt slow and weak. He too had swallowed a lot of water.

The beach was now large before them. When he turned his head for a glance he saw he had only another fifty yards to go. The girl was no longer struggling, she was just dead weight, so he changed to the chest carry, holding her higher, against his left hip. Such a foolish girl! In spite of her foolishness he loved her. He'd soon have her safe on the sand.

Opposite his line of approach, people gathered on the shore. Apparently they'd seen he was bringing in a rescue. He hoped the haole guy had got hold of Queen's Hospital Emergency. The girl would need care.

He was in the warm shallows, his foot grazed the sandy bottom. A few yards more and he got a purchase when he stood upright. The solidity beneath him seemed a blessing almost too good to bear. The crowd waited, watching, on the beach. Turning the limp girl, he stooped under her, smoothly gathering her across his shoulders in the fireman's carry. It took all his effort to rise under the weight. Slowly, almost stumbling, he trudged out of the water, up the incline of the shore. Several dozen people stood silent there. As he approached they drew back, fanned into a circle around him.

Parker noticed the silence. Sometimes people cheered, sometimes there were tears, kisses of gratitude. Now there was just a strange, rapt staring. But he did not really think about this. He was just aware that no one stepped forward to help, no one from Emergency was there. The girl needed artificial respiration and he would have to do it himself.

As he lowered her, face down, on the sand the girl's long legs dropped sidewise in an uncontrolled movement that made his heart sink. Every second counted. His own lungs were heaving, his arms hardly moved in their tortured sockets. Kneeling, he arranged the uncoordinated limbs extending from the bundle of wet yellow and blue rags. His salt–stung vision was so blurred he

36

hardly saw what he was doing. He turned her head to the right, moved astride her thighs and put his hands firmly around her lowest ribs. Her body was familiar to him now. The muscle fibers of his arms and back felt irresponsibly weak but he would insist that they continue to function. Drawing a deep breath, he shook his head and began.

Out goes the bad air, in comes the good. And between the echoes of those lines in his mind were others. His own. Please take in air. Help her take air. Help this poor girl. She's not breathing properly.

Her cold bulk yielded to his pressings but he did not feel a responding elasticity, the swelling of an intaken breath. Water oozed from her nose and mouth. Her eyes were almost closed, as if she were asleep.

Help this girl. Give her the air she needs on this next one. Help this poor haole girl. She's in trouble.

Half an hour later the crowd around him, now grown larger, was still strangely silent. Mute, they watched as he leaned, then released and sat back on his heels, timing his own breath with the stroke as if he and the girl were one in the reach for oxygen.

Someone broke through the circle of spectators, moved deliberately toward him. The shoes came first into Parker's periphery of vision. Well–made black oxfords, grey slacks. This man was not from the emergency unit. He knelt and Parker saw a middle–aged haole wearing glasses. With a practiced gesture the man reached for the girl's wrist. Parker did not break his rhythm, did not speak. He had work to do, strong and slow, and every atom of his energy, even his thoughts, was needed to do it.

Now the man was pressing the carotid in the girl's throat, lifting her right eyelid in a familiar way. Parker rejected what the man was going to say before he said it. In another rescue he had heard the words before, but in the end his perseverance had won. The man's voice was distant, dry.

"There's no use continuing," the voice said. "Her skin is purple. She's quite dead."

His head bent, Parker did not respond. He continued his rhythmical stroke, determined to break the sea's claim on this poor haole girl's life.

Chapter Five

THE POLICE AND CORONER LEFT. THE REPORTERS GOT THEIR STO-ries and the crowd dispersed. Still Parker was unable to quit the scene. Even when the sun set he stayed, walking slowly, baffled and exhausted, from Kuhio past the Moana and the Royal to Fort De Russy and back. The board had not yet come in. He did not want it to smash on the rocks in front of the Waikiki Bowling Alley and Tongg's. Finally he found it near the Ulu Niu Club.

But even with the board back safe at Hale Auau and the light going out of the sky he didn't leave. Speaking to no one he paced in the darkening air, aching, cold, his skin stiff with salt. Without thinking he was aware of the tide coming in, the change in the night breeze as Waikiki made its gentle transition at the end of the day.

Across the crescent of the beach, lights began to be reflected in the water. On the Royal's terrace people were dining. Soon they'd be dancing, and the girl was dead. The world was going on and there was no chance for the girl to enjoy anything, ever again.

Mourning, Parker forced himself at last to leave. As he headed for Melvin's for a hot shower his knees would hardly move. He was too tired to eat, he'd just listen to Hawaiian music. For an hour he stared at the ceiling, listening to old favorites. But nothing eased the pain of his regret. He wished he'd met the girl earlier so he could have taught her to swim.

❂   ❂

Parker grieved for the girl for days afterwards. He didn't see how such a thing could happen right there in Waikiki in the shadow of wise old Diamond Head. In his twelve years of work he'd had all kinds of victims, young and old, from skinny as sandpipers to so fat he didn't think they could sink if they tried. And then there were the little kids with their strong, rubbery arms and legs. He'd held each of them close, made them part of himself as he swam them in. Now this girl had died in his arms.

At the Parks office Kanekini had stood by him. In fact Kanekini had praised him. "Don't feel bad, Kealii. No one could have done better."

Parker had almost broken down as he recounted the facts, Yuki sitting there with them, taking notes to type up for his report.

"I nevah los' anyone who was alive when I got to 'em before." Parker's voice kept cracking.

Kanekini's kindly eye drooped, his face was full of sympathy as he said, "I know you did your very best, Kealii. *I* know that. You always do."

That's what Kanekini had said. "No one can blame you." And, "I know you did your very best."

In the investigation that followed it turned out that the haole whose boat was involved was the son of a prominent kamaaina family. The newspapers played down the story. A small terse item on page one noted that a mainland visitor, Patricia Watson, 22, of El Paso, Texas, had lost her life in a boating accident. In spite of a hard fought rescue in heavy seas by the head lifeguard, Parker Kealii, the county coroner had pronounced Miss Watson dead at 6 p.m. on Friday, June 4, 1949. Artificial respiration had been administered by Kealii for more than an hour without success. The stories did not say that the little boat did not carry life preservers although they did mention that the girl did not know how to swim.

Parker tried to console himself with his boss's words. But the memory of the girl was a stone on his heart as he put in his hours on the beach. When he caught sight of Anne at the Lagoon he walked away, pretended he hadn't seen her.

❂ ❂

Around the Lagoon's tables when talk turned to the girl's death there was anger at the haole whose boat it was. Apparently he was not going to be charged with manslaughter. Among the old–timers, memories of the Massie case were revived. There were remarks that if the boat had belonged to a Hawaiian or an Oriental or in fact anyone who was not from a rich haole family that had been around since the monarchy, a lot more would have been said about it in the papers. There would have been a full scale inquiry in court.

But then, the summer surf was up. What with being tuckered out at the end of hours of glorious struggles in the waves and surfers not being given to dwelling on ugly things anyhow, the incident soon retreated into ancient history. Which was every thing behind yesterday. What was left was just one more story attached to Parker's reputation for being a good guy with bad luck.

⚙   ⚙

A few nights later Parker had an unexpected encounter. Melvin, who was still fighting with his regular wahine, came back to his room late, with a new wahine. So Parker had to leave. Feeling rotten and alone he sleepily headed for the beach and the canoes.

He was walking down Prince Edward in the quiet dark when he became aware of a figure in white, on the other side of Ulu Niu, among the coconut palms. It seemed to be a woman, in a long gown of white, crossing the broad lawn of the Koa Cottages. She moved in a soft, leisurely fashion as if enjoying the stroll.

The sight of a serene lone figure out late was nothing special. People walked around Waikiki at all hours of the night. They went to or from lovers, they went to or from parties. They went to the beach for a swim. Waikiki was a fine place just to roam, for that matter. There was little traffic on the Ala Wai or Kalakaua and the only sounds were the rustling of the coconut fronds in the trades and the distant sighing of the sea. Tonight an almost full moon cast shadows of the long stemmed palms across the spacious lawns. The cottages slept in the silvery quiet, most of them nestled in fresh smelling foliage—ti leaves, croton and ginger, comfortable clumps of dark forms on this mild, ordinary night.

Across the stretch of grass surrounding the Koa Cottages the figure in white came, almost ghostly, completing the beauty of

40

the shadows. Past one, then another of the palm trees she drifted, like a sleepwalker in a dream.

On the corner of Ulu Niu was a street light, and here Parker recognized details of the figure. The slender body, the straight dark hair cut off at the shoulders, the way she wore it on one side. She walked slowly toward him as if every moment were a pleasure she didn't want to end. Parker's first reaction was to head in another direction. But he couldn't. His feet kept going straight ahead. So as not to startle her, he increased the slap slap of his thongs on the sidewalk.

The light was behind Anne as she approached. Within the folds of the garment's fine fabric he could see the outline of her body, a shifting line of light between her legs as she moved.

When they were still several yards apart, to show her who it was, he greeted her. "Hullo!"

"Oh, it's you!" She drew near, her manner unhurried.

"M'yeah," he acknowledged, his voice polite. "It's me."

She stopped, stood there smiling, as if meeting him like this was fine with her. It was a nightgown she was wearing, apparently. A white cotton nightgown with long sleeves, wide like bells at the wrists. Around her neck was a lei of three strands of pikake. He had the feeling she was happy. The flowers' scent reached him faintly, perfuming the encounter.

"I saw you the other day on the beach," she said.

With the light on her face like that he couldn't help but notice her cheeks and lips.

"I watched you giving artificial respiration to that girl."

Anne had seen his disgrace! Now he was lost.

"You worked so long and hard. Just wouldn't give up."

He would say good night and leave before it got any worse.

"I thought you were wonderful."

Quite possibly he hadn't heard right.

"I thought you deserved a medal."

Parker stared at her, unable to reply. In all his years of work no one had ever said such a thing. He was just a man who did his job.

Awkwardly he glanced about. "D'you stay aroun' here?" he finally managed to ask.

41

"Down there." She pointed toward the Ala Wai. "Liliuokalani." As if an explanation were in order, she went on. "I hung my lei beside the bed. But then it smelled so nice I couldn't sleep." She lifted the strands of blossoms which were to blame. "So I decided just to walk around and enjoy it." She dropped her nose into the small creamy flowers as if she still hadn't had enough.

Above them the coconut fronds stirred. The words of an old Hawaiian song came back to him. 'She and I are two. With the rustle of the sea's spray we are three.' He'd change that to 'with the scent of her flowers.'

"It's a nice lei," he offered. "Smells nice. Pikake."

"I know. The flowers were named after Cleghorn's peacocks. He used to live around here."

"He did?" There was a Cleghorn Street, Parker knew. It must be an old family. "Lotta people I don' know their name," he apologized. "Jus' their faces."

"Are you going for a swim?" She had noticed the towel on his shoulder. He used it to cover his head against blowing sand when he slept between the canoes. But this didn't seem like something she needed to know. "Swim? No. Well. I *might* need it," he said cheerfully.

"Yes," she agreed, then seemed to forget the towel, looking about as if bemused by the soft night. Not at all embarrassed for the nightgown. He wasn't sure about catching her like that. Although she was more covered than she would be at the beach, he felt a little apologetic. If he had a proper place to stay he wouldn't have surprised her like this.

"Well," he said, shifting his weight without moving away. Not really wanting to leave. Not wishing to seem to abandon her, either.

The shadows breathed their earth scents. Anne stood touching the pale loops of the lei, her lips in a faint smile. There seemed to be many choices in the night around them.

An owl called. They turned to listen. But the call was not repeated.

She had nothing he could carry for her and she wasn't going anywhere so he couldn't offer to walk her there.

"Well," he said again. Remembering that after all, she was a malihini so he should be extra nice to her. Mainland people led terrible lives apparently, with some kind of crime going on every week and snow storms, too. The Advertiser wrote about those things. He'd heard that snow bleached your skin. She was so pale, this poor girl who hadn't the luck to be born local. He'd like to say the right thing to her.

Unfortunately, he began to move away. His legs seemed to have a mind of their own. As if he had to be somewhere, which was not at all the case.

"Aloha," he brought out at last. "Aloha, Anne." Astonished to hear her name in his own voice, like that.

"Aloha, Parker!" She said it quite easily. Not at all sorry they'd met, it seemed.

"Oh, you know my name!"

"Of course. Everyone knows *you!*"

As he was carried away down Ulu Niu he was struck again by what Anne had said. Thought he should have a medal! A stone that had pressed his chest seemed to ease. He felt very light as he crossed Kalakaua Avenue.

Chapter Six

NEXT NIGHT AT THE LAGOON PARKER LOOKED FOR ANNE AGAIN. But when he saw her inside, alone at a small table reading her book, he hadn't the nerve to go in and speak. With two of his life guards, Morgan and Squidley, he loafed under the umbrellas, joshing with Ah Lee, enjoying the evening. Not unaware of its beauty but lulled by the ordinariness of it—the palms, the trades, the kind sky.

As usual, the phone in front of the Lagoon was busy.

"'Ey, look at Dede! Combin' his hair b'fore he calls his wahine!"

Dede turned, showed his fist before he dropped in his nickel.

Parker couldn't let on that his thoughts were inside the Lagoon at a certain small table. When the Niu Cottages landlady paraded by with her black and white terrier, a pink hibiscus stuck proudly in its collar, he chuckled at the hibiscus. "I wonder," he said to Morgan, "did she step on someone's lawn to pick it?" That got applause.

"Socks' wahine is lookin' for him. Says she's goin' to kill herself if he doesn' come back."

Parker hooted at that.

"She was sayin' that about Kunia a coupla months ago."

There was laughter. Kunia looked irked.

Rose and Mieko scudded around in their thongs, carrying dishes, singing out orders to Hiro in the kitchen. "One corn beef hash, two da kine on top." "Teriyaki, three scoops a rice."

Wipeout's powder blue jeep appeared. He buzzed around the corner, a moment later his great bulk appeared, ambling slowly, sadly toward them. He was wearing the orange Primo Beer tee shirt that did not quite meet his jeans over his big opu. His dark curly hair was as unruly as ever. Wipeout was something to look at, with his wild hair, powerful arms and huge fists. He was gentle as an ox. His name had been acquired years earlier in a famous surf wipeout that nearly killed him. But his troubles hadn't ended there. He had bad luck with wahines, was divorced from a wife to whom he was apparently very attached. Now, at thirty-six, he was with a wahine who, it was rumored, hit him when he was asleep.

Howzzits were exchanged all around.

"Parker, I wanna talk t'yuh," Wipeout rumbled.

Just then Hike, the beach clown, pranced up. To look at him you knew he had a story and it would be funny.

"Whistlin's out!" he roared.

"Out of where?" There was puzzlement.

"Jail. He's been in jail."

"What for?"

"Borrowed a car without tellin' the owner."

Grins were exchanged.

"He got out in twenty-four hours with jus' a lecture. The owner didn' press charges. They *begged* him to leave. He used his secret weapon."

Ah Lee and Dede began to laugh before the last sentence. Whistling's puhios were famous. They could clear half an acre of beach even with the trades blowing.

"He stank up the city jail so much they opened the door and begged him to go."

There were hoots, cheers. Other stories of Whistling's puhios were offered.

"No shame!" the group cried, revelling in it. "No shame!"

"You eat?" Parker asked Wipeout. Thinking they could go inside, sit near Anne.

"Yeah. No. Well, I might have a bowl of poi."

A bowl of poi. That struck Parker as odd. Wipeout must be broke. Leading the way he chose a table where he could face Anne, in case she looked up from her book.

"You' wahine okay?" Parker asked hopefully, his eye on Anne.

"Naw. She lef' las' week." Wipeout tried to act disgusted. "Wase' time that wahine."

Parker waited. In the old days when he was a Kakaako Wharf Rat diving for coins, Wipeout had dived for the rival Palama Gang. Their gang fights had been wonderful. He and Wipeout shared memories that went way back.

Wipeout nodded to Lois and Payoff, then gazed into space. He sighed heavily. At last he said, "My las' paycheck was more'n two months ago."

"The layoff wasn' nuthin' personal," Parker reminded him. "Jus' a reduction in force. The army's doin' it all over."

"M'yeah. But nobody's hirin' truck drivers now. Every day I try."

Parker had got his city–county paycheck that morning, was feeling good at having money again. He'd squared his account with Hiro for the meals he'd been charging. Tomorrow he'd start looking for a room of his own.

Mary–san came with the menu but Wipeout made a gesture he didn't need it. "A bowl of poi," he said solemnly.

"Have a laulau. My treat." Hiro's laulau were twice the size of anyone else's.

"Well, okay," Wipeout weakened.

"Four laulau, two poi," Parker ordered.

"I know," Mary–san said. "Large poi."

Wipeout got to the point at last. "I can' make the payment on my jeep. I'm behind already."

Parker's heart sank. This week, at last, he'd thought he'd have a room of his own.

"The finance company is 'bout to take it back."

"M'yeah?" Dreading what Wipeout would say next.

"So I'll give it to you, if you wanna take over the payments."

"You givin' it away?" Dumbfounded, not understanding at all. He'd always thought the jeep was cute, painted baby blue, like that.

"M'yeah. You wan' it?" The expression on Wipeout's face was pure misery.

"Me? The jeep?" Parker couldn't believe it.

"You could keep up the payments. You got a steady job. You' 'bout the only one 'roun here who does. All the military goin' away…." Wipeout's deep voice trailed off.

Parker knew nothing about finance companies. They sounded scary to him. Polly always took care of the family's money matters. It was her parents who fixed them up with the house in Palolo, made the down payment. He'd never even had a checking account. Didn't trust banks. Felt there was something sneaky about the way banks took people's money, said they'd keep care of it for them. Clearly, there was something in it for them. The idea of someone making money on his money was offensive to him. He was a cash man.

"I don' know," he said doubtfully. "How much is the payment?"

"Twenty four dollahs a month."

Pekuela, them, paid about twenty–two dollars a month for their rooms. If he got a room he could not pay for the jeep with the same paycheck. He'd have to wait two weeks for one or the other.

The poi and laulaus came. In half a dozen spoonfuls or so Wipeout's portions melted away.

"Look," he said. "I'll go home and get the papers so you'll see. All I hav'ta do is sign the registration to you."

"How much more you owe?"

"'Bout a hunnerd twenty."

Parker was tempted. Polly had their old black Chevrolet. She'd been using it since he left home. Several times he'd thought of going and getting it but hadn't wanted to face the fight it would bring on with Polly.

Sunshine breezed in, tall, handsome on his proud neck. He glanced about, looking like a caramel–colored Joel Macrae. On the Red Cross Lifesaving test he'd gotten the highest score. Now it was for Parker and Kanekini to decide, from among the top applicants, which two would get the jobs. Parker didn't see how Sunshine could miss. Feeling mean, he watched Sunshine handing out the howzzits as he moved among the small tables.

Parker tried to keep his mind on this important conversation he was having with Wipeout but saw Sunshine stop beside Anne.

"'Ey, beautiful!"

Anne put her finger at a place on the page, held it there as she looked up. Her expression was a mix of friendliness and reserve. "Sunshine!" she said.

Parker did not hear their next words but he watched Sunshine's abominable good looks as he stood there, smiling with his shiny teeth, turning his profile this way and that as he talked.

Making the moment seem like such fun, and just between the two of them. He patted Anne's shoulder as if she were a good girl. Asked her something, bent and looked right into her eyes as if her answer were the only thing in the world that mattered. Then he burst into a laugh, patted her in that repulsive way again. Why did she let him do such things? But he had finished, apparently other plans were on his mind. With a salute to Anne and a glance around that ignored Parker's stinkeye, he headed for the door, still on a big smile, clearly a man with a fine evening ahead.

Across the table Wipeout stared at nothing. He looked wretched, even desperate.

Parker was suddenly aware of decisions to be made, life to be lived. "I'll take the jeep." His voice was firm. "It'll be good for my work. Jus' right for goin' aroun' t'th' beaches. Thanks, Wipeout. Thanks!"

Wipeout said nothing, just turned his head away. After some moments he heaved his great bulk up out of the chair. "I'll tune it up for you first," he said. "It's in good shape already."

Wipeout's word on cars was solid. He had driven and repaired everything on wheels during the war.

"I'll go to my room, get the papers for you." With the dignity of a bereaved bear he made his way through the tables, out.

Anne was reading again so Parker had time to study her. She was still pale as a moth, her arms as bad as he remembered them, in a short–sleeved palaka shirt. She wore the white saila–mokus and gold sandals. One hand rested on her book on the table, the other held one foot comfortably in her lap. Her dark, straight hair, too heavy for the bobby pin, fell forward as she read. She turned a page, smoothed her cheek. A lot of her height, Parker thought, was in that long neck, which wasn't good for anything in sports. But it was her paleness that he kept noticing. Apparently she didn't swim. Perhaps she didn't know how. Like the girl he'd tried to save. Maybe there were more people in the world who couldn't swim than he'd guessed. He stared at her, hoping she wouldn't be dumb enough to go out in a boat without a life preserver.

Anne looked up. With a smile she beckoned him over.

Grinning at his luck he went to her table. He was going to say, "I never see you at the beach," when she spoke first.

"Did you save anybody today?" There was grave mischief in her eyes as he sat down.

"Jus' one li'l kid," he admitted. He didn't know why he even mentioned it since it wasn't a real rescue. The mother wasn't watching when her four year old floated too far out in her life jacket. The little girl was having a fine time when he brought her in, warned the mother to be more careful.

"You' readin'." He apologized, with a glance at the book.

Anne pulled the bobby pin out of her hair and put it between the pages, closing the covers. As her hands moved on the book he was struck again by how colorless they were. Up close like this, in the restaurant's bright light, he had a new impression of how she looked. Her blue eyes seemed important. When they looked at you, you really felt it. Her white skin made a big contrast with her dark hair and black eyebrows. Made them very noticeable. He didn't remember being aware of this sort of thing on girls before.

"You never come to the beach. Kin you swim?"

"Sure," she said, looking surprised. "Sure. I can swim. I'm a good swimmer." She made a gesture, "Why?"

"A good swimmer?" He found it hard to believe that.

"Yes. Well, not fast. But good."

She pronounced each word real plain, the way people from the mainland had a habit of doing.

He looked at her white arms and throat. "What beach do you swim at?"

She got it, and laughed. Her small, even teeth had a space between the two front ones.

"I don't *like* to swim." She shook her head "no," still smiling. "I had to swim so much when I was a child that I got to hate it. Every day, two times a day, at the club pool. Now it just bores me."

Parker considered what she'd said. He could understand getting bored with swimming in a pool, although of course it was better than not swimming at all.

"You *had* to swim?"

"My father made me. He wanted me to be good at it."

49

"He did?" Parker was stumped by that one. His father always beat him when he found out he'd been swimming.

"So I don't go to the beach."

Parker stared around the nearly full room, trying to adjust to the idea of swimming as boring. Well, Pekuela, them—sometimes the beachboys said they had so much sex it got boring. All those girls scrambling after them all the time. They'd hang up for awhile, just for something different. Maybe it could get that way with swimming, too, although he didn't really see how. The ocean changed so much. There was so much new each time to notice and enjoy.

"You're a beautiful swimmer," she complimented him. "I've seen you doing laps in front of the beach after work. Such a smooth, easy stroke."

"Well," Parker fumbled. Again this wahine had surprised him. "I started soon as I was old enough to run away from home, to the sea."

"Yes?"

"When I was five, six. I was living in Kakaako then. So I ran down to the piers. I wanted to be a coin diver when I grew up. That was my ambition. To go out to meet the ships."

"Did you?"

"M'yeah. But that was much later. You gotta be a strong swimmer for that. The big boys wouldn't let little kids go out. It's too dangerous. They'd beat us up. You had to earn the right to dive."

"How?" Anne moved her book to one side, leaned her cheek on one hand, as if quite content to hear what he had to say.

"Well, you had to be big," he repeated. "At least eighteen or twenty. And strong in the water. Us kids—we wanted so much to dive that we had our own way to practice. We din't have any money to practice with so we got soft drink bottle caps and put 'em on the street car tracks to mash 'em flat. Then we'd throw 'em in the water, aroun' the piers, and practice catchin' 'em on the way down."

Anne's watching him like that made him feel more and more enthusiastic as he talked. He wished he could make her know how it had been, how pretty the bright little disc was as it zigzagged, dropping through the green water. "It goes like this," he made a swinging gesture. Back and forth his hand moved down.

Her black eyebrows lifted, waiting for more.

"Only you can't learn the whole thing with bottle caps. Because diff'rent pieces of money have diff'rent speeds and diff'rent patterns. Like a dime goes back and forth faster, and with a shorter swing than a nickel. And a quarter is still slower, with a wider swing. You have to know that so you can figure where it's going to be." He traced the different arcs in the air. "When we see it swingin' to the right, we know how far down it will be when it zags to the left. So we can reach for it over there."

"And fifty cents was the slowest of all?"

"We din't get many of *them*. In those days money was hard to come by. We'd dive even for a penny." He chuckled. "One time a boy dove for a penny—he thought it was a penny. Turned out to be a two and a half dollar gold piece!"

"How far down would you go for a coin?"

"Whatever it took. We'd go ten feet, fifteen, even twenty. But down there the water is dark and dirty. We can' see the money real good."

"How much did you get, meeting a boat?"

"Three, four dollahs. Five dollahs, we was *happy*." It was funny how happy he felt, telling her about those things. Actually, they'd been hard days. But good, too. Although he couldn't expect her to understand that.

"We stuff' the money in our mouths." He puffed out his cheeks, waved an arm to show her. "Then we yell to the tourist, 'Way out here! Way out here!'"

"What was that for—'Way out here?'"

"So another boy wouldn't get it. We'd spread out an' shout for the tourist to throw it down to *us*."

"Did you ever fight over the coins?"

"Oh sure. We'd pull hair, hold legs. Bes' man wins! Sometimes two, three go after the same coin, knock heads, make so much white water you can' see the coin. But once you get a coin, it's yours. No hard feelin's. Sometimes we could even catch the coin in the air."

Parker laughed, reached for a coin, to show her how it was done. "Drop it down, missus! Way out here!"

A familiar figure filled the restaurant's doorway. Wipeout had papers in his hand. Parker was never so sorry to see Wipeout in his life.

"Oh," he said. "There's my frien'." He rose. "Well, I gotta go."

Anne seemed disappointed. She straightened, looking up at him. "Too bad," she said. "I enjoyed hearing about your nickel diving."

He liked the way her lips curved when she smiled.

"M'yeah. Well." For a moment the world seemed to be going just about right. "Talk t'ya again."

Outside, under the umbrellas, Wipeout explained about the papers and signed the registration over to him. Parker felt honored that Wipeout wanted him to have the jeep. They shook hands. "I'll keep good care of it," he promised.

As Wipeout started to leave Parker tried to make his friend feel better. "You' wahine—she'll prob'ly come back pretty soon."

Wipeout shook his head, barely acknowledging. "No, it's the end."

A few days later Parker was stricken to discover the worst thing that had ever happened among the regulars of the Lagoon. His friend had killed himself. He had dashed his brains out against the banyan at Kuhio.

Chapter Seven

PARKER WAS IN CHARGE OF ORGANIZING THE FUNERAL. THEY would say good–bye to Wipeout the Hawaiian way. A gathering of canoes would take his ashes out beyond the reef. Parker felt so rotten about Wipeout's death that he could hardly keep his mind on what he had to do.

Wipeout hadn't talked about his problems. He'd looked sad around the Lagoon of late, but then he'd always had a mournful, heavy look. Like it was heavy to lift his hand, heavy even to raise his eyes. He'd been a powerful swimmer back in their nickel diving days. And a powerful fighter when the Kakaako Wharf Rats tangled with the Palama Gang. Wipeout could smash two heads together like coconuts. At one time he'd been a salvage diver. After the blitz he was one of those who brought up the bodies in Pearl Harbor. Pulled open the doors of cabins under water, dragged out trapped sailors. Later he'd become a truck driver, on contract to the Navy.

His heart aching as he made the funeral arrangements, Parker had little time to think of Anne. He was glad Anne had not been around the morning he discovered Wipeout's body. He'd spent the night on the beach again, between the canoes.

Next morning as he approached the banyan tree, alive with screeching mynahs and sparrows, he'd seen something lumpy and orange at its foot. Denying what his eyes told him, he'd made out as he drew near, that it was Wipeout's orange Primo shirt, that Wipeout lay face down on the cement with his arms flung out as if to embrace the tree. But Wipeout was not a heavy drinker, he told himself. A few steps more, then the truth, the horror. Wipeout's skull broken open, the grey brains visible, creeping with flies.

Vomit in his throat, Parker had done what needed to be done. Covered Wipeout's head with his tee shirt. Phoned the police and the morgue.

It was almost an hour later, at the Lagoon, that he'd broken down. Telling Hiro and Rose and Mary–san his voice had made a lot of funny sounds and what he said had stuff from the old gang fights mixed up in it. "At firs' I thought someone mus' have clubbed him. But who would want to?" Parker found himself sobbing. "He nevah hurt nobody. 'Cept if he was smashin' 'em up in a fight."

The police had shown him the evidence on the tree, the dent in the smooth grey trunk of the banyan, about five feet off the ground. Then a snatch of dark hair on a twig below the dent, and a brown smear, the dried blood, where his head had slid down. Apparently Wipeout had run, carrying himself low, in a head–on charge, like a freight train. He had done it himself, Wipeout had smashed his own skull.

The ceremony would be held on Sunday so everyone could be there. Wipeout's ashes would be committed to the sea a little before sunset. There was a Hawaiian tradition about being taken away into the great eyeball of the sun.

A calabash was set up at the Lagoon. The boys went outside for contributions, too. They contacted nearly every Hawaiian in town—the firemen and the police, the boys at the Gas Company and Mutual Telephone, the stevedores at Castle and Cooke Terminals and everyone on the beach from the shacks of Kalia Road to the beachboys at the Royal. Most of the money came in as one dollar bills although there were two twenty dollar bills which Ah Lee was suspected of contributing although he denied it.

Expeditions were made to the graveyards for plumeria flowers and to Tantalus and Manoa Valley for yellow and white ginger. Leis were constantly being strung under umbrellas. Everyone wanted the canoes to be heaped with flowers for Wipeout. Anne was drawn into the activity, stringing the fragrant blossoms with the rest of them.

❂　❂

Parker got the use of eight canoes from the Outrigger; the ceremony would be held on the sand in front of the club. Each canoe took six paddlers. On Sunday at four o'clock the canoes were lined up side by side facing the sea, their dark bodies gleaming in the late afternoon sunshine, the graceful silhouettes repeating one another. Behind them the dense, powerful bulk of Diamond Head anchored the far end of the beach's curve. A flotilla of luminous, flat–bottomed clouds lay across the horizon. Surveying the scene Parker was happy for Wipeout that he had such a nice day.

Parker had been through the sprinkling of ashes several times, for Jake the Seahorse and others. But for many of the younger boys it was the first time. They would be watching him. Parker prayed for the strength to carry off his part in the affair with honor and thanked God he was Hawaiian.

Tension mounted as the cartons of leis piled up and the paddlers, wearing their best trunks, arrived. Besides the flowers there was also a carton of ti leaves. Ti was a magical plant that soothed headaches, cooled babies' fevers and was used in wrapping broken bones. It also exorcised evil spirits. The paddlers would tie on the long green leaves as wristbands to protect themselves against the destructive spirit that had taken Wipeout from them.

With such heaps of leis it was suggested that the paddlers wear a plumeria lei each. Parker objected. It might look as though the paddlers were decorating themselves. But after talking about it they decided that to decorate the paddlers did not honor the paddlers, it honored the occasion. Each of the boys placed a lei on his bare shoulders.

"You'll be in the *Oio*," Parker told Sunshine.

Sunshine frowned. "I thought Beef was gonna steer the *Oio*."

"He is."

"Whad'ya mean? I'm jus' a paddler?" Sunshine's face, his body went tight.

"Yup."

"I'm a steersman. You know that. I always steer. Every time I take tourists for the hotels it's me that steers."

"Thass' fine. Here you' a paddler."

Sunshine's body was moving around like he couldn't find the right place in the air to put it. His expression was mean.

"You sayin' Beef's the steersman?"

"Thass' what I'm sayin'."

Parker looked at him coolly. It was too bad he had to raise his eyes a couple of inches to do so, Sunshine out–topping him as he did. "You wanna paddle, or you wanna drop out?"

Sunshine glared. But it was clear he was also thinking. The lifeguard appointments would be announced in a few days.

Parker watched Sunshine narrowly. He was still wearing his gold cross on a chain as if he'd turned religious all of a sudden.

"Well?" Parker lifted his chin, to have the matter settled.

"Don' matter to me...." Sunshine stepped backward on the sand, colliding with a tourist. "It's nuthin'...Oh! Sorry, Missus. That's a nice camera you got there." He gave her a big, cheesy smile as she clicked.

By armfuls the leis were lifted from the cartons and hung over the prows of the canoes, then the sterns. Now the eight slender dark forms were muffled at both ends in clouds of pink, white and gold blossoms. Their scent sweetened the air, adding another presence to the occasion.

The sun was still two hands above the horizon, a light trade stirring the palms when Parker placed a table on the sand with a large Hawaiian Bible and a spray of white gladiolas. They were from the ex–wife, the only family of Wipeout's anyone could find. She was pretty cut up by Wipeout's death. It was decided that she should stand with the kahuna for the ceremony, as a sort of symbol, since no other relation was available.

Smash Walker's musical group took places nearby, the great bass fiddle gleaming in the late afternoon sunlight. On signal the group struck up the Hui Nalu Club song, a call to the brother-hood to which Wipeout, in the old days, had belonged. The paddlers, who had retreated to the Outrigger parking lot, filed in, two by two. They walked toward the table, then separated to make a wide semi–circle, down to the water's edge. The kahuna, in a red malo, followed, carrying the urn with the ashes, over which was folded the American flag. Last to appear was the ex–wife wearing a white holoku and carrying a pikake lei of many strands.

The kahuna took his place at the table, facing the sea. He was tall, an old man with a massive head of grey hair that seemed to bow the slim, withered frame that carried it. On his bare chest he wore a curved hook of bone pendant, the symbol of his office.

All were assembled, the music ended. Solemn–faced, the kahuna lifted his arms and asked for a ho'omalu, a period of silence. The crowd grew still, even the tourists who had been tramping around on the outskirts of the scene. Nothing was heard but the snapping of the Outrigger flag in the trades, and the sighing of the small waves, a few yards away. The tide was going out.

After some moments the kahuna took the Bible and read a passage from it slowly, in melodious Hawaiian. He was in no hurry. When he was ready, he set the book down, closed his eyes, folded his hands. In tones lower than those he had spoken, he began a chant, quavery but strong.

The sun dropped lower, its light golden on the phalanx of brown bodies in the semi–circle, standing guard.

Parker recognized a lot of the Hawaiian words, but not enough to get the whole meaning. Still, he trembled at the power of it. He had stationed himself near the table, in case the ex–wife needed him. But she carried it off well. She didn't cry, just looked sad, her eyes down, her long black hair lifting in strands with the breeze. At the right time she handed the pikake lei to the kahuna. He set the flag aside and draped the flowers over the urn. Then he moved to the largest and heaviest of the canoes, the *Hoonaunau*, traditionally used for carrying the ashes and the chief members of the funeral party.

The paddlers broke ranks, each going to the canoe assigned him. Standing by the outrigger poles they waited until all was still. Then the stringed instruments played the opening bars of "Aloha Oe." Someone began to sob. Fifty male voices lifted in the sweet farewell. By the time the chorus ended, many of the singers had dropped out. Sounds of weeping mingled with sounds of the sea as the last chords died away.

The paddlers lifted the canoes by the poles, carried them into the water. Then they took their places. The crews of the *Oio* and *Malama* were ready to go before the *Hoonaunau*. They feathered until it had got under way, to take the lead out. Some of the men had tears streaming down their faces. Parker was glad he wasn't one of them. He'd been holding on tight, fixing his thoughts on what was to be done. He sat behind the kahuna, where he could keep an eye on the fragile old man who was gripping the urn. There were only five to paddle; each one had to pull extra hard.

Arms stroking powerfully, paddles flashing together, the crew of the *Hoonaunau* showed the way. They crossed the reef, went a little beyond. Here the sea was quiet, no white caps today, just bobbing little hills of dark blue water that gently sloshed the sides of the canoe. The other outriggers drew up, then prow to stern, their balancing poles on the outside, they formed a circle around the *Hoonaunau*.

Raising his quavery old voice, the kahuna spoke. His words were in English so that all the paddlers, Portuguese, Japanese, Chinese, Hawaiian, and mixes thereof, would understand. He spoke of their coming together, a gathering of hearts and spirits, in tribute to Wipeout. He spoke of life's oldest mystery, the end of life, which they now faced, with their friend.

To the Hawaiians, how a man died was important. How he faced death. What struck Parker was the way Wipeout had chosen to die. He'd done it like a man. With koa. Courage. Not taking pills or jumping off the Pali, but in charge, himself, through the last, unflinching step.

The Hawaiians of the old days did hard things, he'd heard. When sacrifices were needed they offered themselves in the place of a dear one. Or for their chief. He'd never had such a test given him, Parker thought, although he'd often longed to do something magnificent for Kanekini.

The perfume of the heaped up flowers mingled with the scent of the sea as the kahuna went on in his wonderful old–timer's voice. He spoke of death as a chance to reunite those who had been separated, and a new bonding of the hearts of the living. He spoke of forgiveness. Parker especially noticed that word. He thought of his mother abandoning him at the Salvation Army Home. How he'd struggled with the puzzle of that all these years, still couldn't understand why she did it. He thought of how she'd sent him off, as if she didn't care about him at all. And how he'd left his own kids, now. Well, if his mother was wrong, then wasn't he wrong too? He couldn't bear to think about it.

The kahuna dropped the pikake lei into the sea carefully, so that it spread open, a floating white circle of many strands on the dark blue water. Removing the lid, chanting, he tipped the urn to spill the ashes slowly within the circle. Then he turned and nodded to Parker, who removed the pink plumeria lei from his shoulders and laid it in the water near the circlet of pikake. The water within the white circle was still cloudy, the last visible evidence of his gentle sad friend. The other members of the *Hoonaunau* took off their leis, laid them nearby, and the rest of the crews followed. Inside the ring of canoes dozens of circles of bright flowers floated. Then the men in each prow, and the steersmen, began to cast off the leis that draped the canoes. More and more were added, the pool filling with color, with the scent of carnation, white and yellow ginger, tuberoses and gardenia. The last leis landed on others, hardly touching the water.

Raising his arms to the sky, the kahuna invoked peace for their departed comrade. He leaned and scooped a handful of purifying salt water, which he sprinkled on his own head and chest, signifying to the others to do the same. There was another moment of silence, ho'omalu. The waves slapped gently at the sides of the canoes. In spite of the deft movements of the steersmen, holding the water with their paddles, the canoes began to drift apart. The circle was breaking. The pool of color leaked outward in streaks of pink, gold and white. Still the little flotilla lingered a moment longer between the sea and the sky.

In this last moment, just before the good–bye was over, Parker experienced a rush of feelings different from any he'd ever had before. He was overcome by a sense of closeness to everyone there—the kahuna in front of him, Kunia behind him, the others of the *Hoonaunau*, and all the rest. Morgan, Freitas, Concrete, Hike, even Sunshine. They seemed dear and meaningful to him. And with this sense of closeness came a feeling that everything was all right, after all. That in spite of the sadness and confusion and pain, in the end it would be okay. He had an overwhelming sense of tenderness for them all. People, just doing the best they could. There wasn't much time. That seemed to be the message. The sweetness of the little time they did have. It occurred to him that he might even go home. He could probably bear Polly's foolishness after all. There wasn't much time.

The return to shore was a race to release feelings rarely encountered so close up, so hard. When the canoes were more or less in a line, at Parker's hoarse shout, the paddlers, yelling, dug into the water, pulled furiously.

Crossing the reef, four of the canoes were going fast enough to catch a wave. A churning mass of water lifted their sterns and, smoothly as a locomotive on a track, rushed them shoreward.

The *Hoonaunau*, with only five paddlers for its heavy frame was not one of these. It caught a small wave later, was the last to beach. But the race was to race, not to win. No one cared who the actual winner was. The shouting and joshing was both real and forced. High spirits were no offense to the dead. The living were just doing what they loved to do. This time it was in honor of their missing comrade and there could be no dishonor in that.

The canoes were turned in the shallows. Then, shoulder to shoulder, their faces taut with the effort, dark bodies gleaming in the last rays of sunshine, the crews carried their canoes ashore. In their accustomed places the *Manukai*, *Lanikai* and the *Oio* were gently lowered, their prows toward the orange globe that was to take all human griefs with it into the sea.

"Pau sad," the men assured one another. This was as true as it was not. Then they looked for their clothes and headed off for the funeral spread at The Blue Lagoon.

Chapter Eight

HIRO HAD TRANSFORMED HIS RESTAURANT FOR WIPEOUT'S party. The tables were ranged against the wall in a fifteen-foot buffet and covered with ti leaves. Sparked with pink hibiscus and set with heaps of local foods, the effect was sumptuous.

Hiro and Parker had debated what to serve. Finally they decided just to have what people liked to eat. This turned out to be a terrible chop suey of racial favorites: sashimi, Portuguese sweetbread, hot dogs, pipikaula, four varieties of sushi, octopus cubes in mustard sauce, crisp won tons, malasadas, baked ham. Several of the boys donated jars of opihis and limu. Aoki's Market gave six dozen wienies and buns; Aoki owed Wipeout a favor from way back. A keg of beer was installed under the umbrellas with paper cups handy. Hiro didn't have a liquor license but the event was not open to the public so he could serve it to friends on the premises. Ah Lee had offered to stand for the beer.

Of the spread itself there was little to say because within minutes nothing remained. Most of the paddlers arrived at the same time. Barefoot, in a herd, they trotted the block and a half from the Outrigger and their effect on the tables was that of a giant vacuum cleaner. A hundred brown arms and hands reached, picked, lifted, reached again. Piles of food vanished, were replaced, vanished again. There was almost no talk. Mieko and Rose served steaming wienies out of a cauldron while Mary-san cut open the buns. Hiro sliced sashimi with magically swift strokes, sent new plates of the rosy raw fish to the tables every few seconds.

Anne helped serve. She brought in the heated trays of crisp won tons and hot malasadas. Each time, the one she'd left a moment before was empty.

The Walker group was supposed to provide music for the event but there wasn't time for them to get set up. Suddenly the tables were bare and this time it was the end. The arms and legs eased out the door and were gone. Nothing was left but sugary smears of grease on the still-warm metal trays which had held malasadas.

Parker eyed the stripped scene. "Barracudas," he murmured. He'd barely had time to stuff down a hot dog with an opihi or two.

Hiro wiped his hands on his smudged apron looking defeated. "I shoulda got another ham," he mourned.

"There's no bottom to that gang," Parker assured him. "It was fine."

Anne emerged from the kitchen. Her cheeks were flushed, she looked happy. Parker thought she was extra pretty today with a pink and white striped skirt that hung in many folds. She consoled Hiro. "Wipeout would have loved your spread."

Parker backed her up. "M'yeah, I'm sure he liked it." He eyed the trays Anne held. "What you gonna do with them?"

"Return them to Lau Yee Chai's. They were for the won tons."

"I kin ride you." He took the trays. "My jeep's around the corner."

"Thanks. They are heavy."

He found them light. In fact he had to kind of hold his steps down as he walked with her to the jeep.

"Am I taking you out of your way?" As if she were looking for something to say.

"Not a bit." He could swim ten laps just for nothing the way he felt with her there beside him. At Lau Yee Chai's he drove Anne around to the delivery entrance. The head cook from whom she'd gotten the trays that afternoon had a trickle of sweat in front of his ear. He was nice, didn't count the trays, only asked if the party had gone well.

❂   ❂

Parker drew up to the court Anne indicated on Liliuokalani Avenue. Six cottages faced one another across a wide lawn. Their errand had taken only a minute or two, it seemed. He eased to a stop, cut the motor.

"Smoke?" he offered. Hoping she wouldn't go in right away.

He took a pack from the jeep's compartment. He didn't dare carry them in plain sight.

"No thanks."

They sat in silence as he lit up, inhaled a deep lungful he'd been wanting for some while.

In the bungalows nearby small evenings were in progress. Silverware and dishes clinked. Water splashed. On a radio Sol Hoopii sang "Beautiful Kahana."

"I got mad this afternoon," Anne confessed. "At the funeral." There was an edge to her voice he hadn't heard before.

"Mad?" He couldn't imagine anything at the funeral to be mad about. So many flowers, and all the people turning up to show their affection for Wipeout. The music making people cry.

"The tourists almost wrecked it. Didn't you *notice*?"

"Whadd'ya mean?" Of course he'd noticed the tourists. They'd been everywhere, into everything. He thought they'd been nice, taking an interest, like that. "A lot of 'em come and took pictures," he offered.

"Exactly. They were just terrible. They don't know anything about Hawaiian customs. And they didn't know Wipeout. What right had they to stick their noses in like that?"

Parker thought Anne shouldn't blame the tourists for not knowing Wipeout. Doubtless they would have liked him if they had. Their intentions were good.

"You're a Hawaiian. How can you stand to have them desecrate your ritual like that?"

Parker didn't know the word but he got the idea. He'd noticed this sort of thing before. When haoles were mad they had a need to use big words. "What'd they do so bad?"

"You didn't hear them saying 'I thought it was supposed to begin at five o'clock. Why doesn't it begin?' Complaining! As if it were a show for their benefit."

"Guess they didn' have nuthin' else to do," Parker apologized.

"And those horrible cameras, clicking all over the place. Before it began they asked the paddlers to pose for them, as if they were performers." Anne's voice rose to a strangled sweetness. "'Oh, you're so handsome, you've got so many muscles. Would you mind lining up for me?'"

"They don' know any better," Parker pointed out. "It's prob'ly the firs' time mos' of 'em ever saw a Hawaiian funeral. How they gonna learn? Have to be a firs' time."

"They even asked some of the paddlers to sit in the canoes for pictures. While the canoes were on the beach."

"I know. I tol' 'em it's not allowed," he said quietly. He didn't see why it bothered her so much.

"And they asked the boys to put flowers behind their ears, because it would look 'authentic.'"

Parker had to crow at that one. "Thass' not Hawaiian! We don' wear no flowers like that!" Sitting beside Anne he couldn't help but notice how haole everything about her was. The way she pointed her nose here and there, the way she used her hands to adjust the folds of her full, striped skirt.

"Sometimes the tourists didn't even ask permission to take pictures. They just oozed up real close and shot at their faces against the sky...." Anne made a sharp gesture. "As if the boys had no more right to privacy than a palm tree."

"M'yeah. Well...." Anne seemed to have an awful lot to say on the subject. He hadn't imagined she'd talk so much. Did all haole wahines take on like this?

He could see the curve of her cheek in the shine from the street lamp. Here in the dark he didn't find her as scary as in the light, where you had to keep noticing her white skin and the important eyes and all that.

"Wretched people with their inner tubes and bottles of sun tan oil. Gawking. Delighted. They even took pictures during the ceremony. Click click! So rude!"

Parker said nothing, feeling sorry for how she remembered it. To him it had been wonderful. The boys solemn, thinking about Wipeout. The kahuna's voice reading, and the sea, waiting. How could Anne think about tourists at a time like that? He felt sorry for her. It seemed to him that she was easily hurt. She wanted everything to be just perfect. That was it.

"Don' feel bad," he said. "It turned out okay." He inhaled the last of his cigarette, got rid of the stub with a practiced flick.

"I know. Local people are so patient. Mostly they hardly saw the tourists. Just watched with kind of sad smiles. Like the tourists' silliness couldn't spoil the occasion for them."

"M'yeah. Thass' mostly what they do," Parker agreed.

This seemed to annoy Anne more than ever. "Oh, for heaven's sake," she fumed. "You Hawaiians! Here are strangers, trampling on your island legacy and you don't even care. Actually, it's your fault, the whole thing."

"Me? How, my fault?" There was no end to the surprises in Anne.

"You shouldn't have held the funeral where you did, on the beach between the Royal and the Moana. That's just where all the tourists are. Naturally, they took it as though it were planned for their entertainment."

Parker hadn't thought of it that way. "It's the only place we could hold it," he explained patiently. "The Outrigger is the only place we could get that many canoes."

"Then you should have borrowed the canoes and moved the ceremony off somewhere else," Anne pronounced. "Had it in Kahala, for instance, or Ewa. Or any other place but Waikiki."

"You can' go movin' those canoes aroun' here and there!" he protested.

"Why not?"

"They're too valuable. The Outrigger owns them. They use them every day, nearly every hour. It would take a long time to get crews to paddle around the coast to some other place. And dangerous." The idea of eight canoes going through Honolulu Harbor made him nervous just to think of it. And Kahala was full of coral. Anne had a lot of ideas on things she knew zero about. "Besides," he added, "Waikiki is Wipeout's home. Thass' where his ashes should be." The idea of putting Wipeout's ashes in such alien waters as Ewa or Kahala seemed rather offensive to him.

Anne was quiet a moment. "Well, the tourists are ruining Hawaii, and that's a fact. They're all over the landscape. They wear idiotic hats and colors a parrot would blush to be seen in...."

Parker thought there were too many tourists but he'd never looked at them that way.

"I know they bring in money. But they also bring in a lot of bad things too. Their ugly mainland prejudices. And their stupid materialistic values...."

He was way behind now. The next time she took a breath he was going to make a suggestion.

"We've got thirty–six thousand tourists a year now and the Tourist Bureau wants *more* next year. Can you imagine?" Her voice creaked with indignation.

"You wanna go some place that's got no tourists?" Tomorrow was his day off.

"Where's that?" Anne turned to face him. "They're every-where. They even go up to Laie, to the Mormon Temple."

"You ever heard of Sacred Falls?"

"No. What about it?"

"It's just a nice place, on the windward side."

"Is it sacred?"

"Well, it's s'pose to be the home of the pig god. There's a nice waterfall." He felt a little shy, bragging on it like that. He grinned, to encourage her. "No tourists, anyhow. I kin promise you that. Tomorrow morning?"

"I was going to the Kodak hula show in Kapiolani Park."

"It's over at eleven. I'll pick you up then."

"Where? There'll be a lot of people."

"Don't worry." His voice was very sure. "I'll find you."

Chapter Nine

PARKER STOOD BACK AND LOOKED AT THE JEEP CRITICALLY. IT sparkled, wet, the hose still ran into the grass. He couldn't see a speck of dirt anywhere. Even the tires gleamed, unblemished black. But just to be sure, he rinsed the jeep again with care. Pondering about this excursion with Anne. Wondering how to act with her. He knew what Pekuela, them, would do. But he hadn't their experience in such matters, and his feelings seemed to be different, too. Besides, he had no idea what to expect of Anne. She was unpredictable. She might even bring her book and read in it. With her, anything was possible.

After going over it this way and that, Parker decided to be like a fisherman. A good fisherman never looked ahead to the results. Never admitted he was going fishing, even to his wife. If he met someone on the beach who said, "Nice day for fishing!" he'd turn around and go home. You did your best when you baited your hooks or set your nets, but no matter how wise you were about fish, or how lucky you'd been before, you never expected anything. Each time you went out was always the first time. What happened was between your guardian spirit and the guardian spirit of the fish.

It was the same way, probably, Parker thought, with a wahine. You did everything you could to set it up. You wore clean clothes and had money to treat. But what happened, as when you went to fish, was not up to you.

Although he'd showered the evening before, it seemed the right thing to do to shower again just before meeting Anne. Afterwards he smoothed his body with coconut oil and studied himself in the mirror over Melvin's sink. He was in good shape at least. His stomach was flat, his arms and legs looked strong. Anne could feel safe with him. She'd know he could take about as good care of her as a man could. His faded jeans had a nice crease. He'd slept on them, laid flat, the seams nicely matched, turning carefully during the night so they wouldn't rumple. With his hair neatly parted on the left side and smoothed with water, Parker thought he looked about the best he could.

Fresh as a Sunday morning the blue jeep waited. Parker mounted the flat canvas seat feeling like a prince. The jeep's color had seemed a bit showy to him at first. But then the playfulness of its looks kind of got to him. Strangers smiled and waved as if they liked it and friends always knew where he was. Besides, the color was Wipeout's choice and he'd told Wipeout he'd keep good care of it. To change might seem a little disrespectful. For a moment Parker had a setback as he thought of how he was looking forward to the day, and Wipeout couldn't. But maybe Wipeout was enjoying it another way. Parker gunned the motor as he set off.

❂ ❂

"I'm glad you could make it." Trying to tame the smile all over his face. He couldn't help the way it came up from in the center of him.

He'd picked Anne out of two hundred people sitting in the bleachers with no trouble at all. His eyes had gone right to her head, found the dark hair combed smooth to one side, the white forehead, the serious expression. When the show ended, he was at the edge of the bleachers, watching her descend.

She was wearing clothes he'd never seen before, a pale green shirt sprinkled with small flowers and pants of the same soft green. They stopped just below the knees so he got a good look at her calves when she climbed in the jeep. They were a lot better developed than her arms.

"I thought you didn' like tourist things," he joshed her, as the tourists with their cameras poured by, so many he couldn't move the jeep.

"I came for the hulas," Anne said coolly. "I'm taking lessons myself."

Parker had no hope that a haole like her would ever understand what the hula was really about, but it was nice of her to take an interest. "There's good stories in the hula," he offered. "The old ones, I mean." He got the jeep in motion.

As she sat next to him the pants pulled tight over her thighs. They looked meatier than he'd expected. She was puny on top with that white neck and weak looking arms but from the waist down she seemed about right. In the sunlight her hair had sparks of red in it. Almost straight, it hung thick to her shoulders turning up just a little at the ends where she'd cut it off.

"I'm reading all the books on Hawaiian things," she informed him. "I might even become an expert."

Parker smiled politely. "Thass' nice." Then, so she wouldn't feel bad about not being local, not having his advantages, he said, "The mainland's a nice place too. I went up there once. To Los Angeles." He couldn't find anything nice to say about the experience. "I was young, then. Nineteen." To prove it hadn't been too bad he added, "I stayed almost a month."

Anne did not seem interested in hearing about the mainland.

"I packed a lunch," she said, looking as if she expected him to be real pleased.

Parker was not pleased. "I'm not used to eatin' lunch. It's a rule. We not s'pose to eat anythin' that would weigh us down on duty. So I got out of the habit."

Anne looked put out. "It's just ham sandwiches and fruit."

"Oh, thass' fine," he said easily. A ham sandwich and fruit he could handle almost without noticing.

He took the Ala Wai to town so she could enjoy the unbroken sweep of greenery across the canal and golf course to the magical hills. Clouds lay along the ridges of the Koolaus as if whispering secrets into the valleys. Young fern and sweet bamboo stood in those deep valleys. Since Anne complained about Hawaii being ruined by the tourists he felt like showing her the opposite. He'd prove to her how nice it still was.

As they neared City Hall Parker's eyes automatically turned to the corner of the building where he knew Kanekini would be sitting. His desk would be piled with papers, poor man. And here he was, so light and free on this wonderful day off. Parker's heart squeezed with gratitude every time he thought of Kanekini.

Downtown Honolulu, with its stop lights and bustle was a different world from Waikiki. Some buildings, like Alexander Baldwin and Bishop Bank, were four stories high.

He headed up Nuuanu. Amidst the dark greens of the sheltered valley the sparkling dry plain of Waikiki soon seemed very far away. Here lawns were never watered. Four or five showers a day turned yards into jungle if they were not constantly clipped and groomed. Some of Honolulu's most elegant homes lay in the shadows of giant ear pod trees. Sweeping driveways gave glimpses of superb old kamaaina estates.

"Nuuanu Cemetery." Parker gestured toward the long low wall of grey stone. "Local boys like to come here."

"For the flowers?"

"M'yeah. Pick plumerias. But also for the food."

"Food?"

He gave her a rascal grin. "Lotsa Chinese buried here. They put out food for the dead. Oranges, sweets. After a funeral, even cooked food. Rice cakes. Roast pork. They make a lotta noise, then they leave. The boys come 'n eat 'em for the ancestors." He thumped the steering wheel, enjoying the naughtiness of it. "In the old days when we wanted to make music, we'd go to the cemetery. Nice 'n quiet. Nobody to bother you. Sometimes we'd play all night long...."

"Isn't it kind of spooky in a cemetery at night?"

"Naw. Hawaiians isn't scared of dead people. Used to, Hawaiians buried their relatives in the back yard. So they'd be handy, to share in the family parties, like that. But the Board of Health ruined it. Said they had to put 'em with ever'body else. Have to *pay*. The haoles figure out a way to make money on ever'thing. Even dyin'." Parker hoped Anne understood he wasn't talking about her.

The road began to wind, following the stream. They met few cars. Most of the traffic over the Pali was on Saturdays and Sundays when people went to the other side of the island to their weekend cottages.

Coconut trees hung with luxuriant vines gave way to shorter, scrubbier vegetation. The wind increased, flapping the jeep's top noisily. Here the landscape became wild and primitive, not at all tropical in its aspect. Only hardy evergreens that could take the constant tearing of the wind survived. Some days it would not be safe for a jeep to go over the Pali. Today the wind was strong but not unsafe.

At the Pali lookout he parked. With difficulty they walked, bent against the wind, to the stone wall at the edge of the 1,200 foot drop. "You know about Kamehameha, them?" Parker had to shout to be heard.

"Of course!" Anne held her hair, whipping against her face, with both hands.

"Sometimes people try to commit suicide here, but it doesn' work. When they jump off, the win' so strong it holds 'em up, jus' lets 'em down easy, so they only sprain an ankle, like that." Parker hoped it wasn't disrespectful to mention this, so soon after losing Wipeout. He was saying what he thought the beachboys would say if they had a tourist or wahine up here. For himself, he had no words for what he felt at the view before them. He was almost embarrassed by its wealth. From the mossy palisades on their left, stretching over to Chinaman's Hat, it swept 180 degrees across the coast to Waimanalo. The richness of the color—blues and lavenders and fifty shades of green, each meaning something—it was beyond him to grasp it all. With greedy affection his eyes picked out favorite landmarks—Kaneohe stretching its neck into the sea, the cut out coastline of Kailua, the heaped up hills of Maunawili.

"I've been here before," Anne said, "but it's fantastic, each time."

"M'yeah." He didn't want to seem to brag. The old Hawaiians knew, loved, and named every cliff, every knoll. It was all sacred to them, all worthy of attention. He could spend a long time looking at the scene himself but he didn't want to impose on Anne. After a few minutes they turned their backs on the spears of wind and returned to the jeep.

He eased down the steeply winding road in second. "If it was night time we couldn't come over the Pali," he told her. Sheer walls of lichen-covered granite protected them on their right. "With those ham sandwiches you got."

"Why? What's the matter with ham sandwiches?"

"Never take pork over the Pali at night. A lotta people tried it, goin' home from a luau, like that. Somethin' always happens. An accident. Car turns over. You never can tell. Jus' don' try." He gave a short laugh, went on. "Nuuanu has a lot of things, can' be explained. At night sometimes there's drums, the night marchers. People say it could be the soldiers comin' back, after Kamehameha pushed them over the Pali. You hear the night drums, no matter who you are, Hawaiian or haole, you pull the covers over you' head!"

"You too?" she asked slyly.

"Me too," he admitted with a grin.

The road became straighter, ran in an easy incline toward the sea. "Well, this is the windward side," Parker pronounced. He looked around like an emperor. "It's all diff'runt over here." There was so much new to see he could hardly keep up.

"Doesn't look so different to me. I mean, it's rural, all these little farms, banana patches. But it's still Hawaii."

Parker stared at her, unable to believe such stupidity. "It's windward," he said again, trying to make her understand. "Waikiki is leeward. This is where the wind arrives."

"So?" Anne shrugged her shoulders. "Eventually it gets over to the other side. Same thing. Finally." She looked at him. "Isn't it?"

"No," he said firmly. "It's not the same thing at all." For a moment Parker wondered what he'd got himself into with a wahine who talked like that. How could she be so blind when the evidence was everywhere around them? Why, even the air was different. Heavier, more moist, as if the elements were more connected, the sea and sky with the rich land. And how could you forget for a moment that awesome palisade of dark cliffs looking down on you? How could you possibly feel the same in their presence as with the soft ridges of the other side? If Anne couldn't see the differences, then she couldn't feel the sense of joy and privilege he had at being there. He wondered if it would do any good at all to tell her about some of the old Hawaiian things. Like how the Old Ones felt about the land, and the sea. The sky.

He thought of his grandmother. How she'd taught him the names of the clouds, and their meanings. He doubted if he could remember the words for those things now. The young clouds, the sorrowful clouds. The clouds that piled up like the wrath of a chief, and the clouds that danced and trembled for joy. He remembered his grandmother holding him on her lap when he was small, kissing him frequently as she talked about the clouds and the winds. Often she had a towel on her shoulder, the towel into which she cried because she loved him so much. Each wind had its own name because the wind that sprang down Nuuanu Valley was quite different from the one that sifted through the palms of Waikiki. She had talked about the perfumes in the wind. The wind that was scented with the dawn—that was one he remembered. Moanikeala.

But rattling along in the jeep was not the time to speak of such things. They were almost holy to Hawaiians. Sacred Falls would be a nice place to talk. Anne would probably like to hear about the goddess Pele, too. Pele, who lived in Kilauea, her hair streaming volcanic fire. She went everywhere, even to Windward Oahu. Some of the things she did were so strange he couldn't make out the lesson in them. Often she seemed to be testing people's generosity. Disguised herself as an old woman or a handsome young man beside the road, in need of a ride. John Kaipo had picked up a pitiful old tutu one time, driven some miles and turned to ask if this was where she wanted to stop. No one was in the back seat. Then he'd known who she was. Lots of people could tell stories like that. Especially while headed for Sacred Falls Parker kept a sharp watch for anyone who looked like they needed a ride.

The rare faces visible along the way were mostly Hawaiian, sometimes Japanese. Windward people were for the most part humble farmers. Their cozy wooden shacks, roofed in corrugated metal, stood on the inland side of the road. Red and gold croton bushes brightened their well–used yards, chickens scratched in the bare dirt. Everywhere banana trees hung out their long green banners of promise. A cow grazed next to a white frame church. Parker noticed it all with interest. On the sea side of the road simple cottages awaited weekend guests. Occasionally a fine estate with a spacious lawn announced a wealthy kamaaina's retreat.

Across the long bridge over the marsh at Waikane the jeep trundled. Then past the air strip where military planes had landed during the war, now being reclaimed by thickets of haole koa. The gutted old sugar mill, desolate as a skeleton, was succeeded by the granite headlands of Kaaawa and then the little settlement of Punaluu.

Parker was silent as he drove, thinking about what was ahead, about going into Sacred Falls. He always felt as though he should prepare his heart for the experience. Perhaps more than any words he could say, the valley would affect Anne, teach her what she needed to learn.

At Makao Beach he turned the jeep toward the mountains and said, "We're almost there."

Chapter Ten

THERE WAS NOTHING IN THE DRY, ABANDONED CANE FIELDS where the road ended to hint at the treasures in the valley not far away. Parker did not try to explain anything to Anne as they left the car and followed a well-beaten trail through wild grass and stunted cane. Insects whirred in the quiet. The sun, nearly vertical, pressed on his head and shoulders. His feet felt happy as he scudded in his thongs. In fact, he felt happy all over, his body so strong it almost ached to lift or carry a wonderful burden.

Most of the time it was the sea that made him happy but when he came to a place like Sacred Falls he was astonished all over again at how dear the land was to him. In a wonderful way it reminded him of his Hawaiianness, put him to thinking about things he sometimes forgot.

At the mouth of the steep valley, abruptly, the vegetation changed. The bleached grass disappeared and trees, full size, sprang up in a lovely woodland. The pebbled stream lay ahead of them. Parker took a deep breath. Here the magic began. A green and wonderful silence held the shadows.

They took off their thongs and sandals, stood looking at the stream. The clear water, only a few inches deep in most places, dashed brightly against rounded stones. In small pools minnows and other tiny bits of life flashed. Before crossing Parker twisted a large leaf off a nearby kukui tree. Then he selected three nicely shaped pebbles of about the same size and placed them on the leaf, near the trail.

"Oh!" exclaimed Anne. "A Hawaiian ritual? What's it for?"

"It's to get ready," Parker said quietly. "For going into the valley."

"But why? I mean, what does it mean? Should I do one or is yours enough?" Without waiting for his answer she pulled off a leaf, found three pebbles which she placed like his. "Am I doing it right? Do you say a prayer or what?"

"You keep quiet."

"Oh. Well."

"You jus' do it and keep quiet. This the pig god's home. C'mon." He entered the cool stream.

Anne followed him. "I don't understand," she protested as she waded. "What do the stones symbolize?"

"It's jus' what we do," Parker said, keeping his voice low. "Ever'body. Not jus' Hawaiians." When she had reached the other side he said, "Look...."

On every rock in sight, and even on the ground beside the path, dozens of leaves were set out, each with its offering of three pebbles. Some of the leaves were old, dried and curled. A few looked as if they'd been picked yesterday.

"Japanese and Chinese do it too," he said. "Portagee, Korean."

"Oh my goodness! They're all over the place! Tell me about this pig god? Is he good or bad, or what?"

"He's not good or bad. He's jus' there." The difficulties in explaining to her were going to be worse than he'd thought.

"Well, what'd he do?"

Parker looked at her gravely, made his voice patient, hoping it would calm her, slow her down. "Pele chased a young man here. He didn' want to be her lover. Or maybe he was her lover already and he did something Pele didn' like. Anyway, he ran in here and she changed him into a pig. Sometimes you can hear him in here going,..." He made a snorting, snuffling sound. "Then it's time to leave."

"It's probably a boar," Anne said. Her voice was crisp, practical. "They can be very dangerous. Oughta be shot. They should send in some hunters to clean out the place."

At his look she caught herself. "Well, I mean, if this nice waterfall is where people like to come, they shouldn't have to worry about being gored, should they?"

Parker couldn't believe his ears. He stared at her.

"Oh, all right. I probably shouldn't have said that. But are you sure it's safe? You go first." She glanced around at the ohias. "If there's a wild pig in there, I'm going up the nearest tree."

Even making allowances for her because she was from the mainland where people had to put up with bad weather and rude manners, Parker found Anne's remark revolting. If hunters came in here, and he knew about it, they'd have to shoot over his dead body. Most local people, he thought, would feel the same. That was the kind of thing that made local people local. Either you felt that way or you didn't.

As to the truth of the story about Pele and the pig god, Parker himself wasn't sure how much to believe. Some of the stories about Pele were pretty fantastic. Still, too many people had had experiences with her not to adopt an attitude of respect.

Their path led through stands of greenery near the stream. Heaped up boulders lined its sides. Their smooth, generous shapes invited jumping from one to another.

"Look!" Anne called, clearing five feet of water to land on one. He grinned. She was nice to watch, her body soft and agile in the pale green. Mostly he led the way. They climbed over fallen logs, stopped to look at odd fungus. He didn't know the names of many things, but they made him feel good, all these interesting forms of life put here to share the land.

In a hollow where little light penetrated Anne exclaimed, "Oh!" She had found decayed leaves that were mere webs of themselves. "They're like lace!" She held up one the size of her own hand.

"Kukui," Parker said. "This here's the nut." He held out one of the blackish, mottled balls.

"Good to eat?"

"No. Burn. The old Hawaiians burned them for light."

"I'm going to take some of these leaves home." Stooping, she began to gather the fragile–looking webs.

"Not now," Parker told her.

"Why?"

"We don' pick up anythin' while we're goin' some place. Only comin' back."

"What's that for?"

"You pick the wrong thing, it'll rain."

Anne laughed. "That's a good one!" Then she smoothed it over. "If you say so!" Crinkling her eyes with that look of mischief he already knew. There were so many sides to this wahine. One minute saying the worst things imaginable and the next kind of teasing him with those soft–looking lips in a mocking smile. In spite of the rash things she sometimes brought out, her face, in repose, had a wistful quality. And that pale skin. It looked as though it would scratch if you touched her. He had a feeling he ought to throw a blanket or something over her to keep her from getting damaged.

The damp path narrowed, he went ahead. In shaded places it was muddy from the rains that came every day. Finally they emerged into a small clearing and she drew up beside him. The air was still. Here in the heart of the gorge there was no wind. This was one of the places he particularly wanted her to see, a widening in the stream where the cover broke and you could look around. At their feet the water danced with noisy playfulness among the rocks. On the opposite shore the kukui trees leaned, pale leaves set with a dainty precision so that each one caught the light. But the main sight was above. Around and above their two frail selves rose the shaft of the lava tube. There were no ledges, no descents. Just the vertical face of the rock on both sides, mossed to a velvety green, shooting straight toward heaven.

Anne lifted her eyes, gasped. "Oh, my God!"

Parker said nothing, unable to express what he felt.

Anne turned in a circle, head back, taking it all in. "I feel as though I'm looking up the folds of a curtain. A great emerald velvet curtain. That's it. I'm a mouse looking up this great theater curtain! Oh my gosh!"

He found her voice a little loud.

"The falls can't beat this, I'm sure. Nothing could top this. I mean that sheer rock soaring toward the sky. That wedge of blue up there. You could imagine anything here. Pele! Pig gods! Anything!"

She could enjoy it more if she'd just look. At least that's what the old Hawaiians would do. He himself felt like dropping to his knees. Once, in a fancy church, he'd felt like this when the organ began to play. The sound came roaring out of the pipes along the wall and he'd felt everything within him lift, as if he were going to rise—whoom!—straight up to glory on the power of it.

Anne was still exclaiming about the theater curtain.

"Anne," he reproved her. Just then he saw a movement at her

feet. It was not headed for her. But then it was. He reached for her to pull her away. "Look out!"

She escaped his grasp, leaped onto a nearby boulder. Where she had stood a nine–inch centipede now wound its leisurely course on the hard dirt. The sun gleamed on its coppery plates, in a rippling movement the metallic legs propelled the body of armored segments, one after another. Delicately but powerfully the centipede twined toward the stone ledge on which Parker stood.

"Kill it!" Anne shrieked, scooping up a rock.

Parker did not move. He stood watching as the centipede slid toward him, then disappeared beneath the ledge.

Anne's eyes blazed as she came toward him. Her hand still held, awkwardly, the rock which was too heavy for her wrist.

"Why didn't you kill it?" she gnashed. "You let it get away." She was weakly holding onto the rock as if she'd like to throw it at something. Possibly him.

Parker looked at her, his face impassive. "Put the rock down," he said. "You drop it, you might hurt you'self." He took it from her, set it gently nearby.

She was trembling, he saw.

Sometimes when people on the beach were shaking and upset they threw themselves into his arms. He always had to be prepared for that. Mothers weeping over children, teen–agers with problems. He'd even had a young serviceman hang on his neck, crying, when his buddy was brought in drowned. Parker guessed that was why his shoulders were built so thick and solid, for people to hold on to, if they needed him. When that happened, he always stood very quiet, his face troubled, talking to them in a low voice, saying what they wanted to hear.

Anne did not touch him. Her face seethed, flushing like a bad sunburn. "Why didn't you kill it?" she stormed. "You saw how huge it was. If it'd bitten me, I'd've been lame for a week."

Parker looked at her as he would a barking, frightened puppy. Thinking what to do for her. He had no idea she'd react so badly. If the centipede hadn't headed right for her he wouldn't have mentioned it.

"You should protect me!" Her voice caught as she said it.

Parker had to laugh at that. "I did protect you. You're not hurt."

"But you didn't kill it!"

"This is his home," Parker said quietly. "Not yours." He looked up the stream bed toward the inner cleft of the valley. "You come where he lives. He has a right to live in his home."

She seemed only to get madder at this. "I think I have a right not to get bit by a centipede. Don't I?"

"He was minding his own business. He didn't try to hurt you."

"Well, I'll be damned!" Anne straightened, her jaw hard. "It's like you're defending the centipede. Not me, but the centipede." She took an audible gulp of air. "If you hadn't seen him, he would've bitten me. His business!" she added bitterly.

"He didn't hurt you," Parker reminded her again. That was the main thing. Why couldn't she let it go at that? He was about to lose patience. She wanted things her own way. Haoles were like that. They wanted the world absolutely safe. No mystery, no risk. Dull. It was a wonder they even walked around on the beach. But then, seeing how shaken she was, her face all puffy and pink, eyes scrunched up, blaming him, a wave of softness went through him for anyone so unable to bear a small thing. If she burst into tears he would hold her.

"So he didn't bite me." Her lips trembled, she stuttered a little as she spoke. "What about the next people who come by?" Her voice faltered as if she knew that wasn't her real concern. "Or it could bite us on the way back."

His tone was consoling while he teased. "We'll go back a diff'runt way." Since it was unfair to be playful while she was in such a state he added reasonably, "You kill one won't make the place safer. There's prob'ly thousands more. So why kill one?"

He glanced around the lovely glen. Many of the secrets of nature were hidden in this little valley. "Besides, you can' go roun' killin' ever'thin' doesn' suit you."

"My welfare is certainly more important than a centipede's."

Parker chuckled. "The centipede don' think so."

"Oh, for God's sake!" Anne snapped. She moved away and

sat on a big boulder, drawing her legs up, looking all around, to be sure it was safe.

Parker came to where she sat. He stood resting one bare foot easily on the great stone, thumbs in his jean's pockets, looking down at her. Amused, but at her disposition.

"You not gonna get rid of ever'thin' in the world that might hurt you," he pointed out. "After all," he gave a good–natured laugh, "the main thing might hurt you is you."

Anne scowled at the cliff ahead of her, which she clearly didn't see. "Is what you're saying Hawaiian? Is this what the Hawaiians believe?"

"Guess so," he said simply. "Seems jus' natural to me." He stood watching her face, kind of enjoying the silliness of the argument. Anne was calmer now. Her skin had gone back to its normal, pale color. Of course anyone with skin like hers was going to have more problems.

"I'm trying to look at it your way," she said seriously. "Okay, so I accept...nature. The red ants that sting. The centipedes that pinch and poison. I love them all, like Dr. Schweitzer. What does that change? They're still going to bite, whether I love or hate them. So what good does it do?"

"None, 'cept the way you feel." He didn't know who this doctor was or why she'd mentioned him.

"When? When I get bitten?"

"Then, too. But all the time. If you go around loaded with fear, it's gonna hurt a lot more than if you think it's natural. When I was workin' in the fields at the Home I was always barefoot. Most of the time they didn' have shoes for the boys. I got bit every day. Sometimes two or three times, on the feet and ankles. I got so I thought nothin' of it."

Anne looked down as if for some evidence of what he'd been through. He had good, solid brown feet. Straight, unblemished toes. Nothing wrong there.

"Are you saying you're against killing?"

"Unless you have to, for food."

"Why?"

He had to stop a moment to think about that. When he

brought out the answer he still wasn't certain. "Because it gets to be a habit."

"But it's okay to kill animals for food?"

"Sure. I've killed a lot of pigs. But that's diff'runt. I didn' kill them with my heart."

"Then, why did you do it?"

"Somebody had to."

Anne was quiet, as if somewhere else in her thoughts. Slowly she changed expression as her eyes returned, took him in. "You know," she said carelessly, but there was a spark in it too, "you've got nice hair."

Parker was surprised to hear her say such a thing, although he'd heard the words somewhere before. Not from Polly.

Anne stood, stretched. She looked toward the inner valley, lifted her eyes to the top of the tube again. "It's so beautiful in here. Mysterious. Hawaii has something...I want to learn...." She didn't finish what it was she wanted to learn.

Parker understood this as a kind of apology for what had happened. "Let me go first," he said, to reassure her. "The falls is only about two hundred yards ahead."

He took the lead. There was a dull roar in the narrowing valley. The path became steeper. As they climbed he began to feel uneasy about what had happened. To see a centipede, even to be bitten, was not important. But to have such a scene in that particular place! His heart squeezed as if he'd made a mistake. He turned to keep an eye on Anne.

She was stepping in his footprints behind him, her face bemused. The falls ahead roared. She said something. He paused to hear her.

"I was wondering...maybe the pig god doesn't like mainland haoles. Could the centipede be a warning? We're so different, you and I...."

A twang of alarm shot through Parker at the words, so close to his own thoughts. A warning? Of what? The old Hawaiians found symbols, meanings everywhere. He glanced around the gorge, where a calm twilight reigned.

It was then Anne let out a strange cry.

The sound pierced his chest as well as his ears. In a reflex he reached for her arm, glanced at her feet to see if she'd got bit.

"Someone *hit* me," she yelped. She pulled away from him, wheeled around furiously.

"Hit you? Who...where?" Unable to believe it. He glanced up at the forbidding granite cliffs, at the gnarled trees, as if someone might be hiding there. Then he saw it, on the path behind them, still rolling, a pebble about the size of the ones they'd placed on their leaves. A fresh grey, it came to a stop, exposed, alone on the hard dirt path.

On the way up they'd heard only the cry of an occasional bird. No traces had been visible, like a fresh footprint in the mud, of a human in the valley.

Anne wiggled, reached for her back. "Damn, that hurt!" She sounded on the verge of tears.

"Where?" He moved to look. Lifting the back of her loose shirt he saw between her shoulder blades, above her white brassiere elastic, a dab of pink on the otherwise unblemished fairness.

"The skin's not broken," he informed her. He pulled her shirt down, rubbed the spot. "It's gonna be okay," he said. But his own body was tingling, gooseflesh stood on his arms.

He glanced up at the soaring, unscalable cliffs, knowing the pebble had not come from that height. No one could be up there. But nothing moved in the eerie stillness around them. The leaves of the trees remained poised, immobile, set out for the sun.

"I'm scared," Anne whimpered. "I feel like I'm not wanted."

"Don' be scared," he said. But he knew they must leave at once. Anne was his responsibility.

She moved to pick up the pebble.

"Don'," he said sharply. Not knowing why. Feeling that it was not for them to question. Seizing her wrist to put her into motion, he stepped over the pebble. She did the same.

Only when they were well down the path did he release her wrist. The way back, now familiar, seemed shorter than coming up. They did not see anyone on the trail. Just the narrow valley with its stillness and alternating patches of sun and shade. They passed the place where they'd seen the centipede, Parker choosing a path a few feet from where they'd walked before. At the glen where Anne had found the webs of kukui leaves she did not stop or try to pick them up.

They crossed the stream at the entrance to the canyon, found their slippers and made their way back through the tall grass in silence. No one else was in the clearing, where they'd parked.

Not until they were in the jeep, spinning down the coastal road could Parker take a deep breath again. But even then he felt different. The sense of joy and power he'd had earlier with Anne had been replaced by something else.

Chapter Eleven

THEY SAT ON THE SAND AT HANAUMA BAY AFTER LUNCH. Around them on three sides rose the sheltering walls of the volcano. Dry, a hard brown, the ancient crater held the bay like a jewel in a rough setting. Parker and Anne did not have the place to themselves. A dozen or so swimmers and snorkelers combed the shallows. But there was beauty enough for everyone. The afternoon sun spangled the surface of the water, little waves gently shushed the shore. In this tranquil scene the events of the shadowed valley seemed very far away.

Still Parker felt on edge, wary. He and Anne had had a scare and an argument. They had not seen the falls. Things were not going as expected.

The centipede—what that meant was not clear to him since Anne had not been harmed. But the pebble, he felt sure, had been a warning. Somehow it involved Anne. Since she was in his charge it was his duty to protect her. But from whom? In what way? Or could the message be for him? To mark Anne? He dismissed the idea the instant it flickered in his mind. Danger in Anne? This absurd creature, lost as an orphan? Why even his own daughters didn't seem as helpless, as in need of watching as Anne.

He glanced about the walls of the old crater which he loved but today made him feel penned in. He longed to go in the water. They should wait at least another half hour.

"Y'see those beans?" They'd spread the towel for their lunch under a kiawe tree. He pointed up at the long, slender yellow pods among the feathery foliage.

"Yes."

He lit a cigarette.

"Smoking's bad for you, you know."

"Tell me some more!" Laughing at her. "You haoles gave us cigarettes in the first place. Now you say they're not good for us. Why don' you make up you min'?" Eyeing her, one eye half closed against his plume of smoke.

He had a feeling she'd put this pale green outfit on for him. Did that mean she liked him? If so, would she be like the girls Pekuela, them, found so ready to go to bed with a beachboy? Anne wasn't at all like the girl with the long red fingernails. The way she'd looked at him had been scary. Sticky. Like ant bait. He had no idea what Anne's thoughts about him might be.

Anne bridled. "Really, I'm not just an ordinary haole, Parker."

"I didn' say you was."

"Well, you know how I hate what the haoles are doing to Hawaii. We talked about that last night."

"I know." Parker stretched out on his side, blew a long, steady stream of smoke, letting the tobacco soothe him. "You're not like mos' haoles. 'S true. You wouldn' be here if you was."

What had Anne said before the pebble struck? "We're so different, you and I...." He did not choose to pursue the idea. They had not spoken of the pebble since they left. "Go on. What about the beans?"

That was one thing about Anne. She was interested in everything he said.

"Inside is somethin' like molasses. It's good for horses and cows, but it's not s'pose' to be for people. Thass' what I useta eat when I was a kid."

"You did? Why?"

"I was hungry. I was *starvin'*. I was *glad* to eat 'em, when I didn' have anythin' else."

"Was your family very poor?" She sounded almost hopeful.

"No. Not poor. Tight. My father was a stevedore. He made good money, but he drank a lot. 'Specially on weekends, he drank. But we had enough money for poi, at least. You know how much poi they would give me? One cup. One tin cup. They would fill it up to the handle, that's all. If the poi came above the handle, they'd scoop some back out." He shook his head. Even now he found it hard to believe. "They'd give me this one cup of poi and sea salt. That was my dinner." He took a long draw on his cigarette. The memory still hurt.

"How strange!"

"M'yeah. My father and mother, they ate stew with their poi.

After they finish', they gave me their dishes to wash. I'd wash 'em at the pipe outside with a piece of coconut fiber. Make 'em nice an' clean. That was my job, while they was sittin' roun', enjoyin' theirselves after a good dinner."

"What a story!" The sympathy in Anne's eyes was very enjoyable.

"But...I don't understand. Why did they do it? Did you have a very big family? Lots of brothers and sisters?"

"No, jus' me."

"Just one child? And they treated you like that?" Anne frowned. "Hawaiians usually have big families. Eight or ten kids. And they're generous about food. Generous about everything, but especially food. It's one of the failings of the race. They're always giving things away. Even to strangers. *Why* didn't they give you more to eat?"

"Dunno. That was my mother's idea. She was Hawaiian. Pure. Spoke only Hawaiian at home. When I was little she useta tie me with a rope to the couch when she went out. I'd be there for hours. My grandmother, her mother, didn' like that. She useta come to the house 'special to see me. She loved me a lot. Useta hold me in her arms and cry." He flashed Anne a smile, so the story wouldn't seem as bad as it sounded. "My gran'mother wanted to adopt me," he added, "but my mother wouldn' let her."

"I know a lot of grandparents take their first grandchildren to raise," Anne said. "Hanai."

Parker stubbed his cigarette in the short manini grass. "That was on the Big Island, where I was born, in Kamuela. At the Parker Ranch. Thass' why I was named Parker, I guess."

Now that he'd got started he felt like going on. Anne's eyes did not leave his face.

"When I was about six my mother and father moved to Honolulu. My grandmother followed them here, trying to get me. But my mother...you know what she did? She found out that the Salvation Army had a Home for orphan boys in Manoa. So that's where she put me. In the Home. I was seven years old."

"How could she put you in an orphan's home when you weren't an orphan?"

"The judge signed the order. Judge Deshay. That's where I lived until I was about sixteen, seventeen."

"But *why?*"

"Didn' want me, I guess. I was too rascal. Thass' why she had to tie me up."

"Good grief! Maybe she didn't like children, since she stopped after you."

"Well, I have one sister, sort of. After my mother put me in the Home, she adopted this one girl."

Anne's chin dropped. "You're kidding!"

"The daughter of her best friend. When the friend died my mother adopted her daughter." He'd forgotten how stunned he was when he found out.

"Was your family nice to this—adopted sister?"

"I guess so. Everything was okay when I went home. Sometimes on weekends, holidays, like that, I'd go home for a few days."

"What an awful story! I could cry."

"M'yeah. My grandmother useta cry a lot. Cry and chant. She loved me so much. But she couldn' do nothin'."

Now that he'd told Anne he felt ashamed. "Hawaiians say it's not good to 'bleach bones in the sun,'" he apologized. "That means you shouldn' talk about your family. Even if it hurts, you' s'pose to keep it inside."

"It's all right," Anne protested. "It's fascinating. I mean, gosh, I'm so sorry. You really suffered a lot. You have a right to talk."

"Well, it turned out okay. I got this good job. I really like my job. So it's okay."

Anne touched his wrist. "I'm glad you told me...about your mother. In my family it's my father...." Her features clouded as she paused a moment, stared at the bay. "I'm still mad at him for things that happened years ago."

"Because he made you go swimmin'?" Parker still couldn't see that as a hardship.

"No," Anne's fingers dismissed. "He wanted me to be a doctor. Made me study chemistry, physics, stuff like that I just couldn't stand. My grades were miserable. That upset him. Finally he understood I would never make it into medical school and he gave up. Then one day he said he didn't think much of women doctors anyhow."

"Oh." Parker had never heard of this kind of family.

"I didn't speak to him for a week. I've never been able to forget that." She sighed, went on. "My father's family has always been very strong on schooling. His sister has more advanced degrees than any other woman in the United States. She's the only one with a Th.D., which is something you get after a Ph.D."

It all sounded terrible to him. He'd spent three years in the seventh grade, looking out the window, waiting for P.E. to begin.

"I'm so glad to be in Hawaii, away from all that." Anne glowered at the sand. Then, as if she'd said more than she meant to, too, she turned and smiled. A soft smile, right at him.

Suddenly Parker felt very unusual. Didn't know where to look, what to do next. His legs felt so fidgety he had to get up. Just had to move. As if all this talk, all this scenery was just too much. Fortunately, a clump of naupaka bushes nearby gave him something to do. He strode to it, broke off one of the insignificant little white flowers.

"You know this?" Showing it to Anne.

"No." She examined it. "Oh, this one's damaged. It's only half a flower."

"That's it," he chuckled. "They're all like that." He showed her two more.

Anne studied one of the flowers. "It's as though someone tore it in half. The petals are only on one side of the stem."

"It's a curse was put on the flower. A wahine's lover left her. On the beach she saw the naupaka bushes, cursed 'em for makin' flowers when she felt so bad. Tore one of the blossoms in two. They been like that ever since. Won' change, won' be whole 'till he comes back."

"The beaches are full of naupaka," Anne murmured.

"They's all waitin'."

"Sad little flower!" Anne looked at it tenderly. "Sad curse."

"Hawaiians is strong," Parker assured her. "They kin do anythin'."

Chapter Twelve

SINCE PARKER WORE HIS TRUNKS UNDER HIS JEANS AT ALL TIMES, just in case of an emergency, he was already stripped down when Anne stepped out of the bathhouse. At first he thought she had nothing on. As she drew nearer he saw that she was wearing a pale apricot one–piece suit that was nearly the color of her skin. Still, he got something of a shock seeing her at last—the essential Anne—after looking at her in her clothes and wondering, all this time. Her body was about what he expected, built like a mermaid, all the meat on the bottom. The long supple torso didn't look nearly substantial enough to him. She could use a diet of poi for awhile.

"You' suit's a nice color," he said, since it was so evident he was looking at her.

"Yes," she said simply. There was no bathing cap in sight. Her bobby pin was gone, her dark hair swung freely about her face.

"In the water, the fish gonna think you one big lobster," he teased.

"Already cooked!" she laughed, swishing her hair as if she liked the feel of it.

"You ever used these?" Parker had borrowed masks and swim fins from Dede.

"I've used fins, not a mask."

"You gonna see a lotta nice things. Here the fish so tame you can almost pick 'em like mangoes. Now, the mask...."

"Wait. I want to get wet first." She ran down to the water, waded up to her thighs. "It's not at all cold," she called. She sank down to her shoulders, then went all the way under. The water closed over her head. When she came up in a graceful rise, her hair swept back clean from her face, Parker knew all he needed to know. Without seeing her take a stroke he knew she was a swimmer. Anyone who came out of the water like that, slowly, nose first, was a swimmer. She turned and smiled, blinking at the shock to her eyes. For a moment she remained there, moving her arms with pleasure, her white shoulders barely showing in the green. Then she rose and trudged toward him, laughing, dripping, shaking the fishtail of her wet, dark hair.

He showed her how to put the mask on, fitting the edges closely around the sides of her face. It seemed necessary to touch her face and hair a bit to be sure it was snug. She did what he told her to, smeared spit around on the inner glass and rinsed it before she fitted it on for good. He put on his own mask and flippers at the water's edge, then she followed him in.

Heads down, almost on the surface of the water they moved slowly toward the reef. There was one place he particularly wanted her to see, a steep, enclosing coral formation that reminded him, with its arches and niches, of a cathedral. It had the same kind of mystery and religious feeling, only without the statues of people suffering with arrows and thorns and crosses so that your eyes hurt to look at them. The coral grotto was not sad like that. Still, it was as wonderful to see with all the magic little pukas where eels could slither and lobster babies could hide. That's one thing a cathedral didn't have, no matter how decorated and pretty—all the marvelous things of the sea, living and bearing and getting fat for people to eat them. Though of course that wasn't true in Hanauma where they were protected and were just there for people to see.

Anne used her fins correctly, fluttering from the hips instead of the knees. Most beginners kicked like cross babies, getting no power at all. In a slow glide she cruised, looking like a one-eyed mermaid, her dark hair fanning out fantastically around her shoulders when she ceased moving forward, her white arms and legs luminous in the delicate green water. The light rippled on her body as she turned, bent and straightened in the motions of the underwater dream. She seemed to relish the experience, poking along, as if she were photographing everything in her mind.

Scanning a coral head, Parker saw a wirelike shape protruding from a hole, extended his arm to point it out to her, a lobster's antenna. He looked closer. If only one antenna were in view it would mean the lobster was sharing his hole with an eel. He saw a second antenna so, showing off a little, he reached for the brittle feelers and gently drew the lobster forth. Immediately it began doubling and flapping its rear end in a frantic effort to get free. Anne nodded and he returned the struggling little fellow—he was only half–grown—to his hole.

They continued to cruise and float just below the surface of the water, sharing without words the fabulous landscape. Once he spotted an eel loafing by a deep cleft in the coral hedge. It was a thin brown moray, about eighteen inches long. He did not want to have anything to do with it. Putting out his hand to Anne in a cautionary gesture, he held quite still until it had moved away. Occasionally, when she drew near to inspect the same coral head as he, their shoulders gently rubbed. Reaching to touch a giant, filmy limu, their arms crossed, were almost entwined. It was all in dreamy slow motion. Another time, in a shift of currents his legs drifted across hers, smoothing them in a dreamy caress. More than once he felt like turning and pulling Anne to him, making things clear right then and there. But caught in the gentle tug and drift of the water, enjoying the crackling and thumps in his ears, the shifting patterns of webby light on the sandy floor, he continued, indulgently, to float with her, outside of time. The bay seemed to hold them in its embrace like wayward children among the rest of its sumptuous treasures.

Then, what he hoped would happen, did. Suddenly they were surrounded by a school of fish. Hundreds of small grey mullet all the same size and color, all with the same expressions on their small pouty faces, enveloped them. He stopped moving and Anne did too. They were immersed in a bath of the untouch-ing, wide–eyed little forms. He could feel them within millimeters of his arms and knees. Flickering this way and that, all at the same time, with split–second daintiness, the fish lingered around them. He and Anne drifted, their flippers still, within the cloud of silvery motion. Then, with tranquil delibera-tion the mullet began to move on. The pool of forms diminished, then disappeared. As he and Anne floated, the current brought her body against his so that her breast and stomach slid across his shoulder.

Pekuela, them, said they often began with their wahines in the sea. It seemed like a natural place to begin, the water being such a loving place, caressing you, making everything so soft and easy. You couldn't be in the water and not be aware of your body. How good it felt. How natural it was to feel good things with your body. Still, he did not make a move with Anne. Something held him back. With all there was to see and feel it did not yet seem the right moment. Without purpose, enjoying the sunlight filtering through the water, they continued to float and glide.

Time got away from him in the sea, and especially here at Hanauma. After he showed her his cathedral and they saw some larger fish where the waves were breaking on the coral, he raised his mask and found that the shadow of the western rim of the crater had advanced more than halfway across the bay. It was about five–thirty. Slowly they made their way back to the beach. Only half a dozen people were still there.

Anne was ecstatic, laughing and shaking her arms. "Oh, that was beautiful!" She threw herself on the warm sand, not bothering with a towel, letting the grains cake her wet skin. "I didn't notice I was getting cold. This feels so good." She wiggled in the sand's warmth.

Parker lowered himself next to her, carefully, face down, his movements deliberate so his legs wouldn't touch hers. It wouldn't be the same as in the sea. Propped on his elbows he asked, "Did you like it?" Fishing. Wanting to hear her say she was glad they came to Hanauma.

"Oh yes! It was magic. It's a whole new magical kingdom! I felt like…" Anne rested her chin on her crossed wrists, "I was in a dimension I didn't even know existed!"

"Oh." All he asked was did she like it.

"It was like a glimpse into the mystery of the universe."

"M'yeah."

"It's been a wonderful day. I'd never have seen all these things without you." She turned her head, gave him a sweet look, as if she were really grateful. "There's something so special here. I don't understand it—what the Hawaiians have that the haoles don't."

That, he thought, was the most intelligent thing he'd heard her say yet. Possibly the most intelligent thing any haole had ever said.

"When I first came here, everything I knew about the islands came from 'Hawaii Calls.' And the pictures from Matson menus. I just thought it would be a nice, inexpensive place to spend a year." She sighed, staring at the miniature hills of sand a few inches from her nose.

A year! Parker couldn't help but react to that. "I'm glad you gonna be here awhile!" A sense of happiness swarmed through him like golden bees.

"I'm in the middle of a divorce," she backtracked. "In California you have to wait a year. So I came and got my little cottage on Liliuokalani for thirty-five dollars a month. I didn't know what I wanted. All I knew was what I didn't want. I didn't want my family's kind of social life. So I avoided their friends here. Then I began eating at the Lagoon. Gosh!" She shook her head, giggled. "The local people! They are something!"

"Wha'd'ya mean?"

"I don't know. The way they enjoy themselves. They're so natural. So much at ease. But kind. It's like...they're so privileged. I feel as though they have a lot more than I did, the way I was raised."

It was okay with him if she wanted to talk like that. Since it seemed to mean that she liked local people.

"I began to think about—the difference. Aloha. How it really does make people different. So I began reading books. I spend five or six hours a day at the library."

No wonder she was so confused about the most basic things, like windward and leeward. Anyone who spent five or six hours a day in a library was bound to have their brains messed up. He was surprised she was as good as she was.

"Here," she went on, "it's as if it's natural for people to be friends. As if strangers are friends you just haven't met yet. It's extraordinary...."

"M'yeah. Well...."

"And today—seeing the island with you—you've given me a lot of new things to think about." She traced a doodle in the sand with the tip of her forefinger. "I'll even look at centipedes a little differently." Mocking, she looked at him sidewise.

Did haoles talk like this when they were with each other? He'd never heard a Hawaiian go on like that.

Anne's upper arm rested its entire length against his. It felt cool, and small. One–fourth of Polly's. Polly was built square as an ice house. Well, having all those children hadn't helped her shape any. But even when he first knew her, when he was eighteen and she was seventeen, she'd been packed solid as an aku.

One of the reasons Pekuela, them, had such success with their wahines was that they kidded a lot. They insulted everyone, left and right. Cracked jokes about the haoles, the Hawaiians, Portagees, rich people, broke people. They even cracked jokes about their dark skins. Asked the wahines if they were scared to touch. "Try," they would tease, holding out a big brown arm. "It feels same like white." No shame. Going into howls of laughter at their confusion. Knowing the wahines were dying to go to bed with them. "In the dark you can' tell the difference. Wanna try?" Parker had seen Pek, them, operating at the Moana, under the banyan. It all seemed like such fun. Unfortunately, with Anne he couldn't seem to be lively and jokey the way he was with other people. Why?

"Anne," he said, seriously.

She was still smiling at him, a soft, rascal smile that was also like she was waiting. Like the next move was up to him.

Some sand was stuck on the side of her cheek and chin. Up close like this, just inches away, he could see each of her eyelashes, plain as the leaves of a palm frond. He put out his hand, with one finger rubbed a little of the sand off her chin. Killing time. He thought of asking her. But then he just did it. Curved his hand around her jaw and leaned and kissed her.

Since she didn't pull away from his hand he had an idea she was going to let him. That their mouths were going to meet the way he wanted. They did. The effect was even better than he'd expected. In fact he didn't want to let go. And Anne sort of helped, aiming her face just right. Her lips were cool and soft. Almost at once she turned on her side and drew to him. He put his arms around her and turned on his side also. This made it possible for them to continue to kiss without any effort at all. Parker was amazed at the effect this produced. He'd never kissed like this. Kissing had always seemed to him about what sniffing was to a meal. Like a clue. A signal. It had never occurred to him that it might be like the first bite. This kissing with Anne—for now there were little stops and new beginnings—was like nothing he'd ever had in his life. He and Polly didn't kiss, except as a ritual, on holidays, since he could remember.

Both his arms went around Anne easily, and more. When he squeezed, her bones sort of clumped together, soft, like a stand of bamboo. With Polly it was like hugging a sofa.

Gosh, he thought, this is wonderful! Hoping the kissing would go on a lot longer. Anne's lips had changed temperature. Warm now, they were doing sensational things, breaking off, coming back, clinging. They teased, they explored. It was really extraordinary the variety of things four lips could find to do.

As for his part, he felt that he was doing things right. It seemed to come to him quite naturally. He felt he even had a talent for it. There was nothing he wanted to do more than to see what other enjoyable variations he and she could come up with.

He hadn't forgotten about the main thing, of course. His body was giving him signals about that. But he was so absorbed in this new invention, their marvelous new game, that he was able, for the moment, to set aside thoughts of the rest.

He'd had no idea this sort of thing was available. For years he'd seen people necking on the beach without guessing what was going on. Having sex more or less regularly with Polly and taking care of things himself when he wasn't, he'd supposed that was all there was to it. Or almost all. He felt brilliant. A Captain Cook! He had this new discovery. The newspapers should carry a headline on it. He was an idiot. All these years! He could have kicked himself a mile out to sea.

Anne turned her head away, buried her nose in the hollow of his shoulder. He settled himself on one side, pulling her to him so that his thick arm could pillow her neck. He continued to hold her close, his head bent so that his lips were against her wet hair. He couldn't get over the enormousness of what had happened. If the island of Maui had cruised up and joined Oahu it wouldn't have astonished him more. The crater walls around them looked odd.

96

Lying there, savoring the length of her body against him, his hand moved over her shoulders and back. Relishing the feel of her flesh, but not satisfied. Pressing, moving on, down to the hollow at the bottom of the scoop–back suit, then returning to the fragile neck and ears. One of his thick thighs lay between hers. If he saw a couple doing this at Waikiki he'd have to break it up. This really was not what the head lifeguard should be doing on a public beach. But when he glanced around he saw only three figures straggling up the zigzag road to the rim's top. The color had faded out of the water. The rocks were turning grey. The air itself was greying.

He and Anne hadn't spoken since they began to kiss. He drew away a little to look at her. Her expression was soft. Contented, he would say. He smoothed her chin where, as a test, he had rubbed off the sand. Revelling that her face now was available to his touch.

"Anne," his voice cracked on her name. "I . . . wanna be alone with you. You know what I mean?"

Out at the mouth of the bay the big combers from the sea dashed against the rocks, making geysers of foam. Sparrows were settling for the evening in the nearby kiawe trees.

"I know," she said.

"Does that scare you?"

"No." Her glance dropped to the level of his collarbone, hiding the expression in her eyes. Her lips were pouty, swollen. "I want to be with you too. But...." She stopped.

But? The word seemed to grow, to take on enormous proportions. To fill the bay. But? It was an obstacle that reached all the way to the moon. But? But what?

He could not imagine anything so unnatural, so unjust as to cut off the intent of what she'd just said. "I want to be with you, too...but." The yes turned around to the exact opposite. To a no. A piece was missing. Something he didn't know about. He had to know what it was. Dreaded learning it. But he had to know.

"M'yeah?"

"I feel so rotten...about my divorce. I'm still shaken from it."

He heard her words as if they were slowed down, announced over the loudspeaker at the Natatorium. Each somehow against him. One after another they rolled over him with the punishment of a train of cane cars. Each bearing her undebatable verdict of "No."

"I like you, a lot." Her voice was thin, but clear. "It's just that...I'm not ready, to go that far...yet."

Yet! She'd said 'yet'! He took a breath as if his lungs hadn't had air for an hour. Yet! That mean not now, but *someday*. Not this evening, but some other time. A future lay ahead. A future did exist! However long it might take, the hope was there. She said she wanted to, but not yet.

Not yet. Not yet! He could have shouted with the joy of it. His lungs were so stuffed he had to let go. He did. With a whoop he pulled her against him, hard. He crushed her, rocking from side to side. The wonderfulness of it! The earth itself seemed to be rocking with them. The volcano, the greying sky, the whole world rocked with joy. He couldn't contain it. Shouting, he threw himself on his back, pulling her over on top of him. Then he rolled over on top of her. They continued to tumble, over and over, down the incline of the beach to the water's edge. She screeched and flailed, kicking when she could, but not really hard, to get away. In the shallows they came to a stop, gritty and bruised, laughing.

Breathless, they floundered, the water sloshing their bodies. He pulled her up. On their knees, not yet recovered enough to get to their feet, Anne leaned against him. Her arms were around his neck as they knelt together in the coarse sand.

He wanted her to know how it was for his part. On her shoulders his hands were strong. "Thass' all right, Anne," he said. "Take you' time. I'm not gonna change."

Chapter Thirteen

H E AND ANNE STOOD BEFORE ANNE'S STUDIO COTTAGE IN THE peaceful courtyard. Anne's front door opened into the dark. She'd forgotten to close it when she left that morning. People in Waikiki were careless about that sort of thing. A large hibiscus bush flanked the entrance. The flowers of the day were folding shut as the twilight deepened. From a radio nearby came the shimmering notes of Sol Hoopii's slack key "Maui Chimes."

He held Anne's hands, hating to let her go, but not wishing to jeopardize in any way the promise of her wonderful "yet." Willing to do whatever it would take to bridge the necessary lapse of time until the "yet" became "now." Holding on to her, but also showing, by the way he stood, that he was ready to move away at her first sign.

"Well, I hope you didn' get too much sun today." The smell of her hair, still damp at the roots, came to him.

"No. I think my nose got burned...." She touched it, then returned her hand to his. "I'll be okay."

"M'yeah. Well."

"It was a lovely day."

He said nothing, just feeling her hands in his, thinking how wonderful it was that he'd be standing here again soon, that soon they'd be riding somewhere in his jeep again. He had so much to look forward to.

"You sure you don' wanna get somethin' to eat at the Lagoon?"

"No. Thanks. Not tonight."

Still she didn't move away from him. An airplane's drone made them lift their eyes above the palms. In the sky over Steamer Lane, its red and green wing lights blinking, the plane passed Waikiki coming from the airport near Ewa. In a moment it would be near the dark silhouette of Diamond Head, taking another load of mainland tourists home. There was a tradition, for visitors aboard ships, of tossing a lei overboard as they passed Diamond Head. If the lei floated back to the beach it meant they would return some day. Many an aching heart, mainland bound, had found solace in the gesture. Since visitors returning in planes couldn't drop a lei overboard, the pilots offered them the next best thing. Passing before Diamond Head, they tipped the wings of the plane in a last salute.

Parker watched for a long moment as the DC–6 crossed from right to left in his field of vision, its drone diminishing. He thought he saw a change in the blinking red and green lights, thought he saw the plane's wings dip.

But that was people leaving Hawaii. That had nothing to do with him, and what he had now. Anne was here, and they had Hawaii. There was no connection between those sad people and what he and Anne could look forward to. He was smiling, in spite of himself, at the thought of his riches. He lifted Anne's hand to his chest, placed it near his heart in an unconscious gesture. His other hand drew her to him. She did not resist.

"Well, okay...."

He was going to say "Good–bye," but instead he kissed her. In the shelter of the cottage with its dark hibiscus bush, her lips, her body were familiar to him now. Still, in the freshness of his good fortune they seemed awesomely new, too.

The kiss went on longer than he, or anyone in the world would have guessed. When they broke apart it was to press through Anne's open door. They barely made it across the ten feet of her lauhala mat, to the bed.

Chapter Fourteen

THE BED WAS ONLY THIRTY INCHES WIDE, PARKER DISCOVERED when he was at last able to notice. Actually, it was a punee, since a rough cotton spread made it a daytime couch. There was room for both of them on it only if they were on their sides or stacked one over the other. The springs were so soft that it sloped in the middle like a hammock. They lay cradled together in the bottom of the slough, facing each other.

"How much do you weigh?"

"A hunerd seventy–five," Parker said modestly.

"The way the mattress sags I'm squashed between you and a hill. Let me try the other side." Anne scrambled over him, her knees and elbows digging into his flesh. He moved to take her place, not minding her gouging although he did put his hand down so his ule wouldn't catch it.

"Now I'm rolling down this side. Oh well." She settled her head on the inside of his upper arm, arranged her legs between his.

"You feel like a kaku." Smoothing the long fine bones of her arms, her fragile rib cage. "That's a very bony fish." Then, in case she might not like the comparison he added, "But I like you that way, since that's the way you are." Polly, he couldn't help remembering—it was hard to find a bone in Polly's body. She was solid as a tire all over, except for her breasts which were more like bags of day–old poi.

Anne's breasts were so small they didn't hang down at all. Just sort of stuck out, soft and dainty, like mud pies thrown against a wall. His hand more than covered one. He held her right breast now, the nipple caught between his third and fourth fingers. This gave him a great sense of luxury and privilege, even though it was such a small thing.

In the dark room he could smell a stalk of yellow ginger. Its scent mingled with that of the lauhala mat and their own brine. For the moment the heavy air in the dim little cottage seemed to be at the exact center of the universe.

The first time they made love Parker hardly knew what happened it was such a blaze. He'd had a terrible sense of his own power. Yet even the simplest things seemed beyond his grasp. Kisses were not the sweet nibbles they'd been earlier, they were infuriating; they dragged miles behind the feeling that galloped over him. He gave up on the kissing, tried to keep his jaws from hurting her too much as he chewed on her hair, her ear, her neck. It was incredible the violence that he wanted to do to this frail-looking creature. And it was wonderful how well she held up to it. Didn't seem to feel in any danger at all. Murmuring "Go on, go on." And then "Oh, yes!" when he began to say things in Hawaiian to her, growling words he'd forgotten he knew. Because much as his body was doing, it still didn't seem to be enough to show her what he meant. He had to use his voice too.

But in spite of all that was happening—at one moment the walls of the cottage seemed to be banging against one another—he did not forget the hardest lesson of his life. At the right time—he knew just when to do it—he pulled backwards and lay on her stomach. The last convulsions wrung him. Then he lay quiet.

Anne gave a funny cry and a moment later he felt her sobbing against his shoulder. "Oh, you're so nice. That was so nice of you. I know it wasn't easy." He could feel tears running down his neck. "Thank you," she wept. "Thank you so much, Parker."

"I don' wan' you to hapai," he said softly. Happy that she was glad. Polly always trounced him no matter what he did. If he didn't pull out, as in the early days, she jumped on him for doing her wrong, getting her hapai for sure. And later, when, religiously he'd taken care every time, she'd complained bitterly of not having her satisfaction. He couldn't win with Polly. Anne appreciated what he did. That made him feel good. He'd be glad to do it a lot more. He'd show her what good care he could take of her. This was one thing he felt he knew how to do pretty well. Even though he'd never say it was easy, especially this first time with everything so new and building up so powerfully and fast.

The roaring around them subsided. Or at least from the new sense of stillness it seemed that there had been a roaring. Things became more distinct for Parker, things he hadn't had time to notice before. Like how soft and flexible her body was, her arms thin and light on his back. There was a kind of elusiveness to her, an elasticity which made it hard to seize all he wanted. He was able to remember how it had been when he first got hold of her with his ule. He'd felt so strong. Strong enough to lift her with it. Strong enough to carry her on a long, long trip from which they would never return.

Now he lay dreaming with her in his arms after a second, longer, sweeter journey, in which the travel more than the getting there had preoccupied him. His feelings were subsiding into little wavelets like at Hanauma Bay, friendly reminders of what he'd been through. His body was telling him that he was happy, unashamedly happy.

"All this time I seen the beachboys goin' after the girls at the Moana, I never knew what it was," Parker sighed. Thinking of how he'd watched Pekuela, Sunshine, them, in their adventures, and almost pitied the way they chased around, as if standing still weren't good enough. Now he had a glimpse of what the chase was all about. If what they felt with their wahines was what he had with Anne, he had a new admiration for the way they managed to live. Anyone who fixed it so he felt like the top of his head was going to blow off—regular—was *smart*.

"I don't understand how the beachboys live," Anne said. "Doing nothing but having fun."

"Understand what? How they get wahines?"

"Not just that. How they live. Live so well. Without working."

"Don' worry 'bout the beachboys," Parker advised her. "They doin' okay." His voice had an edge to it.

"I know. But a lot of them aren't even very good looking. Of course Sunshine is. And Morgan and Pekuela. But some of them even have missing front teeth. And still they have wahines all over the place."

"D'you ever go out with Sunshine?" Holding very still as he waited for her reply.

"No. Sunshine's not my type," Anne yawned. "He's chasing bigger fish over at the Moana." In the gloom her white hand looked like a starfish on his chest.

"I seen him hangin' 'roun' you coupla times," Parker offered.

"Oh, he just does it with me to keep in practice," she said lightly.

"He won't be chasing wahines so much pretty soon. He wants to be a lifeguard. Probably will be," Parker added gloomily. He didn't see how he could turn Sunshine down since he came out tops in the tests. Sunshine knew how to do everything just right.

"A lifeguard!" Anne sounded so surprised Parker was jogged.

"Whassa matter? Why not?" What was it to her?

Sunshine was slippery as the seaweed of Manu'akepa, Parker thought. Why did the guy aggravate him so much? "Sunshine's always lookin' out for Sunshine," he advised Anne. "He's got a reason, for sure."

Why talk about Sunshine? Here was Anne lying in his arms and all these extraordinary sensations washing over him. "This is so ono." He tightened his arms around her. "I want it to go on and on. All I want is more."

They were quiet a moment, the darkness silken around them. He kissed Anne's face, pressed against his, as best he could. Unfortunately he couldn't get to her mouth.

"I'm glad you kin swim," he murmured at last. "But if you couldn't, I could teach you."

"I told you I was a good swimmer," she scoffed.

"That still beats me that your father *wanted* you to swim." Parker had never heard of such a thing. All the families he knew hated to lose their kids to the water. "Why?"

"He was a doctor." Anne turned her head away. With a sigh she rearranged her limbs in the opposite direction.

"A doctor? Did he take out people's tonsils, like that?"

"I guess so. At first. He had his own clinic. When I was old enough to notice he didn't do anything. Just sat in an office. Walked around the clinic scaring people to death."

"What's that got to do with swimmin'?"

"He thought it would keep me healthy. Swimming is supposed to be healthy for you."

Parker chuckled. "Swimmin' didn't make me healthier. I got

104

beaten for it. Getting whomped with a broomstick didn' improve my health."

"Who did that? Who beat you with a broomstick?"

"My father. He was a powerful man. He could swing a broomstick like a newspaper."

It was strange. He liked telling Anne about his life, even things that were painful.

"My father did everything he could to keep me home. He'd take my clothes—my only clothes I had—and soak 'em and hang 'em on the line in back of the house, to keep me from leaving. But I'd sneak out, get my clothes off the line and put 'em on wet. I'd go anyhow. When I got back I'd get a licking but then I'd go again next day too." He shook his head, gave a rueful laugh. "Nothin' could stop me."

He began to smooth Anne's back and side in the new position she'd taken, his hand still learning her curves. "There was one time…." He had a nice story for her. "Once when I ran away to the water I didn't get beaten. It was a very special time for Hawaiians. Prince Kuhio died. He was the last of the royalty. When Hawaiian royalty die, the red fish run. At night, for three nights. That was way back in 1925 or 1926. I went down to Pier Two and caught a whole sackful of these fish. About this big." He opened his hand to show the span, barely visible in the gloom, from little fingertip to thumb.

"How'd you catch them?"

"With a bamboo pole I'd cut. And a strong thread with a bare hook. Bare hook! I didn't have bait, but other people did and fish were biting at anything. People had lanterns, flashlights. The fish came crowding into the harbor by the thousands, like they wanted to be caught. I pulled up a coupla dozen."

"Were there any like that this afternoon, at Hanauma?"

"No. They only come with the death of royalty. My father was so happy to see the fish—they're real ono to fry. *That* time he didn't give me a licking." Parker sat up, leaned for his cigarettes and matches on the floor. Lighting up, he inhaled deeply.

"Wait a minute," Anne objected. "How old were you?"

"'Bout fourteen."

"I thought you were living at the Salvation Army Home."

"I was. But I went home sometimes. For weekends. Or Christmas to New Year's, like that. I still went home."

"I don't understand why your mother did that—put you in the Home. Did she ever give you any reason?"

"Nope. Not that I know of."

"Maybe your mother had a terrible time in childbirth," Anne suggested. "I've heard of that. Women who almost died delivering a child—and then had a grudge against it ever afterwards."

Parker was silent, smoking. He had nothing to add to the idea.

"Or maybe she was very young," Anne continued. "Maybe she was only sixteen or seventeen when you were born. Didn't know how to take care of a small child. Resented the responsibility. It could have been that, you know."

Parker thought of how it was with his own first child. How alarmed and furious he'd been when he learned that Polly intended to go through with having the baby after he'd given her money to buy quinine pills. How offended he'd been at the sight of the little creature, even though she looked like him. And then how, bit by bit, he'd gotten used to Daisy, found things to do to make her smile. Later he'd walk all the way from the harbor to upper Kalihi just to spend an hour or two playing with Daisy.

"Why don't you ask your mother what her reason was? Is she still alive?"

"I don't know." Something painful moved around inside him. "When my father died she moved to Kauai. I didn' hear from her anymore after that. Maybe she married, changed names. Maybe she died. No way of tellin'."

Anne was quiet, as if she were sorry. Then she said, "You could probably find out from the court records why she put you in the Home. Your mother must have told the judge something."

"It was Judge Deshay's court. I 'member that. He wrote the order."

"Why don't you look it up? If you knew the reason you might feel better. I can tell it bothers you."

"It doesn't bother me," he denied. "I don' know nuthin' 'bout court records, like that." He didn't like the idea at all.

"It wouldn't be difficult," Anne insisted. "You just go to the court building, behind the statue of Kamehameha, and ask."

He was not going to the courthouse. It was bad enough to have to go to the Parks and Recreation Office to see Kanekini every few weeks on something relating to the beach. All those papers and files. People acting like what was on those papers was more important than anything. He couldn't stand the feel of such places. He was not going to the courthouse for something as personal as why his mother didn't want him.

"Naw." He was firm about it. "What happened was a long time ago. Almost thirty years. Ol' stuff like that, it's *gone*."

She didn't seem to catch on at all. "Look, I'll go with you. How's that? We'll go together and see what we can find." She was pronouncing her words real plain, the way people from the mainland did when their minds were made up. He wished he'd never mentioned the Home. It wasn't really important. He hardly ever thought about it, except sometimes when he was listening to Hawaiian music. Then, longing for something—he didn't know what—he'd think of his mother. Find himself puzzling again over why she'd done it. Why did his mind keep tracking back to something that made him feel bad?

As for Anne's idea, he wouldn't argue now. Not for anything would he spoil what they had.

A gecko chirped. Around them the soft dissonances of the end of an evening in Waikiki continued. Somewhere chairs scraped, voices rose in tones preparatory to farewells. A car door slammed. In the cottage on the other side of the panax hedge a wire coat hanger dropped on a wooden floor.

"I'm happy with you, Anne." He stubbed out his cigarette, turned to gather her in his arms again. "You feel so good to me. Your breast feels so soft...I love it. Mmm. Ono."

Anne's hands were caressing his hair as if she found what he was doing ono, too. He raised his head. "You know, we have a hula that tells how beautiful the queen is, her eyes and hands, and how soft her breasts are."

"The queen?" Anne giggled.

"And there are songs about the king too, about how powerful his ule is."

"No kidding? The king didn't mind if they talked about his ule?"

"It's a compliment. Hawaiians think those things are nice. They're not ashamed, the way the haoles are. The way the haoles talk you'd think the men don't even have an ule."

Anne's laughter encouraged him to go on.

"In the newspaper when they want to say nice things about an important man they say, Oh, Mr. Bellingham made this railroad company and he has a nice house on Diamond Head, but they will never say he has a wonderful ule."

Anne gave a shriek at that.

"That's the difference between the haoles and the Hawaiians. Except now the Hawaiians are getting so much like the haoles you'd think they don't have ules anymore either. Everything is shame, shame." He chuckled ruefully. "That's progress."

"In the song do they really come right out and say the king has a big ule?"

"No. They change it a little to make it nice. They say, Oh, the king is so great and the Pali is a wonderful thing to see. And then you know already what they mean."

"Oh dear! Now every time I hear how magnificent the Pali is, I'll be thinking about the king's ule."

"Well, it *is* a nice view," he reproved her. Firm about that.

"It must be late. Are you hungry?"

"I'm not hungry while I got you." Squeezing her to show his appreciation.

Anne lifted on her elbow. The luminous dial on the clock near the bed showed it was after ten.

"Shall we go eat?"

"The Lagoon's closed." Hating for the moment to end.

"There are other places. Kau Kau Korner."

Parker got up, began to pull on his trunks, then his jeans. Anne stood. He could see her moving around, slim and white, in the gloom. That was one good thing, he supposed, about skin like hers.

"I don' think they have poi at Kau Kau Korner," he grumbled. "We'll prob'ly have to eat hamburgers."

Chapter Fifteen

As the jeep trundled down Kalakaua Avenue the Royal Hawaiian Hotel lay almost invisible behind its lush gardens. The lights of the hospitable porte cochère could barely be seen in the distance. Lately the Advertiser had been running stories on what to do about the mynah birds at the Royal. They made such a racket in the early morning, waking up guests, that the newspaper was asking for ideas on how to make the birds go away. Or at least be quiet. One suggestion was firecrackers. It was said that mynah birds disliked firecrackers. Another was to play a recording of a mynah bird being tormented. That would warn off the others.

Parker's hand showed off his little empire. "Thass' where Kamehameha useta live. In that grove of palm trees. I hear he had a house there. Jus' a plain brown house."

Anne leaned to look.

"Waikiki useta be for Hawaiians. But not anymore. It's gettin' too dear for us. Pretty soon we'll have to live somewhere else."

"What would the beach be without Hawaiians?"

"It already happen' in Kakaako. That useta be the bes' place for Hawaiians. We could walk a coupla blocks, swim, fish off the piers. Then the haoles tore down the Hawaiians' shacks to put in warehouses. Handy to the docks. Not so far to haul stuff from the ships. Now, 'stead of Hawaiians usin' the land, and the sea, they got boxes of car parts, canned goods sittin' there." His voice was loaded with scorn. "Savin' the haoles money."

"So they move' the Hawaiians up on a hill—in Papakolea—where no one else wants to be. Now if they wanna fish, swim, they gotta ride the bus. That hurts Hawaiians a lot. They *need* the sea. Sometimes they don' *have* bus fare to go catch a fish for dinner."

"That's awful!" Anne exclaimed. "Really, it's heartless."

The light changed, he moved on at a leisurely pace. "Waikiki, it's the same, only it's for tourists." He made a gesture at the little shops around them. "Used to, when I saw strangers, I wanted to

make them feel at home. Now I don' have that kind of feelin's."
He had a sense of shame about this. "There's so many people
come in on the Lurline alla time. Las' week, four hundred twenty.
They print all their names in the Advertiser. I'm gettin' sort of
wore out with it—all the new faces that keep showin' up on the
beach." This lack of aloha for the newcomer was spreading. He
found it sickening. The tourists weren't to blame. They'd been
told it was okay to come.

John Ena Road gave him a chance to change the conversation. "In there—that's where Mrs. Massie said she got raped. You
heard about her?"

"Yes. I know. She blamed the local boys."

"Poor thing, she lied."

"Really? You know that for sure?"

"For sure."

"How do you know?"

"Benny Ahakuelo is a frien' of mine. I ask' him once did he
do it. Gang rape this lady. He said no, they never saw her before
the line–up. He woulda tol' me if it was true."

"When was that?"

"A long time after. He'd been free a long time." Parker
gripped the steering wheel, remembering how mad everyone
was in those days, when the trial was going on. "Benny was a
wun'erful athlete. A boxer—champion. An' a great football
player. That's why they wanted to bring him down. Make him
look like a savage. They knew it would hurt the Hawaiian
people, because he was very popular."

"Hurt them—you mean, because they liked him so much?"

"M'yeah, that too. An' also, it made the Hawaiians look like
savages. Don' you see? Then nobody cares if they get chase' out
of Kakaako." For a moment he felt hateful.

"Oh, yes. I see it now."

The lights of Kau Kau Korner lay ahead, a pool of fluorescent
brightness in the quiet streets. Around the building three rings of
cars parked, facing inward. Parker saw an empty slot in the
middle ring, slid the jeep into it with a sense of triumph. This was
a new experience for him. Although he'd driven by Kau Kau
Korner hundreds of times, had seen girls in short dresses waiting

on the cars, it had never occurred to him to stop. The girls, he saw, were mostly haole. That gave the place class. They wore red aprons and red perky caps, something like nurses. Their white uniforms were so short they looked like bathing suits with little skirts. The girls walked fast. They took tablets out of apron pockets, wrote orders, picked up trays of heavy crockery, attached the braces of trays to the driver's side of the cars, strode quickly back into the lights. Parker had a sense of luxury being here. He put his foot on the frame of the jeep, high, in a royal stance. A meal might cost twice as much as at Hiro's but he had to admit it was very ritzy. Here he was, sitting in the privacy of his own car, looking at people from a distance, like a king in his own castle. And being waited on by haoles in their very short dresses while Anne sat with him. This was the most extraordinary night of his life.

Anne slumped, at ease, in her seat, watching the girls hurrying to and from the cars.

"It's funny how much more you look at a wahine's legs when she's wearing a short dress," she said. "On the beach it would be nothing to see all those legs. Here it seems real...noticeable."

"M'yeah? I'm sure they don' have poi."

The girl who came to the jeep was one of the few who was not a haole. She was Portuguese, slender, with a gentle face. "Order?"

"I s'pose you don' have laulau," Parker suggested without much hope.

"Here's the menu," she said, handing him two big folded cardboards. "I'll be back."

The menu had pictures drawn on it of sodas and hamburgers, and at the bottom it said, "Mahalo for your patronage. Aloha." But there was no poi, no laulau, no Hawaiian food at all.

"I'll have a hamburger," he said at last.

"Me too," Anne agreed.

When she took the order the Portuguese girl asked, "With or without onions?"

Parker looked at Anne. Such a question had never been put to him before.

"With. Everything. Pickle too," Anne said, sounding confident.

"Same for me."

"Drink?"

Parker had no ideas on the subject outside of coffee. When Anne said, "Milkshake, chocolate," he said, "M'yeah."

"Two?"

He nodded, not looking at her, it being such a ritzy place. When the girl went away he leaned to Anne and said, "This is nice, but even more I like to be back there in the bed with you."

Anne turned her head away, but he could tell by the curve of her cheek she was smiling. He was getting to know her.

The tray with their order couldn't be attached to the jeep, as to a car, so Parker held it on his lap. Carefully he handed Anne her hamburger, and when she was ready, her drink. One taste of the gummy milkshake and he wished he'd ordered coffee instead.

"Do you still go nickel diving?" Anne asked around a mouthful.

"Naw, not since the war." He worked on his own big bite. "There's prob'ly a whole new gang diving now. In the ol' days we was real stric' about who dived. Because we was in gangs. The Kakaako Wharf Rats against the Palama Gang." Hardly wanting to say the words, he added, "Wipeout was in the Palama Gang."

He went on. "You shoulda seen us when the police try to stop our gang fights. We dive in the water, keep on fightin'. If the police come after us we'd li'l more drown 'em."

"Drown the police?" Anne giggled.

"We had our own territories we defended. The Wharf Rats had from Pier Two to Pier Ten. We got the Japanese and British ships, and the Dollar Line. The Palama boys had the water from Pier Ten to Sixteen. They only had the Matson ships and Inter Island."

Talking about the old days helped him to forget about this hamburger he was obliged to eat instead of food. The milkshake was terrible. He didn't know why the haoles made themselves drink such sickening things.

"If a new kid tried to dive with us and we didn' think he was ready, we wouldn' let him. Even if he was from Kakaako. We'd

112

chew–beef his clothes. Tie 'em in knots so hard, li'l more you have to cut off the sleeves to get 'em out. Or we'd duck 'em in the water till li'l more he'd drown. We had to control who dived. It's too dangerous out there. You can' have jus' anyone divin'." He'd got half the milkshake down, anyhow.

"When the ship comes into the harbor its propeller is still turnin'. The tug is jus' to guide it, mostly. The propeller still creates a suction. You have to stay away from the water feeding into the propeller or you'll get sucked under. When we're out near that dangerous water, we keep our heads down."

"What do you mean 'heads down'? What's that for?"

"Because if we look up, the passengers will throw coins to us. But we can't dive for them because we'll get killed. If they throw coins and we don't dive for them, they get mad. They won't throw anymore. So we don' pay attention. We keep our heads down so they don' throw."

"Did any coin divers ever get killed?"

"Sure. Two I know of. Two new boys. Good swimmers, but they never dive' before. They got caught in the suction behin' the tug, takin' the ship out of port and they never came up. We didn't know they was gone 'til we was gettin' dressed. We went back in the harbor to look for them but the water was muddy as coffee. We couldn' fin' the bodies. Nex' day we found them under Pier Seven."

"It sounds terribly dangerous!"

Since Anne found it scary he had a good one for her. "You know where the anchor is on a ship?"

"It's up in the front, isn't it?"

"M'yeah. Hangin' in a hole right over the bow."

"Could it hit you?"

"Can't miss," he said cheerfully. "That's jus' where we are, mos'ly, right there by the bow."

"Oh, my God!"

"But mos'ly a captain wouldn't drop the anchor without warnin' us, because he knows we're there. Only, sometimes, when it's windy, the captain can' judge the speed of the ship so good. Then he has to drop the anchor at any time, to slow down."

"Good grief! I'm glad you're not diving anymore." Anne

reached for his arm, smoothed it, her fingertips cold from holding her milkshake. No poi and now this stuff. But it was worth it.

"There's a lotta money at the bottom of Pier Eleven," he went on. "Lots. The things they dredge outta there! Rings. Money. Opium."

"Opium?" Anne shot him an alarmed look.

"M'yeah. The boys use to make a lotta money going through the dredge material on the barge. Sometimes they find a coffee can fulla opium. They get good money for it in Chinatown. Twenty-five dollars a can." Remembering how proud Kunia was one time with his find.

"But there was never a real connection between the opium dealers and the coin divers. Funny, they never trusted us. If they had thrown waterproof packets to us, a lotta times they coulda avoided gettin' caught. But the dealers never trusted us."

"Just as well," Anne dismissed it stiffly.

He hadn't realized how much he missed the harbor until now. Remembering how it was, heading out for a big ship with the boys, feisty as brothers. Compared to that, his life on the beach was tame. Of course he wasn't going to admit it.

Anne seemed to enjoy her milkshake, sucking loudly on the straws for the last in her glass, so that was what counted. He managed to down the last of his by mixing it with the hamburger. The pickle was beyond him. When the Portuguese girl came for the tray he kept up his end of the show with a grin and a fifty-cent tip.

"Nowadays coin divin' is a ruined business," he grumbled, pleased, preparing to set off. "In the old days, when a tourist threw a coin, he got somethin' for his money. We was *professionals*! Today anybody can pretend to dive. You know the stone wall there on the beach at Kuhio? You see these kids—ten year olds—hollerin' at servicemen, 'Throw a coin, mister? Throw a coin?' And they're standin' in three feet of water with a glass mask on. Thass' not divin'!" His voice was rough with scorn. "Might as well throw it in the street!"

Anne leaned toward him. There was something special in her eyes. He thought she was going to say he could spend the night at her place. But what she said, her face real close to his was, "I'll throw coins for you sometime. Would you like that?"

He felt shy with her leaning like this, here in the light, where anyone could see. But tickled, too. "You know where I'd like you to throw you' coins?"

"Where?" Her lips right beside his ear.

"In the bathtub. Thass' enough for me."

Chapter Sixteen

ONE REASON PARKER KEALII FELT LIKE SUCH A LUCKY MAN WAS because he had Kanekini for a boss. Every time he thought about Kanekini he felt good, as if a wise and kind uncle were watching over him. Parker would have done anything for Kanekini.

In spite of his horror of offices Parker always felt happy when he entered the glass cubicle that was Kanekini's own private space. Kanekini's aging face would light up as if the sunshine of the beach had just appeared. His desk would be piled high with folders and the phone ringing every few minutes—it was terrible how busy he always seemed to be—but unless he was in conference with someone, Kanekini always signaled Yuki to take his calls and looked at Parker with his face shining and interested. Glad to see him. As if being with Parker was like a few minutes of vacation.

Parker loved to look at his boss's face, the friendly, drooping eyelid, the courteous smile, the big, heavy frame in the swivel chair behind the desk full of papers. And he enjoyed the deep, kind voice of this man who was probably sixty, an old–timer in the city–county system and wise in its political ways. So Parker not only tried to do his job the very best he could, always on time at the beach, and writing his reports without a single smudge or mistake, he also tried to spare Kanekini any problems that would be disagreeable to him. He did not, for instance, tell him of the difficulties he was having now with Morgan's drinking. He wanted his boss to feel that at the beach, at least, all was well.

That was why, against his own judgement, Parker had accepted Sunshine as the new lifeguard. Kanekini had seemed so enthusiastic about him. Then it came out that Sunshine had gone to Saint Louis, which was also Kanekini's old school. Parker hadn't known that Sunshine was a high school graduate and had even gone to the University of Hawaii for two years, until Sunshine's application form had come in.

Well, it was natural for Catholics to stick together like that, and Parker wouldn't have minded having Sunshine so much except that he couldn't make out *why* Sunshine wanted to be a lifeguard. It was okay with him if Sunshine scooped wahines right and left and gave haoles something to talk about just by walking by. But this changing from beachboy to lifeguard smelled like week-old squid.

Nothing was more important than the safety of the beaches. Parker knew that. He'd protect Kanekini's reputation all right. Every Friday morning at the Natatorium before the boys' workout he reminded them of what they owed their boss. Even if they didn't like some of the rules that came down from the office they were not to forget the duty and respect they owed Kanekini.

Parker sat in Kanekini's office, feeling good. The two men were smiling at one another. Each had said, "How's it goin'?" a couple of times, just to get things started.

"Fine, fine. Same old rat race. How's it on the beach?"

"Fine. How's it with the big wheels up here in City Hall?"

"Fine. Fine. Terrible. Gets worse every day. But we're fine."

Overhead the fluorescent tube hummed, between them the messy, stacked up desk loomed. Kanekini's friendly, droopy eye looked at him with interest and affection. Parker knew that Kanekini would always do the best he could for him. There was no doubt about that.

Whenever he was with his chief Parker paid great attention to every word he said, just in case he should mention something he needed, some way Parker could serve. In the old days the chiefs gave their men wonderful ways to serve. Kamehameha, for instance, loved to eat fresh mullet. But his camp was four miles from the mullet ponds, on the Big Island. When he wanted mullet, his fastest runner was sent to bring one, still alive, to place on the ground before him. It thrilled Parker to think of how the man must have felt as he ran, doing something that only he could do, for his chief. Those were great days, because then there were great opportunities to serve.

Sometimes while standing guard at the beach Parker wished he could save Kanekini, or a member of his family, in a sea storm, or a boat wreck. He could imagine no more wonderful privilege. Another thing he could do would be to fight for him. But he

117

didn't see how he'd get a chance to do that. There were, of course, other ways to fight besides with your fists. If Kanekini needed help, he'd go with him to the Board of Supervisors, or to the mayor. He'd be proud to do that. In his Hawaiian way he might not use fancy English, but when he spoke from the heart, he noticed people always listened. Perhaps some day it would be given to him to do something fine for his chief. Every time he walked into the office Parker's blood was up. He was always on the lookout for the chance that might come.

Unfortunately, Kanekini's main problem seemed to be his piles of horrible papers. Paper, as Parker saw it, was the enemy. He didn't see how he could help Kanekini fight an enemy like that. One time, joking, he'd asked, "What kin I do to help you, Boss? Seems like you' always at the bottom of a pit with all these papers."

Kanekini had made a gesture toward the stacks of folders on his desk. "You're right. I'm their slave. Sometimes I think I'll make a revolt. Just rise up and walk out a free man. But then all these projects I've been working on for years wouldn't get done. I can't let them go now. We're on the verge of a big change in our system, Parker. The city and county has more money than it's ever had before, because of the dollars the tourists are bringing in. We can do things we've been wanting to do for a long time. Acquire lands for parks, develop the lands we do have. It's very exciting. I can't quit now. Every piece of paper means something."

"Well," Parker had said, "if you ever decide to make your revolt, I'll help you, Boss. I'll take all those papers—and those too," he gestured to the files behind Kanekini, "and carry 'em out beyond the reef for you. They won't bother you no moah!"

Kanekini had enjoyed a good laugh at that one. Still, the glance he turned on the papers had been wistful, almost fond. As if, in spite of their being such a burden, he couldn't imagine being without them.

Now Kanekini asked, "How's it goin' at work?" The warm glance, the conversational tone made it much more than a boss's checkup.

"Fine!" Parker lied. Not wanting to hurt Kanekini by telling him that Morgan's drinking had reached a point where something had to be done. Kanekini liked Morgan, liked all the boys. Parker knew it would pain Kanekini to let Morgan go, or even to reprimand him. Morgan had been drunk on duty twice last week.

Sunday Parker had warned Morgan. Told him that if he showed up drunk again he'd be suspended. Two days later Morgan's breath had been heavy with liquor and his eyes red, but he walked all right. Parker had pretended not to notice. Thinking he'd talk to Morgan one last time when he wasn't under the influence. If he was suspended, Parker feared he'd just drink more than ever. He had a wife and little daughter. It was a lousy situation.

Then Parker got the idea of calling all the boys together to talk with Morgan, having an old style ho'oponopono. With everyone gathered around, talking with aloha, maybe he'd find the strength to stop. It might turn out that Morgan had something to say too. He might be carrying something in his heart which, if he could release it, then he wouldn't have to drink. The old Hawaiians knew a lot about how to live.

"Well, Kealii, I asked you to come in because I have some news for you."

Parker waited, happy to be there because his boss had called him.

"Terrible as it was, the death of that girl you brought in produced some changes here in the department."

A wave of feeling swept over Parker at the mention of the girl. He still thought about her in his quiet moments, when he first awoke, or just before he slept.

"Because of the attention the case got we're going to have more funds for beach safety. We're going to have the money for five new lifeguard towers along the beach in Waikiki and Ala Moana."

"That sounds great, Chief."

"And we'll be getting more equipment, too. We'll have uniforms for the boys, so they'll be easy to spot. And crank telephones to connect with the Natatorium so all calls will funnel through there."

At Parker's interested grin Kanekini nodded. "Not only that, the Territory is turning some land over to us. It's been on the books a long time but now we'll have new beaches, and we'll put in new facilities for them."

"You can count on me, Chief."

"I know I can, Kealii. I'll need everybody's kokua for a program this big, making the transition. Times are changing, you know. It's not like the old days." Kanekini tipped back in his squeaky swivel chair so his big opu showed. Poor Kanekini probably didn't have the time to get out and swim. Always stuck in that chair with those papers.

"Used to, we could get by Hawaiian style," Kanekini rumbled, as if he were saying just whatever came into his head. "If someone didn't do something quite right—so what? We could let it go. Hana malie. Take it easy. In the end everything turned out about right, so why step on anybody's toes, why fuss? But now we can't be as easy going as we used to be. Our work is being judged by mainland standards now. You're not only supposed to do good work, you're supposed to make the work you do *look* good. Public relations. We never thought about that before. The politicians are watching the city–county employees and the public is watching the politicians."

Kanekini gave a chuckle. "Used to, a man could get elected to the Board of Supervisors if he had a good music group when he campaigned. He'd do a hula, kid around with the audience, and be elected for being a good guy. Now a new kind of politician is coming in. They're talking about *issues*. The Japanese are getting into the political arena. They're hungry young lions, back from the war where they more than proved themselves. They want a hand in running the islands. No, Parker," Kanekini sighed, "things aren't like they used to be. Hawaii can never go back to what it was before the war. In some ways that's good. We'll have more parks and services than ever before. But we've got to do our jobs real well, or someone else will jump in there and do it for us."

At first Kanekini sounded enthusiastic. Then his face clouded and his voice turned sober. He tapped his thumb with a pencil. Parker had never seen Kanekini like this before. He seemed lost

120

inside some worrisome thoughts. His belt looked tight; it seemed to be cutting into his poor opu.

"Sumthin' came up, Boss?"

"No. Not really. Well, yes, in a way. It doesn't have anything to do with *us*. But just a couple of hours ago we learned that the head of the Department of Public Works was fired."

"Bill Leong? He got fired?" Parker was astonished. Bill Leong had been Chief of Public Works since as long as anyone could remember. His name was in the paper nearly every day about some project or other.

"Did he do somethin' wrong?"

"Not exactly. There're always a lot of pros and cons on everything public works does, you know. Even widening a road that people agree needs to be widened will make *somebody* mad. So he gets a lot of complaints from these new neighborhood associations that are being formed around town. Leong has been right in the middle of projects people both want and don't want. The politicians are always looking for material to complain about in the present administration. I guess the mayor decided he made too many unpopular decisions. So he fired him."

"He can do that? Jus' because a few people's complainin'?"

"The mayor can fire a department head without cause. It's his right."

This seemed pretty terrible to Parker. He pondered what it might mean to Kanekini.

"And you, Boss? Does that mean the mayor could fire you, too?"

"Oh sure! If he decided I was more of a liability than an asset. I'd get sixty days notice, something like that, and it would be all over." Kanekini looked through the glass wall that separated his office from the rest of his office staff, as if he'd really like to keep sitting where he was.

"It's always been the mayor's right. It's just never been exercised before. The fact that he did it is a sign of how things are changing. People are talking more and more about statehood. They want us to show that we're up to the privilege of becoming a state. That we're not just a bunch of lazy kanakas lying around on the beaches. We have to prove that we're good Americans, with American standards and ideals."

Parker felt so sorry for Kanekini he didn't know what to say. He'd always thought that a chief should have less to do than his workers. After all, he was the chief. But no. Kanekini seemed to have more, with all these piled up papers. And, as if that weren't enough, now he had to act like an efficient American for fear of getting fired. It seemed to Parker that being Hawaiian and being a chief ought to be enough.

Kanekini's manner changed. As if he didn't want to burden Parker with his problems, he made his voice cheerful.

"A lot of changes coming up, Parker, and I think you'll be pleased. Eventually the beach will have its own emergency vehicle with up–to–date resuscitation equipment. You'll see! Your job will have a lot more responsibilities in the future. We'll talk about that next time." He pushed at a desk drawer so Parker knew their talk was coming to an end. "But for the moment there's one new thing I'd like to ask you to do."

"What's that, Chief?" Parker's gaze was steady, his chin tucked down, firm. He might not be able to run until his heart burst for Kanekini, but he was ready, however he could serve.

"We're going to be needing supplies for these five new lifeguard towers, life preservers, rope, first–aid kits...that sort of thing. And uniforms. I'd like you to make a list of what you'd need for each of the five towers."

"M'yeah?" Parker's heart dropped in his chest.

"Would you make out the request sheets for me, in triplicate? Here are some sheets...." Kanekini turned and opened a file drawer, pulled out some mimeographed forms. "Make one for each stand, since they might have different needs. Got it?"

Parker swallowed. "Sure, Chief. Got it."

Chapter Seventeen

PARKER HAD TOLD THE BOYS TO BE AT THE NATATORIUM AN hour before their regular training time. He hadn't said that it was to deal with Morgan's problem but all of them were aware of his drinking and seemed to guess what the meeting was for. Now the great clock showed almost eight. Sunshine, Whistling and Freitas were already there. Squidley, Ah Sook and Ellings showed a few minutes later. But no Morgan. At eight forty–five Parker sent the boys in the water for their swim of a mile.

It was after nine when Morgan, bleary–eyed and unsteady, came through the Natatorium's golden archway. Furious, Parker put him in the tank for his laps at once. Hoping the water, the action, would clear his head although Parker doubted he could even count his laps.

Several of the other boys were coming out of the water after going through their breaks and holds. Parker hoped they wouldn't notice Morgan's condition. But Sunshine did. Most of them did. They muttered, glanced at him as they took their outdoor showers, headed to get dressed.

Parker let them leave. They still had to get breakfast before beginning duty at ten. It was too late to try to talk to Morgan even if he were sober. Sunshine was the only one who didn't leave. He loafed near the arch of the entrance looking around at the bleachers, the golden walls with their urns and decorations, as if he wouldn't mind owning the place.

Then he walked back to Parker who was at the door of the guards' dressing room disgustedly watching Morgan's laps. Parker remained where he stood at Sunshine's approach although he felt like turning on his heel. He always felt like he'd be short something when Sunshine came around. Today was Sunshine's day off. He'd asked for it expressly. Gave him the time to line up his stuff for the weekend, probably.

"Morgan's a disgrace. He can't work like that."

Parker had never heard Sunshine use such words before. Now he knew where he got them. Saint Louis and the University.

If it had been anyone else he would probably have agreed that Morgan was unfit to work. With Sunshine, his reaction at once was to make him wrong.

"He'll be all right when he's done his laps."

"You gonna let him go on duty like that?"

"Like what? You don' know what he'll be like when he finishes."

"You can smell his breath...that's not gonna change. It's worse than one of Whistling's puhios."

Parker didn't bother to grin.

"I'll take care of Morgan." Bristling at Sunshine's nerve. The newest man on the team and he had something to say? The fact that Sunshine was wearing his shirt, which it didn't look like he was ready to return yet, didn't help either. Months earlier Sunshine had borrowed Parker's best red and gold aloha shirt. Anne had been furious when she found out. She didn't seem to realize that when someone asked to borrow something you couldn't really refuse. Also, you couldn't ask for it back unless it was an emergency. Like a musical instrument when you were scheduled to play that night. It was also true that when a shirt was borrowed it rarely came back until there were just threads left. But he didn't see any way around that. It was just how things were done. Now Sunshine was wearing his nice shirt on his day off, getting ready to go take care of the wahines up Moana side, no doubt. The way Sunshine idled there, elegant, on top of it all, was infuriating.

Sunshine had been a surprise in more ways than one since he joined the lifeguards. He not only rose early and got to work on time, he'd talked to Parker about procedures in a way that showed real interest. He'd even offered to deliver the boys' time sheets to the office for him. And one day when Parker had been staring at the request sheets in triplicate, at the Lagoon, Sunshine had offered his kokua. Parker didn't want to owe Sunshine for anything so he didn't let him help with the triplicates but he did let him deliver the time sheets to the office, since he was already going by there, he said.

"I'll take care of my boys," Parker said so sharply it revealed a hostility lying in wait. "You go take care of the girls." It could have been just a joke, a brave exchange that brought a laugh at another time, but it wasn't funny now.

"The girls I take care of don' get in trouble, at leas'," Sunshine returned.

For a moment Parker thought he was referring to Anne, in which case he needed punching out on the spot. But there was something so pointed about the way Sunshine said it, Parker had to ask. "What's that mean? Whatcha mean by that?" Advancing toward him slowly, just in case Sunshine needed a lesson.

"The las' girl you took care of—it's a shame—she happened to die."

Parker stopped in his tracks.

Now it was out in the open. Ugly as a white eel's grin, it was there between them. No one had ever said it before. To his face, no one had been anything but sympathetic about the loss. Kanekini had stuck by him at the inquest; the coroner and police had accepted his explanation. And Anne had said he should have a medal. But in an almost ignored corner of his mind there had always lain, in secret, the question: how could a girl who was alive when he started to bring her in, arrive, in his arms, dead? "What're you sayin', huh? What're you sayin'?" Ready to knock Sunshine's block off. But holding it in. Needing to know more. Trapped by the need to know something kept secret all this time. "S'plain!" he shouted. "S'plain what you mean by that."

"Sure. I'll explain...."

"Go ahead...." So angry he couldn't wait an instant. "Jus' say it."

"You shouldn't of brought her in." Sunshine was not loafing elegantly now. His feet were well planted, his body tense, eyes locked hard in Parker's own.

"The girl couldn' swim!" Parker yelled. "Don'cha unnerstan' that? She couldn' swim! She didn' know what to do when we came through the waves. Her mouth was open. She kep' yellin'!"

Wishing he could smash Sunshine's mouth right then. As if he hadn't done his very best, talking to the girl, praying for her. If she'd been his own Daisy he couldn't have put more of himself into the rescue.

"That's not the point. You shouldn' of *tried* to bring her in."

125

Parker had to stop at that. Something he'd never faced was in the idea. That he shouldn't have tried to bring, through that heavy surf, a girl who couldn't swim. Remembering how it was out there in the dark blue water. Cold. Big fish. They'd already been there some time. All he could think of was getting her to shore.

"I had the board when I started out," Parker protested.

"You knew she couldn't swim when you headed for shore."

That was true. He also knew that nonswimmers and even poor swimmers are unpredictable, capable of any kind of nonsense when they panic. But he had the board, and he was so glad to get rid of the haole, he'd thought it would be okay with just the girl.

"You don' know how it was." Parker's voice dropped. Feeling he didn't owe Sunshine, of all people, an explanation. But also aware that Sunshine might be saying what other people said behind his back.

Morgan was messily slogging in a diagonal toward this end of the pool. The water was a hard green in the sun. Just at that moment a pair of tourists in coconut hats appeared at the entrance. Before Parker could speak Sunshine raised his voice to them. "Natatorium's not open 'till ten." One of them waved. Obediently they turned and left.

Sunshine's head–on stance relaxed somewhat. He was three inches taller than Parker but the bulk of Parker's shoulders made up for the spread of Sunshine's square hard frame. In a more conversational tone Sunshine said, "You shouldn'a gone out in the firs' place. You shoulda called the Coast Guard."

Parker almost tipped forward on the balls of his feet at that. It wasn't until later, late that night in fact, that he'd thought about the Coast Guard. At once he'd dismissed the idea, confirmed what he'd done. When a lifeguard got a call, it was his duty to do what he could, not to look for someone to do it for him.

"When I went out I didn' know *what* I'd find. This Filipino kid comes in says a boat turn' over. How'd I know it's even true or not? A boat turns over, usually a coupla people can turn it back over. I thought I could help them." Remembering the great pitching hills of water that day. The lack of control when he wanted to approach them on his board.

"Usually a boat's got lifesavers. I didn' know this girl can' help him, can' do nuthin', that they got no lifesavers. I don' know this kid, what he's tellin' me is true. I'm not gonna call the Coast Guard I don' even *know* if sumpthin's wrong."

But as the words poured out, something caught at him. The knowledge that the thought of calling the Coast Guard, if it had flashed through his mind then—he honestly couldn't remember if it had or not—had been dismissed at once because he loathed calling government services. Loathed their style of talking, their questions, the kinds of words they used. He would not call them if he could possibly help it. He was an action man, he did his own work.

"You don' know nuthin' about it," Parker hammered. "You wasn' there. If it was a stormy day, a lot of wind, really cold, like that—*then* I might call the Coast Guard, if I need help. But it was a nice day. Warm. Quiet. The surf was up, but on the board that shouldn'a been a problem. On the board I coulda gone a mile outa the way of the breaks. But swimmin'—well—I tried to go in as direct as I could without gettin' in the worst breaks." Remembering the sickening sense of the board wheeling over, nose down in that first break when the girl threw herself forward. The whole thing had been lost, right there.

"Besides, you call the Coast Guard, it takes 'em a long time to respond. A *long* time. Once I call' 'em, it was nearly a hour b'fore they show up. I knew I could be out there in ten, fifteen minutes. I kin see for myself what to do."

"The Coast Guard picked 'em up, the girl would be alive today."

Stung, Parker bellowed, "The guy took lifesavers on his boat, she'd be alive today!"

Sunshine's smooth features, with an Oriental look at the eyes, were less confrontational now, but still keen.

"You don' know nuthin' yet," Parker rammed at him. "You *new*. I had to act *fas'*. Sometimes you have to act when you don' have all the facts. Still you have to act, jus' do the bes' you can."

He took a couple of angry paces, returned. "You get several

people drownin' at once—what you gonna do?—get the facts? You gonna find out who got kids at home, stuff like that? No. You jus' gotta act. Do what you can." He made a motion of disgust, his eyes smoldering. "You wait. You gotta lot to learn."

"Okay, Parker," Sunshine backed down. He seemed suddenly to decide not to pursue the matter. "Okay for you. Cool head main thing." He gave a snort of laughter as Morgan pulled up out of the pool, trudged toward them. "Here's our most sober lifeguard. It's the salt water makes his eyes red."

Morgan grinned sheepishly. Hopped on one foot, hitting his head to clear his ear of water. He could probably take care of his beach after he'd eaten, Parker thought.

He wasn't going to let Sunshine one up him by teasing Morgan, so cool, as if nothing at all had happened. Adopting his own tone of banter, although it wasn't easy, his jaw still stiff, he lifted his chin at the perfect morning around them. "Nice day for the kumu," he ragged Sunshine. "You can't miss." Kumu being slang for the wahines you catch.

"How's that?" Sunshine's banter matched his own.

"Day off—an' you got such a nice aloha shirt!"

"Oh!" Sunshine gave him a dazzling grin. "M'yeah, I really like this shirt. Goes with my tan!" He sauntered off, tall, lean, sure of himself. The shirt was starched, his saila–mokus clean and creased. He ought to work in a Kapiolani used car lot, Parker thought.

Morgan still looked awful. "You gotta eat b'fore you go on duty," Parker said. "C'mon. I'll treat you."

Parker had a lot to think about as he stood his duty under the banyan. Sunshine's dreadful words, "She could be alive today," returned again and again.

Chapter Eighteen

PARKER STARED AT THE SLICE OF FRIED ULUA ON HIS PLATE. EVEN the Lagoon's best fish didn't taste like much. That wasn't Hiro's fault. In spite of his happiness with Anne, Parker missed his kids. Especially in the evening he missed them and tonight Anne had her hula class so he was eating alone. The last few years at home, while Polly roared off to her music engagements, he did most of the family's cooking. The kids loved hanging around him then. It was a nice time, he thought, the radio playing Hawaiian music and the kids taking their showers, one after another, coming into the kitchen hungry, their hair wet. The girls even stopped bickering among themselves to do what he said. Ruth set the table, Daisy mixed the poi, Lani washed the dishes left over from earlier in the day. Willing to do the chores he gave them, just to be around.

He'd turned his back on all that. Walked away from it. Same as his mother had walked away from him. Put him in the Home. Gone off to Kauai. He wondered if his mother had missed him the way he missed his kids. Had ever regretted that she only gave him poi up to the handle of the little tin cup. No kid of his had ever lacked for food, Parker thought with a surge of defiance. That was one thing sure. They were all crazy for his corn beef and cabbage. He had to make a big pot full at least once a week.

At the next table Payoff had broken a handful of crackers into a bowl of cold water and sprinkled sugar over them. He was eating the concoction with chili peppers and Hawaiian salt. Hiro put up with a lot.

"Why d'ya have to eat such awful rubbish?" Lois's lips curled. "Makes me sick to look at it."

"Nobody's askin' ya to look," Payoff observed.

A few days earlier he'd caught her drinking with another man at the Tavern and beat her up on the spot. She loved it. She was jealous of him, too. Her left eye was still a bruised blue. Now she watched his every move with greedy relish.

A few days earlier Parker had gone home to Palolo for some

clothes and personal things. He'd hoped he would have some time with the kids. Just his luck, Polly wasn't working that night. She hadn't changed a bit. Within a few minutes she started yelling. When she understood that he was leaving for good she'd thrown everything she could get her hands on at him, beginning with a bag of poi. She'd gone on to fishing cold, slimy clothes out of the washing machine and slinging them with all her might. Clothes sometimes sat in the rinse water of the washing machine for a week at a time, now that he was gone. Ducking, trying to soothe the kids who were crying, he'd picked up the items he needed most and piled them in a carton which Polly had tried to set fire to, although that, due to the wet clothes, had fizzled. She'd hit him and kicked him and as he was going down the walk, she'd thrown an alarm clock. It only hit him on the shoulder so he'd got away safely with only a few scratches and a torn tee shirt. But he'd thought a lot about the kids ever since.

Hike, the beach tease, pranced in, trailed by Socks looking like a thundercloud. They threw themselves into empty chairs nearby.

"D'ja hear about Socks' date las' night?" Hike crowed to Parker, but real loud, so everyone in the restaurant could hear.

"Shuddup," Socks growled uselessly. He scowled at the floor, just waiting for Hike to get it over with.

"He pick' up this oriental girl was waitin' for a bus by the Barbecue Inn. Took her out for a big chow. Cos' four bucks. Foun' out she was a mahu!" Hike roared. "Gave the pretty li'l thing a dirty lickin'."

Socks was obliged to bear the hoots and yelps of laughter. Hike was incorrigible. There was nothing you could do about Hike. A few days earlier he had spotted a serviceman asleep—or maybe passed out—up against a coconut tree in the beach park. Hike had skinned up the tree and peed on the guy.

More than once Parker had lectured Hike about his pranks, especially on the shabby old haole man, bent with arthritis, who was one of the Lagoon regulars. He spent his days sitting under the umbrellas, as unnoticed as a shadow. Evenings he ordered tomato juice. Every half hour or so he would go into the little alleyway that led to the Lagoon's bathroom and swig the vanilla extract he carried in his pocket. Hike caught him at it and roared the news.

"It'll kill him," he shouted, while the old man stood there, paralyzed with humiliation. "An' haoles are supposed to be smart!"

Everyone thought the old man would vanish after the exposure. But his habit, apparently, was stronger than his shame. The next night he was back again, with his loneliness and his tomato juice.

"What you do will come back to you some day," Parker reminded Hike. "Wait 'till you' an old man." But he might as well have talked to a coconut.

Anne appeared in the Lagoon's doorway. Her face was fresh and pink from the sun she'd been getting lately. Sticking out of her lauhala sack were the bamboos, puili for her hula class.

As soon as he saw her Parker reacted. It was as though the surge from his heart pulled him up. He stood and took a step toward her as she made her way through the small tables.

"Sit down!" Anne hissed at him when she got close.

"What'd I do wrong?"

"People will look at us!"

Parker didn't know what made his knees spring like that when he laid eyes on her. It just seemed the natural thing to do, to go and meet her, be sure she was all right, get her seated in a good chair.

Anne scowled at him, looked around as if to deny what had happened. She caught Lois's glance, fast pulled into a smile.

"Hi Lois," she said, like everything was just fine.

Unfortunately, Parker had pulled the chair out. Anyone could see that. The messages Anne's eyes sent were crosser than ever. "Nobody else stands up when a wahine comes in," she muttered. "What're people going to think?" Her lips stuck out when she finished saying it.

"They'll think I'm glad to see you," Parker apologized. "But they know that already. They know I love you. Can' keep people from noticin' things like that," he reminded her cheerfully.

"Well, you don't have to make it so obvious!" Anne slumped

down in her chair as if she'd prefer to disappear. "Oh, hi, Kunia. Howzzit!" she nodded.

Rose came up. "Order?"

Anne flashed Rose a smile brighter than usual. "Coffee, please, Rose. I already ate."

Rose took Parker's plate. He lit a cigarette, looked at Anne. Set up, just to have her there. He still couldn't get over his luck. Feeling like a different man. Really, it was extraordinary. Even though Anne was a haole it turned out they were perfect for each other. Perfect. She was crazy about Hawaii and he was Hawaiian. How could it be better? Whatever Anne needed, still, as a haole, was all right with him. He could wait. He wasn't going to change.

At the next table Payoff and Lois were leaving. She managed to touch his arm and shoulder several times as they stood.

"Where's you' book?" Payoff asked Anne.

"No book tonight," Anne said evenly. "Hula." Her glance was annoyed as she watched them move away.

Anne's coffee came. She poured a swirl of condensed milk into it. "Why did Payoff ask about my book?" she grumbled. "He wasn't just asking, it's like he was making a point that it was good I didn't have it."

Parker smoked, thought about that. He had feelings about Anne's book himself. Only recently he'd found out that it was not just one book she carried around, it changed. Sometimes it had a blue cover on it, sometimes brown, or red. Once it had a shiny jacket with a picture. "He can' understand why you read so much, I guess," Parker offered.

"Why? Because I like it, that's why."

"That's what's so strange."

"Strange? All these interesting things that are in books are strange?"

He didn't know what she could be referring to that was so interesting. He himself glanced through the Advertiser nearly every day to see what the politicians were doing, and he enjoyed the sports section. But he could understand why Payoff or anyone would have feelings about her reading in public the way she did. There was something uppity in acting as if the words on a page were better than the live people around you. "Maybe it

132

seems too haole," he suggested gently. He didn't want Anne to feel bad. "Putting importance on wrong things."

"How could reading be wrong?" Not disguising her scorn.

Parker stared about, at a loss. Besides his personal loathing of books and papers, there were other resentments that for Hawaiians went way back. Paper and writing had meant grief to Hawaiians since always. It was the confusion paper brought that cost many of them their land, their homes. Most of what was written on paper turned out to be haole trickery. Rules that had nothing to do with the way Hawaiians lived. But the haoles said it was the way they should live.

The most shocking loss of all—the loss of their queen, had been associated with paper. The haoles had said their papers decided who the islands belonged to. And they had guns to back up those papers. It seemed that the haoles' papers gave them an authority that Hawaiian royalty had once received from their gods. Certainly that was confusing. That paper could give what the gods once gave.

But it was when the haoles insisted that the Bible, the paper from their god, was stronger than all the Hawaiians' gods together that the Hawaiians gave up. Before such a claim the Hawaiian imagination collapsed and they gave in to the haole and his powerful religion.

"Anne, you gotta unnerstan...."

The truth was more complicated still. The one book that a Hawaiian could carry was the Bible. The Hawaiians had an enormous affection for the Bible. When they learned that the rules for pleasing the haoles' god were in the Bible, they transferred to the Papaia Hemolele the same love and awe they once attached to the symbols of their chiefs.

So for Anne to carry a book the way someone else would carry a pack of cigarettes seemed both like more than she should do, and less than what was proper.

"People here's not useta books," he observed shortly. He stubbed his cigarette in the Primo Beer ashtray, glanced around at their riches. Every face in the restaurant except for two sailors at the counter stools was familiar. From the kitchen came the sizzle and smell of good things frying. Rose and Mieko scuffed around, calling orders: "One corn beef hash, hold the vegetable, mash. Teriyaki, three scoopsa rice." And outside was the evening sky. The sea. Diamond Head, quiet, solid. Who could want more? Except for seeing the kids he couldn't imagine anything better than what they had right now. "When you here, why don' you jus' do like the others? Jus' enjoy what we got."

Then he saw the figure in the doorway. It was the closest thing to a carbon copy of himself.

Anne saw her at the same time. "That must be your daughter," she breathed. "My God! She's you all over. Except the eyes. The eyes are different."

Daisy stood there, hands on her hips, studying the room, her chin lifted almost in a pose of defiance. Her faded blue jeans and white tee shirt were the same as his and she had the same chunky build. Even her thick, sturdy bosom, more muscular than fleshy, was like his. Catching sight of him, her manner changed entirely. With a shy smile, she lowered her head. Like a good puppy wagging its tail, she came toward him. Her walk rolled like his.

"Hullo, Daisy!" Parker grinned. He rose and pulled Payoff's chair over to their table. "You here?" he asked for openers.

"M'yeah. Jus' came to see you." Daisy ducked her cropped head, overcome by the moment. Her voice had the same gravelly roughness as his.

"This here is Anne."

"Mmm." Daisy hardly looked at Anne, not interested. "I have sumthin' ta give ya, Dad," she said, barely squeezing out the words. Her large dark eyes were fixed on his face with a liquid sweetness. She made a gesture he might have made, and when her hand came to rest on the table beside his it was a small copy of his own. Thick and powerful–looking for a girl's, with the same surprisingly tapered fingers and nails.

"M'yeah? Okay." Understanding that she wanted to see him outside. Parker rose, gave Anne a complicit wink and followed Daisy out.

When he returned alone a few minutes later he was smiling. "She gave me three dollars," he said, dropping his eyes.

"What for?" Anne looked astonished.

Parker stretched his torso and tucked the folded bills into his

134

front change pocket. "She helped a haole lady clean her garage and got paid five dollars. So she wanted to give this t' me. Came all the way on the bus." His smile just wouldn't stop.

Anne's face wore an expression he'd never seen before. "What's the matter?" he asked.

"I don't know. I just feel funny."

"Funny, how? Because Daisy gave me the money?"

"No. Yes, I guess so. It's so different from anything in my own family. It just seems weird to me."

"Weird? For my daughter to give me part of what she earned?"

"Well, you told me she was down here a few days ago to get two dollars from you for something she needed."

"M'yeah."

"She's always coming to get money from you. But when she gets money, she doesn't save it for when she'd need it, she gives it to you."

"M'yeah." Still not seeing it.

"She'll probably be down next week to get another two or three dollars."

"Prob'ly."

"Why doesn't she manage her money better than that? All those bus fares...."

"She *likes* to get money from me," Parker explained. "She *likes* me to give it to her. And then she likes to give it to me."

Anne looked ready to burst into tears. "Seems like a dumb way to do things," she mumbled. "In my family we were supposed to keep our accounts straight. Be thrifty. Plan ahead. Pay our debts. It was a matter of honor. This way,..." Anne kind of tossed her head, her lips compressed. "It's so messy. It's like the giving is more important than the money."

Parker didn't know what to say to that.

"I guess I'll have sliced pineapple for dessert," Anne decided suddenly.

She took a long time eating it, cutting it up into tiny bites, looking around a lot, but not at him.

Parker waited comfortably, watching Rose fill the sugar

shakers, the regulars paying and leaving. The Useless Bunch were eating their catsup sandwiches.

Parker made a mime of writing to ask Rose for the check when Anne finished. "I told Daisy I'd take her home," he said as he took out his wallet. "Ya wanna come? I won' go in," he added pointedly.

"Daisy?" Anne registered surprise. "I thought she left!"

"No. She's outside, waitin'."

"Outside? Why? Why didn't she wait in here, with us?"

"She didn't want to. She's shame'. Rather be out in the air, on the sidewalk."

"But—it might have been an hour—if you started talking with some of the boys!"

"Thass' all right," he laughed. "She wouldn' min'."

Anne stared at him.

"She's enjoyin' herself. She's waitin' for me."

Anne looked like she could yelp with pain.

He fished around for something to take her mind off whatever it was that was eating her. Then he remembered. "Don' feel bad," he said. "I have some good news."

"What's that?" As if sure it couldn't be good.

"I gotta lead on a place to stay."

"Oh! Where?" Her expression serious.

"Jus' a few blocks from here. Corner of Kuhio and Kaiulani."

"Have you been there? What's it like?"

"Not yet. The lady doesn' like to see people at night."

"A room, or what?"

"It's a gardener's cottage. Hasn' been used in years. It needs cleaning, fixing up."

"Sounds good. We can do that." Nodding. Interested.

"It's a big place. A widow lives there by herself. She doesn' like people, doesn' want them around. But now she decided she wants somebody on the grounds. You know that big property, covers half the block, on the corner. Makai ewa. It's all dry, deserted looking. Big croton hedge aroun' it."

"Oh, that's the place!"

"In there."

"When are you going to see her?"

"Tomorrow, firs' thing. Before I start work."

"Gosh, I hope you get it."

"Kanekini tol' me about it. He lives next door to the widow's sister in Manoa. Nobody else knows about it yet."

"What's the widow's name?"

"Randal."

Anne was quiet a moment. "I've heard of her," she said at last.

"Heard what?"

"Nothing good," Anne replied gloomily. "Nothing good."

Chapter Nineteen

THE WIDOW'S PROPERTY WAS ALMOST CONCEALED BY A MASSIVE hedge of flamboyant croton bushes, higher than Parker's head. The driveway seemed to provide the only access, so Parker entered there. He skirted a faded blue Packard and looked about, impressed by the size of the place, here in the heart of Waikiki. Hot, flat and forsaken–looking, it was the equivalent of at least eight normal lots and as desolate as if it were on a lonely country road.

There were no coconut palms. In fact there were no trees at all except for two or three dead things he did not recognize, perhaps fruit trees, untended in this strange wasteland. The place had once been a sumptuous estate. That could be seen, in spite of the brown, knee–high grass. Whoever planned it had not sought the usual Hawaiian effect of palm and lawn, fringed by voluptuous tropical leafage. The grounds had been laid out like a mainland country garden with flower beds and geometrical gravel walks. But the plants that remained, brittle survivors of years of neglect, were unfamiliar to Parker's eyes. Near the driveway, clumps of overgrown rose bushes, ragged and woody, raised thorny brakes toward intruders.

The house, a large, peaked bungalow, stood exposed at the center of the lonely acreage. Of a pleasant Victorian design, it might have been the cottage of a sea captain at the turn of the century. Its paint, grey or white, was now mostly gone, the generous, swooping roof in bad repair. A gracious veranda surrounding two sides of the front had been screened, giving it a blind and secretive air, concealing the windows and doorway.

To one side of the house several rusting iron chairs and a tipsy table held a conference of ghosts. In the arc of the drive lay a fallen cement bird–bath. There was no sign of life, not even a cat in the clumps of dead ferns by the entrance stairs.

A stealthy silence held the place. The sound of an occasional car passing in the street hardly penetrated the distant, thickly grown hedge. Parker felt alone and vulnerable at nine in the morning as he mounted the three wooden steps, wide and welcoming, to knock at the screen door.

No sound came from within. Thinking it not polite to peer into the screen porch Parker turned his back and studied the forlorn grounds as he waited. He would enjoy fixing the place up, he thought. Trimming the walks, cutting back the roses, watering, tending the lawn of the front circle. In a few months he could have the yard looking spruce again.

But then the widow might not want that. She was said to be strange. "Sort of a recluse," Kanekini had said. "One of the last of an old Scottish family." It was her younger sister who had told him that Mrs. Randal might rent out her gardener's room, to the right person.

In a fresh white tee shirt and clean saila–mokus, his hair carefully combed, Parker hoped he would look like the right person.

A creaking, as of wicker furniture, came from the porch. Turning, Parker saw a woman had been there, stretched out on a chaise lounge, watching him the whole time. She lit a match and put it to her cigarette. "Come in," she said in a rich contralto.

A little shaken to find that unknowingly he had been observed, Parker opened the screen door and took a few steps toward Mrs. Randal. She was in her fifties, he guessed. Her curly grey hair was short, her dark brown eyes handsomely shaped, although her gaze was blurred and distant. It was hard to tell much about her other features, concealed as they were by the puffiness of her pink skin, crisscrossed by countless fine lines. She wore a pale, sleeveless garment that revealed arms and legs thin as sticks although she appeared to be thick about the middle.

Beside the lounge stretched a low table littered with lotions, creams, medicine bottles and glasses. An oversized heaping ashtray spilled onto candy bars and books. On the floor around the table and chaise lay open packages of Lucky Strikes, dirty dishes and more books. Clouds of cigarette smoke did not disguise the strong odor of gin which a half–empty bottle at hand documented.

"Mrs. Randal?" Parker began, pressing his hands politely at his sides. Not approaching. Letting her keep her distance, in case that was what she wanted.

"You're here for the room, aren't you?" she muttered through the smoke.

"Yes. My boss, Ted Kanekini...."

"I know Ted," she said abruptly. "You're Hawaiian, aren't you?"

"Mostly," he said modestly.

"I like Hawaiians." She was quiet a moment, staring at him in an unfocused way through the smoke. "They've had a rotten deal."

Parker wasn't sure whether it would be courteous to agree with that or not.

"My family's been in Hawaii for forty–five years." Now that he was here she seemed pleased to have someone to talk to. "My father was one of the first managers on the Baldwin estate in Maui...." She interrupted herself, "You're a lifeguard?"

"Yes, ma'am."

"Well, go look at the room, if you're interested. It's out back, to the side of the garage. The door's not locked. It hasn't been opened in a long time. Everything's overgrown...but I can't be bothered. There're tools in the garage, if you need something."

"Thanks. I'll take a look."

She did not move. Clearly she had no intention of going with him to see how it was.

Parker made his way around the side of the house to the garage in back. On the side entrance steps were mounds of old yellowed newspapers. Cartons of bottles stood about. Everywhere he saw wonderful stretches of work to be done.

As she had warned, a cascading bougainvillea vine had overgrown the roof of the gardener's cottage and now blocked the low wooden door. In the open garage he found a dull saw with which he crudely roughed away some of the foliage. Mindful that the heavy dry undergrowth might contain scorpions, he gingerly pulled free half a dozen woody branches. A heap of thorny tangle with purple blossoms lay on the ground before he was able to drag open the creaking door. Parker felt good. It had been a long time since he'd worked like this with his hands, done things in the yard. Even before he stepped into the room he knew he'd take it, just for the chance of the work that needed to be

140

done. Already he had a feeling that Mrs. Randal wouldn't mind if he cleaned the place up. She said she liked Hawaiians.

The room was a decent size. It had a cement floor and two nice windows for cross ventilation. There was a narrow iron bed and a rickety table, that was all. No chest of drawers or closet. All of a gardener's clothes, it seemed, went on two large nails. In the tiny bathroom the toilet stood dry. The cold water shower worked unsteadily; the holes of the head needed cleaning. He'd coax the plumbing to work again, paint the room. It was a wonderful place, as he considered it. He would not be bothered by the other beachboys here, or by Polly. Mrs. Randal couldn't stand having people on her property, Kanekini had told him. The children—Daisy, them—could always find him on the beach.

For a moment Parker stood in the low doorway, surveying the dry yard, imagining how nice he could make it look. Anne might enjoy gardening too. He must tell Mrs. Randal about Anne. He would not let other people come on the property but he would have to make it clear to Mrs. Randal that Anne was part of his life.

He turned for a final look at the room. If he had a chair he could write his reports at that table. On the floor, a short, dark line, about the size of a pencil, caught his eye. It was moving. For a moment he hesitated, trying to think how to scoop it up and throw it in a far corner of the yard. As a child he had sometimes held down a big centipede, pulled out its pincers and let it crawl on his arms and neck, to make people scream. Kids in those days did that. Turned centipedes loose in the classroom, put them in people's clothing. The cruelty of the game had finally got to him. The centipede couldn't eat without its teeth. Or so he'd been told.

Parker watched, thinking of many things as the segmented body in a rippling movement eased across the cement floor. It took a serious effort for him to raise his foot, in its thong sandal. He stamped down hard. What perverse impulse blocked his intent at the last moment? How many times, in barefoot football, had he placed a field goal, his stiff toes connecting at just the right angle with the ball to send it between the posts? But now that same foot, in the simplest movement of all, came late on the mark he'd given it. The thong landed with a jarring crunch not on the

141

front of the centipede but its tail. Four inches of its front half lashed over the top of his thong, catching the cleft between his big and second toes.

The pain jolted him. He hopped with it, the ropey thing dangling from its grip on his flesh. When he pulled it free, paste oozed from the flattened center of its coppery body. The middle scales were utterly crushed. Still the head thrashed, reaching blindly for his fingers. He hurried to the door, threw it far to the side of the cottage.

Between his toes the red puncture marks showed plainly. The tip of one of the claws was embedded still. With a quick hard squeeze he exposed it more, picked it out. He couldn't remember a bite hurting so much in all the times he'd got bit at the Home and the reform school. Couldn't remember a pain this mean. The fierceness of its burn brought water to his eyes. Within seconds the burn streaked up his foot into his leg. He squeezed the spot to milk out the poison, rinsed it in the shower. Nothing helped much. He'd just have to wait. Leaning against the wall he held his foot, gave himself time until he was steady enough to go back and see Mrs. Randal.

At least it wasn't Anne, he kept telling himself. It wasn't Anne. He felt terribly lucky that it had happened now, and to him. A small war had just been declared between him and the centipedes around the place. This was not the wilds, like Sacred Falls. But the real difference was Anne. He could not bear the thought of Anne suffering what he had now. He would do everything he could to make the cottage safe. Bracing himself against the doorway he bore down on the pain, getting used to it, getting on top of it.

He could not let Anne know he'd been bit. Just to hear about it might set her against the place. He'd have to take care of the centipedes—there were surely more—without her guessing.

When he could set his foot down and walk on it so you'd hardly notice anything different about him, he headed for the screen porch to tell Mrs. Randal he wanted the cottage.

❁   ❁

"It's enchanting," Anne pronounced. "In a spooky kind of way. Like a Charles Adams cartoon. You'd expect anyone who lived in such a place to be weird. I could tell she hated me on sight, Mrs. Randal."

"She doesn't hate you," Parker's tone was reproving. "She just doesn't like people."

Mrs. Randal had not been rude to Anne. In fact she had risen from the chaise lounge and tottered across the screen porch to greet her, or more likely, to look her over, the first day Anne appeared. With her cigarette down to a nub in one hand, a pained smile on her face, Mrs. Randal had stood in the doorway, perhaps to block entrance to the house. Her eyes caught Anne's for a second, then fixed on a point a few inches above Anne's head.

"Anne...?"

"Anne Blair," Anne supplied.

"Yes. Well, please don't bring your friends here. I can't stand having people around. What state are you from?"

"California."

"That's nice, I'm sure. Excuse me." Mrs. Randal needed an ashtray, that was clear.

The signal was provided for Anne and Parker to withdraw and continue to the cottage with their load of rags, brushes and cans of paint.

The bougainvillea had been trimmed so the windows could be flung wide. Inside, Anne kept her voice low. "Eight feet away I could smell the booze. And she could hardly walk. At ten in the morning!"

"M'yeah. Thass' the way she is, all right," Parker agreed. He pried open a gallon of white paint, began to stir it with a stick.

"One good thing," Anne sniffed. "She won't bother us. She hasn't the strength. It's a wonderful hideaway."

Parker had swept the cottage and painted the doorway and baseboards with a heavy duty insecticide which he'd also poured down the shower drain. His cleanup had netted a dozen centipedes of varying sizes but now he felt the place was as safe as he could make it for Anne.

"On the other hand," Anne continued, "alcoholics are unpredictable. I ought to know. They can be terribly nasty. Awful swings of mood. You never can tell what they'll do. Or say."

Parker continued to stir the paint. "She'll probably be okay. She said she liked Hawaiians."

Anne stood near, watching the swirls in the layer of thinner on top. "Why'd she have to ask what state I was from, anyhow. D'you notice? Wants to show she knows I'm not local."

"Oh, she's prob'ly jus' tryin' to take an interest. Sump'n to say."

"She said it to put me in my place, that's what," Anne fumed. "To show she had me figured out. How'd she know I wasn't from here, anyway?" Anne straightened, put her hands on her hips. "Did you tell her?"

"No, I jus' said 'My girl friend, Anne's gonna be comin' here. You gotta know that.' An' then I promised I wouldn't let no one else come on the place." Parker looked up at her, his face puckered with concern at her annoyance.

"Then how'd she know?"

Parker returned to his stirring. "They know. These kamaainas, they can jus' tell."

144

Chapter Twenty

"**H**AS MRS. RANDAL OFFERED TO PAY YOU FOR THIS YARD WORK you've been doing?"

Parker looked around, feeling good at what he'd already accomplished. He'd gotten rid of the bottles and newspapers and other rubbish he'd found piled around the house and laced through the grass. And he'd pruned the bougainvillea so it was a graceful swoop of color across the cottage instead of a top–heavy bundle crushing one end. Lately he'd been clearing the cracked gravel paths of knee–high brown grass, cutting back the invading shrubs. Today he was resetting stones that bordered the walks. On his knees he trowelled out holes, tapped the dark lava rocks into place. Nearby, Anne pulled weeds from an ornamental bed, threw them in a condensed milk carton. Her head was bent. The back of her neck, exposed through her divided hair, was vulnerable and pale. Her slim hands, so weak and impractical–looking, capably dug and twisted out the coarse weedy tufts. For a moment he stopped and filled his eyes with her. After three months she still seemed like a miracle to him. He'd never got used to the feel of her in bed, a soft clump of bones that yielded so astonishingly to his embraces.

"Not yet," he answered cheerfully. Not admitting he worried more that Mrs. Randal might stop his work than that he should be paid.

"She really ought to lower your rent." Anne's voice held an edge. She tired easily in the sun. In a minute he'd tell her to go sit in the shade.

"Maybe next month, when she sees how good the place looks," he placated her. "It's not important."

"It *is* important to you," Anne pointed out. "You said you wanted a side job to earn some extra money. But on your day off you're always working for *her*." Anne lifted her chin in the direction of the house. "For free."

"I know," Parker said stolidly.

"And now you've got me doing it too. She's got two free gardeners, fixing up her property."

Parker looked around, as if he owned the place, which, in a way, he did. He wondered if, when Hawaiians once lived here, they had buried members of the family on the land. That was the way they kept folks close in the old days. So they could enjoy the keikis, the luaus, like that. Wipeout hadn't had a family. Or a yard.

The air was drowsy. When the trades were still the heat gathered. Beyond the red and gold croton hedge rose the hills, their magical heights sheltered by clouds from the bright skies. Up there lay Palolo.

The news about the kids was not good. Every time Parker phoned home he learned something else that worried him. The third girl, Lani, was becoming more and more moody. Wouldn't talk for days at a time. Lately she'd been refusing to go to school. Daisy was in trouble for fighting. The school counselor wanted to talk to him about that. The other three girls were all right but his son was as bad as he had been at twelve, running away, staying out nights. Polly managed to make everything that went wrong seem like it was Parker's fault. He'd made an appointment with the school counselor but out of sheer stubbornness refused to go home and talk to Polly.

He wouldn't think about Palolo, he'd just look at the hills. Whenever he felt rotten about Polly, or rather, since she didn't count, about the kids because of his situation with Polly, he could always look at the hills. It was strange how something as common as that—looking at the hills, which he had looked at a thousand times before—could make his eyes, in fact his whole body so happy. It made him feel strong and light at the same time. That was part of his luck, he supposed, in being Hawaiian, this smoothing on of sweetness, like the blessings they were always giving in the Bible.

He remembered how he felt when he came in on the old *Matsonia* after being away for a month in Los Angeles. He hadn't looked at the hills, he had *drunk* them, drunk their greens, their contours, as if his very life depended on it. He could have swum through the air to kiss them.

He'd never heard words in English to explain how you felt when you ran your eyes over a piece of land you loved, in the morning. Or words to tell how it was if you couldn't see that piece of land. A hollowness like not having eaten, or maybe worse. He'd gotten so used to looking at the green of the Koolaus he couldn't imagine a day without them, now. He even felt as though he owed the hills something, which was strange because he couldn't really do anything for the hills, except to look at them.

It was Polly's folks, who were Chinese Hawaiian, who insisted they buy the house up there in Palolo. Parker's feelings about owning that house and lot were quite different from his feelings about the hills which he owned by looking at them. The house and lot had papers on them. Payments had to be made each month, or else. There was a risky, uneasy feeling to that, as though a gate might at any time clang shut if certain things, which he didn't understand too well, weren't done. The hills, on the contrary, presented no such difficulties. They were simply there, to be enjoyed each day. That meant that the pleasure they gave was meant for him. The Palolo property, while certainly useful, he was not so sure about. It was his only because it was being paid for by him. Which meant it could be lost by him or paid for by someone else. This seemed tricky and false. Temporary. Not solid, like the hills. He couldn't take the property in Palolo too seriously.

He returned to the lava stones before him, selected one. Handling it with pleasure, feeling its weight, he set it in place, measuring the shape of hole needed. Then he began to scoop out the dirt. He was relishing the smell of the sandy soil when a drone in the sky made him raise his eyes to a plane coming from ewa. Poor people, inside, he thought, going back to the states. One of the reasons he enjoyed looking at the Advertiser was to check on all the terrible things that took place stateside: snow storms, floods, burglaries. Nothing good ever happened up there, the way it sounded. This gave him a cozy sense of his own good fortune. He really should be extra nice to people who had to put up with such a life.

Anne stopped digging weeds to look up with him as the

plane, like a giant silvery minnow against the blue, neared Diamond Head. They both saw it: the plane gently tipped its wings, leveled, then tipped again.

Anne broke into a smile at the sight. "Aloha!" she breathed. When the plane was gone she crawled over to him, kissed his cheek. "I've been learning 'Kaimana Hila' at my hula class," she said, nuzzling him. "It's given me a new feeling about Diamond Head."

"M'yeah?" He was not going to let on how much it meant to him to have her spontaneously kiss him like that. Her arm lay across his shoulders.

"I look at it more. I really love it now. When I arrived in the summer, it was a hard, dark brown. Now the rains have given it a coverlet of soft green."

There were other changes since then. Anne's hair was longer and her skin bloomed with a light tan. He was glad she was learning the hula. He was in favor of anything that would help her get past being a haole.

"Hawaiian songs has nice meanings," he offered. "They all talk about the beauty of the land." His grandmother had taught him that. A song about a beautiful wahine always spoke of her indirectly, through praise of flowers, or the land. Even "Kaulana Na Pua"—"Famous Are the Flowers"—which was a lament about annexation, spoke of the queen's "children" as flowers. The "bitter stones" were the terms of the document in which she lost her throne.

"And every song has the word 'aloha' in it," he added. "You can' have a Hawaiian song...."

"Uh–oh! Look! We've got company." Anne managed to make a little space between herself and Parker, without exactly moving away.

Mrs. Randal tottered toward them on the walk that led from the house. Her unsteady figure, sticklike but lumpy, was closely wrapped in a navy yukata kimono. The hand with her cigarette was extended, apparently guiding her, providing balance and poise.

She drew to within a few yards of them. Parker stood, to

catch her in case she fell or anything. He flashed her his grin. "Hullo."

"Mrs. Randal," Anne said deferentially.

"The yard has needed work for quite awhile," Mrs. Randal announced. She stood there, not exactly noticing what they were achieving but in a proprietary stance regarding their activity. "It's very good of you to help out." She did not look at what had been accomplished, as if it didn't matter.

"That's a pink shirt you're wearing," she informed Anne.

Anne's face brightened expectantly, as if the comment were a preface to something more, on pink, or shirts, but all the amenities appeared to have been taken care of.

Tiny ragged holes, once molten bubbles, dabbled the lava rocks. Parker's hands were cut in several places.

His torn thumb came to Mrs. Randal's attention. "You've hurt yourself," she accused.

Parker gave a happy shrug. "Work!" He knelt to continue, setting a stone the size of a rabbit in line with the others, his thick hands, almost the color of the rock, finding the position that seemed right for its form.

For some moments Mrs. Randal stood there, skinny as a scarecrow in the late afternoon sunshine, a light breeze from the Ala Wai carrying off her cigarette smoke. Then she said, "The difference between a Chinese and a Hawaiian is that a Hawaiian will work only with his heart. A Hawaiian only does what he wants to. And if he doesn't want to, money won't change his mind. Right?"

Parker raised his head, gave her a disarming smile. "Thass' right. I guess."

"On the other hand, Chinese work only for money. That's what makes him want to work. Even if he doesn't like the job. Right again?"

"Mmm. Guess so."

"I know what I'm talking about," Mrs. Randal pronounced. "We had Chinese on our plantations, then Portuguese...the Hawaiians wouldn't work in the fields."

Anne's expression, which had been glum, cheered. "I'll bet you had some fascinating experiences in those old days. I mean—

before the war, when things were different," she corrected herself.

Mrs. Randal's magnificent, blurred eyes wandered toward the valleys. She drew on her cigarette, released smoke as she spoke. "I know stories about the Hawaiians...what the haoles did...."

Anne's face was lifted, her eyes hopeful, but Mrs. Randal turned and began to move unsteadily toward the garage. A pair of mynah birds landed in the dead apricot tree, squawking furiously.

"Damn mynahs!" she muttered as she teetered away. "Messengers from hell."

When Mrs. Randal returned from the garage she had several tools in her hands. They did not contribute to the reliability of her walk. As she came up the path she said, "Would you carry these for me, Keoni? I dislike this sort of thing so much."

Parker rose obediently, took the tools, and adopting a slowed pace to suit hers, followed her back to the house.

Anne was waiting for him when he returned. "Let's go inside," she said in a fierce whisper.

Once in the room she turned on him, blazing. "What's this business of her calling you 'Keoni'? Why'd she do that?"

"Well, it's my name," he admitted.

"Your name? How come I didn't know it?"

"It never came up. You never asked me."

"How was I to know you had more names? Did *she* ask you?"

"Sort of. When she said 'What's your name?' I said 'Parker Kealii.' Then she said, 'Oh, like John Parker, of the ranch.' I said, 'M'yeah, I was named after him, John Parker Kealii.' So sometimes she call me Keoni."

"When was this?"

"Oh, weeks ago."

"Where?" Wanting all the details. As if they counted.

"In the house."

"You go in her house now?"

"Jus' on the screen porch. Why you gettin' so excited?"

"I don't know. I feel like I can't stand it. Having that woman know something I didn't know. Worse yet, use the Hawaiian. Not 'John' but 'Keoni.'"

"Aw…it's nuthin'. You can call me Keoni if you wan'. I'd *like* for you to call me Keoni. On the beach ev'body jus' knows me as 'Parker.' They don' even know 'Kealii' mos' of 'em. Those things aren't important."

"They are to me." Now she was crying.

Parker pulled her to him, his hands gritty on her arms. "Don' be mad," he said, kissing her face earnestly. "Don' be mad. I'm sorry." He was obliged to wash his hands before he could finish making things right.

Night had fallen when they headed for the Blue Lagoon for dinner. As they passed the screen porch the house was silent and unlit. But they knew Mrs. Randal was in her usual chair. The smell of cigarette smoke and a creak of wicker showed that the kamaaina was alive, and there.

Chapter Twenty-one

PARKER THOUGHT KALAKAUA AVENUE LOOKED TERRIBLE. IT WAS boarded up with signs saying "kapu—construction" for most of two blocks. A row of swanky shops was to replace the Moana Cottages, and there were to be new restaurants, too. On Ulu Niu, the bungalows he used to pass going to work were gone. No more jokes from their radios about "hot coffee and doughtnuts" by Aku–head. A big pit yawned where the bungalows had stood and during the day a bulldozer roared in circles, deepening the pit. A hotel was to go there, it seemed.

Waikiki was making itself over, for the tourists. Parker eyed the confusion, the losses, with distrust. New was supposed to be better than old. Shinier, more efficient. Made things easier, which was what made people happier, it was said.

Perhaps he'd get used to the changes, as he had before. But Waikiki didn't seem as good to him as it was before the war. Nothing taller than a palm tree except the Moorish curves of the Royal's pink towers. People nodding to everyone they met.

Even standing guard at the beach was discouragingly tame. Hedged around with rules and more rules. Every other week, it seemed, he got a bulletin about something new that wasn't permitted. The latest was no dogs. Successively it had been no fires, no drinking, no camping, no playing ball, and now no dogs. Pop Guthrie couldn't take his black lab, Satan, for a swim as they had every day for so long. Parker hated to break the news about that to Pop. But with more and more tourists in view every day, you now had to be careful about every little thing.

How different it was from when he was a Wharf Rat! The gang at the harbor! The fights! Going out to meet a big ship! That was *life*! That was the real thing. Whether you ate or starved was up to you. That was when your very bones felt alive in your body. Not like today, with haole limits everywhere. Haole rules.

Remembering the old excitement of Boat Day. Swimming out in the blue to meet a big ship. The boys rambunctious, the ship huge, scary. High days, those. He wasn't complaining about his life now with Anne. No. He'd never been so happy. Never known such happiness existed. But there was a cost to it. He'd changed. In belonging so much to Anne he'd lost something of what he had been. He hardly recognized himself as the Kakaako Wharf Rat of the old days.

✿　✿

Anne wanted him to go to the courthouse to look for the order that sent him to the orphanage. She couldn't understand why he wanted nothing to do with a place that fixed people's lives with pieces of paper. Where paper controlled people's lives instead of the people. Terrible things happened in that courthouse. It was where folks got rid of husbands and wives, and children—legally. It was where people who didn't pay the taxes lost their property. The place reeked of misery. It was where he'd been sent to reform school, and where other folks were sentenced to Oahu prison or signed over to Kaneohe.

Even if Kamehameha was standing out front, all shiny and gold, his arm extended as though to see if it were raining, it didn't make him feel any better about the courthouse. He would have nothing to do with a place where people were paid to stick their noses into all the rotten things that happened to human beings.

He was the head lifeguard and his grandmother had taught him respect for the right things. This was the kind of haole foolishness he felt he should not encourage in Anne and he had flat out refused.

One cross word led to another and Anne suggested he spend the night at his own place. It was the first he'd passed alone since they began. During the long hours he made up his mind. Next morning the *Lurline* would arrive. He rose early and headed the jeep toward the harbor. Knowing how Anne would feel about it only made it better. Delighting in the dangers that scared her so much. The propeller with its deadly suction. The murderous anchor hanging in the bow, directly overhead.

With a naughty sense of freedom he sped toward Pier Ten. Thinking of things he hadn't thought about in a long time. How it was, out in the water, with a huge ship bearing down on you. Awesome, unstoppable. Coming right at you, and you no more than a gnat in its path. That was a feeling like no other.

But the ship was your friend, too, and the boys had their own ways of making her a part of the romp. He was getting older and all that, but he'd go out one more time. He'd show Anne!

    ✪ ✪

It was not yet seven when Parker entered the great shed under the Aloha Tower. The *Lurline* was due in at eight.

Around him on the pier, lei vendors held out their colorful strands, sang their bargains. "Plumerias, t'ree foah dollah. Nice plumeria!" The sweet scent of the flowers mixed with the dockside smells of brine, creosote, hemp and heavy machinery, wonderful to breathe. He hadn't realized how much he'd missed these smells.

A Chinese Hawaiian tutu whom he knew by sight held out a string of gardenias and ferns to him. "You like one nice lei?"

Parker hiked his eyebrows, gave her his Huck Finn grin. "You give, I like. No give, I no like." They both chuckled at the standard answer.

Members of the Royal Hawaiian Band were setting up in their accustomed place. They looked sleepy in their rumpled white uniforms. Parker chaffed a few he knew from his diving days.

He probably looked like a happy man, he thought, in his nice aloha shirt and jeans with no patches. But as he stepped out of the shed onto the dock, a sensation he hadn't expected—like termites swarming through his guts—took over. It had been so long. Who was diving now? Remembering how, in the old days, the gang nearly drowned newcomers they didn't want.

He looked down at the green water of the empty slip. Knowing how the other divers might react to his cutting in on their take. The fact that he was an old–timer wouldn't count. He had to be prepared for a gang–up. In the water and out.

Stripping to his trunks, he wedged his shirt and jeans under the barrier near the band. When he glanced up he saw two kids he'd never seen dive, outside the barrier. They watched him, expressions sharp, surly. One was a tall, lanky Portuguese Hawaiian whom he recognized from somewhere. The other was a Japanese kid, solid as a tugboat, his neck as thick as his head, which wasn't small. His hair stuck out straight all over in a long crew cut. As he took off his skivvy shirt and pants, every movement suggested the ease of great strength. In his faded, raggedy red trunks even his okole looked powerful.

Parker hiked his own waistband. In the water he would want to know where these two were at all times. His lifeguard trunks had the Water Safety Instructor's patch on the left leg. But that probably meant nothing to those kids. They threw him dark looks as they made their clothes into tight bundles, stuffed them under the barrier. He wished Wipeout were with him. Wipeout going out with him as he never could in the old days.

With the band tooting and the hubbub of haole voices nearby Parker didn't recognize who was calling. Then he saw Nuts waving, headed toward him.

"Nuts! Good ol' Nuts! 'Ey!"

He never thought he'd be so glad to see Nuts. It was a miracle he was still alive. Nuts would do anything. He'd dive off the roof of Pier Eleven, clearing the cement wharf by inches. And not even for money. Just to do it. They shook hands, as it had been a long time since they'd seen each other.

"There's Jocko! An' the Parson!"

"Howzzit! Howzzit!"

The Parson still didn't smile, after all these years. Then Naki, of all people, showed up. Parker felt good. He'd be all right. Still, he'd keep an eye on those two kids and the other new ones who joined them.

It was time to head out for the channel. The water's surface had an oily shine, in the old days it was usually cleaner. The trades chilled the top layer of water during the night. Underneath it wasn't much warmer. It was too deep ever to get warm like Waikiki. When he was young he had skin like an alligator. They all did. They could stay in the sea for hours.

To get a little extra heat for that first chilly plunge he jogged and flexed a moment. Before he came he'd had a cup of coffee. He remembered when he didn't have a nickel for such a luxury, when he'd been cold to the bone from sleeping on a wooden bench in the Wharf Rats' shack. Not even a towel to put over his shoulders.

Running, yelling, Naki and Jocko threw themselves headlong into the water. Parker followed. With an exhilarated snort he surfaced, leveled off to swim. There were plunges around him but the Hawaiian–Portuguese kid and the Japanese were already on their way out so he didn't have to worry about them. His feet in a gentle flutter, barely rolling his head for air on the left side, his arms going over like wheels, he settled into his easy stroke. He had about ten city blocks to go between the harbor and Sand Island, to meet the ship outside the channel. The water was smooth but heavy. When he got outside the harbor it would be fresher.

Heading out to meet a big ship again! As he plowed forward Jocko and a new kid were in view when he took air. Jocko's big, bony elbows, like windmills, were unmistakable. The other one, an Oriental, chugged along as if he could go for hours.

He'd forgotten to tell Anne about the sharks. Outside the channel the water was so clear it was easy to see everything under water, even your own toenails. When a shark swam by the texture of its skin was visible. Once a woman passenger had dropped in a dead faint on the ship's rail when she saw a shark swim under a diver. Thought it was going to take off his legs. But the sharks around Sand Island were just lazy scavengers, after the ships' slops. They weren't likely to go for live meat.

He began to think ahead, how it would be when the diving began. If they got to dive. He'd heard the captains didn't slow up much now, they were in a hurry to get in and dock. Not many boys were going out, for that reason.

In the old days he'd learned to pick out the passengers who really enjoyed throwing coins to the boys. A lot were just lookers, probably couldn't believe their money wouldn't be lost. The thing was to get one of the good throwers to pitch directly to you. Laughing and calling, "'Ey, mistah, drop it down!" "Ovah heah, missus! Way out heah!" You could get a kind of link across the space between the two of you. Then the passenger would make it easy, let you know where he was going to throw his coin. "Here's one! Here it comes!"

When you got the coin you held it up to catch the light so he'd see his money wasn't wasted.

Laughter and good feeling went back and forth with the coins across the water. When the ship moved on you could see the passengers were sad that the game was over.

But diving was a fight, too. There were boys who, when you held up your coin before putting it in your cheek, would knock the coin out of your hand. You'd have another scramble as the coin went down again. Some of the tourists enjoyed that kind of action. They'd throw a coin not to a boy, but in the middle of three, to see them thrash the water white. The divers were rough then, pulling hair, grabbing legs so the other boy couldn't swim. But there were no hard feelings. If someone scooped your coin before it was tucked safe in your cheek, that was just his good luck. Back on land everyone shook hands, laughed, in good spirits. Often they got into a crap game while they were still wet. Lost their money another way within an hour. More than once he'd been dumb enough to do that himself. Lost the four or five dollars he'd risked his life for.

But not today. He'd show Anne what a professional nickel diver could do. Might even take her to Kau Kau Korner as a treat, in spite of the dreadful food.

He passed the Sand Island entrance of the channel. Now he was getting close. Cutting his stroke he looked ahead and to the left. Just a few hundred yards away, sliding toward him, there she came, the *Lurline*. The sight made him catch his breath. She dominated the horizon off Waikiki, her proud bow lifting, crisp and white, out of the water's dark blue. The sun seemed to shine directly on her, like a queen. In her own way, he found the *Lurline* as awesome as Diamond Head. He was inclined to believe she had a mana of her own.

Gliding imperially, the ship grew larger, more distinct. In a few moments she would be here.

Using the breast stroke he kept his eye on the ship's course and speed. Around him the other boys did the same. From now on his life depended on knowing every instant exactly where he was in relation to the ship. As she sliced through the water, twin white waves curling back from the bow, the waves looked like mere lines of foam. But he knew the power they contained.

Larger and larger, the bow filled his horizon. He felt very small with all that tonnage plowing toward him. High overhead, the two huge wings of white metal arched, bearing forward. Up on the decks the passengers squeezed shoulder to shoulder at the railing. They wore brightly colored clothes, their faces were alive as they laughed and pointed below. If they had a chance, they would throw coins, he thought.

It didn't look like they'd get a chance. From the size and speed of the bow wave the ship didn't seem to be slowing.

On she came, hard toward them. Still hard, not easing at all. There wasn't going to be a pause. The divers were poho.

Nearby, Naki made a noise of disgust. "Tsah!"

Around them several boys cursed.

"No moah chance!" Parker groaned.

Rotten luck! The old aloha was out. Damn! If the ship didn't stop before the channel, the boys would never get to dive. In the harbor they couldn't compete with the band playing, the hula girls dancing and friends with leis waving and calling.

Before the war the ships spent ten or fifteen minutes waiting for the Young Brothers tug to guide them into the harbor. There had been a stately sense of pleasure to arrivals then and the passengers had time to admire Honolulu, with its palm–lined strees spread out at the foot of the green hills. The nickel divers had been a welcome part of the scene.

Now their one chance was gone! Getting landed quickly— efficiency—was all that mattered. When he was younger he would have had to go without eating.

The bow was only fifteen or twenty yards away; the great fold of water curling back from its point would hit him in a moment. Treading water, tossing his head to clear hair and water from his eyes, Parker made a decision. He took a few strokes to the left, out of the path of the point, but within touching distance of the ship's side. Anne would see! He wasn't going to be cheated out of the whole thing.

The bow loomed over him, its tip slightly to his right. Tons of water rolled away from the slice of the ship. He braced for the blow, ready for action the moment it passed. There was a marvelous crash, then he went into his fastest stroke, paralleling the ship only an arm's length from its side. Some of the boys caught grips in the holes along the side for their ride. But he wasn't satisfied with that. Furiously he churned in the trough next to the ship, about two yards behind the point of the bow. He had to make up those two yards.

The water drove like sand against his flailing arms. He'd forgotten the feeling of racing a ship. Unable to see where he was, he had to rely on his knuckles grazing the ship's side occasionally to tell him his position. Reaching and pulling fiercely he felt he was gaining by inches, toward the point. But the price was terrible. He couldn't last long. He was losing wind. Smoking hadn't helped any.

A softening in the water meant the engines had slowed a bit. Encouraged, he poured on his hardest stroke.

Directly over his head the anchor was poised in its hole. But the captain probably wouldn't drop it without warning, especially this far from the pier. At one moment he heard yelling, which might be the passengers, hoping he'd make it. He probably looked like a dolphin, plowing along near the point of the bow. Unless they were old–timers they wouldn't know why he was racing, what he intended to do.

His lungs were on fire, his arms weakening. He couldn't keep it up. He was about to quit, slide back to one of the holes in the side, and say he'd had another kind of fun, racing his big friend. But then, through the blinding foam, he saw he was only about a foot from the bow point. He couldn't let the *Lurline* have it then. In spite of his scorched lungs he told himself just to go ahead. Then his left hand hit, not the flat side of the ship but sharply, the point. On the next quick stroke his hand, spread wide, caught it. His grasp held. The wedge solid in his hand, the ship's mighty pull took him. His body went so slack with relief that it cost enormous effort to bring his right hand up and over, to double his purchase on the point.

Limp with gratitude he hung there, his body trailing in the white–laced trough. It was some moments before he had the strength to pull higher, so as not to take the smothering foam. His heart pounded so hard he thought it would burst. He hoped no one would come and drag on him for a moment. He was too used up.

But the exhilaration of the stunt didn't let him rest long. He pulled forward until his armpit held the point of the bow, then worked his torso across it. With the water driving against him, the two-inch wedge of the metal point cut into his chest, bruised his ribs. Fortunately, the ship's paint was not slimy. He had a good grip, whatever he did. The water beating on his shoulders felt stiff enough to stand on. Carefully he stretched his right foot and knee across. Then he pulled his body around so the point was headed vertically into him. This was when your ule and laho could catch it. He particularly wanted to keep them in good condition now.

Holding the point hard, his wrists stiff as crowbars, he drew up his legs, planted one foot on each side of the point, just below the waterline. His heels overlapped, both insteps across the point for a solid hold.

When his feet were set he prepared to let go with his hands. He lifted his head above the white water piling up on his spine, and with a push straightened backwards. Locking his body stiff, he made his position good. Stretched on his back, arms at his sides, he made his own little wake, ahead of the *Lurline* as the ship plowed steadily ahead.

The water roared around his ears but he became aware of another sound too. Then he remembered the people on the ship. Up above the anchor in its hole, above the flaring arch of the bow, the passengers leaned on the railings of the decks. Through the flying water he saw the passengers waving, cheering. Laughing, he lifted his hand, waved back. Now he was feeling good. Back in his old stunt, he was having his sport. Anne should see him now!

The ship was slowing. Jocko had got up to the point. He wanted to be in it too. They had done this together many times. Jocko pulled himself up Parker's stiff body, got behind his head and planted his feet on Parker's shoulders. Then, with a thrust, he straightened backwards.

It was easy for the other swimmers now. Parker couldn't see

them as they took places behind him, just watched as they scrambled up his body, to stand on one another's shoulders, one more and one more. The hulk of a Japanese kid was among those who pulled up past him. Lying on their backs, making a stiff human chain, they laughed and shouted with the mischief of it. Sometimes there were as many as ten boys stretched like a stick ahead of the ship as it pushed into the harbor.

It was a win, after all. He and the *Lurline* were doing it together. The boys got their free ride in, the passengers applauding. He hadn't had the fun of chasing the coins, zigzagging through the pretty green water. But Anne would have seen something if she'd been there.

Chapter Twenty-two

THAT EVENING ANNE CAME OVER AND APOLOGIZED. PARKER felt so set up from his fun of the day that he took her in his arms at once.

She sniffled a little and said she had no business trying to make him find out about his family if he didn't want to. He said she was the first person who cared enough to be interested in those things. It was his fault, he should be grateful she was trying to help.

When she heard he'd been out to meet the *Lurline*, Anne was thunderstruck. Wanted to hear all about it.

"Sharks?" She acted so alarmed and proud that he changed his mind about going to the courthouse. Decided it might not be so bad after all. He could overcome his personal feelings against the place since she seemed to want it so much. She would go with him. They'd do it on his next day off.

It took a beautiful night of making love to get all their little thoughts and feelings patted back into place after a night apart. Privately Parker resolved not to let quarrels like that come between them again. One thing he had to be careful about was his relationship with Mrs. Randal. Anne tended to think that Mrs. Randal's interest in him was personal, which of course it wasn't.

He understood that Mrs. Randal, having grown up on Maui, had special feelings for Hawaiians, believed you could count on their aloha. He didn't want to betray that trust. Apparently she had suffered a lot with all the changes that had taken place. It seemed to him that she was the suffering type, so allowances should be made for her and her gin. Since he was on her property he considered her one of his responsibilities. He wanted her health and happiness, inasmuch as such things were possible to her. If she'd been ill he would have fetched medicines, sat with her, whatever was needed. Planting half a dozen sprouted coconuts to replace the dead mainland–type trees was part of showing his appreciation for being there. He'd also put in pakalana vines near the screen porch so it would smell nice next May.

He found it natural for Mrs. Randal to lean on his presence since she was so wobbly and alone, but he determined not to let her do anything that would hurt Anne. So when he walked up the driveway after work he always had an excuse not to linger.

If Anne weren't with him Mrs. Randal had got the habit of coming to the door to say a few words. Ordinary things like, "Did it rain at Kuhio? We had a few sprinkles here." If it hadn't been for Anne's feelings he would have been glad to stop a minute and give her news of the beach. Like the time Kunia brought in a squid and a lady tourist had rushed over demanding to know what the ugly thing was and where he'd got it. Kunia had laughed, bitten off one of the still-wiggling tentacles just to upset her. Told her he'd got the squid "right out there where you was swimmin' awhile ago." The lady tourist had flounced over to Parker to complain. Informed him that the waters should be cleaned out and made safe for swimmers. Otherwise she wasn't going to swim anymore.

Mrs. Randal would've had a good laugh at that one. But he saved the stories for Anne, instead, breezing by Mrs. Randal at her screen door. Lately, however, she'd begun asking him to pick up things at the store for her. Most of her groceries were delivered by Aoki's but she'd forget small items like milk or matches. Usually she remembered to pay him so he was glad to do this.

"Come in, I want to talk to you." Mrs. Randal did not leave her chair as he slowly opened the screen door, a carton of Luckies in his outstretched hand.

His trunks were still wet from his swim. Worse yet, Anne would be along in a minute. He did not want her to find him inside the widow's house.

"Sit down!" Mrs. Randal commanded, waving toward a wicker chair.

"I better not. Thanks, uh? My trunks's still wet."

"That's all right. Damp trunks won't hurt that chair." Even if her words were slurred, she was going to have her way.

Gingerly, he seated himself on the chair's edge. Fearing she might tell him she'd changed her mind, she wanted him to leave. Even though she liked him she might do it. She could do anything. You couldn't tell about a lady like Mrs. Randal. She was stretched out, as usual, in the chaise, with a Hawaiian quilt over her legs and more junk than ever collected around on the table and floor. He couldn't hand the carton to her because she was busy lighting a fresh cigarette even though she already had one burning in the ashtray which was spilling over with butts. So he continued to hold the carton and to look at her politely.

"This is a valuable piece of property," she informed him, when she'd got the cigarette going.

"That's why I like to make it look nice for you," Parker put in, hoping that would count for something.

"That's not the point. *How* it looks doesn't matter. It's the land that's valuable. And where it is."

"It's a good location," he had to agree. "Handy to the beach."

"For years people have been trying to buy it from me."

"I'll bet you could get good money for it."

"I don't want money. They want the whole thing, these real estate developers. I've told them that's out of the question. I *live* here. I'm not leaving until they carry me out. So now they're trying to get me to subdivide it. Cut it in half. Take the mauka side of the yard, including your cottage."

"Oh," said Parker soberly. "What for?"

"They want to build a huge apartment house, half a block long and three stories high. Forty–five units. Did you ever hear of anything so grotesque?"

"They got some apartments two stories high already, on the Ala Wai," he pointed out.

She ignored him. "Almost every week someone is phoning me or writing me about it. I feel so persecuted...."

He did not know what that meant exactly but it sounded as though she felt bad.

"I know just how the early Hawaiians felt when the missionaries were taking their land away from them. Of course it's not exactly the same, but I mean, it's *my land!*" She raised her alto voice, lifted her chin in a dramatic way he'd never seen before. "I've lived here twenty–six years, ever since I moved in with my husband. And now they're trying to get me out." She gave a dry little sniff, reached for some kleenex which she didn't need.

Haoles had these feelings, he knew, about owning property.

Since they seemed to need their patches of land, they should have them. For himself, he had his own way of owning things.

"I'm being *hounded*. They even go bother my sister."

Parker could not imagine Mrs. Randal doing anything she didn't want to do. In fact he couldn't imagine very many people brave enough to face her down if she got mad. She was scary enough without being mad. He was silent, wondering why she was telling him these things, what she wanted from him.

"I'm thinking of having gates installed on the place. I want these people to know I mean what I say. That I won't have them snooping around. There was someone here the other day—walked right up the driveway."

"I'll run 'em off, Mrs. Randal. If anyone comes on the place, I'll see they don't bother you."

He was so relieved to find she wasn't going to make him leave that it seemed like an easy bargain. He rose. "You kin count on me."

But she wasn't through yet.

"About the gates. I'd like to have gates. But I know it would look strange. People would think I'd gone soft, like the Bard sisters...."

Parker couldn't imagine gates. He'd never seen gates in Honolulu, except, as she said, on the Bard estate. They had a stone wall all around their property with shards of glass on top. Like a prison, poor things.

"You gonna put in a fence?"

"No. That's not necessary. The croton hedge is enough. It's just that gates would...make a point. We could close them sometimes," she added.

Parker tried to look at things from her point of view. It was difficult.

"The thought of getting the work done, having people around for several days makes me ill."

"Don' worry, Mrs. Randal. You don' need gates. It'll be all right."

"That's very kind of you, Keoni. You're a real Hawaiian. You've got the old style spirit of kokua...."

She probably would have said more but he handed her the

carton of cigarettes and began to move toward the door. "M'yeah. Well, I gotta go. Anne's comin' over in a minute."

An expression passed over Mrs. Randal's face. There was no doubt about it. She reacted badly to Anne's name. Anne was not just imagining things.

That was why Parker was so surprised at Mrs. Randal's next move. She invited them both—Anne was with him one Saturday morning as she said the words—to dinner on Thanksgiving.

Chapter Twenty-three

"WHY WOULD MRS. RANDAL INVITE US TO THANKSGIVING dinner? There must be a reason."

"Don' hav'ta be a reason. She's havin' turkey. I live here. So she invites us."

"You know she hates me."

"She don' hate you. She jus' don' care much for mainlan' folks." Parker smoothed Anne's sweet shoulder. "She's ol' style, that's all. Ol' style kamaaina. Don' trus' all these new folks comin' in now, since the war."

"I thought old style was to show aloha. She acts like I don't exist."

"Thass' jus' her way. She prob'ly forgits. With all her drinkin' she forgits a lot of things."

Anne's toes switched back and forth against Parker's instep, agitated. "You mean that milk and stuff she's always sending you to the store for?"

"Well, it's not far."

"Three blocks each way," Anne scoffed. She flopped on her side, swashing him in the face with her straight hair. Carefully he smoothed it before laying his head next to hers. When he pressed it wrong she squawked.

"She disapproves of me for sleeping with you. But she doesn't disapprove of you for sleeping with me."

"Missionary influence, prob'ly."

"Her family wasn't missionary."

Parker reached for his Chesterfields, lit one, drew on it deeply. He had his smoke, he had Anne, he had everything.

"I wish you could find another place to live. That's what I wish."

"Awww...." Rebuking her on this one. "I'm *lucky* to have this place. It's *hard* to find a place in Waikiki now."

"Every time we go in and out we have to walk by the screen porch where she's sitting."

"Well, she has to sit somewhere to drink. That's her life."

Anne turned her head. "Did she say who else is coming?"

"Nope."

"When she said, 'I'm having turkey for Thanksgiving' I thought she meant for us to keep out of sight."

"You see, you was wrong!" he crowed.

"You always look on the bright side," Anne mumbled.

Parker laid his cigarette in the saucer, pulled her close against him. "I'm happy I got you." The glee in his tone was incorrigible.

"That's the trouble with you Hawaiians. Let people push you around. Never stick up for your rights." Her voice had an I-told-you-so tone.

Parker smoked, staring contentedly at the ceiling of the gardener's primitive room. Yesterday he'd built some shelves. One thing at a time he'd fix it into a real little home.

"You don' unnerstan'," he said. "She *likes* to have us here. She's not so lonely. Even though she likes to be alone."

"It's *you* she likes," Anne scolded. "Because you're Hawaiian. And then there's all this work you've done around the place."

"Naw. She don' care 'bout my work. She don' care how the place looks."

"And that's another thing!" Anne rose from the pillow, her eyebrows set to show how she felt. "You really ought to...."

He cut her off. "Maybe this dinner she's gonna make is like—you know—to say 'mahalo.'" Before Anne could argue about that he sat up, planted his feet on the cool concrete floor. "You wanna shower first?"

"We can take it together." Anne slid around him, put her feet down next to his. "You just wait," she threatened. "I'm going to eat all the turkey skin I can get."

❁ ❁

At five after three there were no sounds of voices, no unfamiliar cars in the driveway. Parker in a starched aloha shirt and Anne in a pale linen dress mounted the steps to the big house.

Some moments after their knock Mrs. Randal appeared, unsteady on her long, swamp-bird's legs. She was festive in a green taffeta holoku and wore a navel length strand of polished kukui beads. For the occasion she had applied an acid–bright orange lipstick which also ringed the fresh cigarette in her hand. Her bobbed, grey hair was quite neat, her puffed webby skin less noticeable than usual, Parker thought, with all the other things that were going on.

"Oh, hello, you two!" she gushed in her husky voice. Her tone managed to be both welcoming and remote at the same time. "Come in! Come in! I'm just flying out. I have to run over to my sister's for a minute to wish her a happy Thanksgiving."

Parker stepped aside, confused, to let Mrs. Randal pass.

"Oh!" She turned and gave them a benign, unfocused smile. "I haven't had the time. Would you…just pop the turkey in the oven? That would be so good of you." She made a gracious gesture toward what presumably was the kitchen. "It's on the table."

"You gonna drive?" Parker asked in alarm.

But she was concentrating on maneuvering down the steps, the train of her holoku in one hand, cigarette in the other. "So good of you," she murmured again.

In the driveway, where the rose bushes raked the far side of the car, the motor turned over, was gunned hugely. With a roar close to an airplane's, the car backed out.

"Good grief!" Anne exclaimed.

The gears stripped. Then, with both the gas and clutch on the floorboard apparently, the faded old Packard, booming like a B–29, began to creep down Kuhio Avenue.

Anne turned to Parker, her expression stunned. "It takes hours to cook a turkey! Why are we here at three if the turkey isn't in the oven?"

Parker grinned, shook his head. "Mrs. Randal. Let's go look."

Now that she was gone, a thick silence enclosed them. They moved through the screen porch, past the stretched out chair surrounded by a yard–wide spread of the things Mrs. Randal needed for her days. "I never been inside," Parker said as they stepped within.

"Theater," Anne murmured. On a table by the door a volume of Eugene O'Neill lay among New York theater magazines.

The living room itself had theatrical touches. An oversized peacock chair faced the bay window and garden. Beside it stood a large dead palm. A stuffed elephant's foot served as a stool. One wall was mostly books, hundreds of them, many stacked in toppling piles.

Exotic objects, many of them brasses, some with a nautical air, were placed about. There was a great, tarnished hibachi, a curious old astrolabe, a brass tray that would have served for the head of John the Baptist. A pukkah fan hung on a wall against a gorgeous cloth, a huge Chinese jar held a fountain of peacock feathers. Over a wicker settee was flung a silken paisley faded to the colors of dead leaves. To one side an enormous, spotted gilt mirror reflected the empty clutter of the room.

"She has some lovely things," Anne murmured, picking up a Chinese snuff bottle in which a miniature landscape had been painted from the inside. "My family has a collection of these."

Here and there were objects out of place, like candy wrappers, or a box of corn flakes, but nothing was sleazy or fake. An eclectic but sure hand had assembled these possessions.

Parker had never seen anything like the furnishings of this house. They did not impress him as worthwhile, being both useless and old. He himself would take a fine Waianae sunset over that metal stuff any day. However, since Mrs. Randal seemed to value such objects he would protect them for her, if necessary. There were things that might tempt a thief. Like the peacock feathers. Hawaiians esteemed the feathers for hat leis. No one would ever learn from him what Mrs. Randal had in her house. Mostly, as he moved through the rooms, he noted objects that might booby trap Mrs. Randal, unsteady as she was on her feet.

In the dining room a huge oval table, probably solid koa, was loaded to near spilling with an accumulation of perhaps months. Coffee cups stacked four high, bottles of milk in various stages of souring, vases of dead flowers, cereal bowls, ashtrays.

Parker let out a muted whoop. "Hu–i! We' s'ppose' to eat here?"

Anne stopped dead at the sight. "Oh no!"

They'd been quiet at first, speaking almost in whispers, as if not to disturb some ghostly invalid in a nearby room. Now they became bolder.

"Look at this!" In a corner, almost concealed by an Oriental screen, stood a harp, once silver, now mottled and stained. As if torn by a furious hand, its strings dangled in mute waste.

At the door of the kitchen Anne's voice rose in disbelief. "Oh, this is too much!" An avalanche could hardly have done a better job of burying every horizontal surface. Sacks of groceries leaned and spilled. Fruit rotted under heaps of canned goods and newspapers. Dirty dishes slid over everything. In the center of the room stood a big country worktable and there the turkey lay, pink–skinned, barely visible among the piles around it. To make space, Mrs. Randal had pushed plates and pans aside, a few were balanced on the edge.

Anne crossed to the turkey, touched it. "The flesh is warm," she said. "It's been sitting here since yesterday, at least." Wrinkling her nose, she wiped her fingers on a brown paper sack.

"Honey," she turned to Parker, pleading, "she has no intention of giving us a Thanksgiving dinner. She's just toying with us."

"She bought the turkey," Parker pointed out. "She *did* buy it."

"It was just a whim. She had this whim and then she changed her mind. She didn't mean anything by that invitation." Anne lifted the lids of several pots on the large, old–fashioned range. Nothing fit to eat lay within. Burnt rice, congealed grease, dark lumps that, from the rancid smell, could have been rotted prunes or worse. "She hasn't done a thing toward a dinner."

Hands on his hips, Parker stood wagging his head, grinning. One didn't find such opportunities often.

"She can't treat us like this." Anne's voice dripped disgust. "Come on. Let's go!"

"Leave?" You couldn't have dragged him away. The afternoon was turning out better than he'd hoped. "We not leavin'. We got work to do."

"You mean…you're going to let her do this to us?"

Parker's mouth took a stubborn set. "She *did* invite us. And she *asked* us to put the turkey in the oven. We can jus' do that. Later, when it's cooked, we eat some. The trimmin's don' matter. Maybe all she eats at Thanksgiving is turkey." He studied the confusion on the counter tops. "Too bad she don' have poi, at least, to go with it."

"You saw the dining table! We can't even sit down for a slice of turkey without cleaning the table!"

"We got nuthin' else to do. Le's jus' put the turkey in the oven, like she said."

"It'll take at least three hours to cook!"

"So, le's get started. Find a big pan," he said decisively, picking up the turkey, handling it as he had handled many luau pigs. "Gosh, it's still got the organs inside."

"Sitting here for two days with the things inside? She wants to poison us!"

Parker sniffed. "Smells all right. It's still good."

"Oh, you!" Anne gave a sigh of resignation that was also a compliment to his male authority. Wrapping a soiled dish towel around her middle for an apron, she began to search for a basting pan, opening the cabinet doors and drawers, of which there were many. It was a fine old kitchen. Splendid meals for grand parties might have emerged from it in better times. A number of items not usually found in a kitchen turned up. Cans of motor oil, a ouija board, a box of Achilles condoms. Platoons of fearless, fifty-cent–sized cockroaches waved their antennae at the disturbance. There was no roaster or any kind of receptacle large enough for a ten–pound turkey.

"If the condoms are in the kitchen maybe the turkey pan is in the bedroom," Anne joked.

"Try the frige," Parker suggested sensibly.

The heavy door swung open. Anne gasped.

While the kitchen was like a shipwreck, at least a certain amount of maneuvering space remained. The refrigerator had no such space. It was stuffed like a cabbage, a solid mass within which one could barely make out recognizable objects—bottles, cans, stained packages, clumps of decomposed fruits and vegetables.

"I'm afraid to touch it!" Anne breathed. "Anything could be in there!"

Parker came to see. "Ain' that sumpthin'!" he marveled.

"I don't know what I can take out without ten pounds of garbage hitting the floor."

"Here, use this." He brought a Gilbeys Gin carton from the back porch, set it before the refrigerator. "Start at the top."

"Sweetheart!" Anne put her hand to his cheek. "We can get a complete turkey dinner at the Tavern for two–fifty each."

"Nevah min'. We got nuthin' else planned. Jus' go ahead." he had already cleared the sink so he could begin to wash.

Gingerly, Anne began to pluck the most identifiable objects from the top of the heap. Feeling used, she also had a sneaky sense of glee at discovering Mrs. Randal's disgraceful habits.

The first items to go were a crushed egg carton with several broken, drained eggs and a pot of cottage cheese, its putrid contents gone green. Then a parcel of slime that might once have been lettuce, an empty peanut butter jar and several cupcakes apparently tasted and thrown back in. A petrified pork chop. Two ginger ale bottles with less than a swallow in each.

When Anne found a bowl of potato salad at least a year old she felt she was getting into mother lode territory. Under it three pots nested, their dried nameless contents—blood, perhaps, or molasses—looked as though they would yield only to weeks of soaking in hot water. "Look, honey," she showed one to Parker.

"A pick axe would fix it," he chuckled. He had stacked dishes toppling high on the drainboard. With a soapy rag he methodically scrubbed each piece, set it aside, sudsy, to rinse later. Since there was no other space, he put the dishrack on the kitchen chair.

With gagging noises that were only slightly exaggerated Anne gave him a running account of her discoveries. "Ugh! Tainted rice pudding.... Ick! Canned soup from the Middle Ages.... Empty pimento jar.... What's this? Pew! Dog throw-up.... Calcified spaghetti.... I never knew archaeology could be so fascinating. What are these, guavas?" Holding out some round, darkish hard objects.

"Might be limes. Or some kind of nut."

"Could be cockroach bait."

"If only we could throw out sad memories like we clean a refrigerator, huh?"

Parker hummed at the sink.

Half an hour later success seemed to be in view. As she worked her way down from the upper shelves, Anne saw near

173

the bottom what appeared to be a large tray in which corn bread or biscuits had once been baked. She worked it loose, scraped off the fungus–encrusted newspapers on the bottom which had apparently held fish, then gave it to Parker to wash. "I think this'll do. Shall we make dressing?" She looked around the kitchen for ingredients without much hope. "Sweet potatoes? Corn flakes? Maybe I shouldn't have thrown out those cupcakes."

"There's a package of bread on the screen porch near her chair."

"Super! Did you find a skillet? How do you feel about liver and heart in the stuffing?" Her lips lifted away from her teeth as she asked.

"It's food," he said curtly.

Anne groaned. "Okay. Have you seen any onions?"

At four–thirty when they put the turkey in the oven Mrs. Randal still had not appeared. For the sheer charm of it Anne continued to clean the refrigerator. When she'd removed everything that was either useless or unfit for human consumption the shelves were almost bare. She put back a cube of butter, three bottles of coke, and a dill pickle floating in its jar like an embryo in alcohol. The machinery, crusted with two inches of frost, loomed in the emptiness but she saw no reason to overdo a good thing.

Parker continued to restore order, throwing out traps with dead mice, stacking the canned goods together. Anne dried the kitchen chair, sat down and watched him as he continued to wipe surfaces, his brown face absorbed, at peace.

"Oh! The dining room!"

When the table had been cleared she set three places with real silver around a large polished nautilus shell mounted on teak. At seven o'clock, when Mrs. Randal still hadn't arrived, she added golden candles, and lit them.

A roaring in the driveway announced the return of their hostess. Anne, nursing a singed knuckle from basting the turkey, sat in the peacock chair reading *Emperor Jones*. Parker, half–asleep, was tuned to the Hawaiian music on KGMB.

The green holoku appeared in the living room door frame. A strong scent of liquor floated toward them. Parker stood, in acknowledgement of Mrs. Randal's arrival.

"Oh!" She paused at the sight of the candles glowing in the dim adjoining room. Then, lurching, she crossed and threw herself into Parker's arms, which he put out to keep her from falling.

"You angel!" she cried. "Here you are, taking care of everything!"

"M'yeah. Well,...." Parker looked uncomfortably at Anne.

"Did you find the turkey?" Drawing back unsteadily to see his face, Mrs. Randal focused on the top of his forehead. "Oh, it smells so good!"

Gently Parker disengaged himself. "We—ah—threw out some empty bottles and stuff in the frige," he confessed. Keeping his hand out to catch her, just in case.

"Threw out...Oh, those old things. I've been meaning to do it. You darling! You're just what I needed to put this place in order!"

Anne came toward them, glaring.

"He's not here to put your place in order, Mrs. Randal. We were invited here as guests, remember?"

Mrs. Randal's hair was untidy, her eyes redder than the chewed-off remains of her lipstick. She frowned at Anne as though remembering her, slightly.

"Why are you hanging on to Parker? Are you about to fall down?"

Slowly, as if another thought had gained her attention, Mrs. Randal released his arm and turned away. "I love candles," she murmured. "Little flames of God. Or is it the devil? You've made everything look so nice...."

With a dreamy smile she wandered toward the bookcase, found an open cigarette package on one of the shelves. "Actually, I'm not very hungry. I ate so many pupus at Dorothy's house."

She turned to Anne as she put a cigarette between her stained teeth. "Of course if you're hungry, you may eat." Concentrating, she guided a lit match to the cigarette's end.

"I *may* eat!" Anne yelped. "I don't know what you were thinking of when you invited us. The turkey wasn't even stuffed. Not even a pan to cook it in."

Mrs. Randal blew smoke more or less in Anne's direction. She made an airy gesture with her cigarette. "Why are you complaining? All's well that ends well." She gave a dirty little chuckle. "But she wouldn't understand that, would she, Keoni? She doesn't understand us Hawaiians."

Parker flashed Mrs. Randal a placating version of his Huck Finn grin. "Hawaiians..." he began. Anne's furious look cut him off.

With the cigarette in her hand leading, a sort of ballast, Mrs. Randal moved away, heading toward the screen porch.

"The Hawaiians have had a rotten deal," she announced as she maneuvered across the living room floor. "Keoni knows I understand...how the haoles took away the Hawaiians' birthright."

"He's only thirty-six," Anne protested. "Perhaps *you* remember the days of the monarchy."

Mrs. Randal seemed not to hear her.

"Hawaiians...," Mrs. Randal nodded with heavy-headed authority, "are a kind people. They understand that different people are...sometimes different. Hawaiians aren't like haoles."

Passing Anne, she looked at her as if suspecting her neck were dirty.

"Hawaiians invented aloha. Which a haole like you could never really understand."

"Haole? And what are you?"

Keoni looked from one to the other as if hurting for them both.

Mrs. Randal drifted unsteadily onto the screen porch, headed toward her chaise lounge.

Anne's slim frame seethed. She opened her mouth. Parker made signs to her. He shook his head, tapped his temple, trying to ward her off.

"You're just a malihini," Mrs. Randal continued mildly, in her husky voice, as if they were hanging on her every word.

Anne blushed to her elbows. This was probably the vilest thing Mrs. Randal could call anyone.

Parker followed Anne to the porch, put his arm around her waist in a gesture of comfort and restraint.

Could Mrs. Randal possibly negotiate her way through the collection of flotsam and jetsam around the chaise? Anne watched, hoping for the worst. It occurred to her that perhaps she even slept there.

Mrs. Randal reached the edge of the chaise, turned, and holding her cigarette aloft, aimed her rear end at the pillows, then dropped in among them.

"For your information," Anne stormed, "the turkey is ready. What are we supposed to do now?"

"Just one of those malihinis...," Mrs. Randal lifted her nose, blew out smoke, "who takes a few hula lessons and then thinks they're real island folks."

The air was tight. Parker squeezed Anne's waist in a plea that was also a warning.

"Think you know something about Hawaiians because you're sleeping with one."

"I don't have to take this!" Anne cried. She pushed away Parker's arm as if she were mad at him too. "You...vicious...."

Parker took a reproving step forward. "Mrs. Randal...." His voice sounding cross.

"That's all right Keoni," Mrs. Randal leaned back, gazing at Anne with a serenity that dripped disdain. "Don't worry about her. She'll soon be going back."

"How dare you presume!" Anne screamed. Her face screwed up into a parody of itself. "How *dare* you, you poisonous old kamaaina...serpent!"

Mrs. Randal closed her eyes as if longing for a little nap.

"I'll never come back here again. Never!"

Mrs. Randal adjusted her head slightly on her deep pillow. A pleasant little half–smile crossed her lips.

Anne seized Parker's arm. With a last hateful look at the reclining figure, so at ease in the chaise, she flung out, dragging him with her. She tried to slam the door, but Parker, fearing Mrs. Randal was already asleep, caught it in time and closed it with care.

Chapter Twenty-four

A NNE INSISTED THAT HE MOVE, INSISTED THAT HE GET HIS things out of the cottage at once. Her eyes flashed, she twisted her thumbs. Parker didn't think she'd throw things like Polly but he understood he better just do it: leave.

Tracking back and forth in the darkness, their stomachs grinding from not having eaten lunch or dinner, they loaded his belongings in the jeep and took them to Anne's cottage.

The following day Anne broke out in a case of hives. "It's *her* fault," she fumed, making a paste of baking soda to rub on her throat, between her breasts and along her underarms.

"She's pupule," Parker tried to explain, gently smearing the paste in swirls with his brown fingertips. "Why you care what she says? You know how she drinks every day."

"All day, every day!" Anne added, still furious.

They had fled, leaving the turkey in the oven at 350 degrees fahrenheit; quite probably it was still there. Parker couldn't imagine Mrs. Randal turning off the gas and removing the bird.

He felt bad about leaving her place with all the wonderful yard work that still remained to be done. Especially, he regretted not having pruned the rose bushes that scratched Mrs. Randal's car going in and out the driveway. He himself saw no reason to leave just because of a few drunken remarks. Of course Anne wasn't going to leave Hawaii. So why take Mrs. Randal's words seriously?

❂   ❂

Two days later Parker had a lead on a room of his own. While he spent his nights at Anne's, for the looks of the thing at the office he needed his own place. And too, he didn't want Polly bothering Anne. Polly was capable of anything.

Ah Lee was giving up his room at the beachboys' hangout on Koa Avenue. Ah Lee, often known as Lonesome Ah Lee, for the cloud of gloom he habitually carried around with him, was at last happy. After more than a year of watching Kawehi he'd finally got up nerve enough to talk to her and then ask her to go to bed with him. For the last few weeks they'd been inseparable. Now he was going to live with her at her parents' house. The parents were pleased and Ah Lee was glad to give Parker his room.

Ah Lee was actually a haole whose great grief was that he had not been born Hawaiian. Tall, angular, with straight, baby blond hair, his real name was Robert Lee Weiss. His family was high in official circles in Washington, D.C. Cheated by his parents of his desired heritage, he did everything he could to disassociate himself from being a haole. Refused to own a wallet or wear sandals or even thongs. He was among Waikiki's best surfers. His nose peeled constantly—one of the defects of not being Hawaiian—so he was obliged to wear heavy daubs of zinc. A year earlier he had taken to saying his name was Ah Lee. If he couldn't be Hawaiian he could at least be Chinese. It was a compromise that satisfied everyone.

The room he was leaving was in a rambling, termite–ridden structure on Koa that was a sort of headquarters for the beachboys. Once an elegant private residence, the high–ceilinged old rooms had been chopped up into smaller rooms for rent. Parker had often slept there at Spam or Kunia's while getting away from Palolo. Ah Lee's room was the former pantry, next to what had been the kitchen but was now the communal bathroom. The location meant extra noise outside the door at all hours as the beachboys and their wahines came and went but that wouldn't bother Parker.

He would move in over the weekend. Anne saw the room and liked it. Liked the big closet and long speckled mirror over what had been the built–in sideboard. The bed was a handy three–quarter size and the room was a freshly painted cream.

"Don't forget—this Thursday we're going to the courthouse," Anne reminded him after they'd tried out the new bed.

"Oh, I meant to tell yuh. Sumthin's come up. I can't go this week. I gotta talk to the matron at the girls' detention home."

"What for?"

"Daisy's bein' released."

"Daisy's in a detention home? Whatever for?"

Parker hung his head. "Fightin'."

"She fights? Who?"

"Other girls. She beats them up in the bathroom at school and then eats their lunches."

"Sounds like she's hungry."

"She's not hungry."

"Then why does she do it?"

"She's jus' like me when I was young. She *likes* to fight. But me, all the other boys was doin' it too, so it wasn' so bad. It's worse for a girl," he mourned. "An' then she eats the lunches."

Anne had to give up plans for Thursday. But they agreed that Parker's next day off, without fail, they would go together to the courthouse.

❂ ❂

Anne had put on weight. A big bowl of poi each evening had added six pounds, most of it around her thighs and hips. She had difficulty pulling off her one–piece woolen bathing suit when it was wet. One evening when she was having trouble with the obstinate, ropy thing, stuck over the largest part of her rump, Parker offered to help. He inserted his warm, dry hand between the clammy suit and her stomach, sticky with salt, smoothing the suit free, did the same thing behind. Then he pulled downward, held it for her to step clear.

Anne was lifting her foot out of the soggy lump, her hand on his shoulder, when the phone rang. It was Mrs. Randal and she asked to speak to Parker. Anne was so astonished she gave him the phone without a word.

"M'yeah?" His stomach tightened at the sound of the familiar slurred voice.

"The pull chain for the lamp beside my chair came out," Mrs. Randal announced.

"M'yeah?"

"When can you fix it?"

Anne stood looking at him, her suit around her ankles.

"Well...uh...."

"I need it right now," Mrs. Randal insisted. "I can't read without it."

"I'm busy," he fumbled.

"I'll be waiting for you. In a few minutes." She hung up.

Anne was glowering. "Now what?"

"Her light's broke. I gotta fix it."

"Of all the nerve...."

He laid his hand on Anne's breast. "It won't take long."

"What a terrible time to call! Shall I put my suit back on and we'll start over?"

⊙　⊙

When Parker arrived, well over an hour later, Mrs. Randal had dabbed on lipstick to meet him. He noticed this because when she greeted him at the screen door she smiled. This was the first time he'd ever seen her smile.

Also, she used a voice he hadn't heard before, sort of babyish and wheedling. "I only gave my normal little pull and the chain just fell out." As if she was so surprised.

He doubted this was true and also he doubted that Mrs. Randal needed the light to read by. Mostly, when it was dark, she just sat staring at the night, smoking and sipping her gin.

She turned on the porch's dim ceiling light and unfolded a cloth kit of small tools, each in its own slot.

"That's a nice little collection you have there," he said admiring the screwdrivers, graduated wrenches and pliers. There was even a tiny hammer.

"It was my husband's. He used to make little machines. Sort of mechanical toys. He had a workshop under the house."

"This house got a basement?" Parker marveled.

"It's the only private basement in Waikiki. You can't see the trapdoor on the back porch because there's...too much stuff."

He'd heard of basements. Now he knew someone who had one.

He pulled the standing lamp away from the lake of objects around her stretched out chair. The litter was worse than ever. It was beginning to pile up now, in layers. Mail and cookie boxes on top of gin bottles, glasses and books. There was loose food, too. Bananas, an open can of beans.

It didn't take a minute to find and close the opening over the beads of the pull chain so it worked nicely. If Mrs. Randal's hands weren't so shaky and useless he'd have thought she widened the opening herself.

"There you are!" He gave the chain a couple of smart pulls, off and on, placed the lamp back next to her chair. Then he turned and smiled at her, glad he was able to help.

"Here!" Mrs. Randal scrinched up her eyes, and the rest of her face too. Holding out the tool kit to him. "I want you to have this."

A pang of alarm shot through Parker. "Oh, thanks anyhow, Mrs. Randal. Thass' you' husban's. You better keep it. I don' know much about tools an' fixin' stuff, anyhow, hardly."

"No. I've decided, Keoni. You keep it." Fingers shaking, she tied the tape binding the kit together, as he held it.

"Well, thank you, Mrs. Randal. Why don' you keep them here for me? In case you' lamp gets broke again, like that...."

"No, they're for you." She pressed his hand away. "In case you need to fix the jeep or something. How would you like to come back and live in the cottage again?"

He almost put the tools down. But then he thought, "She's just trying to be nice."

She went on. "I'll reduce the rent to twenty dollars. You'll be saving ten dollars a month," she encouraged. "Think of it! I'd be willing to do that, just for you!" Again she smiled. This time he had the feeling it was because she was happy.

"Thanks, I gotta place," he lied. Well he'd have it in a few days.

Mrs. Randal's blurred eyes went hard. She turned away in a movement that surprised him with its swiftness and precision. Facing the wall, after a moment, she said, "So...why are you standing around? The light's fixed. You can see that."

"Here's you' tools, Mrs. Randal."

"Don't be an ass," she said to the wall.

He'd never heard a lady say that before.

"Well, then. I'll keep good care of 'em. G'bye Mrs. Randal."

She was still standing like a tree, facing the wall, when he eased out the door, kit in his hand.

❁　　❁

Parker rarely thought of Mrs. Randal's warning that Anne was just a malihini who would be leaving soon, but when he did, he reasoned that the fact that Anne got so mad proved how untrue it was.

Anne didn't talk about the mainland or her family, although he knew she received letters from them at the post office general delivery. Mostly she liked to talk about Hawaiian things. When he told her what his grandmother taught him about the winds and clouds she had listened intently.

Anne was sweet as a weke. She still had some terrible haole ideas, of course. Like on the subject of borrowing. Sunshine still hadn't returned his red and gold aloha shirt, and now Payoff had borrowed his blue one with the maninis on it to go to a baby luau.

"He's wearing it every day now," Anne complained. "It'll be in shreds if you don't get it soon."

Parker knew this was true. But then he'd had Kunia's swim fins and mask for months. That was the way it went.

One day Anne couldn't stop laughing at a story in the *Star Bulletin*. "Did you see what happened to Duke? Big headline: 'Sheriff Kahanamoku loses hood ornament to thief.' Someone sawed it off his car yesterday!"

"Melvin stole it," Parker said mildly.

Anne stopped laughing. "Melvin?" She was so astonished it took her a moment to ask, "His own cousin, Melvin? *Why?*"

"Ev'body knows. He jus' did it for rascal. Melvin's real rascal."

"What do you mean, 'everybody knows?' You mean he's *talking* about it?"

"Sure. He brags about it. He showed it to us. It's in his room."

"Melvin can't do anything with it. Everyone in Honolulu knows that hood ornament." It was a small sculpture of Duke himself, surfing, in gold. Duke's car was recognizable anywhere because of the gold trophy on the front.

"He's not gonna do anythin' with it." Anne looked so upset Parker tried to smooth her down. "It's not serious."

"Duke was upset enough to report it to the police. It was on the front page."

"That was jus' for one day."

"Well, if Melvin's bragging about it to the beachboys, isn't it going to get back to Duke?"

"Prob'ly."

"So what will happen?"

"Nuthin'."

"You mean Duke won't do anything to Melvin? Won't try to get it back?"

"He's not gonna do anythin' agains' his own *cousin*." Parker was appalled by the thought.

"The whole police department is looking for Duke's hood ornament, but Duke's not going to do anything to get it back! That's a good one!" Anne's face was rosy with indignation.

"Duke doesn't *need* the hood ornament," Parker pointed out.

"Why, he's very attached to it. The newspaper story said it was made by a famous sculptor."

"Duke don' care about that."

Anne still has some haole ways to get past. She continued to read in her book although not at the Lagoon. It made him uncomfortable when she was absorbed like that, paying no attention to him. He eyed a new pile of books in her cottage with the same distaste he felt for the beach reports. He still hadn't written up the requisitions for Kanekini.

Still Anne was making progress. She knew how to mix poi and the best way to keep a bottle of limu from going bad. How to soothe a mosquito bite with papaia juice and what to do if you stepped on a spiny sea urchin. She could make a hibiscus open at night and knew better than to take bananas on a fishing boat. Little by little he'd get her past being a haole. She loved Hawaii and he was Hawaiian. Those were the main things. Clearly they were meant to be together. She was not going to leave.

Sometimes before they went to sleep Anne would ask him to bring her a glass of water. In the gloom he would stare at her body stretched out on the punee, pale and mysterious. Pretty as moonlight. He never really got used to the sight of her. Never knew how, really, to show what he felt about her. At times she seemed like a run–away orphan given to him to take care of. But she was a lot more than just an orphan. She was a woman, too. When they made love, her briny scent, like lipoa seaweed, maddened him. Sometimes he tasted his fingers after touching her. But he never dared say what he'd really like to do.

Chapter Twenty-five

PARKER DRESSED IN A NICE ALOHA SHIRT AND WORE SANDALS INstead of thongs to go to the courthouse. His feelings about the place hadn't changed any. All those important doorways and signs lettered in gold looked just as bad as he feared.

"What good is some old papers?" he grumbled.

"There must be a reason why the judge agreed to put you in the Home. I'm sure you'll feel better if you find out why."

But the trip didn't do any good after all. When he and Anne found the department that kept the records, a Chinese woman with a jade bracelet gave them the bad news. All the court files before 1930 had been destroyed several years earlier.

Anne was very disappointed as they walked away. "This is important," she insisted.

"Naw, I hardly ever think about it."

"It's not true. Do you know how many times you've told me about the little tin cup with the poi up to the handle?"

"No." He was startled at the question.

"Nearly every night. Nearly every time you start to eat poi."

"I nevah thought of that. I guess I do," he said soberly.

"There must be more information about your past, somewhere," Anne pointed out. "On an island this small, where everybody knows each other, there's bound to be someone who can help."

Parker looked doubtful. He wasn't sure he even wanted to meet someone from the past, at that.

"One of these days—maybe soon," Anne predicted rashly, "we'll learn something worthwhile."

❊ ❊

Mrs. Randal phoned him at Anne's again. Said she needed him to set some mouse traps for her.

Anne exploded. "She has no right! Who does she think she

186

is? You aren't even living there and she acts like you're her personal handyman!"

"Well, she's got no one else to help her," Parker apologized.

"I don't think...I think there's more to it than just fixing things. That's what I think."

"You' not *jealous*, are you?" Parker confronted the idea squarely. "You' not jealous of *her*?"

"Of course not!" Anne retorted. "How could I be? Drunken, tottery old scarecrow! It's just that I can't *stand* her!"

"You got nuthin' to be jealous about."

Anne twisted a lock of her hair furiously. "Snobby old kamaaina, without much to be snobby about, either."

He had already kissed her several times when he walked in the door. He probably shouldn't kiss her again. "You know you got me. I'm not gonna change."

Anne's green eyes fixed him for a moment. "I know," she said, her voice gone soft.

"I'll tell her not to call me anymore," Parker promised. "I'll tell her to get someone else, nex' time, if she needs sum'thin' done."

This time when he arrived Mrs. Randal did not smile. In fact she acted like someone had stepped on her sore toe. "Oh, there you are." Swinging her chin in the opposite direction from the screen door as he came in, as if the sight of him hurt her eyes. Not getting up from her chair.

"Where's the traps?" he asked at once. Wanting to get the work over with so he could tell her not to phone Anne's anymore.

Mrs. Randal could point out only one trap, with a mouse already in it, in the dining room. When he'd taken out the dried little body and set the spring with a scrap of raw bacon, since there was no cheese, they could find no more traps.

"I told Aoki's to send me half a dozen," Mrs. Randal insisted. "I'll give them a piece of my mind."

They stood in the kitchen. It looked like a shipwreck again, but not quite as bad as on Thanksgiving. There wasn't a square inch of free space on the big table in the center of the room.

"Mrs. Randal," Parker began earnestly, "I hav'ta tell you I don' want you to phone Anne's house anymore. Please? Huh?"

"Why? Is she complaining?"

"It makes Anne mad when you call me."

"I was perfectly courteous to her."

"When she gets mad at you she gets mad at me, too."

"She's heartless and inconsiderate, that's why." Mrs. Randal sniffed. "No understanding of how things are in the Islands."

"Please don' talk about Anne."

"Poor Keoni! Well, all right. When will you be back?"

He stared at her. He had no plans at all to come back.

"I want to know," she bore down, "when you'll be back."

He shifted around uncomfortably. "That's hard to say. We're real busy at the beach these days...." Some kind of assurance that she hadn't been abandoned seemed required. "I'll stop by, see how you doin' real soon, how's that? Okay?" The words seemed vague enough not to go back on what he owed Anne.

He moved toward the door. The lake of stuff around Mrs. Randal's stretched out chair was piling higher. And lots of loose food, too. Apple cores, orange peels, spilled corn flakes. Mrs. Randal would soon have the mice right in her lap if she didn't start tidying up. To reach the chair she had made a trail through the debris.

He had to get to the door before Mrs. Randal so she couldn't lean on it and keep him there.

"Be seein' you," he said cheerfully as he pulled the screen open.

"I don't see why you have to rush off. You just got here. Did I ever tell you about the Hawaiian woman who took care of me when I was a baby? She used to feed me poi out of her own mouth."

"Bye!" Backing his way down the top steps.

"And bananas, too. She used to chew up my bananas for me."

Mrs. Randal's face was so disappointed as he hurried away it took him about a block to get his balance back. He felt as if he'd had a close escape. Mrs. Randal was getting scarier and scarier. This "soon" was going to take awhile.

❂　　❂

The jeep key was not where it should be, in the ignition. He'd reminded Anne about this a number of times. She'd forgotten and taken the key into the cottage.

Hurrying, Parker cut across the lawn instead of coming up the sidewalk. As he bounded up to the open door he found her on the punee, pushing her book to one side. The expression on her face was guilty.

"You was readin'!"

Anne said nothing. Her mouth twitched.

At six–thirty he was supposed to lift weights with Kunia. Suddenly, that didn't matter. "You told me you was tired," he accused her. "You was gonna take a nap."

"I was," she retorted. "But then I changed my mind."

"You lied," he charged her. "You was plannin' all along to read you' book."

"Okay. I was. So what?"

"Why did you lie to me?" Not understanding, himself, why he was so mad at this.

Anne said nothing. She picked up the book, fiddled with the pages as if she were just waiting for him to leave.

"You lie 'bout one thing, you start lyin' 'bout all kindsa things." He felt a chill as he said it. Not wanting to believe this. Hoping she'd prove him wrong.

"I feel like I have to lie," Anne said stubbornly. "You make me feel like I'm doing something wrong if I read when you're around." Her lips stuck out; she wasn't giving an inch on this. "I know you hate it."

"I don' hate it," he denied. Realizing he was lying as he said it.

"You make me feel like you hate it. You make me feel like I'm doing something bad. So the only way I can do it is to sneak."

"You don' have to sneak. Jus' say you' gonna read. Jus' read."

"You say that now. But when I'm trying to read I can just feel what you're thinking. You walk around, you talk to me. You ask questions. You *try* to keep me from reading."

"I don't try nuthin'!" he stormed. "If I talk it's cause I wanna say somethin'."

"You interrupt, that's what you do."

"If I'm mixin' poi an' you ask questions I don' mind."

"It's not the same thing."

"It is the same thing."

"It's not!" she said. There was a new tone to her voice, as if she were close to tears. "When I'm reading I'm thinking about something else. It's not like mixing poi."

"Thass' the trouble. You read that book, you' always thinkin' 'bout other stuff, not what's goin' on now."

"There it is!" she cried. "You can't stand to have me think about other things."

"Why not jus' think about now? All that old stuff in the book, thass' *gone*. Thass' not important. Now is what's important."

"Oh, you're hopeless!" Her head dropped, her voice cracked.

Parker stood glaring at her. Then he gave in. He went to the punee, took her in his arms like a hurt child. "Don' do that," he said, his voice still rough but now kinder. "I jus' can' stand you lie to me. Ei nei. Please. Don' lie to me. It makes me feel like I'm crazy, I catch you lyin' to me. Ei nei."

Anne turned her head away so he couldn't kiss her.

"If you wanna read, jus' tell me, okay? I'll try not to bother you."

"You're just saying that, now," Anne insisted. But she let him pull her chin around and kiss her.

"You read you' book. I'll be back in about a hour, okay?"

"Okay," she said. Not really agreeing. Just ending it.

❂   ❂

Parker worried about his family. Polly was threatening divorce. That was fine by him. She also said she would take the car, house and everything in it. The idea of losing everything they'd collected over eighteen years didn't matter, but his status with the kids did. Polly was bad–mouthing him to the kids. He felt as though he was losing his influence with them. The last time he'd been home they hardly had anything to say and he'd found the place a shambles. No one was doing any chores. The love of cleanliness and order he'd learned at the Salvation Army Boys' Home and tried to teach them seemed completely lost. The beds were unmade, the dishes were piled high and the washing machine had been running for two days. Five wahines who ought to know better—he wouldn't count the eight year old—and not one of them could push the button to stop it. Lani had been lying in bed for days, not speaking, and her mother was threatening to send her to Kaneohe.

At work he had other problems. Sunshine was agitating for a change in the schedule that would give him Sunday off, although all the guards were supposed to work weekends. Said he wanted to go to Mass, keep the Sabbath. As if Sunshine cared about things like that!

It seemed like Sunshine was going down to the office almost every week, now. At the last Friday meeting with the boys, Sunshine had told about the new sand they were going to put in at Kuhio Beach. Parker hadn't known about it. Thousands of tons were to be brought in from Molokai to replace what had washed out, because the hotels were complaining. And Sunshine had known about it first.

Parker still hadn't written up those terrible requisitions. But then everything in the government took a long time. It would probably be months before the sand was brought in. They'd been arguing about the puka in the Pali at the Public Works Department for years. That's the way things went at the city and county. Kanekini surely didn't expect him to hand the requisitions in right away. The lifeguard shacks probably wouldn't be built for some time yet. He'd get the forms done next week.

The trouble was that there were so many appealing things to do on his day off, with Anne. Some of her suggestions astonished him. She wanted, for instance, to go to Hanauma and make love in broad daylight. "It would be so beautiful," she said, "with the sun on us, and the colors, and the water." He couldn't help grinning as she slid her hand down inside his trunks to hold him, so cozy, wheedling, kissing the corners of his mouth.

He'd been tempted rotten, of course. Lots of the boys took care of wahines on their surfboards out past the main breaks at Waikiki. But in Hanauma there was the view from above, as people came down into the crater. He wasn't against the idea. It seemed like a natural thing to him, to make love in a beautiful place that you loved.

But in the end he'd put his foot down, on account of Kanekini. He didn't want to do anything that might reflect badly on Kanekini. Anne's daring was really scandalous. They not only made love in Kapiolani Park, during a walk one night, Anne had suggested they make love on Thanksgiving, after they finished fixing the turkey at Mrs. Randal's. Wanted to do it in her bed, while they waited. "It would serve her right if she walked in and caught us," Anne had chuckled. "The old kamaaina douche bag."

Anne had another surprise for him. He'd thought himself so clever, scooping her after the funeral.

"Actually, I was taken with you, long before that."

They were sitting in the jeep in front of her court, at dusk, the way they had that first evening. He was remembering how he'd felt, driving a haole wahine like her for the first time ever. Remembering how she turned her nose this way and that. Then it turned out she'd had her own ideas all along.

"I thought: him! He's the one."

"When? When was that?"

"I can tell you the exact moment. It was when you were working on the wahine who drowned."

Parker almost swung his feet out of the jeep to leave. He was thinking these nice things and then she had to come up with that.

"It was your hands." Anne took his hand, keeping him for what she had to say. "I noticed your hands as you worked on the girl. They looked so powerful. Dark and strong. But kind. At one moment, between strokes, you pulled the girl's shirt smooth, the way a mother would a child. So the wrinkles wouldn't chafe."

My hands kin bus' things up good, too, he thought, looking on the positive side.

"Here, put your hand in the second best place." Anne pulled up her tee shirt, brought his hand to her breast, with hardly a glance around. Passersby in the twilight were rare. Although he'd rather be in the cottage, he obligingly slipped his fingers inside the webby brassiere he knew so well to hold her nipple properly.

"You had scratches on your body. There was a long bleeding

192

streak on your jaw and throat. Your eyes were closed, as if all your attention were within."

"It was. I was prayin'. Hard." He'd really prefer to be in the cottage where he could take care of things better while she talked.

Anne's Portuguese neighbor came down the sidewalk, turned into the court. Recognizing the jeep, he gave an absent-minded salute to the two in their embrace. "Hi, folks!"

"Oh, hi!" Anne continued. "You seemed almost to be in a trance, pouring yourself through your hands into her body."

Parker tried to keep his mind on what she was saying. "That's what you do when you give artificial respiration."

"No, it was...more than the procedure. It was like you...were trying to follow the girl to wherever she was, to bring her back."

He didn't see her point. You did the best you could.

"Your face was so lost.... I thought I'd never seen a human being give so much to another."

He was pleased by that. Yes, he did give everything he had.

"To me it was something Hawaiian. The completeness of it. I saw you as a Hawaiian of the old days. As if you were wearing a malo, kneeling in some ancient rite. I'd been looking for what the Hawaiians have, in my books. And here was the real thing."

She'd lost him there. It was Red Cross training.

"What you were giving that girl, I wanted. To pour your strength into me."

"Why don' we go inside?"

"That night, as I lay in bed, I realized...that I wanted to feel your hands on me."

"Look, we can do better inside," he urged her.

"I wanted you right then! Wanted you to use the mysteries of your race on me the way you did to that girl."

"Le's go inside, okay?" Giving her a tweak before he took back his hand. His legs were over the side of the jeep. "I wanna see about those mysteries."

"From then on, at the Lagoon, secretly I watched you!"

Chapter Twenty-six

PARKER REVELED IN HIS NIGHTS WITH ANNE, EVEN THOUGH THEY were not always peaceful. Anne's studio cottage was furnished with two narrow punees, or daybeds, one against the waikiki wall, the other against the makai wall. Every night they slept in the one along the waikiki wall. The bed, a thirty-inch iron frame with a sagging web of steel bands held a soft mattress with a lengthwise gully and a bend in the center. When Parker lowered his hundred seventy-five pound bulk into it, the bed had no more support than a hammock. With almost no space left around the edges, Anne was obliged to sleep in a pile on top of him. He learned to remain on his back the whole night, filling up the pit, while she restlessly swam over his body. He stayed as quiet as he could, but Anne said she got bruises on her thighs and stomach from his knees and hip bones. During the long hours they perspired. Their skin stuck together and stung. On his back, Parker tended to snore. Sometimes he got loud.

"Hush!" Anne would hiss, pinching his nose shut. "The neighbors will hear you. There's nothing but screen between us and the Hall's." As if there was anyone left in the court who didn't know he slept there every night.

"Yes, yes," he would murmur, hugging her gratefully.

Occasionally, exasperated, Anne suggested putting the mattress on the floor where, flat, it gave them room to spread out and be cool. But she had a horror of centipedes and besides she'd got used to having the lumps of his body, which she said felt like a collection of car tires, under her. She found the floor dismayingly hard and level. "I feel like I'm lost out in a meadow somewhere," she complained, unable to sleep.

They tried putting the punees side by side. But it was a lot of trouble to fix at night and unfix in the morning and besides they never got used to sleeping on the second bed. The crack was uncomfortable and as the second bed eased away, it got wider. The other side of the crack was too far away so they always wound up in a heap on the same old waikiki bed anyhow, with just a lot of nuisance to push things back into place and straighten out the bed clothes. Anne claimed the lack of sleep gave her dark circles under the eyes and frequently resolved to be more reasonable.

"Whassa matta?" Parker growled one night when she dug her elbow into his chest as she got up. She'd been thrashing about for an hour. He didn't mind her jabbing and gouging since she seemed to need to do it, but he worried about her not being able to sleep.

"I can't stand the stickiness."

"Can' help it. Whatcha gonna do?"

"Put the sheet between us."

She spread the top sheet so he and the bed were covered entirely. Then she climbed back on him in her usual position, lying over his left side, her legs stretched along his, toes hooked around his ankle and instep.

The sheet covered Parker's face. When she had wiggled her weight into its accustomed corners, he shook his face free, chuckling at her whimsy.

"This is much better," she assured him. "Much cooler."

But an hour later she decided she didn't enjoy being separated from him and pulled the sheet away to lie down on his bare body.

He thought she was ready to give up and accept their skin burning and sticking for the rest of the night, but no. In a little while, crosser than ever, she told him to go home. "I've got to get some sleep," she whimpered. "You'll just have to leave. I can't sleep while you're here."

"If you say so. Can' go agains' what you say."

He kissed her, pulled on his trunks, jeans and shirt in the dark. Stepping into his thongs on the doorstep, he headed back to his room on Koa. He didn't much like his cold, lonely bed, but just as he was falling asleep he heard a noise at his door. It was Anne, whispering and scratching. "I can't stand it," she accused, bumping into things as she felt her way toward the bed. She pulled off her muumuu, threw herself down beside him.

"What a horrible night!"

But the wide, flat bed presented the same problems they'd had with the mattress on the floor. Anne couldn't sleep on top of him where she belonged, because he was so lumpy she'd fall off the edge and she couldn't sleep any other way. She complained about the voices and banging around of the beachboys coming and going with their wahines, and the smell and feel of the bed. At last, unable to deal with the oddness of the situation any longer, at Anne's insistence, they got up, dressed, and left.

Liliuokalani was deserted as, bumping into one another with weariness, they shuffled past the dark and silent cottages. In the friendly, perfumed gloom of Anne's cottage they returned to the waikiki bed, to sleep at last.

From this experience Anne learned how dependent she was on Parker. Parker learned nothing at all. What suited Anne was what he wanted. His greatest joy came from feeling that she was having things her way.

One day at Hiro's she told him not to eat the fat in his laulau. Much as he loved the fat, he set it aside when he opened the steaming leaves thereafter, even if Anne weren't with him, his pride in pleasing her stronger than his lust for the familiar juicy sweetness.

❁   ❁

Their hours of intimacy, deep, permeable chunks of time, often stretched into whole days. Although he wanted to show Anne the island, teach her the Hawaiian things that would help her get over her haoleness, on his free day they usually went nowhere. They began making love as they awoke and the self–indulgent fulfillment went on and on, morning slipping into afternoon in spirals of passion, tenderness, rest and talk.

The blinds were kept closed. In the dimness the cottage became steamy from their frequent showers. For a cooling change they spread the white sheet on the lauhala mat. There they stretched indolently, drifting in and out of naps that were dreamy extensions of their caresses. With all the time in the world, they bent to refining each sensation to its sweetest peak. Sometimes they lay in their deepest embrace, not moving, for long, long minutes. The elegant waiting seemed to squeeze pleasure from the farthest corners of the universe.

"You know what I like about the way you make love to me?"

They were resting, facing each other. Anne leaned on her elbow, her feet laced with his.

"It's your authority."

He thought of authority as what he needed with his boys.

"I like your authority when you separate my legs. Not rough at all, just easily. As though it were your natural right."

Hawaiians didn't talk like this. Some of the things haoles said were really interesting.

"And then, there's another thing. I've noticed that just at the last moment, just before you take me, you wait a moment. I'm not talking about the teasing—I know we sometimes do that to each other. Like you make me wait when I think I can't bear it another second. Or you kind of play with me, to make me beg for more. I don't mean those things."

"M'yeah."

"I mean, before you enter me at all. When you're on your knees over me and you know I'm just aching for you, but still— there's a moment when you wait. As if to ask for that last confirming 'yes.'"

He hadn't supposed she'd noticed, but that was, in fact, a really special moment for him. Even though the agreement was there, still, it was like he caught his breath at the thought of what he was going to do—take Anne. A crazy sense of gratitude, as if it were the greatest thing that could happen. He'd never got over the feeling. Couldn't forget that out of all the world, it was Anne. Anne the beloved, Anne the miracle. Couldn't get past that. The extraordinary privilege that Anne bestowed on him with her body.

But wasn't it normal, after all, to pause before doing anything that meant a lot? You looked at the surf before you plunged into it. You kissed the waves with your eyes before the sea touched your lips.

"It's like..." she went on, "a gift you're putting into my hands. Since you're so much stronger than I am you *could* have it your way. So you're making it my choice."

Well, that was true. Since he wanted sex so often, and so much, he felt it should be up to her to make the final decision.

"And I love it when you talk to me in Hawaiian...growling those words. It takes me back to the old Hawaii...the power of those days...."

There was still quite a bit of power left these days, she might have noticed.

"I feel as though what we're doing is *huge*. Monstrous even. Big as Hanauma Bay. It's as though all the great men of those days—even Kamehameha—are inside your ule, all charging on me, filling me, making me part of everything—the clouds, the hills, the mana that makes Diamond Head rear up out of the Pacific. All of it, it's all mine, huge, inside me."

She lost him for a minute there, talking about other men, and especially Kamehameha. He wasn't sure that was quite respectful. On the other hand, it was hard to disagree with anything that big. Anne always made him feel like a king.

❂   ❂

One day, after hours of fulfillment, Parker sat on the edge of the wrecked bed. He was thinking of getting dressed and heading for the beach for a swim—it was almost five in the afternoon. Anne came and knelt in front of him. Taking his laho in her hands, she cupped them prayerfully. "They're so cuddly and nice."

"Not much left," he apologized. Every cell in his body felt drained, but saturated, too. "Tomorrow I'll be o.k. again."

"I love your ule," she said, looking at it tenderly. "Even when it's soft it's beautiful."

"Oh? You think so?" Tickled by such conversation.

"It looks like a poi pounder."

He chuckled at that.

"It's shaped like a bell. Short, massive. The head is molded smooth like a primeval boulder, worn by the sea. And I like its color."

Color? He'd always thought it was normal, not a color.

"It's a primitive color. Earth tones."

The beachboys, kidding with the tourists, spoke of themselves as primitives. He wasn't sure what a primitive color would be. Maybe dark. Well, he was dark; that was true.

"Your ule," Anne closed her eyes as if to see it better by not looking at it, "makes me think of warriors' shields of koa. Dried blood. Nightmarish dark eels...."

He thought she might break into a chant, going on like that. He had his own ideas. Kneeling on the mat beside her, he pushed her down on her back, opened her legs for his own look. She tried to squeeze her knees together. Forgetting about the neighbors, she shrieked. But in the end she let him.

"It's like a jellyfish," he said. His fingers, in an expanding, contracting movement showed her how it looked.

"First you call it my opihi. Now it's a jellyfish!" She pretended exasperation.

"Well, actually, it's more like an abalone," he conceded. But he never dared tell her what he'd really like to do.

❂   ❂

"The states is nice, but I'll never forget how glad I was to come back when I went up there."

Anne had a letter from her mother. Every time this happened she was grumpy for hours. She tore up the letter, and the envelope too, dropped them in the lauhala wastebasket, flopped back down on the sheet beside him.

"We just don't fit, she and I," Anne mourned. "It's always been like that. What she likes, what she wants for me—oh, you wouldn't understand, angel. I couldn't explain it. Things are just different on the mainland. People are so concerned with how things *look*, with who knows whom."

Parker listened, wondering what that meant. In Hawaii everybody just knew everybody, it seemed to him.

"Sometimes I miss, oh—things like the theater, or talking about a new book. But I'm so glad I'm here now, sweetheart."

"M'yeah. I couldn' stan' it myself. After one month up there, Los Angeles, I had to come back. *Had* to! Even though I din' have money. So I stowed away. On the old *Matsonia*."

"No! How?"

"I jus' walked on board and hid in the men's room 'till the ship was past the breakwater." He'd enjoy telling her this story. He lit a cigarette to go with it. The cottage smelled of plumerias and day–old poi. Hawaiian music played softly on Anne's radio. With pillows and sticky dishes of pineapple strewn about the floor the littered room seemed to be the piko of all the earth's good things.

"The weather was rough and mos' of the people was in the cabins. I knew some Hawaiian boys who had a cabin but I din' wanna get them in trouble. So I found the deck steward and ask' him to take me to the cap'n. The cap'n shook hands with me, real strong and said, 'Well, what can I do for you?' I said, 'Cap'n, I'm a stowaway.' 'A what?' 'That's right.' 'Tsk tsk! You Hawaiian boys! No money?' 'No, sir.' 'An you gotta go home.' 'Yes, sir.'" Parker acted it out for her, changing his voice for the captain's part. "So he call' the steward and tol' him to take me down to the crew's quarters. He gave me a mattress, to sleep on the floor, an' a blanket. I was nice an' warm. Ate with the crew. Every day I sat up on the crew deck and watch' the haoles walkin' aroun' playin' shuffleboard, like that. We'd smile, wave to each other.

"When they foun' out I was a stowaway they had the steward take cigarettes and candy to me. In the evenin's I watched the movies. But I was jus' waitin' to get home."

Anne looked at him steadily.

"When the ship came aroun' Diamond Head, I went out on deck. I was never so happy in my life. I jus' looked and looked. I was wearin' my trunks under my clothes, like always. I thought of divin' overboard...."

Parker couldn't keep from grinning as he remembered how it was. The excitement. The happiness. "I coulda gave my clothes to the other Hawaiian boys, an' dived overboard. Swum alongside the ship, pickin' up nickels with the rest of the coin divers. They nevah woulda caught me."

"Why didn't you do it?"

"I didn' need to. I wasn' afraid. I was comin' back to Hawaii."

Anne said nothing.

"So I jus' stayed on the deck. We pulled into the wharf, I saw cops. When they walk' up the gangplank, I knew they was comin' for me. I was standin' right beside the cap'n, talkin' to him, leanin' over the rail, watchin' everythin'. The cap'n said to the cop, 'That's funny. He was here jus' a minute ago. I wonder where he coulda went.' An' I was standin' right there! I said, 'Cap'n, here I am.' So the cops took me away."

"One of them was Joe Ikeole. He look' at me and said, 'You?' An' I said, 'M'yeah.' He took me to the police station on Bethel and Merchant. The cap'n there look' at me an' saw how I was smilin', so happy to be back. He jus' shook his head. 'Why do you Hawaiian boys do this?' he ask. 'Don' you know they don' have poi in Los Angeles? Why don' you stay where you belong?' I thought they might put me in jail, since I already had a record. I'd been in reform school. But they didn'. The chief jus' talk to me. Thass' all. Then they let me go."

❂   ❂

Later Anne said "I never knew anyone who was in reform school, before. I thought they were terrible people. I mean, it's hard to imagine—you. Doing something terrible."

"Depen's how you look at things."

"Well, why were you sent up?"

"For stealin' a car. One day I ran away from the Home with two other boys an' we stole a car. They was older 'n me—about seventeen—an' one of 'em knew how to drive. We went ridin' aroun' the island. Got caught, of course. Then they sent me to the Kahuku Reform School."

"How long were you there?"

"About a year and a half. How long you stay depends on how good you are at workin'."

"You mean, if you work hard, they let you out sooner?"

"No. Not at all. The opposite. The better you work, the longer they keep you. They don' wanna lose good workers. Me, they wanted to keep me forever. They put me in the taro patch. That's turrible hard work. I mean, brutal. It was *cold* in the mornin', in that mud. An' it was so deep you sank down up to your thighs.

More. Up to your hips. You have to lean to walk. I was leanin' almos' to touch the mud with my face. If the taro was ready, we pull it out. If it wasn', we pull out the weeds.

"The way I got out was, one time we played a baseball game with McKinley High School. Afterwards we got in a fight. They wanted to beat us up because we won. Thass' normal. But the sup'rintendent, he put the whole team in solitary on bread and water for ten days. When I came out I was weak, but they put me back in the taro patch anyway. The gang boss yelled at me because I wasn' goin' fas' enough. I got so mad I chased him with a pick. Two weeks later they let me out."

"A *pick*?" Anne's voice hit a high note, but she was laughing.

✪   ✪

Anne seemed fascinated by his past. As long as he didn't talk about Polly she would listen endlessly to his stories. So he learned to avoid incidents that involved Polly although he didn't see how Anne could be jealous. It was so obvious that he was bursting with love for her.

He stroked her breast, the pale curve that had become so dear to him. She was fleshier now. And her straight, dark hair was longer. It brushed the tops of her nipples.

"It seems like all these years my heart been wasted. I din' know it, but now I know it. I was thinkin'—every time I hear about Kamehameha I think how lucky the Hawaiians was in those days. They had Kamehameha to love and fight for. I never had somethin' like that. You know—someone you could really fix your heart on. Then I found you. Now my heart has you to think about."

"You think with your heart!" Anne giggled.

"What's wrong with that?"

"A lot of people died for Kamehameha," Anne pointed out.

"They was lucky," Parker said shortly.

"Lucky? How can you say that? They made human sacrifices before going off to war."

"They believed it would help the people. Kamehameha believed it."

"Would you let yourself be sacrificed? Would you offer to give your life for Kamehameha?"

"You bet!" he crowed.

"You *would?*" Anne asked, on a sudden intake of breath.

"If he wanted." Parker's tone was triumphant. "I'd be *proud!*"

Anne raised on her elbow and looked at him. "But it would *hurt!*" she insisted. "The way they did things in those old days— you know—with knives made of bamboo, spears of stone...." She shuddered.

"Sometimes things hurt," he acknowledged. "But it's only for a little while. Either you're a man or you're not. And you'd be doing it for your chief."

❂   ❂

One incident in his youth he never told Anne. This was because it was too close to his heart. He hadn't the words to explain why he had not gone to work for the princess.

He had met her at a Hui Nalu swim meet. They were big events in the old days, even royalty attended. Although he was not a speed swimmer, never carried off the prizes, he competed, for the fun of it, for Hui Makani. He was a chunky sixteen then, a butterball of a rascal with high spirits and a white smile.

The princess noticed him as he clowned with the boys, making a lark of the races so each one did his best. She asked who he was. Learning that he lived at the Salvation Army Boys' Home, she sent for him.

He was led to where she was sitting, everyone around her acting very respectful, listening to each word she said. He found her beautiful, pale–skinned in her long dress, her hair swept up. She'd asked him a few kind questions, wished him luck, that was all. But later she'd sent word to the Home that she'd like him to come and live on her estate in Nuuanu. He could work with the gardeners, help with the luaus, that sort of thing.

Parker had been overwhelmed by the offer. Had trembled at the honor of it. But he was afraid he couldn't meet her trust.

Couldn't stay away from the sea, the nickel diving, the gang fights and the harbor. Couldn't bear to live in the valley.

To run away from the Home regularly and be beaten for it was all right. He didn't mind that. But he could not run away from the royalty to whom he, as a Hawaiian, owed his life. To fail in what he owed the princess and her family seemed to him like a mortal sin. Heart aching, he had said he could not. But he never drove up Nuuanu without turning his eyes toward her estate, and thinking how, if he'd been a little steadier, he could once have served his princess.

❂   ❂

"You seem so complete in your brownness," Anne said admiringly.

"To be naked is nuthin' to Hawaiians," Parker said. "Especially they like to swim naked. The sea is their bathin' suit!" He chuckled. "In the old days the Hawaiians took off their clothes as a sign of respect."

"No!"

"Thass' what I heard. If an alii come by, the people took off their clothes and threw their selves on the ground. Because they thought the alii represented—you know—Pele, them."

Anne had been chewing his thumb. She did this at odd moments. Sometimes, while sitting at the table after a meal, she would take his hand and contentedly suck and chew his thumb. Parker did not find it strange, only new, that Anne did this. As they rested, dreamy, in the sultry room Anne often put her mouth to the hard flesh of his bicep or chest and gnawed on it, like an infant massaging itchy gums. Sometimes she produced such teeth marks and swollen purple bruises that he was obliged to wear a tee shirt at work for days at a time. He bore her maulings with a quiet joy, relishing her right to his body. Whatever she did was just Anne. All he wanted was more of her, whatever that was.

"You never seem undressed," she went on. "It's as though your color clothes you. My white seems almost indecent next to you."

He knew what she meant. There was something almost

shocking about white people's bodies. But he didn't want her to feel bad.

"I think your color is nice, too," he assured her as she lay down beside him. "You aren't just plain white." His finger traced a vein that he found at the edge of her jaw. It slid out of sight in her throat, reappearing below her collarbone. There it branched, or joined other blue threads, to become a lacy network in her breasts.

"You know," Anne confessed, "I look at this wonderful color you have all over, and I keep thinking it's something you acquired—you know—like a suntan, over your real skin. So I keep watching to see if there's one little place that got missed. Like Achilles, when his mother dipped him. She held him by the heels. That was the one place she missed. I'm always on the lookout for a spot that's the color of the *real* you." Anne made a small stir out of peering behind his ear, under his arm. "Anyhow, I think you're a beautiful color."

"The Hawaiians that stays indoors is lighter than me," he offered humbly.

"I love you just the way you are," Anne said. "I always pick the brownest cookies, the darkest lamb chops. Mmmmm! Bittersweet chocolate!"

Anne lay down again. Her eyes on his face, she settled her head into his groin, her pale cheek pressed against his laho and soft ule. "And you've got a smile that's worth a thousand words."

"I do?" He had to grin at that. The raffish good nature shining through his pleasure at the compliment.

"M'yeah," she said, imitating him, as she often did now. "You know what you look like? A Norman Rockwell good–bad boy. You look like one of his kids." She lifted her head on her slim, vulnerable neck. "How can you look like an all–American kid and yet so Hawaiian, too?"

"Hawaiian, that's the main thing," he assured her. He didn't care about the rest. Although he had noticed something strange the other day. After looking at her all afternoon, he'd got so used to her face, her light skin, that when he went to the mirror to comb his hair he'd been shocked at the reflection there. For an instant a dark stranger had stared at him. Then he realized that he was not what he'd been looking at those long hours, the fair, precise features on which the earth turned now. That unfamiliar face was his. He was something nearly forgotten out of his own past.

❂   ❂

"What's this?" Anne touched a spot on his right calf.

Parker raised his head and glanced down, even though he knew the scar well, a mottled badge the size of a half dollar.

"That's where a fishhook caught me when I was little, about seven or eight. I was swingin' my fishin' pole and this time, for once, I had a real hook. 'Bout medium size. The hook caught my leg. Oh! I didn' know *what* to do! I tried to pull it out but I couldn't. Somebody said there was an army dispensary at Pier Five so I went there. The doctor cut it out for me, free!" He still marveled as he remembered it. "Today you have to pay for everything, but he did it for me free. These two army guys had to hold me down, because no anesthetic then, you know, and they took a knife and cut all around so they could lift it out, like an apple core."

"Oh, my God!" Anne covered first her ears, then her eyes.

"M'yeah. Today they don' do it that way. They push the hook all the way through and cut off the barb. Then they pull the hook back out. But those day, they cut all the flesh to get the barb out. Don' feel bad. It was free. Think of that!" He was smiling, still happy at the memory.

"It's getting dark," Anne sighed. She rose and went to the window, peered through the blind at the greying sky.

"M'yeah." A wave of self–reproach swept through Parker. He'd planned to spend the afternoon writing up the equipment requests that Kanekini had asked him for so long ago. Every day he promised himself he'd do it. And every day the thought of sitting down with those papers, the writing and thinking that went with them, was so repulsive to him he just didn't do it. Now the afternoon was gone.

The requests weren't the only problems that faced him in his work. He still hadn't figured out what to do about Morgan who was showing up hung over nearly every day. The schedules had all been changed. Sunshine had got Sunday off. He'd gone to Kanekini about it. That hurt. Sunshine had gone over his head and Kanekini, instead of sending him back to Parker, had given in to his story about wanting to go to Mass.

Parker felt sure Sunshine had some advantage in mind. Every time Parker had anything to do with Sunshine he felt short afterwards. Never before had Parker felt so uneasy about his job, so behind in what he wanted to do to please Kanekini.

Anne tilted the blind to let in more light, examined a patch of roughness on her upper arm. "This fungus isn't going away," she grumbled.

Parker went to her, examined the splotch with interest. "Oh, that's ringworm. I'll give you a nice plant for that. The juice cures ringworm."

"Oh, really," Anne complained. "You make everything too easy. It's probably not ringworm."

For a moment Parker was stumped. He saw she was teasing, but also guessed something deeper. "What is it then? What do you want it to be?"

"It's probably leprosy," she pronounced, taking a tone, lifting her nose. "It's the beginning of the end."

"Thass' all right," he said with a chuckle, going along with her. "If they take you to Molokai, I'll go with you." His heart rising at the thought of it. "I won' let it separate us."

Anne turned, gave him a long look. "You'd go to Molokai with me?"

"Of course!" He was happy, just saying the words. Then she'd believe him. Then she'd know how he felt.

Tears came to Anne's eyes. "I believe you would. Ei nei! I believe you would. M'yeah."

Chapter Twenty-seven

FRIDAY, AN HOUR BEFORE HE FINISHED WORK AT THE BEACH, THE delivery boy from Aoki's market found Parker under the banyan. The message was that Mrs. Randal wanted to see him.

"She's not sick, is she?"

The Japanese kid shuffled, glanced around at the bathers. "She's about like usual."

Just to be sure, before going to Anne's, Parker stopped in at Mrs. Randal's.

"Sump'n wrong?" he asked, as if that could be the only reason for the message.

"No." Mrs. Randal said mildly through her cloud of smoke, not bothering to rise from her chair. More stuff than ever was strewn around. Coke and Nehi bottles on top of bills and what looked like legal documents. Coupons, nut shells, the ouija board. New layers of dirty plates, cans and boxes slid around in toppling piles.

"Wassa matter, then? Why'd you send for me?"

"Because you didn't come on your own." She made it sound very logical the way she said it. Inhaling deeply, she studied him with dissatisfaction.

"I tol' you b'fore about this. It makes Anne mad," he reproved her.

Mrs. Randal's lifted eyebrows dismissed that. "I didn't call you at her house," she shrugged. "She's got nothing to be mad at."

"Look, if you need sumthin', I mean, if sumthin's broke, like that, I'll be glad to help if I can. But don' just call me for nuthin'. Anne'll get excited when she knows I came here."

"Why ever would you tell her?"

Parker stopped. The idea of not sharing the variations in his day with Anne seemed sneaky. He felt trampled by the question. "Because I *like* to."

"Well, if you want to ask for trouble...."

He was about to be cross now. "Look, Mrs. Randal. I'm not

208

comin' back anymore, jus' because you call. Is that clear? I don' want you to send for me again." He knew he sounded awfully mean. "Only if it's important," he added.

"Only *if* it's important!" The fury in Mrs. Randal's voice as she said it somehow got her out of her cave of pillows in the chair. She lurched to her feet on the trail through the litter. Paralyzed, Parker watched, unable to believe she'd make it. But she did. Weaving, she stood there, looking more than ever like a scarecrow in a black silk kimono with a dragon embroidered on it. Her head was pulled up high on her neck as if to see over the top of him.

"How dare you trifle with my feelings like that? *If* it's important!" She made that "if" sound like the biggest thing in Waikiki. The other part, he didn't know what she meant.

"Important—like when you couldn' turn on you' light because the pull was broke. I un'nerstand you had to have light."

"I'm not talking about pull chains. I'm talking about...aloha. Have you any idea...I thought you were Hawaiian.... Do you know what that means—aloha?"

He did not think Mrs. Randal had a lot to complain about as far as he was concerned. Worse yet, he was getting the idea that her version of aloha was more complicated than he wanted.

"Jus' say what you mean." Then he asked gently, "What *is* the matter?"

Mrs. Randal took a deep breath. "I've gotten used to you," she announced haughtily. "That's the problem. You *know* how I loathe people. Have an absolute horror of them. Their voices, their faces." Her tone became harder. "Their idiocies. Always wanting something. Intruding. Disturbing me. I can't stand them."

"I know." It was the correct response, but it didn't seem to help much.

She was gearing up for worse. "I kept them all away—until you came along. Then out of the kindness of my heart I did what I'd never done before. I let you have the cottage. Let you live here where I saw you coming and going every day. I thought that because you were Hawaiian...it would be different."

The way she was talking, it was as if she were on a stage, say-

209

ing things that lots of people, far away, were supposed to hear. She stood holding herself together, wobbly but straight, her chin lifted, arms folded close like a moth's wings. A black moth. No, tighter than that, like a black cocoon, holding all these feelings close to her breast while the words trickled out, against her will, through her lips.

"I'm sorry," he said, since it was his fault that they were trickling out.

"Sorry!" Her commanding, deep–set eyes swept him, scorned the offer. "I let you on my property. You were the first. The first! I had to see you every time you came and went. How you looked in the mornings, in your fresh tee shirt, with a towel on your shoulder as you headed for work. Your hair combed, with a straight part, and your legs rubbed with coconut oil. I saw that. And then in the evening, when you came back, your head wet and tousled from your swim. I had to see all that," she blamed him. "Sometimes I even made myself go to the door to speak to you."

"I know," he said softly.

"Just a few words...nothing at all. 'Is that a Kona wind coming up?' or 'I'm out of stamps.' Ordinary things, like that. I got used to it," she said bitterly.

Parker's forehead wrinkled. She couldn't say he'd ever refused to get her matches or stamps.

"But when you brought what I needed, you always had to leave right way—because of *her*." Anne's name never crossed Mrs. Randal's lips.

He felt bad about that. He knew he hadn't been able to give Mrs. Randal the company she needed.

"I had to put up with that, right here on my property where I've lived all these twenty–six years. Right here in my own house that Captain Randal built for me."

"It's a nice house," Parker side–tracked. "I guess he sure loved you. You kin be glad of that."

"Of course he loved me," Mrs. Randal snapped. "He adored me. Couldn't wait to get home, every time he was at sea."

Parker was inching into line with the door so that, as she was comforted by memories, he could slide out.

"You're not going yet," Mrs. Randal informed him. She tottered diagonally across the space so she was closer to the door than he was, and next to the handle, too.

"You've been having things your way long enough. It's time I counted for something here." She managed to bring her frown into a focus around his head and shoulders. "For once you're going to have to listen to me."

"Yes, ma'am."

"Don't you 'yes ma'am' me. I can't stand that kind of servile nonsense. You're a Hawaiian. Don't you have any kind of pride at all?"

"M'yeah. Well...."

"Don't interrupt me. What was I saying?"

"About Hawaiians?" he suggested helpfully.

"I know something about Hawaiians," she warned him. "I grew up with them. They're lazy. Not worth a nickel on a plantation. All they want to do is sit around all day. Won't move except to do something they want to do. Like surf, or raise taro. They're useless, except for what they like." After a moment's thought, she added, "They're good cowboys, though. But that's only because they like horses. And steers."

"I know. I'm from Kamuela. We had some good cowboys down there."

Mrs. Randal was not interested in Kamuela.

"I thought I could count on you for your aloha," she mourned, her nose in the air. "I was wrong."

He had no answer for that.

"No one has any aloha anymore. It's all shot to hell."

His deep sigh agreed with her. He felt sorry about that himself. She probably remembered the days when Hawaiians always ate with the door of the house open so they could call any passerby, even a stranger, to eat with them. Now Hawaiians ate behind closed doors. And as for the tourists, it was "Let's see your money first, then aloha." Mrs. Randal was right. She had a lot to feel bad about.

"And the reason there's no aloha now is because of the new people coming in all the time—like her."

Parker was jabbed by the partial truth in that. Even though

211

he felt he had more aloha, himself, since knowing Anne, than he ever had before. But he couldn't expect Mrs. Randal to understand that. The steady thump of a pile driver echoed through Waikiki eight hours a day now, setting the foundation for the new hotel.

Hiro had received an offer on the lease of The Blue Lagoon. A haole developer wanted to put in a three–story building with shops along the bottom floor. At the end of his block the cottage of the massage parlor was already gone. Concrete for some new business was being poured.

"You need any cigarettes, or matches?" Parker offered.

"Have to get back to *her*, is that it?"

"I said I'd fix dinner tonight." He did not say 'corn beef and cabbage.' It would be criminal to flaunt such happiness. "She might be gettin' hungry."

Mrs. Randal shuddered, as if an icy breeze had touched her shoulder blades.

"My shawl is on a chair in the bedroom," she directed him.

He stood, undecided. "Well," she pushed. "I don't want to take a chill."

The fancy bed with a great carved headboard was not made, and clothes were strewn around. But he had a feeling that she rarely used the room. The shawl was a cream–colored silk with a long fringe.

When he came back she was standing exactly as he'd left her. She turned for him, as if she were used to having a man lay a shawl over her shoulders. Mixed with gin and cigarettes, the scent of a woman's skin, powdery, forbidden, brushed his nostrils.

"You don't know what it's like," she said, speaking away from him, wrapping the shawl close, "to loathe people. And yet to have the days so long." Her words were heavy as stones. "So long. And everything so difficult. Even to reach for a cigarette is hard."

Her shawl was pulled tight, like a defense against what she had to bear.

"But when you were here," her voice became lighter, "things seemed easier. I watched you head for work in the morning and knew that at six–thirty that evening I'd see you coming back again. All day I had that to look forward to. At one o'clock I knew it was only five and a half hours more until you came. I watched the afternoon light change, watched the patterns of light creep across the floor, the shadows longer and softer. I'd be able to bear them because soon you'd be walking up the driveway in that funny, bowlegged walk of yours. From six o'clock on I'd feel so light, I could do anything. Almost fluttery. Just because of that minute when you'd walk up the driveway. Looking around as though you owned the place. I saw that. Yes, you did."

"I was thinkin' what work I'd do next to make the yard nice."

She dismissed that. "Sometimes you didn't come. The shadows went all the way across the floor and the light got so grey there were no more shadows. I wouldn't have the minute I'd waited for all day. Because you were off somewhere with *her*. There was always the problem of *her*. How many times that I waited when you came I had to see her, too?"

Mrs. Randal turned to him. Her face was twisted in a misery that dug at him in spite of himself. He took a step backwards. He was not going to let her throw herself into his arms now, as she had on Thanksgiving. They were in strange waters and she was capable of anything.

Instead, with a disdainful glance, she drifted on her shaky white ankles toward the screen. The black silk kimono, topped by the pale, fringed shawl was a close wrapped bundle of pain.

"The darkness would settle in, the birds in the trees. There was the long night ahead. But it wasn't unbearable. I had my gin, and I knew you weren't gone. Later, that night or next morning, one way or another, I'd see you again. You lived here and you'd be back. The shadows stretching across the floor.... Now...." She threw out a sticklike arm. "There's just the shadows. And at one o'clock there's no use to begin counting. It's too heavy to pick up a magazine. Even to open the mail is too hard, too heavy."

The thought of Wipeout came to him. He had an image of the bearlike figure with the shaggy head. His friend with the gentle, sad ways. He wished Mrs. Randal had met Wipeout. If they'd met perhaps they could have helped each other.

"But worst of all, I think...I got used to the cottage light. The comfort it gave me, that little yellow light over there, shining among the branches of the bougainvillea. The darkness all around, as I sat in my chair, and that one little light, across the way, soft as a candle."

She shouldn't be saying these private things.

"I could tuck down in my chair and feel—safe. Because of that light. Strange!" she marveled, listening to herself. "I'd always enjoyed the dark. It meant I didn't have to put up with people. Their voices. Their laughter. My life was just what I wanted. Perfect quiet. Perfect solitude. My gin. Then *you* came along. You spoiled my perfect life."

She began taking small tottery steps on her thin ankles, first in one direction, then another. Mad at him for making her say such things. Mad at herself for saying them.

"Don't you see the position you forced me into?"

"Well, I was jus' lookin' for a room, is all, when I came here," he reminded her. "Kanekini tol' me you had a room."

"Oh, you're innocent, all right. The Hawaiians are always innocent!" She cackled at that. "The innocent Hawaiians. Don't blame the Hawaiians." She threw back her head, hugging the shawl closer than ever. But there was no laughter in her vague eyes as she broke off and challenged him. "I never asked anything of you, did I? *Did I?*"

He wasn't sure what she referred to but the answer seemed to be no. In a low voice he assured her, "No."

"So you are responsible. *You.* It's your fault." She glared his way, looking mad enough to slap him.

Mrs. Randal was so used to being right, so used to having her way, that nothing he could say would be heard. He couldn't pat her arm. He didn't see what he could do to comfort her without taking too big a chance. It occurred to Parker that she liked him a lot less now that she was in love with him. She was a scary, dangerous woman.

"Look, I'll help you, Mrs. Randal. I'll fin' another Hawaiian for you. There's other fellows needs rooms too. I'll fin' someone good for you."

"I don't *want* someone else, you *idiot!*" The snap of her tone almost took a chip out of his skull.

She clung to one of the screen porch's uprights, her nails long and yellow. "You know what I'm saying." Her chin jerked this way and that. "It's you I want here. Even if *she* comes along. I'll even accept that." Mrs. Randal's head dropped, her last words almost inaudible. Her face against the post. "If you'll come back."

"I can'. I got a place. I tol' you."

"You won't have to pay any rent at all. Just live here."

"Please, Mrs. Randal...." His voice husky.

"I'll pay you, as if you were the gardener." She said it to the post.

Parker took a strong step toward the door. "I'm leavin', Mrs. Randal. I'm sorry. I hope you fin' somebody makes you happy. But I'm not comin' back." His hand reached for the door.

She lifted her head. "You can't leave like this." Eyes furious, frightened. Voice raspy.

The door now wide. "Don' send for me, b'cause I'm not comin' back."

"You're letting yourself be run by that haole wahine! She's running you! A real Hawaiian wouldn't do this!"

"Leave Anne out of this!"

"If it weren't for her, you'd be here!"

"G'bye, Mrs. Randal. I'm not comin' back."

Her screechy voice followed him as he hotfooted it down the gravel driveway. "We'll see about that."

❂   ❂

Forty–eight hours later Parker was under the Lagoon's umbrellas picking his teeth and talking with Ah Lee when a police car drew up to the curb. Nobriga unloaded his big frame and came toward them.

"Parker!" he said.

"Yas suh!" Parker took a step forward with a jaunty grin. Hoping one of his boys wasn't in trouble.

"You're under arrest."

The complaint, filed by Mrs. Randal, charged Parker with the theft of a kit of tools valued at about fourteen dollars, but of great sentimental value, as it belonged to her deceased husband, Captain Jeffrey Randal.

Nobriga went to Parker's room with him and they got the tools.

"This'll look turrible on my record," Parker told Nobriga. "I didn' take 'em. She *gave* 'em to me. *Made* me take 'em. I din' even want these little things."

"She filed the complaint." Nobriga's voice was sympathetic. "That's all we got to go on. You can tell the judge your side of it."

"Maybe if you come with me to see her—give the tools back and talk to her—maybe she'll change her mind."

Nobriga knocked on the door of the screen porch. Mrs. Randal was sitting in the dark but the light was on in the living room. She was wearing lipstick, as if she knew they'd be coming. Also, it seemed planned, the way she led them directly to the living room so Nobriga didn't have time to see what was around her stretched out chair.

"Here's you' tools, Mrs. Randal," Parker said, giving them to her.

"Thank you," she said graciously. She stood there, silent, with an air of satisfaction. In fact looking like a gecko that had swallowed a big bug.

"Mrs. Randal, please tell Nobriga here that I didn't steal you' tools."

Mrs. Randal wasn't listening. She was just eyeing him greedily, triumphantly.

"You gave them to me. Don' you remember? The night you call' me to fix the pull chain for you' lamp? You tol' me to take them. Don' you remember?"

Mrs. Randal studied him for a moment, turned to Nobriga. "I believe he wants me to withdraw the complaint."

"Well, you could, if you wanted to. You'd just have to sign some papers."

"I could if I wanted to?" She said it almost dreamily. "If I *wanted* to?" She looked at Parker.

He got it. She was putting it up to him.

The smile she gave him was sly, but there was something pathetic about it, too. Something sad in the foolishness of her wicked hope.

"Mrs. Randal,..." he began. He gave up, made a gesture to Nobriga. "Let's go. Maybe she'll think about it."

"*I* don't need to think about it." Mrs. Randal's tone had reverted to granite. "It's other people that need to think about it."

In the car again Parker asked Nobriga, "What could the judge give me for this?"

"Well, since you didn't break and enter...."

"Break an' enter? She's always phonin' me, an' I'm tellin' her to *stop*."

"It'll probably be a misdemeanor instead of a felony."

Parker hated those ugly words. They sounded like mainland horrors to him.

"The judge'll probably fine you about thirty dollars."

"The tools is only worth fourteen dollars."

"You can't win against a kamaaina like her, Parker."

"But she's lyin'!" The injustice of it eating him.

"Look at it this way. She could have charged you with rape."

Chapter Twenty-eight

AROUND THE BLUE LAGOON PARKER'S ARREST WAS GENERALLY scoffed at. The problem, it was agreed, had to do with haoles. Mrs. Randal was a haole even if she was a kamaaina, and the other part of it was Anne. The coconut vine had it that Parker lost his place at Mrs. Randal's because she wanted to sleep with him. So she kicked him out. That was Anne's fault. If it weren't for her he could have taken care of the widow and kept the room.

Parker lost no face over the incident. A charge of stealing was considered a bum rap and generally a haole idea. At one moment Ah Lee suggested that Parker could sue Mrs. Randal for defaming his character. But then, for the sake of his reputation as a Chinese, he realized he should keep his mouth shut.

Anne was unaware that she was implicated in the rumors because with her people showed no change. Actually, it wasn't she who was blamed since she herself was generally liked. It was the fact that she was a haole. Haoles, whether they were malihinis or kamaainas were, for locals, a mistake. Malihinis were boring and a waste of time, going back to wherever they came from. Kamaainas couldn't be trusted. They knew all the right things to do—ate poi with you and laughed at Island jokes. But you never knew when or how they would turn up as part of the web that caught locals and made their lives confusing and miserable. At bottom, the haole was the source of everything that had hurt Island people since time began.

In general Parker was seen as an unlucky man, not for being arrested but for having taken up with a haole wahine. A lot of folk suspected that what Parker wanted was a blue-eyed baby. While this was understandable it was unfortunate that he seemed so stuck on Anne. It could never turn out right.

❂   ❂

Anne went with him again to the courthouse. As he parked the jeep he glared around the area, at the library across the way where Anne spent all those peculiar hours with her books. Beyond was City Hall, where poor Kanekini was buried alive in his miserable papers. The whole place had always seemed unwholesome to Parker. Now that he was going to be judged a criminal, it seemed like a haole version of hell. Wearing his best aloha shirt, he tried not to look like a thief. Mrs. Randal had not withdrawn her charges about the tools.

In the dingy courtroom amid the dark rows of depressing benches where murderers and their victims had sat, Parker waited for his case, Anne holding his hand. Mrs. Randal was nowhere in sight. The judge, who turned out to be a lady, was in a sort of pulpit so you had to look up at her. She spoke in a low voice to each criminal standing before her and finished with a case every few minutes. Then a man in a uniform like a cop called the name for the next case. When he said, "John Parker Kealii" in his strong voice, the name seemed to echo all over the building, a sort of preview to the roll call in heaven.

Like the others, Parker's case did not take long. He was sworn in, his hand trembling at the awesomeness of the oath they asked him to take. The judge, wearing a black smock with a small white collar, read the nice report Nobriga had written about him saying that the defendant cooperated in every way. He understood that Mrs. Randal wanted him to keep the tools, since he occasionally returned to do odd jobs for her.

The lady judge's face had not revealed anything but her voice was not unkind as she asked him if he had used Mrs. Randal's tools while he lived there. Being as truthful as possible, he answered yes, thinking of the garden tools. The worst moment came when she asked the clerk if he had a previous record and was told he had been involved in a juvenile car theft and spent fourteen months in Kahuku Reform School.

In the end, she fined him fifteen dollars, not for the tools, which had been restored, but for court costs. As Parker understood it the judge believed him about the tools but thought that a kamaaina wouldn't make a case against him unless *something* was wrong. Even though she got the tools back just by asking for them, she must have *some* grievance against him, and since the case had taken the court's time he was the logical one to pay.

He handed over three five-dollar bills at a table to the side of the pulpit—he'd come provided. Then, with a glance at Anne, among the benches, he headed for the door. Anne jumped up to join him but he was moving fast.

He pulled the courtroom door open with a fierce sweep. At the same moment, a woman in the hall pressed it inward. Off balance, she dropped her hand, gave him a startled look. The look went beyond the shock of the little encounter, was prolonged into something else. It gave Parker a strange feeling. She was Hawaiian—she had that in her favor—and in fact there was even something slightly familiar about her. She had a light skin, hair wavy in front, a bit like his, a slender build. She paid no attention to Anne who piled through after him, just stood staring, as if she had something on her mind. But she was a stranger and he was in a hurry. He wasn't going to sort it out, so he gave her a hasty "Sorry!" and pressed on.

In the round room under the dome, when he turned for Anne, he saw that the woman had not yet entered the courtroom. She stood in the hall watching him with a strange expression, as if she had recognized him, as if his face meant something to her.

He knew this was not true because if she'd been on his beach he would remember her. Women often looked at lifeguards. He was used to that; especially, he was used to long looks from haole wahines. If he'd seen a Hawaiian wahine like her on his beach he would have said a few friendly words. Asked her where she lived, who she was related to. She was not from his beach. So why had she given him a look such as he'd never had before in his life?

"Did you see her?" Anne slipped a hand into his. "Did you see that Hawaiian lady looking at you?"

"M'yeah." He didn't want to talk about it. He'd parked the jeep across the street, in the palace grounds where it was cool, under the banyans. The air today was oppressively hot and damp. Already this morning there had been half a dozen brief, steamy showers. The sun was invisible behind the vapor clinging to the Koolau range.

"Do you know her? Who is she?"

"Nope. Never saw her before in my life."

"There's something familiar about her," Anne insisted.

That was what made him uncomfortable. He seemed to be missing an important fact. As they made their way past the statue of Kamehameha, Parker tried to place what was special about the wahine, besides the way she stopped and stared at him.

Short bobbed hair, going into grey, with a little wave in front. A tomboyish body dressed in an aloha shirt and jeans. Not gone to fat like many Hawaiian women her age. She looked like a lively type, the jokey kind who would do a naughty hula at a party. That was what he'd got out of the two brief glimpses of her, one up close at the door, the other down the hall.

"I thought she was going to speak to you, but you bolted so fast."

"You think I like to be in places like that?" he rebuked Anne. "You think I wanna stay in court, like a thief?"

"But I think this woman...."

"Forget the woman." Anne had slowed. He was pulling her across King Street.

This did not have the right effect at all on Anne. Instead of allowing herself to be pulled she stopped dead in her tracks.

"Stop pulling me! I'm trying to talk to you!"

King Street was one of the city's main connecting threads, stringing together a dozen little districts that lay between Kalihi and Kaimuki. Electric buses whined by every few minutes. Much of Honolulu's traffic passed through the heart of the civic center.

"C'mon! You jammin' up traffic." Several cars had to slow, go around. The drivers threw them puzzled, annoyed looks. It was beginning to rain. Drops big as half dollars hit the macadam in plops, creating steam around them.

Now Anne was pulling him. "Let's go back and get to the bottom of this. I know she wanted to speak to you. She even opened her mouth."

"I don' wanna speak to her. An' I don' wanna talk about it in the middle of the street. Look. Now the bus has to stop. C'mon...." He threw his arm around her shoulders, urging her on. Not clear, himself, why he didn't want to know more about the wahine. Probably, coming after the roll call from heaven, and the oath, meeting anyone was too much.

221

Anne ducked under his arm. "Why are you being so stubborn about this? It won't take five minutes...." Anne looked mad, now. Her hair was getting wet. The sun of the last few days had left scoops of pink under her eyes and across her forehead. Her nose, especially, was a bright burn. The rain pelted them. Steam from the street rose, hot on his ankles.

Turning on her heel, Anne started back across the street. Now it was the cars coming from ewa side that had to slow and drive around. One car even honked.

Maybe the woman was related to Polly, he thought. Or was a neighbor of hers. Maybe she was a spy, getting ready to do him in.

"It's not our business, that wahine!" he shouted, seizing Anne's arm, jerking her to a stop. "C'mon. We' leavin'."

"I'm not!" Anne shouted back. They were standing nose to nose as the traffic eased by. The stoplight at Punchbowl released another handful of cars headed for downtown and Kalihi. Having a fight in the middle of King Street confirmed all his worst fears about the place, about the dangers of being around buildings that dealt in paper. He and Anne had to get away at once.

Anne turned abruptly. "I'm going back," she defied him. "I'm going to speak to her."

Another idea, entirely new, took Parker: A Hawaiian wahine.... This steam, rising around his ankles.... A sense of recognition which was impossible since he'd never seen her before in his life.... A look that went beyond....

His knees almost buckled at the thought of it. The courthouse! Of all the unlikely places in the world. Exactly! If it had been at Hanauma Crater or while driving around the island, he would have got it at once.

There was only one thing to do. Get out of there. He took a hard step after Anne. In a swooping movement he seized her around the thighs and threw her over his shoulder. "You' comin' with me!"

Anne shouted and kicked as he carried her across King Street. But she was kicking only from the knees down, like someone using swim fins for the first time. And her pounding on his back was nothing at all.

A Packard was obliged to stop and let them pass. The driver wore white lace gloves. "Look at that Hawaiian carrying a haole girl, in the rain," she said. "It's rather sweet."

Her companion was not impressed. "We'd have done them both a favor if we hadn't stopped."

Chapter Twenty-nine

"OH NO!" ANNE WAILED. "NOT AGAIN!"

"Wassa matter? I thought you liked laulau."

"I did...the first hundred times."

"You wanna eat salmon with your poi?"

"No, I don't want cold canned salmon with my poi. I don't even want poi." Her lips were puffed up, in a sulk.

"You want rice? It'll take twenty minutes to cook."

"No, I don't want boiled rice, either."

"You' sure picky tonight."

"I'm just tired of always the same stuff, every night, all the time."

"You wanna go to the Lagoon?"

"No, I don't want Hawaiian stew or chopped steak either."

He looked at her in exasperation. "What *do* you want?"

"I want...the kind of food we used to have in San Francisco. All those wonderful restaurants with things like...coq au vin, rack of lamb...." As if she knew those words would mean nothing to him, she added, "Pepper steak."

That sounded easy. "Okay. Tomorrow we'll buy a steak and put pepper on it."

"Oh, no no no! It's not like that. It's foods cooked with sauces, French style. Or...," she went on, "an Italian dinner at North Beach. We'd have a glass of wine with dinner. And heavy white linen napkins." Anne's face was sad, dreamy.

The wine sounded suspicious to him. Only winos drank wine. He didn't want Anne to start going wrong.

"Look!" An inspiration had struck. "We'll eat out tonight!" She needed a treat. They hadn't been back since their first night together. "We'll eat at Kau Kau Korner!"

"A drive-in!" Anne just looked at him.

"You can have a milkshake!" he encouraged her, remembering how she'd noisily sucked her straw for the last drop.

Anne shook her head. She seemed ready to cry.

"Chocolate! You' fav'rite flavor!" he promised.

She turned her head as if to conceal tears. "Open the salmon. It's all right."

Parker busied himself with the can opener, set the tin, its top sprung back, in front of her place with a fresh fork. When she set the table she used her lauhala place mats. But when it was left to him he covered the table with nice fresh newspapers. He knew the proper way to do things.

They sat down to eat. If he told her something nice she might feel better. She was just staring at her bowl of poi.

"There's one song makes me think of you...when I hear it I could li'l more cry."

"What song is that?" Her voice dull.

It was almost hard for Parker to say the words, they meant so much to him. "Beyond the Reef."

"M'yeah?" She didn't seem all that taken with the idea.

"It's so beautiful. So sad."

"Actually, the words are dumb."

"Dumb. How? How could the words be dumb?"

"'My love is gone, and my dreams grow old,' what's that supposed to mean, anyhow?"

"It soun's nice when you' singin'," he insisted. "They match, the words, with 'the sea is dark and cold.'"

"You mean 'rhyme.'"

For a moment they ate in silence. Parker stirred his poi with his tablespoon, brought a hefty load to his mouth. With a quick turn of the wrist he put it smoothly upside down in his mouth. Anne nibbled the salmon glumly, staring at the pink hibiscus bush beside her open front door. She sighed.

Parker tried another subject. "Polly is hapai again." He'd been mulling over the implications of this for several days. There was no way Polly could hang this one on him.

Anne set down her poi spoon, her eyes hard. "Hapai? How much?"

"More'n seven months. You can' see it on her b'fore 'bout seven months."

"Who is it? Who's the man?"

Parker shrugged. "She's a musician. She's out a lot."

"Aren't you *interested*? She's getting a divorce and she's pregnant. Six kids aren't enough?" Anne made it sound like he'd done something wrong.

"The other kids are like mine. This one isn't."

Anne folded her arms, scowling at him. "You *know* I don't like to hear about Polly. What'd she say?"

"Nuthin'. Nuthin' at all. I asked if she was hapai and she jus'—you know—started throwin' stuff." It embarrassed Parker to tell how Polly was. Anne glowered at the table.

He should not have mentioned it. Especially tonight. He fished around in the events of the day for something to distract her.

"Oh, at the beach.... Come on, ei nei. Don' be mad. There was a little girl, so cute, with freckles. I'm talking to you!"

Anne picked up her spoon. "Go on."

"She was 'bout eight years old, blonde. Hair cut off across the forehead."

"Bangs."

"M'yeah. She was goin' aroun' with a mayonnaise jar full of water, sellin' drinks of water to people on the beach. For a nickel."

"So?"

"I bought a drink from her an' I said, 'Whatcha gonna do with all your money you get?' An' you know what she said? 'I'm gonna buy me some play money, for monopoly.'"

"That's a dumb story," Anne pronounced. "Dumb kid. Incidentally...the beach...that wahine who was looking at you was there today. The one that was at the courthouse."

"Courthouse?" he faked it. A handful of ice slid down his spine.

"You know, the one you nearly bumped into. Who looked at you so strangely."

He hadn't told Anne what he went through after the encounter. It was beyond him to explain how the certainty of knowledge had built in him when they left the steaming street. The wahine had not been a friend or relative of Polly's. She had not been spying on him. Not with that brassy stare. She had been *marking* him. He had all the proof he needed in that street, steaming around them like the pit at Kilauea. Just because the wahine

226

didn't have long fiery hair didn't mean a thing. Pele often disguised herself as an ordinary person. Only Pele scared people just by looking at them. Only Pele turned up unpredictably, anywhere.

He had wanted to tell Anne but had a feeling Pele's name shouldn't pass his lips. Anne was strange about Hawaiian things. He never knew how she'd take them. Sometimes she acted like she owned them—the ones she read about in her book. They'd never spoken again about the pebble or the centipede at Sacred Falls.

If Pele were mad at him, he shouldn't make things worse by talking. And to a haole at that. He pushed the thought further. Could Pele be on Polly's side? Did it have to do with his leaving the family? Or with Mrs. Randal, who had already punished him once?

Since there had been no further signs during the week, little by little he had managed to ease away from the terror that first gripped him on King Street. But at one moment—he refused the thought, of course—he wondered if it was because of Anne. That first evening he could not make love to Anne. Just held her tightly the whole night through, wondering if even that could be wrong.

"I finally got to speak to her."

"You *did*? What did you say?"

"Not much. Actually, I was rude to her." Anne said it with satisfaction.

"Rude! Oh my God!" Parker wrapped his arms around his stomach as though he'd been kicked.

"What's the matter? She was being rude too, the way she stared. Like she owned you or something."

"She was in Waikiki? Today?"

"There under the banyan. Why are your eyes popped out like a crab?"

"What was she doin' under the banyan?"

"Nothing. Watching you."

Parker's bowels nearly dropped through their hole. He pressed his arms against the sides of his body, squeezed his buttocks tightly. "When? When was this?"

227

"About five–thirty, quarter of six."

"Tell me what you said."

"I thought she might have something to do with Polly. So, first I went and got right in her line of vision, so she couldn't see you. When she moved and kept on staring, I went to her and said, 'Why are you looking at Parker so much? Who are you, anyhow?'"

Parker could hardly breathe. Chills ran down his arms to his wrists.

"So she said, 'Who are *you*? You look like a haole to me.' She didn't say lousy haole, but it meant the same, the way she said it." Anne sounded almost pleased.

"And then?"

"She said, 'Are you his wife?' So I knew she didn't know who you were." Anne was eating her poi now, as if she were enjoying it. "She just stood there another moment, watching you as you walked Diamond Head on the hard sand. That seemed to make up her mind. She gave me another dirty look, but not as if I really mattered. Then she took off, toward the Tavern."

Parker stared at his laulau as though he'd never seen such a thing before. Pele had looked at him and he hadn't even known! He felt as though she were looking at him now. He glanced around the room to be sure.

The room looked ordinary. But that was Pele's trick. To look ordinary. That was why she often appeared as an old woman, all wrinkled and bent, when people would be looking for a beautiful girl with long hair. Pele's specialty was throwing people off guard.

"She went off?" he repeated. Trying to believe this proved something. She wasn't interested in him. She'd left. She hadn't tried to speak to him.

"I walked down to the hard sand and called you. Remember?"

"You din' say nuthin' 'bout any wahine," he accused.

"There was nothing to say. She'd gone already. She just watched the way you walk. That was it. After she saw you walk, then she left."

Parker's breath was short and choppy.

228

"Well, your walk *is* something to see," Anne reminded him. She teased him about his wide–kneed gait at times. "You look like a cowboy," she said. "You look like you've been in the saddle for years."

For some reason, Anne's saying that reminded him of the ranch at Kamuela. Of his mother.

Maybe Pele was just curious. Niele. She often did things just to provoke people, out of curiosity. Why did he feel as though this had something to do, after all these years, with his mother?

❂ ❂

The next evening Parker had finished his shower and was sitting on his bed, naked, rubbing coconut oil into his ankles and feet when he heard a knock on the frame of his door. A female voice called softly, "Hui!"

He had left the door open. All the boys did. They closed their doors only when they had a wahine with them. Anyone who came in the beachboys' hangout had to be prepared for Hawaiians with or without clothes on.

Anne was at her hula class so he knew before he looked up it wouldn't be Anne. What he saw chilled him all the way to his toenails. It was the wahine from the courthouse. It was Pele.

That he should be naked seemed to Parker a rare piece of luck. If one had to deal with Pele, it should be respectfully, with the full ceremony of nakedness, as a real Hawaiian would. His heart was beating so hard he could hardly rise to his feet to acknowledge her presence. His towel lay on the bed, where it had dropped off as he sat. To his credit, his hands were at his sides as he stood.

Pele's expression was more friendly this time, it seemed to him. But that didn't mean a thing. His hair, he feared, might be sticking straight up on his head. He hoped that this would not be counted against him. He was not a coward in a lot of ways. It would be too bad to be taken for one now. He stood there, brown, complete, Hawaiian, just what he was. He was only a man. More than a man could do could not be expected of him. He was sorry about the kids. He was even sorry about Polly. He could not say he was sorry about Anne. As for that—he'd just have to take whatever was in store, when it came to Anne. No way out of that.

Wordless, he stood before Pele, trying to make out what was in her face, what had brought her to his humble room.

She spoke, and her voice was just like anybody's. "I found out your name," she began. "Found out you're a lifeguard."

He hadn't supposed Pele would need such details, or would talk about them. But then this was his first experience.

"Remember me at the courthouse?" she asked. Backing up, as if she wanted to hear him speak. He hadn't said a word since he raised his head and saw her.

"M'yeah," he said, finding his voice very uneven, rough.

"I been lookin' for you," she went on. "Ever since that day."

She sounded like any Hawaiian wahine might. But that went with the disguise.

"This is my sister."

He had been aware of someone behind Pele but had been too riveted on Pele's face to bring himself to look.

"I brought her to see you too."

Two of them! Was this Hiiaka, the one who boiled her lover and a bunch of other people when she got mad? You couldn't tell it to look at her. In that starched white dress she might be a haole from Manoa Valley. She seemed older than Pele. Outweighed her by forty pounds. Pele was dressed like a tomboy, in white saila-mokus and a dark printed aloha shirt.

Pele turned to the sister. She seemed excited, pleased. "What'd I tell you? His face. The way he's built. His shoulders. Even his legs."

They were studying his body, Hiiaka going over him as closely as Pele. Checking his feet and fat toes. They were clean, anyhow, and nicely oiled.

The sister murmured something he didn't catch, she being behind and to the side, but he thought he caught the word 'papa.'

A sense of his place as the host came to Parker. "Sit down?" he suggested, motioning to the bed.

They accepted. One of them was now on top of his towel. It occurred to him that he probably should be speaking Hawaiian,

230

but he couldn't. Couldn't even remember the words for 'make yourself comfortable.'

There was no chair, and it didn't seem polite to sit on the floor in front of them so he stood there, gravely, trying to look courteous, innocent, and at their disposition. Possibly their visit had something to do with his being a lifeguard. People expected a lot of things of lifeguards. Wanted them to find their boy-friends, or their hats. To know the names of fish, the best Chinese restaurants and when the buses ran. Maybe Pele had something she needed to know, or to ask him to do.

The two wahines sat on his bed, ill at ease, as if something were in the air.

It seemed up to him to provide the right words. Something kind. Something Hawaiian. Then he got it. For sure there was no one more stupid than he. "Aloha," he said. Then more warmly, with a smile. "Aloha nui loa."

The words had a wonderful effect on the wahines. Their faces changed. They rose, embraced him wholeheartedly.

"Aloha! Aloha!" They made such a show of it, hugging and kissing, that not much was required of him for some moments. It made him feel so warm and human he almost forgot who they were.

They pulled him back on the bed, set him down between them, both talking at once.

"The same...."

"Identical...."

"It's got to be...."

"We have to tell Ikua, them...."

"I couldn't believe it," Pele was saying. "When I saw you from the distance, walking, at Kuhio, then I knew. No mistake, that walk."

"He even has the same ears," the sister was saying, handling his ear with what seemed to be delight.

"...uses his hands like papa,..." Pele exclaimed.

"His teeth! Let's see your teeth." The sister bared her own to show him how.

Probably it was the polite thing to do as she wanted. Respect-fully he showed his teeth.

"Papa had two teeth missing this side but the front ones are the same."

"What's this 'papa'?" he finally had to ask, since they were so enthusiastic about it. Except for someone's father, a papa to him was a board. A surfboard or board for pig at a luau. Some kind of board.

"It's our papa," they informed him. "Your papa. We didn't know how to tell you."

"You are our younger brother. We are your sisters."

"Sure," he said. He'd got one end of the towel up from under Pele but the other end was still under the heavy one. The more human this encounter became, the more he began to desire his towel.

"Your sisters," the heavy one said again.

Parker did not think it would be polite to stand up and put on his trunks in front of them. That seemed too private a thing to do.

"When I first saw you at the courthouse, I thought you were a ghost. Really. I thought you were papa come back. How old are you?"

"Thirty-six," Parker answered bravely. He hoped she wouldn't think he'd already lived long enough.

"That's about how old papa was when I ran away. That was my last memory of him."

"He was older, when he died. He was about fifty when he had that fall. So I remember him older. But yes, when papa was around thirty-six, this is how he looked. Our brother!" The heavy one hugged Parker again. "Keoni!"

Parker smiled at the name. "Haven't heard that in awhile."

He was feeling good humored now, almost comfortable. Of course all Hawaiians were brothers and sisters. What they were saying about their papa doubtless was to throw him off guard. He'd recovered presence of mind enough now to ask the heavy one for his towel.

"D'ya mind?" he asked, tugging at it.

She lifted her hip and released it to him. He stood up, wrapped it neatly around the waist and sat down again between them, since that was where they seemed to want him.

Pele put her arm around his shoulders familiarly, her face only a few inches from his. "I'm going to tell all the others and we'll have a big family reunion."

"Sure," he said. "Good idea." What, he kept asking himself, did they really want?

"Start from the beginning," said the heavy one. "This is new for him."

"M'yeah," Parker agreed.

"We heard, even when we were small, that there was another one. That papa had a baby with another wahine. We even knew it was a boy. Named Keoni."

"Where was all this? Where you folks from?" he asked, strange feelings stirring in him.

"Kamuela."

"You from Kamuela?" he asked, pleased, forgetting that Pele was from all over. "Me, I'm from Kamuela too."

"There were eight of us girls and five boys. But we knew there was one more. No one wanted to talk about it. No one would tell us who the mother was. We heard she moved away. Moved to Honolulu."

Parker had the feeling that these were real people they were talking about. That they were talking about his mother.

"Mama, when she was old, got used to the idea. But there was a lot of bitterness at first."

"Worse than bitterness." The sisters looked across at each other.

"You mean," Parker said, "my father was not my father? He was your father?"

"Our own naughty papa." The Pele one grinned in a way that reminded him of something. Then he remembered where he'd seen that grin. It was a picture of himself the police department took when they put up the shack for the Kakaako Wharf Rats, trying to civilize them. They'd been so happy that day, the nickel divers, with a freshwater shower of their very own, and wooden benches to sleep on. They'd flung their arms around each other, standing in a row in front of the shack, grinning delightedly. A policeman had photographed them that way and given each boy a copy of the picture. Parker had looked at it

233

often, with great fondness. It was still around somewhere, if Polly hadn't torn it up.

Yes, Parker thought. The grin of that rascal in the raggedy shorts, third from the left, was just like the grin on the face of this Pele–sister, or whatever she was, here beside him. And now that he thought about it, he could see a resemblance of that grin in the other one, too.

"What's your name?" he asked, suddenly curious, if she was going to be his sister.

"Harriet."

Seemed like a pretty classy name to him. Not to leave the other one out, he asked her too. "You?"

"Emma."

"Emma and Harriet what?"

"Perkins."

"Oh, I've heard of them. Big family. They're all over."

"Oh yeah. On the Big Island we're related to practically everybody. Hanai or marriage, one way or another."

He turned to the Harriet–sister. "D'you say you ran away from home?" he asked. That interested him. "Me, I used to run away a lot, too. Nearly every day," he chuckled.

"When I ran away, it was for good," she answered proudly. "I went to the mainland. For fifteen years."

"No kiddin'!" Parker looked at her with admiration.

"We gotta lot to tell you," the Emma–sister said. "Family history, like that."

"M'yeah. Family history." He'd never heard of such a thing but it sounded good to him.

"Next time we see you, we'll bring some pictures."

It would take awhile to get all this new stuff sorted out in his mind. He needed some time to think about it. But he felt more natural now.

"I'm at Kuhio Beach every day but Thursday," he said, keeping up his end socially. "Why don' you come by? You can catch me any time between ten and six. We can talk about this some more."

"Oh, we don't live here. We live on the Big Island. Sis just came up to see a doctor. We're going back tomorrow morning."

That made him feel bad. He really ought to spend more time with them.

"I'm supposed to meet someone about now," he explained. "I'll go tell them something's come up."

"No. No," they protested together. "Harriet will be back next month."

"Yes, I'll come and see you then."

They were standing, each holding onto his arm in the small room as they moved toward the door.

"And you must come down Kamuela side," Emma urged. "Everybody'll want to meet you. We'll have a party so you can meet all your folks."

"That would be real nice," he agreed. "Yes. Meet my folks." In a way he believed them. In another way, he didn't. The idea of having folks had never occurred to him before. Some people had curly hair, some people didn't. Some people had folks, he didn't. But it seemed like the right thing, now, to act pleased.

Before they went out the two wahines hugged him so enthusiastically that his towel nearly dropped off, which he didn't want to happen, now.

"The courthouse," he muttered to himself as he turned back into the room. "Kamuela. Gee!" He should dress and leave at once for Anne's. Instead, he sat down and looked at his toes. His hands loosely clasped, he leaned on his knees and stared. He wished he had a cigarette. Too many people had got to him at the beach. He was going to have to stop carrying smokes to work.

What an idea, that their father was also his father! He wondered if it were true. He'd never given much thought to the man who was his father. It was his mother he remembered most since it was she who put him in the orphanage. When he went home for weekends or holidays his father was drinking, so he just tried to stay out of the way. When he was about fifteen, an accident at work had killed his father. A crane had turned over. The Kamehameha Lodge came to the funeral wearing their red sashes. That had been nice. Odd bits of memories like the wonderful singing at the funeral, and the white shirts and red sashes, returned to him. His mother had left a year or so later and after that he'd been sent to reform school. Very few boys in the

Kahuku Reform School had had family so his situation hadn't seemed unusual.

So his father, who apparently looked just like him, had been someone else! More and more the idea was taking hold. He'd talk about it with Anne tonight, see what she thought.

Both the wahines had seemed nice. But what if it were just a prank? Pele liked to pretend, play jokes, to see what people would do. To test them. She'd ask for a drink of water, or a ride, just to see if people would be kind. And then she'd vanish, leave them with an empty back seat, or a cup of water in the hand.

The little blonde girl selling drinks of water on the beach— she could be Pele, just turning things around. Pretending to be a haole, pretending that *she* had the water. It was confusing when you started thinking about it. Anybody could be Pele. Anyone could come into your life, just to test you. How could you tell? Maybe Sunshine was Pele. Pele sometimes took the form of a handsome young man. Maybe Sunshine was there to test him. Maybe even Anne. Or Kanekini. All of them, there for a reason, to see how he'd handle it. To see if he was up to the mark.

Chapter Thirty

"WHY ARE YOU LATE?" ANNE ASKED DISTRACTEDLY. "Well, I had my shower and...."

With barely a welcoming kiss she took the square can of corned beef out of his hands. "The potatoes and onions are already done. I've been waiting. Here...." She immediately handed the can back. "Will you open it? Oh, dear, I think they're sticking...." She hurried back to the little two–burner stove.

On the way over he'd had every intention of telling Anne about the extraordinary visit. But as he rolled the little metal strip along the side of the corned beef he changed his mind. Didn't want to talk about it. Not to conceal it from Anne—he would certainly tell her soon—but because he still felt so strange. Although it was not Pele and her sister who had stood there studying the various parts of him with astonishment, what had happened seemed too important, too precious to talk about at once. He needed time to settle his feelings. Needed to keep it for a moment to himself, for his own personal awe. After all these years, sisters! How to react to that?

When they sat down to the steaming plates of hash, Anne immediately launched into her own news from the Lagoon that afternoon.

"Coach Sakamoto raised hell with Miriam yesterday. Because she ate an ice cream cone before a race."

"M'yeah? Where's my poi?"

"Said he'd kick her off the team if she did it again. Here." She set his bowl before him.

"Even with the ice cream cone she won the race."

"She's good."

"You know how Horse's been looking for a job? He got an offer. On the mainland. Managing the pool at a posh country club. Good money." Anne went on. "Easy life. Lots of rich people. Rich wahines."

"Did he say he's goin'?"

"That's what I asked him. He just shrugged. Said, 'What for?'"

"Right. What for?" Listening to Anne, but another part of him still back there in his room with the two wahines saying, "Our own naughty papa...." And, "We were looking for you for a long time...." Feeling happy in a strange new way.

When he and Anne went to bed he still hadn't mentioned it. They settled in their usual heap and tangle, the only way they could sleep now, and Anne kissed him good night several times. After her toes stopped switching along his instep and her breathing had changed he had time to return to the scene of the afternoon. To go over every detail, every word for meanings.

Eight girls, they'd said, and five boys. What a fight it must have been, he thought, keeping clothes on that many kids, even with the hand–me–downs. Then he had a picture of them all seated for a meal at a big plank table in a yard. It would be almost like at an orphanage, all those kids eating together. Except that they were brothers and sisters. And their parents were there with them.

Then it came over him—whoom!—with a rush that made his ears ring: he should have been there, among those kids. He should! If the man was his papa and his mama didn't want to keep him, he should have been there!

For the first time in his life Parker went to sleep with a wonderful new image. He was sitting at a table among a bunch of kids who were his brothers and sisters.

Chapter Thirty-one

A WEEK LATER WHEN PARKER ARRIVED AT HIS ROOM AFTER work he found Polly shredding the next to last of his aloha shirts with a hefty set of steel dressmaker's shears she'd brought along for the purpose. His other three aloha shirts, together with his two jeans, extra swim trunks, and all his tee shirts, lay all over the floor in pieces not big enough to use to wipe a car.

"You!" he bellowed.

His first job was to get the shears away from Polly before she started on the last aloha shirt. Preferably without anyone getting damaged. Also, he had to take care of the situation quickly because Anne was expected at any minute. Polly would never let go of those shears if she saw Anne.

Parker did not want help from anyone else and did not expect it. The beachboys never interfered in crises with one another's wahines. They were too common and besides they were usually resolved without much bloodshed. It was an unwritten law that the police would not be called.

Polly was shouting but no one in the building would pay much attention to that. If the wahines at the Koa Avenue residence changed frequently, what they did and said did not. Their shrieks and plaints were so familiar that the residents hardly noticed them anymore. Day and night women carried on about being abandoned, pregnant, neglected, hungry. They threatened to go to the police, to his wife, to an attorney, or an old boyfriend.

Polly's yells had nothing to notice in them. All the women claimed they would kill, forgive, scratch out eyes, never do it again, do it ten times worse. They swore they would tell, jump off the Pali, leave for good or stay until the door opened. The information was delivered in well-educated mainland accents as well as in dirty, guttural go-for-broke Kakaako howls. Occasionally one of each at the same time.

The boys who lived there knew that at any hour the halls might be booby-trapped by a wahine on her knees in front of a closed door. Or they might be accosted by one pacing and waiting, armed with a fingernail file, a rock or a shoe. Invariably she begged for help to bring some brute to his senses.

Occasionally a beachboy in a trough would relieve some of the wahine's symptoms, if she agreed. But he would not take sides.

Few of the women were really creative, like bringing rope to hang herself with or to tie the cruel one to her car and drag him. The one cry that was not heard in those busy halls was "Rape!" The Massie case eighteen years earlier in which a Navy wife claimed she was raped by four local youths had caused no end of hurt and indignation. Local boys did not rape, Islanders protested. They were paid to do it.

Healthy shrieks of "I'll kill you!" were common as mynah bird squabbles. Among all the threats that were screamed, the only one that drew any attention was "Fire!" But Polly did not seem to have fire on her mind. The scissors seemed to satisfy her.

"I know 'bout you!" she roared. She brandished the points toward his eyes. "I know 'bout you' haole wahine. I *heard*." She made it sound like it deserved brimstone. "Thass' what you went and did. You got a haole wahine."

Parker had always known that that would inflame Polly. If there was anything that would make her worse than she already was it would be to find out that Anne was a haole. Eventually, he knew, word would get back to Polly. He'd been fearing something like this for a long time.

Sternly he closed in on her, reaching for the chubby wrist that, if almost broken, should yield the shears. Knowing however, that Polly's wrist was not easy to break. And she was fast. Somehow she and the wrist both slid out of his grasp.

Polly looked a full nine months, he thought she might drop at any minute. But that didn't stop her. She came at him holding the shears like a dagger and this time it was serious. Using both hands just to be sure, he caught the arm holding the shears. That left her other hand free to pommel him, which was all right. Because of being so hapai, fortunately, she couldn't knee him in the balls, which was the main thing he had to look out for in a close-up with Polly. She had to settle for kicking his ankles.

He tore the shears out of her hand and hurled them out the window into the bushes. With the load she was carrying her scuffle couldn't last long. She was soon reduced to panting jabs. After a few last kicks and a half–hearted attempt to bite his hand she withdrew.

Smoothing the muumuu over her great load, she lifted her chin. There was a glint in her eye.

"I'm gittin' married Sunday," she announced. "So there."

Chapter Thirty-two

"B OSS, YOU' LOOKIN' GOOD!" PARKER FELT LIKE HE LOOKED GOOD himself, in the new brown and gold aloha shirt Anne had given him.

Kanekini extended his hand for a warm shake although usually the smiles and "How's everything?" repeated several times took care of closing the gap, getting things going.

"Well, Kealii! Thanks for coming in. I wanted to talk to you."

"M'yeah. I got your message. Well, here I am. I wanna do what you want, Boss." Grinning like everything was just fine.

"I know! I know!" Kanekini's manner was the same as ever, but his timing seemed a little behind, as if the words were harder to say. There was the same kindly softness behind that drooping eye, Parker noticed, his stomach giving a little turn.

"Sit down! Sit down! Just a minute." Kanekini went to the door of his glass cubicle. "Yuki, don't interrupt us. No calls. I'm going to be busy for a bit." He returned to his chair, sank down in it with a heaviness Parker couldn't help but notice. Maybe it wasn't as bad as they said. Roy Stone of Kaimuki Playground had told him that Kanekini had a muscle disease that was going to kill him. It was only a matter of time.

"Now!" Kanekini pronounced with an enthusiasm that Parker could tell took effort. "I've got some news for you, Kealii. We talked a little about the changes going on last time you were here, I think. The Parks and Recreation Department has some great things coming up. The beach safety program is very much a part of that. Our beaches are one of our prime assets, you know. They're our treasures."

"Yas suh!" Agreeing on that.

"Over at the Board of Supervisors they don't ask me, 'How's Crane Playground?' They ask, 'How're the beaches?' Not everyone cares about the kids' recreation programs but everyone cares about the beaches...."

Parker thought Kanekini was taking longer than usual to get started. Well, he had all the time his boss wanted. Time to look at his chief, feel the kindly presence, feel the aloha well up in him at having a chief like this to work for. Again he wished he could do something wonderful for Kanekini. Find some way to express what he felt for this man. And now, especially, although, of course, the doctors could be wrong.

"We made a large request for our 1950 budget, just hoping we'd get two–thirds of it—you know how that is. And d'you know—they gave us every penny! That's how important they think our department is. We're a great asset to the city, Kealii. The supervisors say so. And the mayor too," Kanekini added thoughtfully, as if he were less sure of that. "He approves of what we're doing, he says." Kanekini gave a short laugh. "Of course, politics—who knows?"

Parker listened, his hands loosely clasped. Watching for signs, studying the movements of the familiar, bulky figure, the heavy, jowled face with the kindly eyes turning to him every sentence or so. He didn't look different. Yes, he did. The warm glances, the diplomatic explanations were the same. But they were costing him. You could see the cost. If Kanekini was mad because the requisitions weren't in yet he wasn't showing it. Parker felt rotten about the requisitions. He'd thought about asking Anne to help him, but that didn't seem to be correct. When your chief asked you to do something it should be *you* who did it. The doing of it for your chief was as important as getting it done. So even though this work seemed almost beyond doing, to be given the task was an honor. It was the act, as much as the living fish that Kamehameha required of his runner. To serve your chief was to express your aloha and respect not only to him but to the gods whom he represented.

"The point is," Kanekini went on, "we need a new approach to beach safety now. It's not just posting a few men in the most used areas, in case someone gets in trouble. No. We're going to have a much more sophisticated network of communications and rescue services." He paused a moment for effect. "We're going to get a van, Kealii. It'll be outfitted with the latest lifesaving equipment. Our own mobile rescue unit!"

"Thass' *great*, Chief!" Feeling a surge of excitement at the thought of it. The boys would certainly like that. At once he began to consider who to assign to the van. Or should such a job be rotated? It would seem like favoritism if one person did it all the time. A job like that would make so many points with the wahines it would go to the driver's head, he thought. Cruising up and down Kalakaua Avenue in a shiny new van with the words Beach Safety Patrol painted on it and maybe the city seal. He'd see they kept the van bright as a dime, all right. Might even drive it himself sometimes!

"We'll need to train the men in the use of the new equipment. The men have absolutely got to be up to the mark. And that brings me," Kanekini's words slowed down, took another tone, "to Morgan. We're going to have to replace Morgan."

Parker's insides gave a thump. He'd never mentioned Morgan's problem to Kanekini. Sunshine had told. For sure, Sunshine, out-of-line, had carried the story. Parker's next thought was pity for Morgan. Out of a job. He blamed himself. If he'd been tougher on Morgan sometime back it might not have come to this. He couldn't say it was unfair. But it was hard.

"Well, Chief. I been meanin' to tell ya…. But I kep' hopin' Morgan would straighten out…."

"I know. I know. But hopes don't change facts. It's hard to be tough on boys you've known all your life. Especially for you. You've got the old style, Hawaiian way. But we can't have men who aren't up to scratch now. It reflects badly on the whole department." Kanekini's eyes held a spark of grimness Parker had never seen before. "Morgan's been warned. More than once."

It sounded like Kanekini himself had spoken to Morgan. "I've talk' to him, Chief. I've warn' him. He wouldn' listen."

"Wouldn't, couldn't…. The point is, we can't keep him. I've asked him to resign, as of tomorrow."

Tomorrow! Parker was thunderstruck. Things were going on that he knew nothing about. Parker felt as though he were standing on sand that the tide was washing out from under him. Things he'd taken for granted weren't holding. He tried to keep his voice normal although it was extra husky when he spoke.

"Guess we'll have to set up another test to replace him. That'll take a coupla weeks, at leas'. Can' we keep Morgan on till then?"

"That won't be necessary. We had a good group of candidates try out last time. Several were equally good, remember? When we decided on Sunshine. We can just take one of them. They're qualified. You yourself were in favor of—who was it? Boursier?"

"M'yeah. I don' know if he still wants it," Parker said, his tone stubborn. Hurting. Feeling the sand ease out from under him, leaving him off–balance, scared.

Kanekini didn't look comfortable either. He glanced around the glass–enclosed cubicle distractedly. He swiveled his chair this way and that, making it squeak, but he did not tip back in his usual comfortable way, at ease, with his opu up.

"Where were we?" He threw himself backward but immediately righted himself again as if gearing up for something else. "Anyhow. Beach safety isn't just an occasional rescue, now. It's *staying* safe. It's programs in safety. It's reports. It's administration. It's political savvy. It's going to involve publicity to get support for our program. The Lions Club wants to give us a bench for the old folks at Kuhio Beach. We should have more of that sort of thing. Community participation. Then we'll have a political base when we ask for money to acquire lands, develop programs."

Parker wasn't following too well. Some awfully big ideas were mixed in with those long words.

"So. Well, Kealii, we're going to need a specially qualified person to handle this new beach safety work. Someone who is comfortable with the kind of planning and records that will go with these new responsibilities."

Parker didn't see the problem. "I know you' awful busy, Chief, but it seems t'me you' doin' a *fine* job, thinkin' of all this new stuff. I gotta hand it to you...." He stopped, remembering. Maybe that was the point. Maybe Kanekini *couldn't* do it anymore. Maybe he had to get rid of some of his work.

"We're going to create an entirely new job, Kealii, at the head of the whole Beach Safety Program."

"A new job?"

Suddenly, Kanekini was talking faster than usual. "The job won't include the regular lifeguard duties—the kind of thing you do so well. No. It will be administrative. You know. Desk work.

245

Papers." Kanekini patted a pile of his own papers, as example. "We're going to make a new office there at the Natatorium, create a regular command post to be in touch with all the support services. The Coast Guard, the police, Red Cross, Queen's Hospital. Even the radio stations, in case there's an emergency like a tidal wave. To get the news to the public. There's so much to do," Kanekini said. His glance was running back and forth across his desk as if it followed a scampering mouse. "But all that's got nothing to do with the work *you* do, Kealii. The rescue work."

Parker got it. Saw what was next. He swallowed before he said the words. "You gonna bring in some smart haole from the mainland for the job?"

Kanekini's eyes caught his. His smile was partly real. "No. No, Kealii. We wouldn't do that to our boys." He said it as if he was glad about that, at least. "No. Not from the mainland. Local."

Parker's body knew before his mind knew. "Who?"

"Sunshine."

There was silence while the blood in Parker's body seemed to rise about twenty suffocating degrees. He had disappointed his boss. And Sunshine had cockroached him.

Two daggers planted simultaneously in his heart.

Faintly, through the glass, a phone rang, a voice said hello. Typewriters tapped. Within the cubicle was the muffled roar of his own blood in his ears. There was a faint squeak of the swivel chair as Kanekini leaned forward. He clasped his hands on the desk, looking at him.

Parker felt like he could start swimming toward the setting sun and never come back. He'd let Kanekini down. And now Kanekini was having a hard time telling him about it. A sick man and Parker had made things worse. He would have crawled to the beach and back on his hands and knees to make things right again.

And then, following the remorse and pain of this terrible thing, came the other, like grey slime in his throat. Sunshine. He'd never guessed. He'd always known.

So that was what all those trips to the office were about. Being glad to carry reports, run errands. Learning every detail of the work, inside out. Sunshine setting himself up with Kanekini.

Picking up on all this political stuff, too, no doubt. Giving the impression he was up to it. Only eight months on the job and six years younger than himself and Sunshine was going to be his boss. Parker didn't know where to look to keep from destroying something with his eyes.

Kanekini had been talking earnestly for some moments. "...well qualified...schooling...do a good job...." Kanekini paused, cleared his throat. "I know it's a shock to you, Kealii. I feel bad about it. Really. I wouldn't do it if I could see any other way...." Kanekini seemed to be squeezing his clasped hands. He looked at Parker, his droopy eye bigger than it had ever been before, almost normal size, the expression intense.

Parker held Kanekini's look for a moment, then glanced away. The thought of bolting occurred to him, but he wasn't sure his legs would carry his weight.

"Of course you will keep all the authority you now have, with the boys. They will be responsible to you, in their training, their schedules, same as ever. Nothing really changes for you." Kanekini's tone was apologetic. "It's just this other, new business that Sunshine will take care of. The liaison work. Giving stories to the newspapers, that sort of thing."

Sunshine would be good at that, Parker thought with a twist of bitterness. What I could tell you about Sunshine. Half a dozen incidents, just borderline in being okay, crossed Parker's mind. Even the way he treated wahines had something calculating about it that Parker disliked. Sunshine had a technique—he laughed about it at the Lagoon—of giving a new wahine a big rush for a few days, as if he were crazy about her. Then he'd drop her, without a word. It drove the wahines crazy. They'd come begging to find out what was wrong, and he'd have them at the crook of his finger after that.

The latest story was that Sunshine was spending a lot of time with the Republicans now. They were looking for some young Hawaiian blood to make their programs look good.

But that was his private life. There had been rumors about him on the beach, too. Parker felt ashamed when he heard about the six year old Sunshine rescued in front of the Halekulani. The kid had drifted out too far in his inner tube. The parents hadn't even missed him when Sunshine brought him back to shore. The story was that Sunshine patted the kid's head and said, "He's too valuable to lose," and the grateful father gave him one hundred bucks. Not that being thanked with money didn't happen occasionally to lifeguards, but Parker could just imagine how Sunshine turned it into something for himself. That was it. The thing didn't just happen, Sunshine made it happen. That was what was scary about Sunshine. Sunshine made things happen.

Parker had never said anything against Sunshine to Kanekini. Not because he wanted to protect Sunshine but because he knew Kanekini was fond of the boys and would be pained to hear bad about any of them. For the same reason Parker never told him of trouble within their ranks. Never mentioned, for example, Freitas and Squidley's feud over some crabbing nets that created tension among the boys for weeks. Or when Ah Sook had a kid cover for him on the beach for a couple of hours while he took care of a wahine dentist helper in her room at the Moana. Parker had lectured Ah Sook, but the incident was not reflected in his efficiency report.

Twice a year Parker was supposed to rate the lifeguards' performance on the job. This he found impossible to do. The idea of writing things against the boys you worked with! Whistling, for example, was chronically late. But no one was more loyal, more ready to do an ugly job than Whistling. And then there was Ellings. People said Ellings was rude on the beach. Had a way of ignoring people who tried to be friendly. He simply didn't like to talk. Not even to the other guards. It was claimed that he smiled only once a year. But he was dependable as the tides.

Parker didn't see the point to efficiency ratings anyhow. People did what they could. In the end, they were all doing the best they could. Everything balanced out in the end. Why not let it go at that? So every six months Parker turned in ratings of excellent on all the boys, including Sunshine.

"I'm so sorry," Kanekini repeated. "I know it's hard on you, Kealii. But I couldn't wait any longer. I had to act. The pressure around here is building every day. We can't string things out the way we used to." His tone pleading for Parker to understand.

"The Tourist Bureau has been on the city's tail for months

about the beach looking so terrible, just a thin little strip with so much of the sand gone out. Today the sand is being loaded in from Molokai. Barges of it. Thousands of tons. Did you see them this morning? They were crossing the channel at six."

Parker had jumped in the jeep and sped down the Ala Wai for his eight–thirty appointment with the boss, arriving at five after eight, just to be sure. It was the first time in years he hadn't gone to the beach before he did anything else.

Something in Parker's face must have struck Kanekini because he said more earnestly than ever, "You've got to understand, Kealii. In a sense the future of the whole department is involved in this appointment. Work was postponed for five years while the war was on. I couldn't do it then. This is my last chance to bring these projects to maturity. I've got to do it now. There isn't much time."

Parker felt like something inside him was stretching to the limit, about to crack. "M'yeah. Sure, Chief. It's okay." What he felt about Sunshine must wait.

"...All the people who have worked so hard with me over the years...."

Parker sat controlling his eyes, holding his fists. What he wanted to do was pick up the desk, heave it through the cubicle's glass. If only Kanekini had asked him to *do* something. To take some action. He'd do anything for Kanekini. If his chief told him to kill, he'd do it. Not for himself, but for his chief he could kill. Fighting would be easy. Fists, body in action. But now, just when he was crazy to use them, he had to keep them quiet. Couldn't show how he felt. It would hurt Kanekini.

Some boys punched out their bosses when they got a raw deal. He couldn't imagine swearing in front of Kanekini. Why was Kanekini given this terrible thing to do? It wasn't Kanekini's fault. But it must be somebody's fault. Sunshine. It was a good thing Sunshine wasn't in view now. In the old days the Wharf Rats took care of anyone who got out–of–line. But his gang now was his boys. And they were no longer his.

He and Kanekini seemed to be in the middle of a shipwreck. A terrible crashing and splintering was going on around them. The splinters were going into his eyes and throat. It had hurt

Kanekini to make this decision and now he was hurt again, telling Parker. Parker saw the pain in Kanekini's eyes, saw the familiar face swollen with earnestness, across the littered desk. Kanekini, with not long to live, was hurting for him. Parker could have cried. He'd failed his chief. But Kanekini still cared enough about him to be hurt. It was beyond bearing.

He'd have to bear it. That was what the moment required. He'd always wanted to do something splendid for Kanekini. Now all he could do was: nothing. The raging in his blood would have to wait.

Parker had never had such a test. His struggles in the sea seemed easy compared with what he was up against now. In a rescue he would swim, search, dive, drag until his heart couldn't muster another beat. Gladly. But he wasn't in the sea. He was in this office with all those horrible papers. At bottom the problem was papers. The treachery, the misery in those harmless–looking things. He could destroy pounds of them with a gesture or two. But they could reduce him to misery just by lying there. Papers were against people. They were against him, anyway. And this time they had won.

Kanekini was squeezing his thick old hands, pleading. "It's for our people, Kealii," he begged. "I wish you could understand. I want to establish water safety programs for people who never learned to swim. Old folks. The handicapped. People who never dared go in the water before. We'll teach them to swim, teach them to enjoy it. In the shallows at Sans Souci we'll have these learn–to–swim programs. It's so calm and safe there...everyone on the island a swimmer.... It's been my dream...we'll take the lead...Hawaii showing the world. Don't you see, Kealii? Every child, every adult. Even mentally handicapped, the mentally ill. Back to the sea. Back to our beginnings. It would be a crime not to...our great birthright...our beaches."

"Sure. Sure." Parker choked. Seeing the cripples, the lolos...easing into the water on the strip at Sans Souci. The wobbly old folks, not ashamed, because they were going into the cool, sweet waters together. Learning the sea's love, with kind people's help. "M'yeah. Good idea."

Kanekini's voice took another tone. "Of course, you have

your rights, Kealii. You have a right to complain. After all your years of service. You can go to the Hawaii Government Employee's Association. They'll help you fight it. If you want to make a case."

"No. No, Chief. Why fight it? Won' change nuthin'. You gotta do your work. I never done the kinda stuff you' talkin' 'bout now. Community programs, like that."

The slaughter in Parker's chest seemed to have subsided into a more manageable pain. He was gripping the seat of his chair, he found. That was what his hands were doing, squeezing the wooden chair seat as if to wring blood out of it. He and Kanekini were fighting this thing out together.

It was his boss's eyes, actually, that he was hanging on to, Kanekini's eyes, one of them at half–mast. Showing his concern and sorrow. He was lucky he had Kanekini.

It seemed to Parker that the thing to do now was to leave. He had to get away. Get out in the air. Back to the beach, the sea. But Kanekini had to stay here. He was stuck here, with the papers. What could he do to make it easier for his boss?

"You gonna give him a raise, Sunshine, I guess, huh?" Parker swayed a little as he backed toward the door. Reaching for the knob.

"Yes. There will be...more...yes, for a job like that...." Kanekini seemed to have some trouble saying it, as if remembering, maybe, Parker's six kids.

"Thass' good, Boss!" Parker joked. "Thass' real good! Then Sunshine kin maybe pay me back my aloha shirt."

It was time for them both to laugh. Since their faces were so stuffed up with the heat and all.

So they laughed.

Chapter Thirty-three

A S HE WALKED AWAY FROM KANEKINI'S OFFICE PARKER HATED everything he laid eyes on: the city and county employees, acting so sure of themselves, which just showed how stupid they were; the handsome building with its tiled halls and courtyard open to the sky and sun; the ferns and palms on the way to the parking lot. And when he mounted the jeep and headed for Waikiki he hated King Street, the electric trolleys, the people who rode in the trolleys and the people who didn't and therefore drove cars that got in his way.

At the stoplight just before the Advertiser on Kapiolani Boulevard, he didn't jump when the light changed, and the car behind honked. That was all he needed. His rear view mirror showed it was a haole. With great deliberation Parker turned off his motor, got out, and in a walk that was a warning, approached the other car. He couldn't say why he was so pleased it was a haole. Just knew that except for hitting Sunshine nothing would suit him better than to hit a haole. The blood coursed in his arms; they itched for action. He knew just how he would do it. Yank the car door open, lift the guy out by his necktie or nose or whatever seemed most attractive for the purpose, give him a good punch wherever he needed it most, then drop him back in the car. Proceeding to Waikiki he'd feel that one thing, at least, had been taken care of.

But when he walked over and saw the haole up close, saw what a pink–faced pitiful twit he was even though by the length of his arms he looked to be taller than himself, the point seemed lost.

"You honk' cause you need help?" he asked with malicious courtesy.

"Oh, no. Not really. Just a—accident—sort of. Sorry."

"Maybe you' a stranger, need some help?"

"Thanks, I'm just going to Kodak Hawaii. Right down the street."

"I kin take you there without no honkin'," Parker insisted.

"Thank you. Sorry. It's okay."

Parker lifted his chin toward the big, light green building nearby, taking his time, although several cars behind them now had to ease around. "The people in the Advertiser, they don' like honkin'," he cautioned seriously. "People honk, they' sorry later."

"As I say, it was an accident."

"Aloha!" Parker didn't know he could make the word sound so mocking and mean. He gave the car's windowsill an advisory thump, sauntered back to the jeep.

As he drove off, he did not feel as though something had been taken care of. Eight hours of duty lay ahead of him. Eventually he was going to have to face Morgan. And Sunshine. And he had to tell Anne that Sunshine was going to be his boss.

❂   ❂

Parker stood under the banyan, watching the beach change before his eyes. When he arrived half a dozen pyramids of sand eight feet high had been unloaded at the water's edge and the grader was at work on the Diamond Head end. Scooping up great masses of the soft sand, the roaring machine pushed it forward in waves like the surf at Queen's, leveling hills into smooth, creamy ribbons. People stood along the sidewalk, shielding their eyes from the glare.

Parker didn't know what to feel about the work. Doubtless it seemed like a good thing to have the beach fifteen or twenty yards wider, if sand was what you like to sit on. But to enlarge a beach suggested a kind of power, an awesome ability to have what you wanted on a scale he'd never imagined before. Change a beach! If you could do that, you could change a mountain too. Maybe even change a view. Like across the flat plain of Waikiki up to the hills. Or toward Diamond Head. But that seemed like the idea of a madman. But if they could put a tunnel through the Pali, as they kept saying they were going to do, apparently anything was possible. Somewhere, somebody always had an idea about how to fix up Hawaii nei.

If it weren't today, when he was feeling so mad and cut up, he would feel proud studying the golden piles, watching the beach grow sleek and fat. He would have been chatting with people, marveling at what the haoles could do, exchanging thoughts on how progress was sometimes good.

The beach hadn't been much to look at for a long time. That was true. The tourists complained when they saw the raggedy strip of sand with the black rock outcropping in front of the Tavern and from the seawall down to Chris Holmes's. They said it didn't look at all like what they imagined, from all the songs and stories. What had once been a long, gentle slope toward the shallows, had been gnawed away until it was only twenty yards from the banyan and steeply banked, with the water lapping at the bottom of the bowl as if ready to eat away the rest of it to the Avenue.

There were kamaainas who said this was only temporary, that the currents that had carried the sand off to Mokuleia would eventually bring it back. But the Tourist Bureau couldn't wait. Said that the forty–five thousand tourists expected in 1950 had a right to the Waikiki of their dreams. Plenty of sand and up–to–date facilities were absolutely required.

So the tourists should be pleased, Parker thought, and maybe even some of the locals. But hurting over changes as he was today already, all he could think of was that the old Hawaiians wouldn't have done it. And if the haoles hadn't built so many groins out into the water earlier, it might never have been needed anyhow.

Change and progress were, in fact, spreading like an epidemic in Waikiki. More and more little bungalows crumpled to bulldozers. Tall palms fell under cruel saws. Curio shops replaced mom–and–pop markets. Where the Moana Cottages had sprawled under fragrant plumerias, a tall hotel was rising. Already the scaffolding was on a level with the fronds of the palms, and still going up. It looked as though it would top the Royal, which was hard to imagine. The towers of the Moorish pink queen had seemed like the last thing in hotel splendor all these years, and now she would be looked down on by the guests in the Biltmore, as the new structure would be called. Prophetically.

The barges were still coming in with sand over by the Outrigger and Ulu Niu. There weren't many people in the water. They'd been warned away on account of the machines, but a few had sneaked in around the side anyhow. There were half a dozen surfers out in Canoe and Popular.

With a twinge of disapproval, Parker watched a kid of twelve or so, goggles pushed back on his head, swim to the stone wall groin, pulling an inner tube. The tube was floating an enamel basin full of heads of coral. He probably had fifteen pounds of the stuff he'd got off the reef. It crossed Parker's mind that the kid—he looked like a Hawaiian Filipino but it was getting harder all the time to tell, with all the mixing up that was going on—should be in school. He watched the kid put the black tube over his shoulder, then, staggering under his load in the soft sand, head off toward Robinson Village.

Tramping in the fresh sand near the banyan, testing it, Parker sincerely hoped he would not run into Sunshine today. For the sake of all three of them: Sunshine, Kanekini and himself. He needed more time. Possibly a lot more time. He couldn't remember when he'd had so much to get past.

Kanekini had suggested he appeal to the government employee's union. Parker thought of the troublemakers around City Hall who would delight in taking such a case to the papers. A Hawaiian with twelve years experience passed over for a rookie of eight months! It would make a good story all right. Especially since he was Hawaiian. The *Advertiser* made a point of sticking up for the Hawaiians, the most local people of all. But then Parker remembered that Kanekini and Sunshine were Hawaiian too, which would make the case less clear. Besides, he had no intention of doing such a thing. He couldn't hurt Kanekini like that. Kanekini, with that kindly drooping eye. And now it turned out that the droop was not kindly after all, it was a symptom of a mortal disease. Ever since he'd learned about it, Parker had grieved for Kanekini. To act against his chief, and especially now, seemed like the most ungrateful thing a man could do.

Thinking of being Hawaiian reminded Parker of his new sister, Harriet. Perkins was a haole name. Maybe her father was half white. That would mean he had haole blood too. He might be a quarter. This was a new, confusing idea. Today everything was getting confused. He'd always thought of himself as a real

Hawaiian, and the head of beach safety. Things that had seemed solid for a long time were getting shifted around. Sunshine, he remembered bitterly, made things happen.

He was back to Sunshine again. Another sly practice of Sunshine's, with wahines, crossed Parker's mind as he glowered at the sea.

Sunshine kept on his dresser, in prominent display, a large studio photo of an unattractive local girl. Sunshine had never met the girl. The picture was just a ploy. When he took a tourist wahine to his room, he'd say, "That's my girlfriend. I should say *was*. She's mad at me because I can't take her on a trip. Have to work. So she's lookin' for someone else." He'd act as if he felt terrible about it. Stranded, in fact. The tourist wahine, reassured by what seemed like paltry competition, would throw herself into comforting Sunshine. More than any protest of being on the loose, which in his case would seem unlikely, the story of the homely, selfish girl set Sunshine up. It would be gravy after that. Sunshine sometimes complained he felt like he was drowning in gravy. Wondered why he kept picking up wahines when he was already up to his eyeballs in gravy.

Thank God Anne had never fallen for Sunshine's games. Parker felt sure of that. Anne was true and good. His body felt as though he'd been beaten with a broomstick there in Kanekini's office. No, poisoned was more like it. But at least he had Anne.

Turning his back on Diamond Head, he tramped through the soft clean sand, so fresh and grainy under his feet. Then he remembered the new lifeguard towers. He'd thought it would take months for them to be built. Maybe it would happen faster than he'd expected. Kanekini hadn't mentioned the requisitions. Maybe he had given them to Sunshine, the St. Louis graduate and don't forget two years at the University, too! Sunshine would get the requisitions done, Parker thought bitterly. Oh yes. Sunshine would be fine with requisitions.

For a moment he could have punched out the banyan tree. He even walked over to it and gave it a mean look like he'd like to kill it. But there was a certain spot on the smooth grey bark, he remembered, a spot with a smear of brown, that would be there, in his mind at least, forever.

At the memory, there came a shift in focus. The things that were hurting receded. Still there, but in a less demanding position in his thoughts. He was alive. He mustn't forget that. That, already, was a lot.

He glanced around at the beach. The grader, roaring, had moved on, leaving the sand, wide and sumptuous as a stretch of golden sugar all the way up to Chris Holmes's curve.

The beach was there. And the sky with its puffs of white clouds, gorgeous as coral heads. He had the sea. And Leahi. What they gave him was more than a lot of folks had in a lifetime.

For the rest of the day, when the sick feelings washed over his heart, when the anger rushed into his throat, he had things like that to hold on to. Where he was. And Anne.

As the hours crept by, Parker thought of something else Kanekini had said. They'd be getting a van, their own mobile rescue unit. That was something to look forward to. Taking care of a shiny new van, with a lot of important new equipment inside. He'd do a good job on that, all right, for Kanekini.

Later, when he stopped by the Natatorium, Ellings had two telephone messages for him, neither of which Parker felt ready to bear. The first was that the authorities had put Lani in Kaneohe. She was beginning a series of thirty electroshock treatments. The second was from his sister, Harriet. She was on Oahu for two days and would meet him under the banyan, in the afternoon, tomorrow.

Chapter Thirty-four

PARKER WAS A LITTLE ANXIOUS ALL DAY AS HE WAITED FOR HIS meeting with Harriet. When she appeared, under the banyan, just before quitting time, he found he was actually happy to see her. She wore a blue aloha shirt with green parrots and her white saila–mokus. This time she seemed like a sister and a really nice one, too. Gravely, she kissed him on the cheek. Then she grinned.

"You move around a lot," he offered, to get things going. He said it admiringly. "Kamuela, Waikiki. Kamuela, Waikiki."

She sat down with him on the edge of the rock wall. People were leaving the water. The heat had gone out of the sky, although the sun still loitered over Waianae. In the last western rays the palm tree fronds looked waxy and golden, stirring gently with the trades.

"That's nuthin'," she scoffed. "I don' min' travelin' at all. I started young. Went up to the mainland when I was a kid."

"How old?" Seeing himself in her tomboyish grin. Thinking he had a story to match hers.

"Thirteen. Barely."

Parker was impressed at that. "Thirteen? How come?"

"I couldn't stand it at home anymore. Couldn't stand papa. His terrible temper."

"Got mad easy, huh?"

"He'd hit first and ask questions afterwards. With all those kids, of course, there was always some kinda ruckus."

"M'yeah. Kids is aggravatin', sometimes." For a moment his thoughts flew to Lani. Poor Lani, in Kaneohe, getting shock treatments, whatever they were. Tomorrow, his day off, he was going over to see her.

"I was third oldest girl so I was 'posed to make the little ones behave. If there was trouble, I caught it too."

"People those days didn' take foolishness off their kids," Parker observed. "Not like today."

"M'yeah. Folks outside the family thought papa was so nice. He smiled, he joked. But he kept us kids scared to death."

258

"What'd he do? What kinda work?"

"He worked in a gravel factory. Oiled the buckets, kept the conveyor belt running."

"He wasn' on the ranch?" Parker had been thinking of his papa as a ranch hand, a paniolo, doing exciting things with the horses, cattle.

"He was when he was young. Then he hurt his back. Couldn't ride all day anymore. So he got this other job, which he hated. I think he was in pain a lot. That made him mean, too."

Parker could see that. A man doing work he didn't like, with his back in misery. And all those kids to feed.

"It didn't pay too good at the stone–crushing plant," Harriet went on, as if she read his thoughts. "We barely had enough to eat. We were always on the lookout for a little extra food. The last thing that happened...why I ran away...it was on account of food."

Parker was thinking how strange it was to hear his sister talk about being short of food when she was young. On another island, with her family, she too knew what it was like to be hungry.

In the banyan the mynahs screeched as they settled for the evening. The sparrows, who outnumbered them, were keeping up their end.

"I was supposed to watch my little brother, Simon. He was about three or four. I was so hungry, and there was nothing to eat in the house. I took a piece of rope and walked a couple of miles to the fish pond trap. To keep Simon out of trouble I tied him to some bamboo with the rope. Then I went fishing with my muumuu. I caught several oopu in my skirt. Then I got really daring, and caught a fat mullet. Going home I was so proud, with all those fish loading down the front of my muumuu. When my father saw the mullet he knew where I'd been. He didn't wait. He pulled a lathe out of the picket fence and let me have it, right then, wet clothes and all."

At least his stepfather hadn't beaten him when he came back with the red fish after Prince Kuhio died.

"I knew I wasn't supposed to go on private property, take a fish from the pond. But I thought he'd be happy if I brought fish to the family. Sometimes we didn't have anything to eat but

259

plaua moku moku, flour dumplings dropped in boiling water." Harriet's voice shook a little as if the memory still hurt.

"Soon after that I ran away. Went to work as a maid for an army captain's family. Mostly I cared for the children. When they transferred back to the mainland they took me with them. I was gone ten years."

Parker saw it exactly. In how she felt they were almost like twins. Only the details were different. The fear, the hunger, the confusion were the same. And finally, the defiance. He only wished he'd been there with her, to share it. Wished he'd had her for his older sister.

"How old are you? When's you' birthday?"

"I'm forty–six. You?" But then she stopped, seemed to catch herself short. Her face changed. Even in the dusk he could see that. "I know how old you are because…that was when…." Harriet's knuckles stopped her lips. "You're the same age as my sister Anna. Just a few months younger." She turned her head away. "It was awful."

Parker shifted uneasily on the wall. Talking about family was interesting, but it also made his stomach feel hard and tight. Harriet seemed to be thinking how to explain, whatever it was that was awful. She had gone silent, looking off at the sea. The sun had disappeared, leaving only a splash of brightness toward the rose and grey clouds. For some moments he listened to the shushing sounds of the waves on the new, piled–up sand. And beyond, toward the reef, the dull roar of the surf.

Harriet's voice changed as she said, "You should know, I guess. About my mother." Her voice dropped lower as she went on. "Mama found out about the other one—your mother. Knew that she was hapai. Mama became terribly depressed. Cried all the time. She was hapai herself with Anna. About six months. Us kids, we thought her crying was because she was hapai. We didn't know until later about the other one, carrying at the same time."

"In those days people didn't know about sleeping pills, or sticking your head in a gas oven. Or carbon monoxide from a car. We didn't have those things. Or a high building to jump off. Mama was a farm girl."

"One afternoon I was playing with Sterling—he was next after me—near the ohia bushes back of the house. Mama came out. For some reason, we hid. Didn't want her to see us. But she wasn't looking for us kids. She left the house, walking slowly, crying. Her hair was long, down to her waist. It was loose. I couldn't see her face because of the way her hair hung forward, but I heard her sobs. She was doing something with her hands. I couldn't see what, because of the hair. Then I saw the movement of her right arm, and I recognized it. She was honing a knife. In her hand was the sharpening stone, and the knife papa used to kill a pig. She didn't head for the chicken pen, but for the little woods back of our place.

"Sterling and I understood at the same moment. We ran from our hiding place behind the ohia bushes, silently. Together we threw ourselves on our little mama. I tore the knife out of her fist. I still have a scar on my cheek where the knife whipped me. Sterling grabbed her arms. The three of us went down in a heap on the ground. I believe I hit her a few times. I know I screamed."

"Anna was born a few months later. And we heard the other baby was born four months after that. I was ten years old then." Harriet's face was turned toward him. The expression in her eyes made him put his arm around her shoulders. His own sister.

"All this time," he said, "I was thinkin' like I was the only one had problems."

For some minutes they sat there, silent, getting to know each other.

"Oh, I have...I brought you something from Kamuela."

From the pocket of her shirt she brought out a sheet of notebook paper with blue lines. On it, large, was written a single word, "Aloha!" Parker took the paper, studied it. Underneath were the signatures, some smooth as a schoolteacher's handwriting, some as scratchy as his own. Carefully, he went over the names, each so different the way it was set down.

Pua, soft and rounded, in nice ink. Ikua, like bird tracks, so it could barely be made out. He must be named for the great cowboy. Lala, careful, like a young girl's. Sterling, with a backward slant and a flourish under it. Anna, she could be the principal of a school, with a period at the end. Harriet, a jokey, light-hearted

261

scrawl. Carter, serious, broad strokes, underlined twice. Simon, barely legible, as if done with the stub of a pencil while the paper was balanced on a lawn mower handle, something like that. Marie, just right, was last.

"Two of the boys were lost in the war. I'll tell you about them sometime. And two are in Hilo. I couldn't reach them before I left." Harriet said it apologetically. "But I phoned them. They're all happy. They want to meet you."

They had put down their names so he could start to know them. Had sent their aloha. Tears sprang to Parker's eyes. He continued to hold the paper—this wonderful paper—as if he were still studying it although the writing was blurred for him now.

"Gosh," he said finally, when he could speak again. "Brothers. Sisters. Like that. An' all this time I thought I was alone."

Chapter Thirty-five

"MAYBE IT WAS RAPE," ANNE SUGGESTED. "MAYBE YOUR MOTHER got pregnant because he forced her."

When he told Harriet's story to Anne she at once tried to connect it with why his mother put him in the Salvation Army Home.

"Maybe your father tried to sweet–talk her at first and when that didn't work, he just forced her."

Ideas like that made Parker uncomfortable. He wasn't thinking about those old things so much as what it was like, right now, to have brothers and sisters.

He sat on the lauhala mat, leaning back against the punee. Anne was still stretched out in the hollow of the bed. "Maybe your mother knew your father had a lot of kids, so she didn't want to do it…. Harriet said he had a bad temper."

It was hard to believe that would be necessary. Mostly the beachboys had to run away from girls.

"Maybe she fell in love with him. Then found out he was married. Got mad. That makes sense." Anne sat up, asking agreement. "Every time she looked at you, she saw *him*. So she got mad all over again. She wasn't against *you*. She was against *him*."

Anne's talk about this old stuff made him nervous. He didn't want to think about it. Didn't want to mess up the wonderful new feeling that kept coming back: I'm not alone! He'd be standing on the beach looking up at Leahi, for example, and it would sweep over him like a wave—whoom! Sisters! I've got these sisters! And brothers! As astonished as ever. Or he'd be watching kids play, or a pair of mynah birds scrapping over a bit of cigarette foil, and the feeling would come back. Whoom! Gosh! I've got this family. I'm not just me, alone! He stood, looked out at the afternoon light, pulled on his trunks and jeans. "Let's go somewhere, okay?" He didn't want to hear more about the past. Anne had been in a peculiar mood for several days. Now she couldn't seem to let go of the story about the knife. "Let's go for a ride, get some air."

Anne rose, shook out her panties, stepped into them. "Maybe your mother loved Kealii a lot. Regretted she had a child by another man. Did she love him a lot, do you think?"

"It wasn't like that in those days," Parker said impatiently. "People didn't think about love. That was before the movies. I'm tired of talkin' 'bout it." Until he heard his own voice he hadn't realized how edgy he felt. "C'mon," he said, "I'll take you up to Papakolea, on the hill. Show you where the Hawaiians have to live now. Poor things, shoved up there, away from the sea."

But as he drove her up Makiki Heights Anne hadn't the right reaction at all. "It's cool up here. And the view is gorgeous. An Arabian prince couldn't buy anything better."

"You don' understand," Parker protested. "It's not the sea. You can' eat a view. Hawaiians need the sea."

Anne pointed out elegant homes, splendid gates, and driveways sweeping back to mansions. "They're living up here with the rich people!" she insisted.

"That don' help the Hawaiians."

"The settlement is shabby," Anne agreed as they drove through Papakolea. "The houses aren't much to look at. But they're as good as those down on Kalia Road. Better!"

Parker shook his head. Anne still had a lot of work to be done on her. Yesterday she wanted to use a hammer at night. Close a crate for her books.

He swung the jeep up the Tantalus–Round Top road to its highest point. Anne wanted to watch the end of the day. See the city's lights come on.

He turned off the road at the lookout point of the great bluff, the parking area marked by a guard rail. They got out and walked to the grassy slope. "You see how far it is to the beach?"

"There's the Moana." Anne pointed far to the left. "And the Royal. Queening it over the palm grove."

Parker studied the landscape before them, dimming in the twilight.

"The pink and white queens of Waikiki. My sweet Waikiki queens."

Why should she sound unhappy about that?

"You can' see the Halekulani or the Niumalu from here.

They're tuck' down in the greenery." At the Halekulani guests still gathered plumerias from the trees by their cottages for leis. The Halekulani was family owned.

Anne's eyes combed the view as if something were about to escape. "And there's the Aloha Tower." Pointing to the right, to the slim spike with the clock at the head of the harbor. "I'll never forget the Aloha Tower."

She sure was talking funny. He didn't like to see Anne sad. "You know the story on Punchbowl?" he blundered. Looking over at Diamond Head's smaller twin, landlocked, its brow rising toward the sea.

"You mean the military cemetery?"

"No. Puowaina. That's what the ol' Hawaiians used to call it. They made human sacrifices there."

"You know I don't like to hear about such things." Anne threw him a glance of reproach. "I prefer to think of the Hawaiians as a noble people." She turned her back on Punchbowl.

The land spread in repose around them, generous and kind as an open palm. A wedge of darkness against the horizon meant a storm far out in the Pacific, but before them the sea lay harmless as a sheet of wrinkled tinfoil. At their feet, sections at a time, the street lights sprang on. Parker put his arm around Anne's waist. The town prickled into new life with strings of golden points.

"The lights go off and on in Waikiki."

"The palm fronds movin' aroun' hide 'em."

Diamond Head on the end was dark as a fortress, heaped up against invaders from the sea.

"There's the Ala Wai, that long straight line of lights."

A gust of warm rain from the Koolaus drifted over them, not enough to make them move. It dimmed the lights below in Makiki for a moment then dispersed toward the harbor. Anne stood within his arm as quiet as if she weren't there.

"Wassa matta, my wahine?" he asked finally. "You got sumthin' on you' mind?"

"It's so beautiful," she said, which was no answer at all.

Around them, on the grassy slopes, night insects had begun to shrill. It would soon be ginger season again. He would bring Anne up here to cut a few stalks of glorious white ginger.

"You know what I've learned in Hawaii? Hawaiians don't just live their lives. They *love* them. They seem to love every minute, every twig, every flower. I think that's why they're so generous. They just can't resist sharing their riches with others."

"M'yeah. You sure talkin' strange tonight."

"Look at King Street, and Beretania." Parallel strings of moving car lights melted into puddles of brightness where shops were dense, in McCully and Moiliili. There was a cluster of brightness where Kalakaua crossed Kapiolani at Kau Kau Korner.

"My beautiful Honolulu! I want to hold every speck of it close."

Why was she talking like this? He'd bring her back whenever she wanted.

"San Francisco has more lights. Taller buildings. Lots more lights. More people. More everything."

She looked out at the ocean's horizon, barely visible against the dark blue sky, as if to see lights on another shore.

"I didn' know you liked it so much. We kin come back. You jus' tell me."

"I know." She sounded sadder than ever.

Whatever could be the matter? She couldn't be pregnant. He'd been so careful. And there was nothing wrong between them. They were perfectly happy together. Perfectly matched in every way.

"Oh, Keoni..." She turned into his arms, buried her nose in the curve of his shoulder. At that moment he too needed to feel her close. Some awful knowledge warning him.

"What is it, ei nei, my baby?"

"I don't know how to tell you."

"You kin tell me anything." How could she doubt that? He pressed her body, stiff with whatever she was holding in.

"It's...Oh, Keoni!" Her voice was faint, as if from a great distance. In the heartbeat before she said it, he knew.

"I'm leaving."

"You goin' somewhere?" he forced himself to say after a moment. People took trips.

"The mainland."

People went to the mainland. Anne came from there. It was natural, possibly, to take a trip to the mainland.

"Why? Why you goin' there?" She'd be back when she'd taken care of whatever it was.

Anne drew away from him. Where she had been pressed, the air was cold on his chest and neck.

"To work," she said quietly.

Anne was sick or something. Even before this evening he thought she did things that were peculiar. Like putting all those books in a crate. What she did with her books didn't interest him, but he could see how that related. Now she was talking crazy.

"You could work here," he said, being sensible in spite of her craziness.

"No, I'm going back."

Back. The insects shrilled. On a road below them the lights of a car swung around a curve. Back. It was the worst word he'd ever heard in his life. The hill seemed to have become mushy under him. Strangely, his voice continued to work. He muttered, "You' not goin' back." Turning from her he walked to the post of the guard rail.

Anne came to him. "Keoni." She put her arms around him from behind. "Keoni, I told you I came for a year. D'you remember that? Remember, at Hanauma, the first time we kissed? I told you then."

"That was before you had me. Ev'thin' changed after that."

Anne's cheek made a warm spot between his shoulder blades. "I know, sweetheart. I know. I wanted to warn you. But then I didn't want to hurt you. I just couldn't talk about it."

"You even got mad when Mrs. Randal said you was goin' to leave."

"I know. I know."

"Made me leave her place on account of it."

"I know." Anne slid around to hold him face to face.

He wanted to push her away. As if he could shove away this horrible new feeling.

"You been drinkin'?" he asked, although he knew she hadn't. She smelled the same as always, of the Jergens lotion she often put on her hands and face before she left the cottage. And mixed with that fragrance, the scent of the roots of her hair. The scent that more than any other meant Anne to him. It was the scent he fell asleep with, the essence of their hours of sleep together. It meant safety, contentment, preciousness. The scent of Anne was the same, she had not been drinking.

"I'm so sorry, Keoni." Her voice creaked.

If she cried he would jump in the jeep and drive off without her. He did not know what violence he was going to commit if she kept on like this.

"Why you sayin' these things?" he yelled, shaking loose of her. "*Why?*"

Her head was down, contrite, in front of him. "Please Keoni. Don't be so mad. I had to tell you."

"You don' have to say this kind of rubbish. D'you know how it makes me *feel*?"

"I know, sweetheart." Trying to nuzzle his shoulder.

He shrugged her off as if her touch would contaminate him. "Then cut it out b'fore I get really mad."

She kept her head down, waiting. Her silence sawed at him. He seized her hair, pulled it back so it tipped her chin up. "What's got into you? I wanna know."

"Keoni, you're hurting...."

Her words commanded his hand more than he did. He stopped pulling, but he did not let go of her hair. "What's makin' you change like this?"

"I have to go back. Listen to me, Keoni! Please try. I ran away from my old life. Now I have to go back...."

"No, you don'! You' life is here, with me."

"I *have* to, Keoni! It's time for me to go back."

"What kinda time is that?" Every time she opened her mouth he felt like killing something.

"Ei nei,..." Anne pleaded.

He gave her hair a yank that threw her to her knees. "You' not goin' back," he yelled as he walked away. "You' not goin' back."

A few minutes later the lights of a car swung around the curve of the lookout. The car's occupants came upon a strange scene. A slender girl in a muumuu leaned on a jeep, weeping, while nearby a guard rail lay smashed and twisted. A madman, for no reason at all, was trying to pull one of the posts out of the ground.

Chapter Thirty-six

THE NATATORIUM WAS BEING READIED FOR THE A.A.U. MEET.
Already the swimmers' lanes were strung with blue and
white floats. A banner announcing the event on Tuesday afternoon hung across the golden arch over the entrance, and colored
pennants snapped in the trades, over the grandstands. The sports
sections of both daily newspapers carried articles about the leading contenders in the various men's and women's events. Ford
Konno and Miriam Manuwai were the favorites. Most of Waikiki
would witness the occasion.

At Kuhio Beach Parker tramped from one end to the other in
the sumptuous fresh sand, rarely speaking to people, lost in his
own black thoughts. Diamond Head wore a robe of tender green
after the showers of winter. The sky changed frequently. One moment the clouds were a luminous fairyland of lather, the next
they had turned to thunderheads of roiling grey. Sometimes it
rained and cleared in five minutes. The surf was lazy. There
hadn't been a good set of waves in weeks. The Lagoon crowd
was grumpy, bored.

Parker hadn't seen Sunshine since his talk with Kanekini.
Mercifully, word had been left at the Natatorium for Sunshine to
report to Kanekini's office the following Friday, when the boys
trained. That morning Parker told the group that a reorganiza-
tion was going on, and that Sunshine would be handling certain
parts of the expanding Beach Safety Program instead of standing
guard at the Halekulani. The boys were very interested to hear
about the mobile rescue unit, the new van. Parker was glad to tell
them about the new van.

But at work he was no longer the lifeguard he had been. He
stared at the sea without seeing the swimmers. Anne had told
him, "I still have twenty–nine days. Sweetheart, that's almost a
month!"

"A month!" He could have stamped on it to show his con-
tempt.

"It's more than most people have. Keoni, think of all the

people who have only ten days before they go back on the *Lurline.*"

"You goin' on the *Lurline?*" The words stabbing him as he said them.

"Yes."

At that, he'd had to give up. More than any reason for going back she'd offered, that detail maimed him. Deprived him of resistance to the idea as truth. With the word *Lurline* he had to accept that she meant it, that she was going to go.

He stood with one foot propped on the stone wall staring out at the reef. Not looking at the waves or surfers, just staring. He found himself doing that a lot. Recovering, he noticed the Filipino–Hawaiian kid he'd seen earlier bringing coral in again. Several times he'd seen him with his inner tube floating the basin of grey coral heads. He came trudging through the shallows, pulling the tube near to where Parker stood. Parker still thought the kid should be in school, although he had to admit he was a good worker. On an impulse Parker said, "Whatcha gonna do with all that coral, son?" Knowing very well he was going to sell it. Coral was a big item with the curio shops nowadays.

Suddenly, close up as he was, he recognized the boy. He was the skinny kid who had come for him the day the little boat overturned. He was padded with ten more pounds, it looked like, and grown some too. His face was filled out and handsome. The difference was a pleasure to see.

"I get paid," the kid grinned. Recognizing him too, probably. "The other lifeguard, Sunshine, pays me."

"Sunshine?" Parker's jaw dropped.

"He's got his own business. He buys all we can bring him."

"He *does?*"

Parker experienced a burst of fury like nothing he could remember. He could not have said why. Didn't need to know why. Something in the very bottom of his being, at a flash point, revolted. Sunshine, a city–county employee making money off of kids who ought to be in school! It was wrong, wrong, wrong, and never mind why. If his life had been on the line for it, Parker could not have been more incensed.

Sunshine hadn't been around the Lagoon in a long time, but

Parker knew he would be at the Natatorium the afternoon of the A.A.U. meet and he laid for him.

❂   ❂

Sunshine, a head taller than most of the people around him, was highly visible at the meet. Looking like a Polynesian movie star with his proud neck and Ipana grin, he walked around the pool, waved to people in the bleachers, was constantly on the move. It wasn't until three–fourths of the events were over that Parker saw Sunshine head to the lifeguards' room and hurried after him.

Parker had been drinking beer all afternoon, enjoying his rage, looking forward to the moment when his fist would connect with Sunshine's face. At last he had a target for the fury that had been building so long. Sunshine and his pretty face! Sunshine and his wahines! Sunshine and his gold cross, acting like a Catholic! Sunshine and his hoomalimali with the tourists and worst of all with a sick man, Kanekini! And now Sunshine making money off of beach kids! Parker needed no more. Just a few minutes alone with Sunshine.

He'd left word, in fact, with Hiro and others that he was looking for Sunshine, but Sunshine, maybe guessing something was up, had stayed away.

Parker stood in the single doorway to the small concrete–walled room where the boys dressed and left their gear. Outside a race was on, the crowd was yelling. Parker had Sunshine to himself.

❂   ❂

Moments later, in line of duty, Ellings hurried to the guards' room, followed by Freitas.

"Stop it!" Ellings yelled, walloping Parker on a pretense of separating them.

"You not s'pose to fight!" Freitas hollered, lacing into Sunshine.

It was too enjoyable to keep cooped up in the narrow dressing room.

Punctuating their shouts with blows, they managed to move out the door onto the cement walk surrounding the pool. Here, where there was toehold space, their actions took on more handsome dimensions.

Almost immediately several envious bystanders joined in. Parker was in the thick of it when, flailing like a ball of snakes, half a dozen of them pitched off the cement walk and into the water. A group of Lagoon regulars loafed nearby. Forgetting the race that was in progress, whooping with joy, they threw themselves in too. Within seconds twenty–five or thirty bodies were engaged. Kamehameha himself would have enjoyed it. Quickly the action spread. Dozens became part of the fray, in the water and out, skirmishes igniting spontaneously on the concrete walkway of the pool's mauka side and seeping upwards into the stands.

At the ewa end of the pool where the two hundred women's freestyle meter race was about to finish, fans leapt to their feet, shouting encouragement at the furiously battling swimmers. On the Diamond Head end of the pool, fans leapt to their feet shouting with delight at the carnage spreading in their midst. The roar from the Natatorium could be heard in the valleys. The race ended as the seven women swimmers swept magnificently to the finish line, one clearly in the lead, the others in a ragged row behind her. The judges compared times. During the lull, the ewa crowd noticed the mayhem at the far end of the pool. At once spectator sports lost their interest. Wasting no time on jealousy of those with a head start, fans seized whatever was useful at hand and hurled themselves into the fray. Pillows, parasols and thongs were wielded. Women who detested one another on sight crossed aisles to pull each others' hair. Spectators with no one in particular to attack took a look at whoever was nearby and stepped back to slug gloriously.

Polly Kealii tied a knot in a towel, ran to the edge of the pool and smacked Parker's head whenever he emerged within reach. She was heaved, shrilling, into the water, but this was no loss. She found plenty to do there with a member of her music group who always played too slow.

At the judges' stand, Mrs. Fullard–Leo, who had presided over every A.A.U. event since Duke won his first race in the slip between Pier Five and Pier Six, took the microphone. Chin high, bosom dauntless against the trades, she announced that Miriam Manuwai had won the women's two hundred meter freestyle, shaving four–fifths of a second off the national record as she did so. Almost no one heard her.

Observing what seemed to be a peak in the pool at the far end where bodies were piling up on the ropes, Mrs. Fullard–Leo suggested that celebrations over the triumph be confined to land. When her words went unheeded, she turned up the loud speakers and graciously reminded those present that although feelings naturally ran high with such thrilling news, another event was about to be called. It never took place.

Some mischievous soul called the cops. A squad of bruisers appeared, grinning. They blew whistles, between grins, and shuffled around the edge of the pool, clobbering one wretch here, extracting another from the water there. It was the best scene they'd been hailed to in years. A number of them wound up in the pool where, stripping off their identifying uniforms, they were enabled, democratically, to enjoy themselves like the rest.

A coconut was thrown at someone in the pool. It was seized and thrown again. More coconuts were brought in and tossed about. The Samoans got into a brawl of their own and the sound of their smashing each other was like the felling of great trees.

The pool no longer seemed to contain water, only a morass of heaving, shrieking humanity. The bleachers seethed like an ant-hill. Shopkeepers clobbered beachboys, journalists mixed it up with politicians, teachers settled scores with bureaucrats, and a representative of the Hawaii Tourist Bureau fled for his life. A lot of people looked around for the Bellinghams.

In the center of the mauka grandstand, low, near the pool's edge, the band of McKinley High School had been installed to add pep and class to the event. No less than anyone, its members had responded to the exhilarating scene. Flailing one another with their metal racks, they provided fans who cared to watch tonic glimpses of youth in action. The bandmaster eased his feelings on the first trombone. Nowhere was the end in sight.

Then an extraordinary event took place. Perhaps in answer to the summons of Pele, the twelve dark winds of Ka–ne, long lost in the mysterious reaches of Po, lifted. Out past Diamond Head, the *Matsonia*, departing, gave a last mournful salute. As the bandmaster raised a heavy shoe, his sensitive ears, that is to say, his heart, was touched. His expression of glee was replaced by something else. He had received a message from the highest god of all, Ku, procreator from slime, of the universe.

Rising to full height the bandmaster shouted into the blitzkrieg of scores flying around him.

"Students!" he roared. "Students! Listen! We will now play...'Aloha Oe!'"

At the sound of his authoritative voice the nearest members of the well–trained group ceased, in mid–air, whatever they were doing. The three divine syllables, A–lo–ha, worked their magic. Faces changed. A transformation took place as the command seeped into dazed and reckless adolescent minds. Arms poised in attack stretched, instead, into movements of peace. "Aloha?" they murmured among themselves. Then, "Goodness! 'Aloha Oe!'"

"E flat!" the bandmaster ordered imperiously.

"Gee!" the first trumpet was heard to mutter. "The majestic key of E flat!" A few of the musicians rolled their eyes. But they put down their chairs and other weapons, seated themselves and picked up their instruments.

The bandmaster lifted his baton. A calm like a baby blanket settled over the McKinley High School Band. The drummer led with a mighty, preliminary roll which, however, almost no one in the stands heard. The bandmaster raised his chin. His arm swept downward in a regal arc.

Few of the embattled crowd heard the first musical phrases. But gradually, as the din near the band was subdued, more and more combatants ceased their furies to listen. In the pool, too, the cries and splashing began to lessen as the spell of the song crept, irresistibly, into the battlers' hearts.

The roiling waters calmed, the crashing of jaws against fists and of heads against feet subsided.

Over the golden wall of the Natatorium the nostalgic notes lifted on the trades. The harmonies of the spheres were evoked. Sweetly sounded the transcending plaint and farewell to love.

In amazement and disbelief the combatants glanced about at one another. How could it be? Harsh looks and trickles of blood in their own alohaland? What was this all about? Heads drooping, they wiped their eyes and cuts. Shamefacedly they rubbed each other's bruises. Before them, in truth, they saw only the aloha faces of family, neighbors, friends. Dragging one another from the pool, they embraced. The roaring dwindled to a few hoarse cries and the slapping of churned waters against the sides of the pool. Abandoning themselves to the bliss of reconciliation, foes saluted, comforted each other. Smiles graced lips. Saimin was suggested, and different colors of shave ice.

In the slow pace of deep fulfillment, murmuring among themselves, the now weary crowd poured outward through the golden arch of the Natatorium's gate. Kapiolani Park welcomed them, there to rest and contemplate the day's glories.

Finally the sun dropped behind the pool's makai wall and the Natatorium lay empty and still. Within the blue and white roped lanes several pieces of police attire drifted, and one or two coconuts bobbed.

❂   ❂

Next day the *Advertiser* reported that the trimming of four–fifths of a second off the national record for the two hundred meter women's freestyle had produced a pandemonium such as had never been seen at an A.A.U. meet. Miriam Manuwai was a national heroine. Hawaii had done it again. Hawaii no ka oi. Hawaii supported, loved its swimmers as did no other community in the world. The celebration had produced some losses, it was confessed. Several teeth were found on the concrete walkway.

But no one tried to deny that at least three years' worth of hostilities had been purged in the marvelous melee. Most of

Waikiki had taken part before it was over. Even the old haole man who drank vanilla in his tomato juice at the Lagoon got in a few good whacks with his cane before he was knocked out. Next day he said "Howzzit" to half a dozen people when he limped in. He'd managed to deal Hike a fierce one before he himself went down.

Parker and Sunshine were never charged. In fact they felt so good afterwards that they apologized to each other and Sunshine returned Parker's red and gold shirt, starched.

It had to be admitted: a lot of bad feelings got cleaned up in that spectacular event and it was remembered with much nostalgia. Noting this, someone at the Tourist Bureau proposed staging such a jubilee every year, charging the visitors hefty admission fees to watch.

"New Orleans has its Mardi Gras, we could have our own Carnival of Aloha," he crowed.

Old–timers, wiping their eyes, scoffed at this. Said it could never be duplicated. Such joys were delivered only by the gods.

For years it was talked about, going down in Hawaiian history as **The Great Aloha Bash.**

But Parker's griefs were not ended. In three weeks Anne would leave.

Chapter Thirty-seven

PARKER LAY ON THE BED IN HIS LITTLE ROOM AND STARED AT THE ceiling. He smoked constantly these days. Beside the bed were several empty bottles of Primo beer. He raised the last to his lips and took a long swig. On the radio he'd borrowed from Pekuela, Hawaiian music promised the sweetness that life could hold.

When Bill Akamahou came on with "Hawaiian Cowboy," Parker smashed the radio off, flopped onto his stomach. Raking over in his mind for the hundredth time what to do about Anne. Convinced, now, she meant what she said. Unable to see yet how to combat this insanity. Every time he was with her he started off trying to be normal, and nice, but within minutes he was talking about it again, back to bitter charges.

"You're not leavin'," he'd said yesterday afternoon on the beach. Laying it out like an order, his voice ragged with all he was holding in.

Anne said nothing, tightening the corners of her mouth as though she wouldn't try to match him with words. She sat beside him, facing the sea, clasping her knees.

"You belong here. You love me. You said you did, at least," he accused.

"I do. I do." She threw her arms around his shoulders before he could get out of the way although he was starved for the feel of her.

"I'm workin'," he reproved her. He disengaged himself, stern.

"I'm trying to make you understand. I do love you. But that doesn't change the fact that I have to go back."

"It's you thass' changin' things. Ev'thing was fine till you got this crazy idea."

"I'm sorry," she said humbly. "Keoni. I don't want to hurt you. My love. I don't want to leave you. I don't know how I'll find the strength."

"Stop tryin'. We'll go back to how we was. Howzzit!" he

greeted a haole old-timer in faded orange trunks, tramping through the sand.

"And I love Hawaii so much...." She was watching the wavelets make little rushes at the shore. Beyond the pale green shallows the turquoise waters blazed, and further out the spangled cobalt sea tossed reflections of the sun. "My Hawaii...." Tears sprang to her eyes.

Parker scowled. Dumb lovey talk. Haole words.

"I don't know how I'll be able to bear it." Anne wiped her cheeks. "Not to be able to see Leahi every day." She raised her eyes to Diamond Head, on their left. "The beach. These colors...." Her hand toward the jewel tones of the sea. "The local people...."

Socks and Kunia nearby were putting on an act for a tourist in a skimpy two-piece suit called a bikini.

"Aloha!" Socks saluted.

"What's that?" Kunia smartmouthed him.

"I dunno." Socks pulled a face of innocence. "It's a kind of shirt, I think. Mostly for men."

Anne began to laugh through her tears. "Local talk. Howzzit!" she greeted the two as they tromped past.

A drone in the sky to the right signaled a plane coming from ewa way. Parker glanced up, quickly looked away. But Anne watched as it crossed from right to left before them.

"Every time I see a plane tip its wings to Leahi, I get a catch in my heart," she said. More tears coming. "It's so beautiful, to show you love Diamond Head, like that."

Parker ignored the ground glass in his stomach. "You cryin' an' you still wanna go." He gave a contemptuous hoot. "I thought haoles was s'pose to be smart."

"Don't call me a haole," Anne wailed. She turned and threw herself face down on her arms in the sand.

"You' actin' like one."

"Next you'll be saying I'm a lousy haole," Anne accused, her voice muffled beneath her arms.

She had turned it around. Now she was making him the one who was wrong. He shouldn't even be sitting here on the beach with her while he was on duty. He still had two hours until he was off.

"You was gettin' some sense until this came along," he back-tracked.

Anne lifted her head, looked at him. Injured but forgiving.

"I have to walk now," he told her, getting to his feet.

"Will you come over tonight? I bought a slab of tchar siu. We can have tchar siu and poi."

"Maybe," he said. Feeling trapped. Determined not to be bought off so easily, but not sure he could stand the evening alone. Before she could pin him down he moved across the sand.

Some nights he stayed away. Partly to make a point, partly because he was so miserable while he was with her that his beer and cigarettes seemed like the easy way out. He'd tried going to the fights with Kunia one night after they'd lifted weights but his heart wasn't in it.

Lying on his bed, listening to the radio, he sometimes imagined scenes which would make Anne sorry, make her change her mind. He saved the son or daughter of one of the Big Five. The mayor himself pinned on the medal. There was a tidal wave and he rescued scores of victims. He discovered a treasure chest that had been carelessly lost in the reef at Waikiki and laid buckets of gold coins at Anne's feet. Punchbowl erupted, the lava wiping out downtown Honolulu. He swam Anne to safety, far out at sea. Could he make Anne jealous? He would rescue a beautiful girl who would cover his face with kisses of gratitude. Anne would step in and lead him away, never to let go of him again. Unfortunately, his real life remained the same.

Confused, numb, angry, and for the first time in his life, secretive, Parker spent hours alone in his little room. He nursed his wounds from the Aloha Bash. They comforted him. He had a dislocated finger, some knots on his head, a swollen ear and a number of cuts on his body. His jaw ached for days. Sunshine hadn't done badly by him. Sunshine enjoyed a fight as much as anyone.

The Lagoon was a walking field ward after the meet. Lacerations and lumps honored nearly everyone, male and female. Bruised and stitched, tapes and slings in evidence, the participants sprawled happily in chairs under the umbrellas and reviewed many times an event which in their sense of history ranked with Pearl Harbor.

Anne hadn't gone to the meet because she was mad at Parker for comparing her with Polly. He'd said she was just as dumb. Parker wished Anne could have seen him fighting Sunshine. That would have impressed her. Sunshine was inches taller and with a longer reach. But Sunshine, he had a feeling, would never forget their first thirty seconds together. Of course things got confused immediately afterwards when Ellings and Freitas, or whoever it was, came in and mixed it up with them. But Anne would have seen a real fighter in action. She would have known why the Kakaako Wharf Rats were so respected, if she'd seen him then.

❁   ❁

In her cottage once Parker seized Anne roughly. "I won't let you go. You belong here, with me. You said so, *you*."

"True. But now I'm going back."

"No, you not!"

"Keoni, I'm warning you." She tried to pull from him.

"Warnin', nothin'."

"You'd better not try to stop me."

"You better not try to go."

They glared at each other, tense as cats. Then Anne slumped against his pull. She turned her head away, sighed. "Keoni, Keoni. What can I say to make you understand? It's my life. I can go if I please."

"That's not the Hawaiian way. This is Hawaii. I'm Hawaiian."

She looked hard at him, at that, as if he'd said something important. But her plans didn't change.

❁   ❁

As his mind ranged morbidly over the things he could do in the face of Anne's stubbornness, it occurred to Parker that he could, one day after work, swim out to the reef and just keep going. He studied the late afternoon horizon with its descending globe of the sun, and thought of how kind it would be out there beyond human voices, beyond human cruelties. He thought of the girl who had died in his arms in the failed rescue. Was she at peace now, more at peace than if she'd learned to swim? And Wipeout? Had he chosen the right way, after all?

On account of the kids Parker did not consider taking his own life with great seriousness. Besides, swimming out beyond the reef seemed to lack some important dramatic elements. His body probably would never be found so Anne would be unable to throw herself upon him with the expressions of grief he would like to hear. Also, he doubted he could drown if he wanted to. He might perish after some days from the cold, and from lack of food, but he could not imagine, even in a storm that tossed him like a balsa chip, not being pillowed by the sea. Besides, with his kind of luck, if he did get into difficulty out there, it would be just like a shark or dolphin to come and carry him into shore.

❂   ❂

Parker developed pains in his body. He'd never had anything like them before. At first he connected them with his fight. But the pain was so random—turning up in his head one hour, in his knee another, in his back that night—he knew it was not an injury from the fight. Besides, the pains resulting from fights seemed almost enjoyable, delicious reminders of some of his best moments. This pain, which often hit him in the chest, shortening his breath, was an enemy. For the first time pain was an intrusion, like a warning signal.

One night when he couldn't sleep for the thoughts and pains and the terrible music on Pek's radio, and the thumps and noises in the other parts of the house, he pulled on his jeans, stuffed his feet into his slippers and headed for the beach. Here he was, he thought as he trudged along Koa, with his own room, his jeep paid off, a raise on his job, and he was headed for the beach at midnight just like the old days when he had no place to sleep but on the sand between the canoes.

Making for Kuhio out of sheer habit, he took Liliuokalani. He passed the corner where he'd seen Anne in her white nightdress, trailing her pikake scent. He wished they hadn't met. He might as well wish he hadn't been born.

On the beach, stumping in the thick sand, he turned, as he always did, to look at Diamond Head, serene and enduring on the left. Overhead the cozy stars clustered in the kind bowl of the sky. Before him rolled the sea, stern but comforting. He walked down to the water's edge, listened to the hiss of the wet sand at his feet, then to the muted roar of the surf over by the Elk's Club. His heart squeezing reminded him the tide was going out.

Healing his eyes with the rough outline of Diamond Head, he thought of how the Old Ones had known and honored every ridge and knoll. Given every notch in the coast its own name. Mystery and meaning, for them, were everywhere.

It was then the idea came to him, with a shock, not at all pleasing, that perhaps other people—in the states, for example, felt the same about their land as he did about Hawaii. That they might love and name their hills and waters, look at them each day too. The idea seemed unlikely at first, given that they did not have the things he had to look at. But there was a certain logic to the thought that whatever you had was what you liked.

And then the thought struck him that there might be a mountain, hills, a bay that Anne loved before she came to Hawaii. She never talked about San Francisco. Could sights exist that she was longing to see? After a year away, was she as starved for the sight of her land as he would be for Waikiki?

Parker glanced toward the range of the Koolaus. Over Manoa Valley, where it so often rained, a quarter moon had brought forth an arch of colors against the dark blue sky. Chief among the colors—he couldn't help but notice the way it dominated the top of the arc—was the red. This signified that his aumakua was watching him. Since he had seen it, since he had been brought from his bed to see this beloved vision of the night, it was a sign that the red eye of his aumakua was upon him. Every Hawaiian had an aumakua. What form his took—fish, animal or bird—he wasn't sure, as he hadn't had a dramatic encounter with it, as some people had. But his aumakua was nearby, now. In his grief at this moment he was being observed.

With a shiver Parker turned, retraced his steps toward his

room, passing again where he had met Anne, trailing her scent, in white. Was she asleep tonight, peaceful, in the hollow that had once been his? How could he let her go? It was impossible. How could he stop her?

Every day half a dozen wicked schemes poisoned his mind. He would kidnap her. He would get her too drunk to leave. Or drug her with sleeping pills. He'd steal her *Lurline* ticket. Run off with her luggage at the last minute. Dynamite the ship.

Madnesses like these were again scuttling through his brain when he heard the low, whirring call of a pueo, an owl. Several of them lived in this neighborhood of Waikiki. Often he listened with a kind of smile in his chest to their haunting cries. Even before Anne, he'd never felt lonely at night because of them, knowing they were there, alert, surveying their gentle domain of darkness. And now, just when he was thinking he should be in Kaneohe himself, here came this healing, muffled cry, repeated several times, as if it were just for him.

By the time Parker reached the sprawling old mansion on Koa a completely new idea had taken him. Not what he *could* do, at this terrible time, but what he *should* do. What would be the correct thing. How to be up to the mark.

This put such a different cast on how he should face Anne's departure that he had to sit down on the wooden front steps just to get used to it. Everything he'd been thinking until now was turned around. As if there might be a meaning beyond the immediate drama of the event. A rule, or a set of rules, against which he was being tested. Not maliciously. Just tested. To see where he was, as a man. Something like the tests Pele gave people.

Parker considered what—with the best of intentions—he'd done until now, for Kanekini, for Anne. Not much came to mind.

The Old Ones, it seemed to Parker, were happier than people today. Not because their lives were easy. No. Certainly they had their griefs and pains. They lost loved ones, died in battle. But they were happy because they found meaning in their lives. It seemed to him that their acts had more feelings, and therefore more meaning.

He remembered the story of a chief, beloved by his people, who suffered terrible pains in his chest. The people grieved, the kahuna chanted, made drinks of herbs, but the pain persisted. One of the chief's warriors came to him and offered to have a stake driven through his own heart, to release the chief's pain.

In the days of the Old Ones, men knew how to love, and die. Compared to such sacrifices, the paltriness of his own life made Parker ashamed. Now he was caught in this agonizing test. He couldn't let Anne go. There had to be a solution. It seemed almost within his grasp.

Chapter Thirty-eight

WITH THE BOYS' KOKUA PARKER HAD ALL HE NEEDED. HE SURveyed himself in his room's speckled mirror and saw a new man.

The one thing not visible in the mirror was his shoes. But he didn't even have to glance down to be aware of them, shiny black leather with toes as round as a light bulb. Squidley had contributed the shoes. Black socks went with them. Rayon, they had a few runs from being stretched over thick luau feet but they matched the shoes nicely.

The black twill pants he'd got from Melvin's brother who was a bus driver for the Honolulu Rapid Transit. But most people probably wouldn't guess that. Pekuela, who swore he would never again under any circumstances allow himself to be wheedled into going up to the mainland, had given him a nice camel's hair jacket. It showed off Parker's dark skin to perfection.

The aloha shirt of red, green and gold, a torch ginger pattern, was his own, replacing the one he thought he'd lost to Sunshine. It didn't match the other clothes, Parker realized. But then he wasn't trying to look like a mainlander. He was a Hawaiian *going* to the mainland. *Ready* for the mainland. That was the effect he wanted to achieve and he didn't see how it could be much better. Later, if he needed a necktie—he'd heard that special care was needed with neckties—he'd ask Anne to help him get one that would be nice. He had no idea how to match a necktie with a shirt of red, green and gold.

Studying himself, Parker wondered if he should have a hat. In winter, when it was cold, apparently people wore hats. The mirror reflected his hair combed smooth, face solemn but ready. His shoulders looked nice in the jacket even if the sleeves were a little long. Here was a man of decision. A man ready to take on a new destiny. Parker had to smile at the thought of how Anne would react. How, at a glance, she would understand. With kisses and maybe even tears they would plan their new future together. The shoes, which at first had seemed too big on his feet now began to rub in a few places. But joyful in his vision of what was to come, he was ready to bear that. Feeling rather conspicuous, holding his arms slightly away from his sides so as not to use up the jacket, Parker set out for Anne's cottage.

❂   ❂

Anne's back was to him as he stepped through the open door. He hardly recognized the room, it was so strewn with unfamiliar objects, mostly clothes he'd never seen. A suitcase stood open on one punee. Nearby was a dark grey wool jacket and skirt. Anne wore a lighter grey silk blouse with long sleeves, a string of pearls, and spiky grey suede pumps. Parrot green shorts revealing bare, tan legs completed the odd look. She was holding up a lilac–colored raincoat that had a belt to tie it with, like a bathrobe. Magazines lay about, open to pictures of ladies in fancy clothes.

"Ei nei!" he announced his arrival.

"I'm so mad!" Anne said without turning around or greeting him. "These mainland colors look just terrible with my tan. And worse yet, they've gone out of style already. There's a new shape...." She turned and saw him. "Oh, my God!"

"It's me!" he grinned.

"Wherever did you get...those clothes?"

"The boys," he said modestly. Trying not to smile too much. "Pek, Melvin's brother, them."

"What? Oh, no, Keoni. No!"

He had expected her to be astonished. He had not expected her to cry 'No' at the sight of him, although his heart had beaten hard as he walked down Liliuokalani Avenue. She was very surprised, of course. And perhaps she preferred him in his usual things, his lifeguard's tee shirt and trunks. The new clothes would take getting used to. And the new man, who was ready for quite a different future on the mainland. With her.

"Are you going to a funeral, or what? But why are you wearing that jacket? I hardly recognized you," she seemed to be short of breath. "Your face looks...so dark, or something."

"Din't recognize me, huh? How d'ja like it?" He gave himself

287

the privilege of pulling a little on the lapels, cocking an eyebrow. Turned around to let her have the full effect. "Not bad, eh? I'm ready!"

"Ready? For what?"

"The same thing you are," he teased. He walked over and patted the shorts, so outlandish with the silky grey shirt. "Is that a new mainland style, shorts with those things? You wear a hat with that too?" He picked up a grey felt pillbox with a veil, lying on a pile of silky underthings. "Try it on. I never seen you in a hat before." Laughing, making a joke of the whole thing.

Then he saw that under the color Anne had acquired in the past year, a rosy tan which he found so nice on her, she'd gone a dead white. For a moment he thought she was going to faint.

He put out his hand, drew her into his arms. The jacket would feel nice, he was sure.

"D'jou think you kin get used to seein' me like this?" he asked gently. Not wanting to put too much on her all at once.

"No, no, no. Keoni! You've got it all wrong!"

"Wrong! How wrong?" The feeling he'd been pushing aside with all these 'no's' was now beyond ignoring. "I thought you'd be happy," he insisted. "Don't you know what it means?" He rushed ahead, not trusting her to see it right on her own. "It means that I'm goin' back with you. It means we won't be separated after all. I won' let you leave me jus' because you gotta leave Hawaii." The joy of what he'd prepared pushed him ahead. "I change'. Now I see things different. I was selfish, wantin' you to stay. You have your place that you love, too, on the mainland. Thass' normal. I'll learn to love San Francisco the way you love Hawaii." He rattled on, making it sound easy so she wouldn't see it as too much of a sacrifice on his part. After all she'd given up for him. "I heard they got some nice hills there, and a bay. And nice people. Orientals. I heard they got a Chinatown. That'll make it easier for me when I get tired of white faces...."

Anne pulled away, dropped onto the punee, leaning against its wall cushions. Her eyes were closed, her face stricken.

"I got fifty dollars saved," he rushed on, to convince her, make it easy. "I'll fin' a job quick 'cause I'll do anything. I'll work in a factory, whatever they got. I kin handle explosives—I did that before—or chemicals—anything they want. So we can be together. We'll do fine. You'll see."

Tears had begun to slip from beneath Anne's closed lids. They ran down her cheeks. "You can't.... Oh, Keoni!" Her pink–rimmed eyes opened, tried to fix him. "The mainland isn't for you. I can't let you...." She leaned on her knees and began to sob. "It's too much. Oh, it's just too much."

"It's not too much. You're worth anything. Besides, you did it for me. You stayed here a whole year and never complain'. Now I'll go to your place. I kin get used to it. You *need* to go back. But you' not in condition for that place. The way I hear it, from the newspapers, it's dangerous up there. Every week or so someone's makin' a robbery. You can' go to a place like that alone. I love you. That means I'm gonna take care of you."

He sat down beside her. In spite of the risk to his jacket, with her tears, he cradled her in his arms. She was more important than a jacket. "You too weak to go up there alone. You cry easy. You get mad easy." He stroked her arms, comforting her as he recited her weaknesses. "You can' stay in the sun for twenty minutes. You need someone to look after you. You know that." Kissing her hair.

Now she was sobbing convulsively. Probably getting the shoulder of the jacket all wet. He didn't care. It proved how much she needed him.

She reached for the box of Kleenex under the punee where they kept it handy, but out of sight.

"Keoni," she said at last, taking deep breaths, her lips moving as if she were trying to find the exact words. "Keoni, you can't go. I won't let you. The mainland is not the place for you. You couldn't stand it."

Before she could go on he reassured her about that. "I know. I been to the mainland already, remember? I know they don' have poi, like that. Well, I guess I'll learn to eat potatoes. I ate potatoes the other day, jus' to practice." The memory was not a very happy one. Only the thought of Anne's pride in him had sustained him through a whole pile of french fries.

"It's not that. It's more than eating potatoes, Keoni. My friends...my life is very different there. *I'm* different up there."

"You, diff'runt...how?"

"Well...with my friends. We go to dinner parties. Sometimes we wear long dresses, go to the opera. We read books, talk about them. The men wear suits. They don't wear aloha shirts except for a barbecue. We all graduated from...." She stopped. "We went to the same school. Don't you see? My life there is completely different from...." She made a gesture in the direction of the street, toward the Lagoon. "That."

An assortment of fractured images tumbled through his mind. In Hawaii wahines wore long dresses, muumuus and holokus. And they ate dinner too. Maybe mainland dinners were fancier. As Anne went on a dreadful sense of separation slid in, like a cold wind that would blow away any words he tried to call out to her. As if he were on a cliff and the wind was between them, carrying off all the familiar kindnesses. He was alone with a word that was the more dreadful because of its vagueness...'that.' As if 'that' were beyond naming. Too different, too little, too much.... He didn't know what. While it didn't say anything bad in itself, in its nothingness he found, somehow, a humiliation.

"What d'ya mean by...'that'?" His voice, his face must have shown how hard the word was on him.

"Oh, you know what I mean. The bare feet, the pidgin, the local style...."

"I though' you like' those things."

"I do! I do! Oh, Keoni! Please don't be hurt. I *love* you. I do! How can I explain? This hasn't been like real life to me here. It's been—delicious. Like a luau. The music and feasting. The jokes. The fun. Being with you. But a luau isn't forever. Now I have to go back to...my real life."

Parker wasn't listening. He'd got it. The jacket was sweltering. The shoes bruised his feet. He looked down at the shoes, so shiny you could catch the shadow of your hand in them. What she meant was, she didn't want him to go.

Anne threw her arms around his neck. Her face, rubbing his, was smeared and salty. Her lips, kissing his cheek, the corners of his mouth, whatever she could get, seemed miles away.

She didn't want him to go. He was set to leave it all. The job, the kids, Diamond Head, the beach, the boys. But she didn't want it.

He felt like the ko'ae bird that perches on the side of a cliff and has nothing but the grip of its tiny toes. In all the world he had nothing but his tiny perch. Shivering in the cold wind that howled through the gulf between himself and Anne.

Chapter Thirty-nine

PARKER HADN'T FELT SO BAD SINCE—EVER. NOT WHEN HIS STEP-father died—that had been only a catch in the throat while the members of Kamehameha Lodge, with their red sashes, sang. Not even when he realized, after a year or so, that his mother wasn't coming back from Kauai. Not when his buddy, Absalom, had been killed in an explosion that was like hell, in the dark, at Pearl Harbor. Not when Wipeout died.

He hadn't felt this bad when he got married to Polly, and that had seemed like the end of his life.

Standing his duty, he wondered how a human could feel so bad and not be in a wheelchair, not have some great wound to show for it. Without violence, with just the breath that it takes to say a few words, everything had changed.

He looked around, astonished at the lack of evidence of what had happened. The plush new beach stretched its lazy self in the sunshine, inviting people to enjoy the sea. The sky was its immaculate blue. Cloudscapes still piled up, as fantastic as the cathedral in the reef; that was cruel, to make you believe that there was a heaven. The breakers still combed toward shore. Their risings and plungings hadn't changed. On the outside, all was as it had always been, while for him it was as though a tidal wave had swept through, not just Waikiki, but the world.

The buses still ran, Parker noticed with surprise. People got on buses, went places, drove cars. As if there were some place to go, a reason to go. The activity on Kalakaua Avenue seemed a madness to him. Wherever did people get the idea that they needed to dodge in here for a bag of rice, or stop there for sandals? Heading off in this direction and that. Walking. Talking.

How could his eyes see color and motion when in truth all was grey, frozen, wrecked? It seemed like a violation of the facts.

He wanted to be off, alone, like an eel in its hole, but all morning long he went through his routine on the beach. He spoke to people with lips too numb to smile. He walked from one end of the beach to the other. He remembered making himself do that. But then at one moment he found himself standing still, looking down at his feet, and he realized he might have been there for some time. He didn't know. A piece of time was missing. That was kind of scary. He felt he should be concerned. But at least during that piece of time he hadn't been hurting.

It occurred to him that if, as he crossed Kalakaua, a truck was going very fast, a lot of things would be solved. And there was still the sea. He wasn't out of choices yet.

The words "dark and cold" came to mind. He hadn't heard "Beyond the Reef" in months. At one time he'd longed for the feelings in the song. Desired such a love! Now he could not imagine life without that feeling and it was the worst thing in the world. No physical pain compared with it. He tried to remember pain he'd been through. As a kid he'd been hit by a car, the rear wheel running over his thigh. His right leg was still a little stiff because of it. But the accident took only a second, and in a few days he was back in the harbor again. He'd never forgotten the beating he got at the Salvation Army after stealing the car. That had hurt him so much, scared him so much, he'd never done anything like it again. But even that hadn't filled his guts with a deposit of black slime, like these days.

Before having Anne he'd supposed that the pain described in love songs was as sweet as the music itself. Sort of a teasing ache, like sore muscles after you used your body hard in something you hadn't done in a long time. Bearable, and with a foreseeable end. It wasn't like that at all. It was not bearable, and he could not foresee the end.

Parker found it strange that such pain was permitted. This was supposed to be a civilized place and they let this kind of thing go on? They warned children about matches didn't they? And electrical plugs? They had stoplights for cars. Posted warnings at beaches: "Dangerous current, don't swim." Hung red rags on trucks with dynamite. But no one ever told him about love. That struck him. No one had ever warned him what could happen in love.

❂   ❂

They were strolling ewa on the sea side of Kalakaua Avenue. This was Anne's idea, for a peaceful evening. It wasn't turning out peaceful. In spite of his good intentions Parker couldn't keep away from the one and only subject. Couldn't keep from saying what was on his mind.

"It was you took an interest in my family, like that. You. You the one wanted to get the records from the court. That means you.... You *can'* go, Anne!"

An electric bus purred by, a little island of light on the thoroughfare. Few passengers were within. On the back seat four local boys were playing music. One blahlah had his bare feet out the open window. Evening sights, evening sounds. The tall coco palms leaned into the dark blue sky. Well–dressed couples strolled, murmured. Anne glanced about as if marking it all to remember.

"I know. My Keoni. I do love you. Since I knew it wasn't forever, I tried to make it as good as I could while we were together."

"That only makes it worse."

Anne groaned. "Oh, angel! Please! Don't look at it that way!"

"How'm I suppose' to look at it?" She couldn't grasp the simplest fact. "You was even jealous of Polly an' my kids. Mad when I went home for sumthin'. Or gave money to Daisy."

Anne sighed, squeezed his hand tight around hers. "I know. That's the way I am. I'm sorry."

She talked like this now. Nicer than she'd ever been. But not changing a bit.

She turned to him, rubbed her cheek on his shoulder, kissed it. "Keoni, you're so good. You think I'm the same as you."

"We are the same!" He pounced on that. "That's why we belong together."

"Oh, Keoni!"

From within the deep, lush grounds of the Royal Hawaiian came music, rhythmic, with the sliding tones of a slack key guitar. On the sidewalk a lei vendor looked up from the tuberoses and carnations she was stringing.

After they'd passed her Anne said, "I didn't know it was going to turn out like this, Keoni. I thought it would be okay...."

"You knew I was goin' to love you. You knew it!" His voice was hot. "The firs' night at Hanauma, in the shallows, I tol' you 'I'm not gonna change.'"

"I thought that—you know—for a year we'd have love and sex and fun. I didn't know it would be so hard. I told you I was here for a year. You didn't pay attention."

"*You* didn' pay attention. You knew you had me. You knew how it was. You knew it wasn' like Sunshine, Pekuela, them, with the tourists. You *knew*." His stomach was beginning to jar and tremble, as it did when he let himself get into these feelings.

Anne burst into tears, as if she couldn't deny his words. "Stop it!" Covering her face with her hands. "Keoni, stop it!"

"I won' stop it. You didn' stop it. Now it's too late. Things is changed. Now you s'pose to stay here. Now you *belong* here. An' you gonna stay." He shouted it, pulling away her shielding hands, as if to mow her down with the truth of it.

"I'm not! I'm not going to stay! I can't!" Now she was yelling too. "I'm leaving. Nothing's going to stop me. Nothing!"

"I'm gonna stop you. Me!"

"You can't!"

"I will!"

"You can't. I'm free."

"You'll see." Grimly. His voice had dropped.

Anne was free, of course. He knew that. But it wasn't true either. She wasn't free because he wasn't free. He felt bound to her hand and foot.

In the gloom Anne's face took a different expression. Her eyes searching, maybe scared.

"You have no right."

"Rights are what you take. Nobody gives 'em to you." They walked on in silence. Enemies. Inhabitants of different islands.

Anne took a new tone. "Keoni, you're being cruel. Don't you see it's terrible for me to leave? Can't you see I'm suffering too? At least you'll still be here. You'll still have Hawaii." Her hands, open, took in the softly lighted street, the tender palms, the lush planting of the Royal's acreage. "I won't. I won't have you, or Hawaii."

"Then stay!"

"I can't, Keoni." More tears. "It's now or never."

"I'll make you."

"No, you won't. I have rights too." She turned and began to walk rapidly away from him.

"Anne, stop!" He lurched after her, caught her arm, pulled her to a rough stop, as if it were now she was leaving. "I tol' you, stop."

"Leave me alone!" She jerked her arm and he let it go.

"Anne," he begged. "Listen to me. I'll change. I'll be better. I'll be what you want me to."

"It's not that."

"Tell me what you want. I'll do it."

"It's not...."

"Tell me.... I'll do anything you want. I'll try to talk better English. Would you like that? I'll try."

Anne gave him a look as though he'd planted a dagger in her heart.

"Help me! Help me to be better."

"Keoni!"

"Help me to be the man you want."

"It's not that. Leave me alone."

"There's gotta be sum'thin'. Tell me!"

"There's nothing to tell. It's just something that happens. Like rain."

"It's not rain. It's you an' me. We kin fix it."

"We can't!"

"We can! Anne, we kin fix it. Tell me how an' I'll fix it."

"I'm going back to the cottage." She turned again and began to walk toward Liliuokalani. He walked rapidly beside her, trying to keep his hands off her.

"I'll leave you alone more. Would you like that? I'll give you all the time you want to read in your book."

Anne didn't answer, just walked harder, breathing harder.

"I'll let you sleep by yourself more. Is that it? I won' do nuthin' 'bout sex. I'll jus' wait for you, if you want it. Anne! You be the boss. I'll do what you like. All your way."

"Stop it!" she shrilled. She broke into a run, almost colliding with an older couple dressed in colonial white.

"Anne! Don' run away from me. Anne!" His blood pounding behind his eyes, desperate, and furious too, at the sight of her leaving him like that. She was turning to grey in the gloom ahead. He tore after her, his thongs slapping hard on the pavement.

To his astonishment, Anne ducked through the hibiscus that hedged the Royal Hawaiian property. He went through after her, saw her cut across the grass toward the beach. In the shadows, among the standing palms, he lost sight of her for a moment, her navy blue and white dress blending with the darkness. Panic stabbed, at her eluding him like that.

When he caught sight of her a moment later she had doubled back toward the sidewalk. What they were doing was crazy. He was stalking her like a wild pig in the forest!

He tore through the scratchy hibiscus hedge, saw her hurry down the street, then take the public right-of-way by the Moana toward the beach. Here he made good time until he lost his thong in the soft sand, took a moment to recover it. When he turned the corner to the Moana he saw a dozen people, in the water and out. The narrow beach was lit by floods that turned the sea to an emerald green in the large pool of light. Anne hastened across the beach, not looking back. She was barefoot now, carrying her sandals. Unless she cut through the banyan courtyard and the hotel, she'd be trapped because there was no passage back to the avenue through Judge Steiner's property, next door. The bowling alley, which came next, butted onto the rocks. She couldn't pick her way through those rocks at night with the surf pounding up on them.

She had to stop, he thought. He'd pull up on her, scold her as she deserved; then they'd turn around and go home. Instead, to his astonishment, she threw her sandals aside and dived into the water. The little fool was going to swim around the rocks to Kuhio Beach.

Anne's taking to the water inflamed Parker as nothing else could. Challenging him in the sea! There was another thing: Hawaiians had beliefs, or rules you might call them, about what you didn't do at night. You didn't pound nails, which might bring a coffin. If you swept the kitchen after dinner you didn't open the door to put the dirt out; you left it in a corner until morning. Also, you did not hide your face from someone. It suggested death. What was a childish game in the daytime you did not do at night. When Anne dove in the water she hid her face. Furious, Parker kicked off his thongs and went after her.

No one on the beach or sitting on the veranda of the Moana paid the slightest heed to the figures flinging themselves fully dressed into the water. People leapt into the sea at all hours in any attire at all. Particularly at night, drinkers from the bar came steaming through the banyan court and hurled into the waves, shrieking with hilarity.

She was on the far edge of the lighted green water when she plunged. A moment later, swimming under the surface into the dark, she was lost to view. Parker knew she could swim a dozen yards without taking a breath. To avoid the rocks she would naturally go to the right, slightly seaward. The sky was overcast, the tide coming in, with waves only a foot high.

Pulling hard in an overhand, he kept his head raised to watch. So heated he barely felt the coolness of the water on his body. A few yards away he spotted Anne's head. She couldn't get away. Using a breast stroke, confident he'd have her in a few seconds, he swam to where he'd seen her. The water was empty, she'd submerged again. In which direction was she swimming? With those weak arms she couldn't be far. Staying low in the water, he tried to skyline her head when she came up. This wasn't easy, against a dark, murky sky, with the intercepting movements of the waves, he himself bobbing in the choppy water. Trying to watch in 180 degrees at once.

Then he saw her to his right, further out to sea, on the Moana side. She'd passed underwater not far from him, apparently changing her mind about the rocks. A good thing too; swimming parallel to them in the dark was dangerous. In a maddened crawl he headed further seaward so that her head, when she emerged, would be silhouetted against the lights of the shore. Thought she could shake him with her dainty little stroke! She was pupule! She reappeared for a breath, her birdlike profile immediately recognizable. Before she could get away he covered the distance to her, pounced on her with more violence than he'd expected. "You!"

"Let me go," she screamed at once. Her voice was drowned out by the cries of those in the shallows. Muumuu floats produced ecstatic shrieks and protests at all hours of the day and night.

"What you think you doin'?" he growled. He held her by the neck in a grip that had defied the drowning struggles of men larger than himself.

"Stop it!" she yelled. "You're hurting me!" When he did not let go, as the water smacked their faces, she gulped, "Stop it or I'll scream."

There was a fury in her voice that did not inspire Parker to do what she said. Perversely, he tried to bring the situation under control. He put his other hand over her mouth.

"Don't yell!" he admonished her.

"Help!" Anne shook her head. "Help! I'm being drowned!" The last words were muffled under his hand, but they produced an electrical effect in Parker's body.

"Keep your mouth shut!" he raged, pinching her nose shut, his hand solid over the lower half of her face. "You crazy, or what?"

A moment after that, before they'd had a chance to have the angry standoff he expected, a wave that had no business being the size it was, struck. Preoccupied as he was with Anne's craziness, Parker hadn't noticed the sea. Hadn't been aware of the surf piling up on the reef, gathering to roll in at Queen's.

When the first big one struck, Parker felt his body lift in the foot of it and instinctively filled his lungs so that when the top curled and crashed over him he had air to expel, keeping his nose and lungs clear. His hand on Anne's nose and mouth did not give her the same freedom. His left hand was clenched in a vise on her neck, the right kept a steely grip on her face. When they went under, pounded toward the sandy bottom, Anne had not had time to take a breath.

For what seemed like minutes they rolled in the smothering foam that deprived Parker of a sense of up or down. There was nothing to do but wait until they floated to the surface when the wave passed. Holding Anne tight, furious to find himself caught so stupidly, though it was not important since they were both good swimmers, Parker relaxed and waited for their bodies to rise to the surface and blessed air.

He had barely the time to recognize the lift of another oncoming breaker and catch another breath before they were seized and tumbled again. Parker hadn't realized they were so close to Queen's. His mindless grip on Anne hadn't changed. He wasn't going to let her get lost, not far from rocks, in these thundering tons of water at night.

Anne was no longer resisting, thank God. She was trusting him to do right by them both. Darling Anne. Stupid little darling. If she weren't so paakiki they wouldn't be taking this beating now. They'd be sore in the morning. Maybe she'd have learned her lesson.

Before the next wave came he had time to lift her, hands under her arms, upward for a good gulp of air. But Anne did not respond as he expected, thrusting to fill her lungs. Only hung there, head lolling. A moment later the wave lifted them, struck. He was in control now, took it vertically and they were quickly free. But his heart squeezed with terror.

He stroked hard, before the next waves, pulling Anne in the chin carry. They reached the shallows before the last of the set came pounding in. They'd been swept to the left, in front of the Outrigger.

Numb with panic he did the things he'd done so many times before, this time on automatic. Stooped and lifted her frail, sagging body across his shoulders, carried it up on the sand between the canoes. Held her in the middle to drain, before he stretched her out. Not wasting a quarter of a second although his lungs were on fire with the exertion.

"Anne!" he breathed over and over, as he laid her in the sand. "Anne! Anne!" With a catch in his breath that was close to a sob. Shaking his head to clear the water streaming into his eyes from his hair.

He knew her body so well, the long, fine bones, their weight and set, even under the cold, matted rag of the dark dress twisted into a lump around her hips. Beyond the canoes, in the club above, he was half–aware of lights, voices on the Hau Terrace, Outrigger members enjoying the evening with music and drinks. But the only reality lay in the dusk before him, Anne, her head turned to the right, her dark, straight hair plastered across her cheek, limp and cold. Without listening for her heart or breath— he hadn't a moment to spare—he knelt astride the familiar form. His hands cupped around her lower ribs, he leaned, pressed, prayed, applying the stroke that brought life.

Out goes the bad air, in comes the good.

"Please, God," he prayed, harder than he'd ever prayed before. "Give Anne breath, and I'll let her go."

Chapter Forty

PARKER KEPT HIS PROMISE. IN THE NINE DAYS THAT REMAINED HE did not by word or look try to keep Anne from leaving.

To do so it was necessary to spend a lot of time thinking about things like Leahi, the winds, the smell of the sea. They all seemed to be a part of the gratitude he felt that Anne had been given back to him. It seemed like the most enormous luck of his life. No, the second. The first being that she had come to him in the first place.

Anne was alive. That was the main thing. The death of his own heart in her coming departure, for the moment, seemed like a lesser event. That he would manage later, alone.

From time to time a sense of horror at what had almost happened overwhelmed Parker. He'd almost lost Anne through a terrible mistake. That was how he saw it. While he felt horror at what might have been, horror at the memory of the purple body of another girl, he did not feel guilt. In his heart he knew he'd always put Anne above everything, including his life. What happened in the sea near the Moana was just something given to them. But the memory of it, particularly the memory of lifting her limp form and laying her on the sand, made his knees buckle.

Anne spent the night at Queen's Hospital under protest. There was no evidence of water in her lungs. It seemed she'd blacked out from lack of air. The emergency unit gave her oxygen, then kept her for observation.

"It was a stupid accident," she insisted from her gurney, when the doctor asked Parker what happened. "I was an idiot...trying to swim at night.

When he left the hospital, after promising to pick her up early the next day, Parker did something he'd never done before in his life. He went to a Catholic church to give thanks. He'd heard they were always open, day and night, and the Fort Street Cathedral stood nearby. Catholics seemed to get a lot out of lighting candles, things like that, and his heart was so full he had to find some way to express it. A Salvation Army Hall wasn't up to what he was feeling now.

A little awkward, shy, Parker entered. The cathedral, dim and empty, smelled of burning wax, incense and gardenias. Approaching the end where the altar, spot–lighted, rose, Parker found it as beautiful as his cave in the reef. Of course it lacked the movement and excitement that the sea provided. Still, there was a lot to look at. Carvings, a cross with a statue on it, gold things, and a long purple tablecloth with a lacy fringe. He couldn't appreciate the unfamiliar objects as much as those in his cathedral of the reef at Hanauma. But for people who couldn't go there, this was very nice.

To one side, before the steps up to the altar, was a bank of little red cups with candles of different sizes burning in them. Some were sputtering, close to going out.

Taking a fresh candle, Parker lit it with the flame of one of the others, dropped a coin in the offering box and sat down with the candle in his hands. He wasn't sure that this was how it was done, but no one was there to notice, anyhow. The red cup began to warm his hands, which he realized were cold. His eyes fixed on the small flame, his gratitude rose with its heat. "Thank you with all my heart. Thank you with all my heart."

Before leaving the cathedral he felt he should do one more thing. What that might be he was not sure. The Virgin with her cape of pale blue spread wide was too high or he would have kissed the cape's hem. But there was a spray of orange gladiolas at her feet. Parker touched one of the flowers with his lips, and left.

❂   ❂

"I don't want you to blame yourself for what happened," Anne told him. "It wasn't your fault. I started the whole thing."

Parker said nothing. Feeling too rotten about it to agree or deny.

"I don't know why I ran away like that. And then, of all dumb things, when I was cornered there on Judge Steiner's property, to go in the water. I was an idiot." She gave a sad little laugh.

"I knew you wouldn't hurt me when you caught me. It was like a bad dream. When I started I couldn't stop." She kissed Parker's cheek tenderly several times. "I'm sorry, Keoni. Truly, I'm sorry. Forgive me." She was weeping again.

Parker kept a mean rein on his feelings, even when she lay crying in his arms at night. Now he held her tight, smoothing her hair, her shoulders, her back. Telling himself over and over: at least she's here. She's alive. I've got her now. I've got her now.

"I'll make a nice lei for your aloha," he said. "Pakalana."

"Oh," Anne breathed, looking at him through swimming eyes. "My favorite! Are they in season already?"

"Almost. I think we can' find enough. Kunia's mother has a vine. I asked her to save the flowers for me."

"You'll need so many. They're so tiny."

"It's for you."

Anne burst out crying again. "How can I leave?"

○　○

Anne wrote in the notebook across her knees. She was sitting on the lauhala mat, her back against their punee.

"I'm making a list of Hawaiian words," she said. "So I won't forget them. The ones we use most. Puka. Pau, kapakahi...."

They had talked before about Hawaiian words. How the most common ones, for the simple pleasures, were doubled. "We like them so much, we say them twice," Parker explained. "Moemoe for sleep, auau for bathing, lomilomi for massage, kaukau for eating."

"It's funny...." Anne's voice seemed softer, more thoughtful, since the accident. "I just realized...that the Hawaiians double words like hilahila for shame, and names like mahimahi...in fact, the names of many fish. But the most common word of all—pau, for stop, or finished—I've never heard that doubled."

"No, we never say pau twice."

"Why? How's that?"

"Nothing's ever *that* finished," Parker observed.

○　○

304

"How can I give it up? I'm thinking about how I'll feel some day in San Francisco. I'll be walking the cold streets, with the fog crawling in from the Pacific—that damp that gets into your bones—and then I'll remember my pink hibiscus bush."

Anne looked toward the open front door where the bush's lush form now crowded the entry way. "I'll remember how it gave me flowers every single day of the year." Anne's eyes filled with tears. "They don't even ask for water when I pick them." She touched one of the large blossoms she'd placed beside the phone. "They stay fresh all day looking at me until it's dark."

"There's lotsa songs about 'em," Parker remarked. "Hawaiians like 'em a lot."

"How can I leave?" Anne wailed. "How can I live without Hawaii?" She threw herself into his arms.

Mute, Parker held her, tried to imagine. Leave Diamond Head, the green hills? Leave Hanauma Bay and the sweet–eyed u'u in the reef?

"My angel! I don't know why I'm leaving. It's true. I could probably find work here."

Parker stopped breathing. She was holding on to him hard, her fingers caught in his hair. But she said nothing more.

❂   ❂

Anne was confined to bed with burned feet. She had half a dozen blisters the size of mynah bird eggs on the soles. It was her own fault. She'd gone to an exhibition of Samoan fire walking and at the end, when the old chief invited members of the audience to follow him on one last trek, she had left her seat and gone to the pit of reddened lava stones.

Actually, as she told Parker about it later, she hadn't done it right. When she approached the pit, forty feet long, smoking and hissing, she quailed before the heat. But several dozen people got in line, among them bone–white tourists, some of them not at all young, cameras dangling from their necks. Anne watched them pick their way through the coals. Finally, humiliation at her own cowardice was worse than the heat. As the others reached the end, she moved forward. The chief, his head wreathed in ti, saw

305

her face as she looked at the glowing stones. In a kind gesture he touched her arm, making it easy for her to change her mind. But she stepped out. "I'm going."

She was alone. There were no cooled footprints to follow. Halfway across she knew she was in trouble. When she leapt onto the far bank the crowd cheered. But by the time she arrived home in the jeep, trembling with pain, her feet were in blisters.

Parker hadn't known she was going to the affair, much less would take part in it. When he saw the condition she was in he shouted. He'd never dreamed of such foolishness. She hadn't the brains of a sparrow. It was the best opportunity to rail at her he'd ever had. She soaked her feet in the strong tea he brewed and that relieved the pain. Once she was no longer suffering, nothing could have suited him more than to have her depend on him for everything. He would have brushed her teeth for her if she'd let him.

"There's nothing wrong with the rest of me," she fumed at his attentions. "I just don't want to pop the blisters."

He carried her to the bathroom, prepared and served the food, brought the magazines she requested. Humoring her whims and laments, he occasionally touched her forehead for fever in hopes of new symptoms. For nearly four days Anne was unable to walk. To Parker it was the happiest four days of his life.

❂   ❂

"You don't talk much when we're together," Anne observed. The reproach was so tender she might have been saying, "I love you."

"M'yeah?" To say what? Mostly he just watched her, filled his eyes with her. Every minute counting.

He left the sexual initiatives to her now. Thinking she might be feeling weak after the accident, then the blisters. And besides she had her mind on a lot of things. The little cottage was a terrible clutter of objects he didn't recognize. Piles of books, back issues of *Paradise of the Pacific*. Obi cloth. Kimonos.

"Only three more days!" Anne shivered as she looked around at the disorder. "I didn't know I'd feel so scared. I thought...." She moved a pile of lacy underthings on the punee to sit down. But as she leaned, looking at her brown toes, she did not say what she thought.

Later, when they finished eating haupia squares, Anne began to talk about her father and her mother. For some reason Parker found it hard to pay attention. He heard, and then he didn't hear. About how it was on the mainland, how it was in her family. Sometimes she choked up as she talked. That got to him, but her words faded in and out. She smoothed his hand, as she often did at the table, squeezed it.

For the first time ever he focused on the fact that Anne had a past. He'd never thought about her that way. It was always his life they talked about. To him she seemed as though she'd been born just minutes before he discovered her. As fresh, as perfect as a gardenia. In spite of things she'd said at different times, he'd never really pictured it. That she too had an early life. That she had her own losses and griefs.

"Now, sweetheart, I feel strong enough to go back to what I left. To go back to my work."

"What work is that?"

"I'm a copy writer."

All this time he hadn't known what she did! Didn't know what a copy writer was. It sounded terrible. He wouldn't ask.

"You have your work that you love, Keoni. I have mine."

She turned his hand over, dropped a kiss into the palm. "You've taught me so much, Keoni." Her eyes deep, soft. "If only I can take back what I've learned! Is it possible—to live in this state of aloha on the mainland? I feel as though I must try."

Parker listened, watched. He wouldn't say a word. Not one.

❂   ❂

His promise escaped him just once. The following morning, tormented, as he awoke he cried out.

"Love me! Love me!" Hugging her fiercely.

But he silenced himself at once. When next he spoke it was of taking her laundry before he went to work.

The minutes seemed to drag, the days flew, as the *Lurline's* departure approached. Nature seemed to conspire to remind Parker of his coming loss. At work, he noticed the naupaka, the most common of beach plants, with its legend of grief. He studied one of the small white flowers, cruelly torn in two, with only half its petals, in memory of a forsaken love. On all the beaches the naupaka waited for a sign from beyond the reef.

He might not look much different, but Parker felt as maimed as the flower. His fingers and toes had all been there when he smoothed the coconut oil into his body before work this morning. But he could not have felt less himself if he'd been chopped off at the knees.

The Hawaiians had a strange hula—it was rarely performed—in honor of a wahine who was maimed. The story was that this wahine, who had no hands or feet, lived on a rocky shelf high above the ocean. The goddess, Hiiaka, in pity for the poor creature, plucked a hala fruit from the wreath around her own neck and threw it to her. With her stumps the maimed woman snatched up the waxy, orange fruit—sweet-scented but not at all good to eat—and danced with fantastic glee. The hula was done on the knees, with the arms folded back so that the movements were made with the elbows, to convey the ecstasy of her gratitude.

✿ ✿

The cute little girl with freckles was selling drinks of water out of her mayonnaise jar again. Parker realized his lips felt thick and dry, almost cracked. He'd had nothing to eat or drink all day.

"Yes," he said as she approached him. "I'm real thirsty."

"That will be five cents, please," she said gravely.

Parker made a bit of mischief looking for his coins, feeling for back pockets, looking under his arms, scratching his head, before he located his change.

The little girl observed his antics politely. "Thank you," she said, as she took his nickel. "I'll be back tomorrow."

She went off, speaking to others, busy with her chosen work. He could have run after her, hugged her. Almost everything brought him close to tears, he noticed, now.

His own kids were mostly okay, he comforted himself. He'd managed to have Lani's shock treatments stopped after she'd had five. She seemed to be better, was cheerful the last time he'd seen her. Paul still ran away a lot but it was usually to spend time with a Japanese boy who was raising carrier pigeons. He'd be all right. Daisy was in the girls' reform school. That was another story and this time it wasn't even her fault. She'd got a job cleaning house in an upper Makiki mansion and one day while the family was gone, Polly had visited. She had paraded through the grand rooms expressing disdain for the paintings and polished floors and other haole junk until she caught sight of the magnificently set out liquor cart. With all those bottles to choose from she didn't think a just–opened bottle of Jack Daniels would be missed. It was. Daisy was blamed. Hanging her head with shame, lips sealed, she'd been turned over to the authorities. Parker loved her so much he didn't see how she could turn out anything but good, eventually.

❂ ❂

From one end of his station to the other Parker tramped, from the banyan to the seawall, reminding himself to nod to the people even though most of them wouldn't be around more than a few days.

Waikiki was changing so fast. In the streets, almost daily, new "Kapu—Construction" signs appeared. Recently the barriers at Kalakaua and Lewers Road had been taken down, revealing a fine new drugstore. Instead of the sound of palm fronds rustling in the trades, now mostly you heard the roar of demolition bulldozers punctuated by crashes as the little cottages went under.

Kalakaua Avenue was more elegant, with sleek new shops between the Moana and the Royal. Restaurants were acting classier. Shoes were required and after six o'clock, neckties, which the management loaned to customers who needed them. The Blue

Lagoon was one of the few cheap eateries for locals left. But Hiro might not be there with his yellow umbrellas much longer. He could retire on what he was being offered for his lease. How long would he choose to work sixteen hours a day for less?

The barefoot, aloha feel of a sleepy village was disappearing. Shiny new cars sped up and down the Avenue. There was more bustle. Excursions offered the tourists included a trip to Hanauma Bay. To go around the island they could sign up for a bus with a guide, instead of having their own beachboy show them the sights. Progress!

More people arrived by planes these days, instead of on the *Lurline*. Soon Pan American would be joined in the skies by United Air Lines. The Hawaii Visitors Bureau, as it was now called, was hoping for fifty thousand tourists next year.

Parker made an effort to believe this was a good thing, although he didn't see how his own personal aloha could stretch over so many newcomers. Possibly some of them would be people he'd seen before, returning. That was about the best he could hope for.

❂   ❂

It was his last day on duty, with Anne to look forward to for the night. Leahi raised her sweet profile to the afternoon sun, the sand was soft as sugar beneath his feet. Far to the right the Waianae range flung its lavender peaks into the sumptuous evening sky. Never had the land seemed more dear, and Anne was leaving.

After tomorrow, when he walked down Liliuokalani Avenue, her presence would not be at the end of that walk. When he went home after work, it would not be to her voice and smile. The thought of his own room, stale and lifeless, was like a tomb.

The Hawaiian word for death was ma–ke. The year had brought such losses. Wipeout. Old friend and gentle giant, Wipeout. The haole girl who couldn't swim, though she had long legs and could have been a good swimmer. It seemed like life was moving along so fast. Ma–ke.

Remembering Anne's talk about doubling Hawaiian words,

Parker stopped. Makemake meant desire. Did the Old Ones see a connection?

Across his inner eye streaked an image like a flash of light. Holding still, looking for what it was, he went back and found it, indistinct at first, then clear enough to recognize. A knife blade. Then the picture, as he had imagined it. A knife in the hand of a young woman with long hair, walking toward a wood. He saw her weeping, honing the knife with which they killed the pigs. Hard times, those. They had their hard times, too. Who knew what his own mother had been through before she turned her face away from a rascal seven year old? Pity for her, for Anne, for them all, swept through Parker. Who knew the real truth of why anything was done?

You had what you had. You did what you could.

Pressing his lips, Parker looked up at Leahi. If being Hawaiian meant something to you, if you felt connected with the Old Ones, you might have one answer. A piece of hala fruit from the hand of Hiiaka might put you to dancing in rapture on the barren ledge of your cliff. Waving your poor stumps ecstatically, you would dance your gratitude, high above the sea.

Chapter Forty-one

IT WAS AFTER FIVE–THIRTY, THE SEA WAS LOSING ITS COLOR, THE AIR its heat. One by one swimmers and sunbathers gathered their things to leave the beach. Those walking by, Parker became aware, were riveted by something behind him. He turned to see. There was Mrs. Randal, standing alone, tottering, her eyes glued on him, looking like a ghost. Amidst all those healthy brown skins, with that pale, drawn face she looked, in fact, worse than he'd ever seen her. She was wearing her kimono, the black shiny one with the dragon on it. Although people wore robes and hapi coats to the beach this long black thing did not look at all right, and especially with her bony white arms and her fragile white ankles sticking into pink cloth slippers. She looked as though she'd got up off her deathbed to come for him. Her intent could not be plainer. She was not looking at anything else on the beach, the rest of it did not matter. She had come for him.

She stood weaving as if she'd been brought to a halt and could not get into motion again although the look in her eye bridged the ten feet between them, strong as any chain. She clutched the black kimono about her, the dragon in red and white embroidery running up the side, furious, as though it would like to bite her head off. Underneath she might have nothing on, or a nightgown; he couldn't imagine her struggling into a bathing suit. Everything about her looked out of place, the pale limbs sticking out of the black wrapper, the frightened, huddled posture, and especially her face. Gone was her usual expression, so haughty and unseeing; she seemed in the grip of terror, alone, in fear and need.

"Mrs. Randal!" As he took an unconscious step toward her, he saw in her eyes something else. Not just whatever it was that had brought her to him but a watchfulness of him, of how he might react to her brassiness in coming there.

"Wha's the matter? You oughta be home. C'mon. I'll take you home."

As he went toward Mrs. Randal he made a point of heading

to one side so they were a full pace apart. He knew, just knew, that with half a chance she would crumple in his arms. But since he stood straight, waiting for her, it was up to her to negotiate the turn in the sand alone and start back toward Kalakaua.

When they reached the street she leaned against a telephone pole and closed her eyes. "The worst thing in the world has happened," she said.

"You kin tell me when you git home. Jus' fix on gittin' there, these short li'l blocks you gotta walk."

When they were safely up the gravel driveway, it was then, going up the four steps to her screen porch that he took her arm. For the first time felt her bones, her body, let her lean on him.

The screen porch, when he opened the door, was a shock. A giant hand had swept through, smashing, scattering every movable object. Hurled books had made dents in the screens, then dropped with broken backs against the baseboard. Loaded ashtrays had been aimed from the chair, scattering butts and ashes everywhere. All the gear and litter that had gathered around her stretched out chair had been thrown and in fact there was more clear floor space around the chair than anywhere else. The wicker table next to the chair, usually piled high, now was clear except for a bottle of gin and half a dozen cigarettes spilling out of a package of Chesterfields. She used to smoke Luckies. He had loaned her his Chesterfields sometimes; she must have changed brands.

The lamp he had fixed was toppled, looked broken. A clock's smashed face showed one thirty–five. The stench of alcohol hung in the air, shards of glass suggested she'd flung her last glass of gin.

Parker saw it all, said nothing. He guided her as best he could, kicking broken glass aside, through the litter of unopened, stained mail, banana skins, pills, spoons, magazines.

A broken bottle of pickles had soaked a bunch of papers that had a lot of mean–looking typing all over them. His thongs crunched on cornflakes, cookies and worse.

At her chair she did not want to turn loose of him, to drop down among her pillows. Gently he pried her free, pressed her bony shoulders down.

At the foot of her chair he took the wicker stool. "What happen', Mrs. Randal? What's the worst thing in the world?" Feeling like he himself could say something about that.

"Those beasts. Those wretched, heartless, vile sons–of–bitches at the tax office. And they're not alone. In fact I think they were put up to it by the developers."

"Developers?"

"Just because I forgot to pay my taxes for a couple of years. How should I know when one of those stupid papers comes, with all the other rubbish that's in the mail now? Why, every week someone I never heard of tries to sell me a carpet or a toaster. I didn't even see these papers they say they've been sending...."

Mrs. Randal lit a cigarette without offering him one.

"Today they sent someone to my door. A man walked up my driveway with papers. Said I'm to go to court because I'm about to lose my land. My land! They want to take what's mine and give it to someone else, because of some old pieces of paper."

A wave of terrible feelings swept through Parker. He'd never lost property as many Hawaiians had; the place in Palolo was now Polly's as part of the divorce agreement. But he remembered when Moses Kamakani lost his home. And easy, too. Sweet–talked out of his waterfront property in Nanakuli by this friendly haole who came visiting. Third time he came, the children, Hawaiian style, were calling him "uncle." And then what did Moses care for a silly piece of paper when the haole asked him to sign after giving him a big new radio? How many other Hawaiians had been done in by a piece of paper?

Parker felt truly sorry for Mrs. Randal. More than at any other time he understood her pain. It did not ease his pain over Anne, or even make it worse—nothing could do that. But it seemed to extend his pain, to give it a sense of wrongness belonging to the whole world. Not limited to a single parting but a piece of a huge, hopeless madness, beyond human resources to repair.

He sat with his hands clasped, ankles politely together, smelling the good tobacco smoke which he found he craved.

"First he asked if I were Mrs. Randal—as if there could be any doubt about that—and then he showed me his deputy's badge and papers. Said, 'This is a subpoena. You're to appear in the Superior Court on Wednesday the twenty–fourth.' Imagine!"

Parker waited. Watching her smoke. He could not tell her that Anne was leaving. It was too private, too huge a grief. And besides, if she knew, Mrs. Randal might say something he'd hate her for. So he just sat there feeling sorry for her and himself both.

"Me, in court, like a common criminal!" She took a deep draft on her cigarette, hardly any smoke came back out.

He waited, watching her use up her cigarette. The ashtray was smashed. "Just hand me that jar of cold cream," she directed, pointing to a white jar that had barely cracked in the melee. The stub hissed as it went in.

"Why don' you talk to you' sister?" Parker offered at last. "Maybe she kin give you some good advice."

"She told me to get a lawyer."

"Thass' a good idea."

"Told me to call Bunky Cooke." She waved in a gesture of dismissal. "We've known him since Punahou but I don't want to talk to Bunky...."

Parker stood. "You do what you' sister says, Mrs. Randal. Call the lawyer. I gotta go now." He started for the door.

With an astonishing rush Mrs. Randal got to her feet. She made her way through the mess toward him.

"I'm leaving' now," he warned her. Turning his back, he reached for the door. As he pulled it open he felt Mrs. Randal's hands on his arms.

"Don't go." Her hands begged him to stay. "I don't want to talk to Bunky." Her voice broke. "I only want to talk to you."

That must be her cheek leaning against his back. He could feel it, warm, through his tee shirt.

"I can' help you, Mrs. Randal. You know that. Things like this, I can' help you."

"I know," she said softly into his back. "I know that. But there's no one I want to talk to, except you."

Parker looked at the yard bounded by the flaming red and gold croton hedge. Soon the great quadrangle as he'd known it would be gone. The gravel walks he'd weeded, the ornamental beds, the little cottage with its crushing bougainvillea vine. Soon, they'd be replaced by something larger, heavier than a cottage. Other voices, lots of them, would replace his and Anne's. Other lovers. Other lives.

"It'll be all right, Mrs. Randal," he said at last, barely audible. "I'm sure it'll be all right."

That must be tears leaking through his shirt, sticking to his back.

He turned. She was indeed weeping. The smell of her liquor and tobacco was strong.

"Oh, Keoni, I have only you."

He took Mrs. Randal in his arms.

Chapter Forty-two

HIS KNEES WEAK WITH MISERY, PARKER SHAMBLED TOWARD Anne's court. He had comforted Mrs. Randal without saying a word about his own feelings. Hadn't dared tell her Anne was leaving. He hoped he hadn't encouraged Mrs. Randal too much. Just holding her, letting her cry in his arms as people sometimes did on the beach. He'd done the best he could with her and now he had nothing left but pity for himself.

Approaching Anne's cottage he dreaded the devastation he knew he'd find within. Her steamer trunk in the middle of the floor. The walls and tables stripped.

In the Hall's cottage, to the right, a typewriter tapped. The Halls were schoolteachers. Poor devils, always messing with papers. In the cottage on the other side of Anne the man who worked at the Humane Society took an evening shower. Through the screen window came the sound of splashing water and baritone humming. Parker had come to know something about nearly everyone in the court. How much longer would the little cottages stand against the bulldozer's crash?

Through the open doorway Parker saw Anne. She knelt by the steamer trunk in shorts and a halter, her birdlike nose that he'd got used to, in profile. Her face was serious. Nearby, two nearly full suitcases waited.

To brighten the empty table beside their punee Anne had set out half a dozen pink hibiscus. But the blossoms had begun to wither and close. Her phone was gone. Sunshine now presided at the Natatorium with a list of twenty important phone numbers, including the radio stations, tacked beside his large desk.

"My Anne?" Parker asked, as he walked in, ready to cry.

"Of course, I'm your Anne," she said, climbing into his arms.

Parker held her close, breathing deeply the roots of her hair. Breathing the scent that defined a feeling like religion to him. The scent that had embodied his greatest happiness and now was his despair.

317

"Oh, your face, my love!" Anne drew back, touched his lips with her forefinger. "My poor darling!"

Gratified that she saw his terrible pain, Parker hung his head like a boy in school.

"What do you want to do tonight, my angel?"

He had no ideas on what to do this last night. He couldn't tell her about Mrs. Randal. Even though Anne should no longer care, one way or another, about Mrs. Randal, he knew he shouldn't.

He turned away from the sight of the suitcases. Still trying to believe, in spite of all the evidence, that Anne might change her mind.

"What do you want to eat?" he asked at last. "I'm not hungry." Hoping it was clear, from the tone, that he'd probably never eat again.

"I cleaned the refrigerator," Anne said, as if that were a perfectly okay thing to do. To get rid of food you no longer needed, or a person, if you decided to leave. "There's nothing but soda crackers here. We can go to The Lagoon."

"The Lagoon!" His voice sounded different from anything he'd ever heard. An animal's howl. A dying animal. To his astonishment Parker threw himself down on their punee. He seized a pillow and pulled it over his head. The Lagoon—never! He would never go to The Lagoon again. He would never again speak to any of those people. He hated them all.

"Oh, my angel! My brown Hawaiian angel! This hurts me so much!"

He was quite capable of dynamiting the world. He would never get up off this punee, no matter what.

Anne threw herself on top of him. He tried to hold the pillow down over his ears but she got a corner of it up. Her insistent words came as murmurs through the pillow. Somehow her lips got to his neck, kissed him pleadingly. He would not be consoled. He was going to rot and die for the rest of his life. Beyond human help anywhere. Everything was ruined forever.

"Darling, my darling Keoni.... Please don't shut me out. Please let me kiss you." Licking his jaw. Trying to get her tongue into his ear. He pulled the pillow tighter. Somehow she came up underneath his arm, in front.

With her kissing him so earnestly like that it began to seem unkind to push her away. It had been more than a week since they made love. These last nights Anne had wanted only to lie close with him. Her head tucked under his chin, crooning sadly against his chest. Once he found her thumb in her mouth. Today she was managing better than he.

At last he released the pillow since Anne so clearly needed the kind of kisses they were good at. He took her in his arms and their bodies relaxed into their favorite side by side embrace in the slump of the little bed.

The kissing helped quite a bit. Things began to develop in a sort of inevitable way, even if he didn't mean for them to. Anne pulled off her top, then her shorts. He made no move so she unbuttoned his trunks, tugged at them. He lifted his hip a little so they'd ease downward but refused to help further. Anne put her foot in the crotch of the trunks to push them to his ankles. Sheer habit brought his hand to his favorite place, which was quite ready. But he would not go further. His hand lingered, sulkily teasing. Anne whimpered. He did not move to take her. How could he? No! Stubbornly he resisted. This was not easy, with every cell of his body craving her. How could they do what they'd done with so much love and joy all those other times? How could they do it today? The day before tomorrow?

Anne refused to wait any longer. She raised her knee to his hip, smoothly slipped the shaft in where it should be. The sensation jolted him. God! He nearly lost it right there. She drew up, to be on top. Taking a deep breath he let Anne drive on him. Her hands gripped the flesh of his chest. Leaning, she pulled, gorging her body on his magnificence.

But then, no longer satisfied by her thrusts, which did not let him use himself, did not give him the sense of command his body craved, he tore away, turned her on her back under him. With hardly a lost count he was back inside her.

Kaimana hila! Now the world was his! This time, however, he could not proceed as they often did, savoring stations along the way. Nothing but more and stronger would do. Just beyond reach blazed the crown, the glory. He was cresting. But still furious. Holding off as the signals raged. Wanting just a little more, wanting to relish just a little longer the awesome, heaped up surge.

Then, with a jolt it came to him: Anne could be his. For the first time, she could be his. And beyond the bliss, the sacred mingling they'd never had, the possibilities that that meant. A vision of Anne growing his seed laid hold of him. The idea had crossed his mind many times, a distant and forbidden image. Now he saw it as clearly as he'd ever seen Anne. Anne with her slim, fair arms, her belly grand with precious child. How she'd carry, how she'd sit, how she'd stand: Anne, round with his child. Anne could.... Praying, he could make it happen. It could happen in just one time.

In the grip of this image he made a decision. Or thought he did.

Was it Ku who laid hold of his shoulder, who joined them in this union, as in all others? Was it the hand of Ku, reaching from the shimmering muck of the world's beginnings, who seized him now?

At the moment when he was ready to act, or rather to remain, instead of acting, he received a countercommand. Not from his old commitment to protect Anne in every way, but from his vow the night Anne was nearly lost forever. He could not break the promise on which her life had depended. He must let her go.

On the crest he hesitated. No matter the craving for completion that rushed through him. No matter that his soul yearned for this already beloved child. His body convulsed in a familiar movement backward. For the first time ever, tears sprang to his eyes in the ecstatic spending, at the sense of loss.

Anne smothered his face with kisses of gratitude. He said nothing, responded as he always did to her outpourings of love. But his mind groped backward, searching, not knowing what had happened in the split second between Anne and the void. Whether he had been clear or whether a fraction of the teeming impulse had begun before he left. His lips sealed by good intentions, and bad, he shuddered, held her close.

Anne's greed was unfinished. She thanked him, devouring his mouth, cheeks, neck, breasts. Now she was thanking his ule. She had kissed it before, caressed it tenderly. But this time there was a difference in what her mouth said. A piggy fury possessed her. Astonished, he abandoned himself to the extraordinary sensations her daring gave him. Soon his daring equalled hers and they were in positions they'd never taken before, their mouths expressing intimacies beyond permission.

Like a novice surfer, lifted and tossed in the waves, he gave himself up to the sweep of astonishing new pleasures. Floating, crashing, confounded, he revelled to find them possible. He hadn't dreamed such things could be done with someone he loved as much as Anne.

In the succeeding hours he learned Anne's body as he never thought it would be his privilege to know any woman. She became part of him, sealed on his tongue, his nose, his eyes, as he was on hers. They belonged to one another in scents, tastes and acts that took them back to the primal reaches of Pele. Joyously, the conviction imprinted itself on Parker: now she's mine. Now and always. Now Anne could never leave. The final gifts had been given. They owned both givers and receivers.

Buoyed by his new happiness, Parker let himself be carried into a dimension beyond all landmarks, perhaps beyond human right. No concern of his now.

The cottage became swollen with their lovemaking. Their bodies filled not just the hollow of the bed but, thickening the air, seemed to press outward against the walls, buckling them. The poor, thin screens stretched, the ceiling arched, all was one in a mindless, swollen womb of heat and lust.

Parker even joked. At one time he lifted his head. "I feel like I'm drownin'! What will people say? So little water, and here's a lifeguard, drowned!"

Time uncounted later, they gave in to sleep. Limbs flung wide, one head going mauka, the other makai, they drifted into a dreamless abyss, beyond hope, beyond grief.

But Parker was wrong. Next day Anne went on with her preparations. She still intended to leave.

Chapter Forty-three

A NNE PROPOSED "LET'S WALK ON THE ULU NIU LAWN ONE more time." They were reaching for little jokes, things to say, as if last night hadn't happened, as if this were just another sunny Hawaiian morning. Parker wasn't afraid of work, or pain, or other men, but he did not know how he would get through putting Anne on the *Lurline*. He had taken the steamer trunk and the crate of books to the pier first thing this morning while Anne returned the key she'd never used to her Chinese landlord. Now they were coming from Koa Street.

The day seemed kindly, mild thus far, but with a sky of such brilliance it would be hot in the afternoon. For the moment the trades skimming the vast gentle palm grove of Waikiki tempered the embrace of the sun. In the next block bulldozers were grinding. The smell of excavation dust crowded the sea air.

Anne's eyes were so swollen from weeping when he returned from the pier that she had a strange new look.

"Just for old times," Anne insisted as they cut across the tough hilo grass.

On schedule the landlady yelled, the dog barked furiously.

"Okay. Okay!" Parker yelled back. "Pau! We won' do it no moah!"

"I'll even miss them," Anne sniffled, tears catching up with her again. "So much in Waikiki is changing. At least this huge lawn is still here. We can thank her for that."

They passed the corner where he had met Anne in her nightgown, wearing the pikake lei. He'd never dreamed then what lay ahead for them in the next eleven months. Or was that true? Had he known something from the very beginning, when he saw her with her book, eating alone, at the Lagoon?

They pulled out chairs under a yellow umbrella, sat staring across Kalakaua at the sea. Rose came to them, braids shining over the top of her head. She smiled, her solid, square body waited, in service for their order. Mieko came from inside and told them the good news.

"Rose is getting married next month."

Anne kissed Rose, "I'm happy for you." Parker turned away, cleared his throat harshly.

"Hiro's giving her a spread."

"I won't be here to heat up the malasadas!" Anne burst into tears. As if that were the worst thing she could think of.

"Order?" Rose asked, her forehead puckered.

"Portagee sausage, two scoopsa rice, egg on top," Anne said at last. She always talked local at the Lagoon now.

"Same for me. Bowl of poi on the side."

"I know," Rose said as she turned away. "Large."

Good things did happen, sometimes, Parker told himself, glad for Rose. Kanekini had had surgery on his eye. It didn't droop as much. He was cheerful last time Parker saw him. Maybe he'd be all right.

Hike galloped in with Hullo, both dripping. They wore trunks over their jeans which were shredded above the ankles. They chose to ignore Anne's embarrassing tears.

"D'ja hear about Whistlin' last night?" Hike celebrated.

Anne wiped her eyes, smiled in spite of herself. Parker knew for sure what was coming.

"He was in a crap game over on Kaiulani. Losing. Worried. Had to do something. He did."

Parker slapped the table, chuckled.

"He broke up the game. Ev'body ran out shoutin' for gas masks."

Hullo leaned confidentially to Anne. "Hike's talkin' 'bout Whistlin' 'cause he wants to forget what happen' to him coupla nights ago."

"Ah, shaddup," Hike growled. But not as if he really cared.

"He was drinkin' with Melvin. He pass' out first. Melvin put egg white on his okole. Hike woke up...so stiff he couldn' hardly move. Yellin'...thought he'd been buggered." Hullo faked the crab-legged walk, the furious face. "Was gonna drown the guy what did it."

Chairs were scraped around in the hilarity. Kunia and Dede, nearby, joined in.

Hullo took off. Parker observed, "Hullo's in a good mood today. Cunha's breakin'."

Payoff and Lois stopped by. Kawehi arrived with a Carnation carton full of plumerias and some lei needles to string them. Lois took a needle and began to help her, pushing the long, slender wire through the buttery yellow and white blossoms.

"Bring me one lomi salmon?" Lois asked Rose, as she cleared dishes from a table nearby.

Payoff clowned when the bowl appeared, bits of salted raw salmon with chopped green onion and tomato in cracked ice. "Is that what the Hawaiians eat?"

"Better'n your Portagee junk stuffs."

"I might take a taste." Payoff seized a tablespoon and began downing it. Lois pretended exasperation.

"Miriam is going to the Olympics," Kunia remarked.

"M'yeah. We all knew she would."

"Spam is on 'Hawaii Calls' regular now."

Ah Lee, his nose smeared with zinc oxide, pale blond hair stiff with salt, sat down next to Kawehi. Silent, as usual, his expression was contented, intimate as he untangled Kawehi's hair from the panax hedge behind her. Her hair was almost to her knees now and in more trouble than ever.

"We're going to have a baby," Kawehi announced. "December."

A lot of excitement was expressed about that. Parker was happy for both of them. Ah Lee would have Hawaiian blood at last and Kawehi might get a blue–eyed baby.

Indirectly, Parker had heard that Polly had delivered. A boy, or maybe it was a girl. Her new husband took the responsibility for that one.

"Don't forget to throw one of your leis overboard when you pass Diamond Head," Lois reminded Anne.

Anne gave her a wounded look.

"The airplane goin' by don' tip their wings no more now," Payoff informed them.

"Izzat so?"

"M'yeah. Some tourist wahine complained. Said it gave her

an uneasy feelin'. I read it in the *Bulletin*. So they stopped. Pan Am told their pilots to stop doin' it."

"The tourist's the one gotta be satisfied," Parker remarked.

"I hear United's coming in pretty soon. Two airlines. Twice as many people."

"More people, less aloha."

"M'yeah. Used to, people said, 'If it moves, say Aloha, if it smiles, kiss it! Now it's 'Let's see your money, then Aloha.'"

It was an old litany. Secure in their own good feelings they grumbled cheerfully among themselves.

Parker glanced up at dark Leahi, rising over the sad ironwoods of Kapiolani Park. The regulars scudded in and out of the restaurant in their bare feet and wet trunks. Zarko and Jojo gave them 'Howzzits' as they went by. On the tables the coils of yellow plumeria blossoms piled up. Payoff tormented Lois, who loved it. The baby was growing inside Kawehi. Ah Lee looked happy. Anne's bare foot was on his own as she sat staring at the beach. Wasn't it perfect? Wasn't it the way it was supposed to be? Deep in the valleys yellow–feathered birds once had lived.

People began to come in for lunch. Tables were filling. It was time to give their places to others.

Anne took the jeep, went to say good–bye to her haole friends, the doctor's family she knew up on the Pali road. Parker and Payoff went to Tongg's for a few beers. At two Anne would be back to say her good–byes at the Lagoon. She didn't want people to go to the ship.

❂   ❂

Anne didn't stay long with her father's friends. She returned to Kuhio, seated herself on one of the painted green benches to wait for Parker to emerge from Tongg's. Nursing her swollen eyes behind dark glasses, she was glad to have a few moments to herself under the banyan.

Unfortunately, she did not remain alone long. A man in an aloha shirt of many colors, matching shorts, and black oxfords came to stand near her bench and then to sit with her. His knees were burned so pink it stung Anne's eyes to look at them.

"Great scene, don't you agree?" As if taking credit for the discovery.

The scalded pink face gave her a delighted smile. "I love it here." Looking around as if they were Sunday afternoon visitors at a zoo. Naturalists sharing a specific taste.

"I came to rest," he informed her, "but I'm sickened by the way this place is run. Look at that...." He gestured toward the sea. "A million dollars worth of surfing talent out there in the waves, performing for free. And nobody's even paying attention."

"Well, it happens almost every day," Anne murmured. "Every day that the surf is up."

"It's criminal!" the man protested. "All that talent given away free. Why anybody can look at it! Anybody at all! Without paying a nickel! How can they let such a thing happen?"

"What do you suggest?"

"It should be controlled. They shouldn't let people surf just any time they want to. It cuts spectator interest. They should surf only at certain times, and then people should pay to watch."

"Pay to watch?" Anne swallowed.

"Absolutely! A fortune could be made! I don't know what the hotels are thinking of not taking advantage of it." The man wiped his moist face, clearly grieving.

"It wouldn't be easy," Anne volunteered. "The beach is public, you know."

"That's the trouble! The beach should be declared a national resource and boarded off. Only let people enter if they pay, like a museum. And on the days when surfers are doing these beautiful stunts, riding the waves, they should pay double. A mint could be made!" The man glowed. "People here are throwing away money hand over fist. No respect at all for the country's natural beauties and attractions. Makes a businessman like myself sick."

"I'll bet you could really make some changes," Anne suggested.

"Indeed I would! Believe me!" The man's smile was radiant.

"Maybe you could promote the surfing shows with advertising," Anne offered, straight-faced. "Say, on Diamond Head. You could outline Diamond Head in neon, light it up the night before there was to be surfing, with a message: 'Primo Beer. Surfing to-morrow.' So people would know to buy their tickets."

"Young lady," he congratulated her, "you have an eye for public relations! If I were running things here, I'd put you on my team! Unfortunately, I have to get back to my company's business."

"I'm leaving myself today," Anne said. "Although," she added slowly, "there are times when I think maybe I should stay."

❂   ❂

Through the coconut vine nearly everyone knew that Anne was leaving. Parker was astonished at how many people showed up with leis. Even the lifeguards snatched moments from their jobs to drop in, one by one, and say good–bye. Most of them had flowers. It turned out that Hiro had been storing leis in the restaurant refrigerator, including his own, a double vanda, made from orchids grown in his family's back yard.

Sunshine, unfortunately, also showed up with a huge, showy lei that was just like him, scarlet double carnation. With its puffy red ribbon it looked to Parker as though it were professionally made, although Sunshine claimed his sister did it. When he arrived, the lei dripped lushly from his arm like the blood of a terrible wound, Parker thought, repelled, although a lot of people seemed to like it. When Sunshine placed the lei on Anne's shoulders, on top of the growing pile of plumerias, tuberoses and vandas, he got to kiss Anne's cheek, making a little performance of it. Parker was obliged to witness that, although it didn't seem to make much of an impression on Anne, caved in as she was from so much crying.

Parker stood with Anne under the umbrellas, overwhelmed with gratitude at how nice everyone was. He thanked each one with her, wrung their hands, tears springing often to his eyes with his thanks. Unaware that although people liked Anne, it was for him that they turned out in such loving numbers. That the real aloha was for him, since he was so cut up about Anne's leaving.

One after another they came to Anne with their garlands of scent, and kisses, and kind words. The leis heaped higher and higher on her shoulders until her ears were buried. Parker stood holding his own five strands of pakalana for last. His daughter Ruth, peaceful Ruth, so different from all her sisters, had helped him make the lei. It took many hours to string the tiny green and gold blossoms with the fresh and fragile scent that Anne loved best of all.

At two–thirty, his throat scalded with unshed tears, Parker lifted Anne's two bags into the jeep and they left. It was difficult to find parking downtown before a sailing, and Anne had to go through some last minute boarding formalities. If that was what she still wanted to do.

The *Lurline* would leave at four.

Chapter Forty-four

T HE ALOHA TOWER CLOCK SHOWED FIVE OF THREE.
Carrying Anne's two bags, Parker moved with the crowd streaming into Pier Ten. This was his first time to see someone off. Every step, every moment bringing him closer to the thing for which he had no name—when the gangplank rose, and Anne was on the other side.

In spite of everything, he couldn't give up a last faint hope that Anne might change her mind. In spite of the bags weighing him down, in spite of the way she pinched her lips between her teeth as she walked beside him, he still believed it could happen. She could still say, "I'm not going." She could still come to her senses and say, "Take me home, I can't go through with it."

If he did exactly what he should, true to his promise, fate might yet save him from the abyss.

Legs moving mechanically, he stepped into the cavernous shed of the pier. The perfume of thousands of sickening flowers drenched its air. There were twice as many leis for a departure as an arrival. Shrilling passengers lined up at long tables, baggage was carried off with bustle and thump. The tumult, the activity seemed hysterical. From far corners of the shed came yells, the rattle and grind of machinery. Fork lifts chased about in roped off areas, wheeling boxes and bales.

With Anne he pressed through the crowd to a large standard that said "Matson." Affixed to it was the sign he wanted to destroy. "Sailing 4:00 p.m." They stood in line to check through her last pieces of luggage. Around them swirled kamaainas in white, the locals in bright colors and the tourists in the gaudy get–ups they'd acquired at Watumull's and McInerny's. Parties had been in progress aboard the ship since noon. Perspiring, laden with flowers, late arrivals in various states of festivity shouted, hurled themselves into final excesses of aloha.

Through the shed the great white expanse of the ship's side filled the rectangle of view. Lei sellers circulated, holding out their wares, calling their bargains. "Nice gardenia, two foah a dollah. Two foah a dollah." The scent of tuberose and jasmine mixed with the coarse odors of hemp and brine. People continued to pour into the teeming shed. As the crowd increased, the temperature rose. Steamy and clamorous, the room's air acquired the intensity of a hallucination.

Everyone here, it seemed to Parker, was insane. Every one of these passengers, like Anne, had decided to leave. And their friends were letting them go. A lunatic asylum. Next to him in the line a mainland wahine chirped and grinned idiotically. He felt like stomping on her silly coconut–frond hat. Anne was right about how terrible tourists were. They should all be strangled at birth.

Anne's luggage was seized, tagged and carried off. As it disappeared, Anne shot him a stricken look.

"It's cooler out on the wharf," he said. Guiding her by the arm, he pressed though the crowd to the wooden barriers.

Over them loomed the presence of the great ship. From here it was only a cliff of white; he couldn't make out the familiar crisp shape that bore down on him in the blue water. He looked at the bow, the huge mass coming to a point that his feet knew well. This ship that he'd watched for and loved: what was it going to do to him today?

Parker disliked the looks of the Royal Hawaiian Band. They were in place on the dock, white uniforms rumpled, faces damp with exertion as they pumped out old favorites like "Imi Au Ia Oe." Of course they would save "Aloha Oe" until last.

"Come, see my cabin?"

Parker looked at the gangplank. It struck him as the ugliest thing he'd ever laid eyes on. Pekuela, them, talked a lot about the parties they went to on the *Lurline*. It was then the beachboys picked up their biggest tips. The husband slipping them extra, without the wife's knowing, and the wife on her side, doing the same. Sometimes the boys drank so much they had to be carried off the ship. Best sport of all were the last minute quickies, even with married wahines, locking the cabin door, taking a chance they could finish before the husband found a steward with a key. The boys even scooped new ones in the final moments before a sailing. The stories were endless.

"No. I guess not."

"Maybe we should decide on a place for me to stand, so you can see me when I wave." Anne looked up at the great sheer of the ship. "Where, do you think?"

"How 'bout there," he pointed. "The second post back on the first deck. You see that ship's officer, the white uniform?"

"Okay. I'll go directly there."

"You wanna take off some of your leis? Carry them on your arm?"

They stood facing one another, holding both hands, heads close, drawing out the tiny exchanges. The fragrance of the heaped up flowers dizzied them. Perspiration stood on Anne's upper lip.

Parker looked down at the green water of the slip. Its surface was oily, rubbish floated on it. The water was always dirtier when a ship left than when one arrived. Several of the boys had stripped to trunks, were preparing to dive. He lifted his chin to the Parson, Soapy and good old Nuts. The Japanese boy was there, hiked his eyebrows at him as he went by. It was a new feeling, being on this side of the barrier at a sailing.

"Only a few more minutes." Anne's voice broke.

"M'yeah." *But there was still time!*

Crowding the deck railings, passengers called to friends on shore. Voices bridging the few yards of water that were soon to widen into two thousand miles. Streamers were thrown from the ship. The spirals uncoiled, drifted downward, lacing the distance between deck and dock. Showers of confetti burst through the air, twinkling, powdering heads and shoulders, spattering the green water with the look of a sad New Year's party.

"I can't believe it," Anne moaned. "I still can't believe this is the end."

Parker's jaws, clamped hard, seemed stuck. The Royal Hawaiian Band was playing "O Makalapua."

"Keoni, what'll I do? Help me!" Anne threw her arms around him, fingers digging into his shoulders and neck. Her face, smeary with tears, rubbed his. Strands of her hair strayed, got in the way. The scent from the flowers rose between them, poisonously sweet. Her lips, swollen and twisted were kissing him, not kissing him, just sobbing against his.

Parker held her, rubbing the familiar spine and shoulders under the great ruff of cool petals. Feeling her pelvis and thighs against him, as they had been for so many hundreds of hours, ankles entwined, in the hollow of the little bed.

Unspeakable memories. His own knees were shaking.

Link and Squidley went by with their tourist couples, Jordan with his current wahine. She held on to his arm as if fearing he might bolt.

When I was young I went to Los Angeles. Anne has to do it her way.

Around them, fractured images of faces. Strong whiffs of liquor. Sobs and promises. And above, looming over them, the cool white presence of the *Lurline*. Crisp as a nurse, it waited beside the carnage on the dock.

Anne wants to go. I have to let her go.

The ship's deep whistle bellowed once. On a loudspeaker a male voice announced: "Fifteen minutes to departure time. Visitors will please leave the ship."

"Oh no!" Anne swooned against him, so heavy in his arms it was like on the beach in front of the Moana. He was holding her up. She wasn't capable of going aboard on her own. He would have to carry her. Well, there was nothing special in that. The way Squidley and his people were staggering, it would be a miracle if they made it up the gangplank. Kunia had once fallen into the slot of green water.

"Ei nei," he pleaded, trying to rouse her. "C'mon. You gotta be strong." Shaking her a little. Trying to get her on her feet again. But even as he did the right things, mad thoughts took him. He would pick her up and carry her away from the pier. The way he did on King Street. She was too sick to leave. Once the ship sailed she would be over her idea. Realize it was all a mistake, she hadn't wanted to go after all. She'd be glad he stopped her. He'd have her for keeps.

"You all right?" Holding her away from him to peer into her face. Supporting her by her frail rib cage. She was close to dead weight. "Kin you walk? Shall I carry you?"

Anne raised her head, took a shuddering breath. "I can walk. I'll have to."

The confetti, the streamers around them were like a shattered rainbow. The gaiety of the bright web, the sweetness of the wheezy music were as unreal as the brave voices. The starchy white *Lurline* waited to bear away the wounded, with five days of healing ahead.

Parker moved to Anne's side, his left arm surrounding her, his right ready to catch her if she stumbled.

"Thank you, my angel. For a minute I thought I wasn't going to make it."

"You'll make it. Be strong," he said gently.

"You give me strength," she whispered.

The post of the gangplank was within reach. Visitors were coming back down, to the dock.

"I can make it by myself. I'll hold on to the ropes."

Stay! Stay! I'll take an interest in you' book! I'll read it, even! I'll stop smoking! He wouldn't say a word.

Insanely, the band struck up "California, Here I Come."

Anne turned to face him. What was death but the absence of life? Life was Anne.

Visitors came down the gangplank, heads bent into handkerchiefs, trailing clouds of bourbon.

No. Life was more than Anne. He had the kids. He had his job, the boys, the van. He had brothers and sisters to meet. But it felt like death.

"Ahoha!" someone near them was calling. "Aloha!"

Aloha meant "hello" and "I love you" as well as "good–bye." The most heartless, corny joke of all. Anne's eyes streamed. His jaws felt like iron gates that had rusted shut. With a terrible effort he forced them open, made his cruel tongue speak.

"You'll be back."

Chapter Forty-five

A T THE LAST MOMENT, PARKER WENT ABOARD WITH ANNE, TO get her safely up the dreadful gangplank. They pressed through the thronging deck, made their way to the second post, where he could pick her out from below. When Parker said Anne was shaky, the ship's officer promised to keep an eye on her.

Parker glanced down at the scene below. "Reminds me of when I came in as a stowaway," he said, trying to grin. He waved at the boys in the water.

Now he was back on the pier again, in the crowd, looking up. Suddenly the ship's horn gave three lacerating blasts. The voices around him reached a feverish new pitch. Rattling like prison chains, the gangplanks were torn away. Only paper, the bright, fragile web of streamers, held the departing to those on shore. The last visible connection. Brasses sputtering, the Royal Hawaiian Band wheezed into "Aloha Oe." Near Parker a lovely alto sang "Ha–aheo e ka ua i na pali." "Proudly, the rain on the cliffs." Tears checked until now could not be stopped.

A barely perceptible shudder ran through the colored net sloping down to the pier. Then there was another. The great ship moved an inch. The biggest inch in the world. The next seconds brought more inches. Slowly the *Lurline* began to ease away. The streamers pulled sidewise. Voices shouted the usual words across the space. "Come back soon." And "I love you."

The strands tugged loose, scarlet, yellow, blue and white. They broke, trailed into the sea. Calls, yearning looks were the only connections now.

Several yards of green water stretched between the ship's white bow and the end of its berth. Near the piles the coin divers splashed, shouted for attention, trying to get the coins to drop. Dark heads, animated faces, vying with the rest of the scene for a toss.

Parker watched Anne, beside the second post. She waved, pressed her hand to her mouth, waved, covered her face, shook her head. Parker tore his eyes away, glanced at the boys in the water. They were whooping it up. The ship's movement was visible now.

Furiously he stripped to his trunks, stuffed his clothes under the barrier. With a leap he hurdled it. In a long dive he was on his way.

The ship had almost cleared the pier, still going slowly, but accelerating. He had to swim hard so as to be out there, waiting in the channel, when the great bow passed.

Shaking the salt water out of his eyes, he looked up to the second post back from the bow. He waved. A lady tourist once told him he had a smile like thunder. He shouted. The big ship slid by.

"Way out here! Way out here!"

Glossary

aku—tuna

aku-head—smelly fish bait

aloha—greeting of hello, good-bye, love, welcome

aloha nui loa—a very big aloha

"Aloha Oe"—"Goodbye to You," song composed by Queen Liliuokalani

aumakua—an animal spirit which is a personal guardian

blahlah—corruption of "brother," a Hawaiian roughneck

ei nei—expression of endearment, my dear

ewa—a direction, toward ewa district

hana malie—take it easy

hanai—foster child, to adopt or raise

haole—white person

hapai—pregnant

hapi coat—short beach jacket

haupia—coconut pudding

Hawaii nei—this Hawaii, an endearment meaning "our Hawaii"

hilahila—shame

holoku—a formal gown, with a train

ho'omalimali—to flatter, persuade with soft words

ho'omalu—to be quiet, be peaceful

ho'oponopono—traditional method of settling wrongs, problems

hui!—a call to attract attention

kahuna—Hawaiian priest

kaku—barracuda

Kane—one of the major Hawaiian gods

Kaneohe—where the institution for the insane is located

kapakahi—upside down or confused (popular usage)

kapu—taboo, forbidden, on construction sites "keep out"

keiki—child

kokua—help, cooperation

Ku—one of the four major Hawaiian gods

Kuhio, Prince—Hawaiian royalty, died in 1922

kukui—Hawaiian candlenut tree, *Aleurites molucca*

laho—testicles

laulau—pieces of beef, pork, fish and taro greens baked in ti
leaves

Leahi—the highest point on the brow of Diamond Head

Liliuokalani—last queen of Hawaii, lost her throne in 1893

limu lipoa—a popular, edible brown seaweed

lolo—feeble minded

lomi—massage (usually doubled to lomilomi)

lomi salmon—fish that's broken into small pieces

luau—Hawaiian feast with roast pig, poi

mahalo—thank you

mahu—homosexual

makai—a direction, toward the sea

ma-ke—death, dead

malasadas—Portuguese doughnut holes

malihini—newcomer

manini—fish, member of angel or coral fish family, also
colloquial for manienie grass

mauka—toward the hills (opposite of makai)

muumuu—long dress, the missionary cover-up

naupaka—beach shrub, *Scaevola frutescens* var. *sericea*

niele—curious

niu—palm

no ka oi—"is the best"

ohia—a flowering bush, *Metrosideros collina polymorpha* (also
called lehua)

okole—buttocks

ono—good, sweet, delicious (often doubled, onoono)

o'opu—goby fish

opihi—limpet, shellfish

opu—stomach, belly

paakiki—stubborn

pakalana—Chinese violet, *Telosma odoratissima*

pali—cliff

Pali—steep cleft in the Koolau range

paniolo—Hawaiian cowboy, a corruption of *espanol*; Spaniards were the first cowboys

pau—finish, end

Pele—goddess of fire and volcanoes, disguises herself in many forms

pikake—a fragrant white flower, *Jasminum sabac*; the word is a Hawaiian corruption of peacock

plaua moku moku—flour dumplings dropped in boiling water

poho—out of luck

poi—Hawaiian staple, a paste made from baked, pounded taro root

pueo—owl

puhio—bad smell, breaking wind

puili—split bamboo instruments used in hula

puka—hole

punee—day bed

pupu—hors d'oeuvres, literally sea shells

pupule—crazy

saila moku—work jeans

saimin—noodle soup, sold at curbside stands

shave ice—shaved ice with colored syrups poured over it

tchar siu—Chinese sweet red pork

ti—a plant with glossy, leathery, blade-shaped leaves, used for many purposes, *Cordyline terminalis*

ule—penis

ulu—to grow or increase

ulua—an inshore game fish of the pompano family

u'u—squirrel fish

wahine—girl, woman

waikiki—a direction, opposite of ewa, toward Diamond Head

weke—a goatfish